"Engaging . . . An enjoyable yarn with characters who leave you wanting more."
—*Locus*

"Shinn's novels are always surprising . . . [She] breathes life into the old tropes and spins off in new directions . . . Shinn is an engaging storyteller who moves believable characters through a fascinating landscape and interesting adventures [and] manages to do it with deep insights that make us reach into our own souls and wonder: If we were placed in the world of these characters, what would we do, and what would we believe in?"
—*St. Louis Post-Dispatch*

"*Mystic and Rider* . . . is that rarity, the opening book of a series that stands solidly as a read-alone novel. The resolution is strong enough that the reader is satisfied, and yet the potential for more will leave me looking forward to the next volume. Well-developed and engaging characters, an intriguing plot, plenty of action, and unforeseen twists make *Mystic and Rider* a great book."
—Robin Hobb, author of *Fool's Fate*

"Strong, charismatic male and female protagonists make this an excellent choice for most fantasy collections." —*Library Journal*

"Clean, elegant prose . . . Shinn gives us an easy, absorbing, high-quality read."
—*Booklist*

"Tailor-made for the growing audience of fantasy fans who like a good juicy romance . . . Spellbinding characterizations . . . A rich beginning." —*Publishers Weekly*

"Shinn's most successful book." —*SFRevu*

"Shinn excels at strong characterization and enthralling stories, and this first in a new series is no exception. Primary and secondary characters alike jump off the page, and the standard quest fantasy is transformed into a journey of personal discovery."
—*Romantic Times*

continued . . .

More praise for Sharon Shinn and her novels

"Shinn demonstrates her amazing writing talent ... in a great new fantasy series. The world of Gillengaria is so realistically portrayed, readers will be convinced that this world actually exists."
—*The Best Reviews*

"The most promising and original writer of fantasy to come along since Robin McKinley."
—Peter S. Beagle

"Taut, inventive, often mesmerizing."
—*Kirkus Reviews*

"It doesn't get much better than [this]—interesting characters, an intriguing mystery, a believable love story, and a satisfying ending."
—*Starlog*

"Smoothly written. Shinn has a talent for creating vivid, sympathetic characters. Nuanced and intelligent. A thoroughly entertaining reading experience."
—*SF Site*

"A delightful world to escape into."
—*Locus*

"A solid read."
—*Booklist*

"Rich with texture and diversity, and genuine characters."
—Anne McCaffrey

"Romantic ... delightful. I'm eagerly awaiting her next novel."
—*The Magazine of Fantasy and Science Fiction*

"Warm and triumphant."
—*Publishers Weekly*

"Inventive and compelling."
—*Library Journal*

MYSTIC AND RIDER

SHARON SHINN

ACE BOOKS, NEW YORK

THE BERKLEY PUBLISHING GROUP
Published by the Penguin Group
Penguin Group (USA) Inc.
375 Hudson Street, New York, New York 10014, USA
Penguin Group (Canada), 90 Eglinton Avenue East, Suite 700, Toronto, Ontario M4P 2Y3, Canada
(a division of Pearson Penguin Canada Inc.)
Penguin Books Ltd., 80 Strand, London WC2R 0RL, England
Penguin Group Ireland, 25 St. Stephen's Green, Dublin 2, Ireland (a division of Penguin Books Ltd.)
Penguin Group (Australia), 250 Camberwell Road, Camberwell, Victoria 3124, Australia
(a division of Pearson Australia Group Pty. Ltd.)
Penguin Books India Pvt. Ltd., 11 Community Centre, Panchsheel Park, New Delhi—110 017, India
Penguin Group (NZ), Cnr. Airborne and Rosedale Roads, Albany, Auckland 1310, New Zealand
(a division of Pearson New Zealand Ltd.)
Penguin Books (South Africa) (Pty.) Ltd., 24 Sturdee Avenue, Rosebank, Johannesburg 2196,
South Africa

Penguin Books Ltd., Registered Offices: 80 Strand, London WC2R 0RL, England

MYSTIC AND RIDER

An Ace Book / published by arrangement with the author

PRINTING HISTORY
Ace hardcover edition / March 2005
Ace mass market edition / March 2006

Copyright © 2005 by Sharon Shinn.
Map by Kathryn Tongay-Carr.
Cover art by Donato Giancola.
Cover design by Annette Fiore.
Interior text design by Kristin del Rosario.

ISBN: 0-441-01303-1

ACE
Ace Books are published by The Berkley Publishing Group,
a division of Penguin Group (USA) Inc.,
375 Hudson Street, New York, New York 10014.
ACE and the "A" design are trademarks belonging to Penguin Group (USA) Inc.

PRINTED IN THE UNITED STATES OF AMERICA

10 9 8 7 6 5 4 3 2

For two women, sisters to each other,
who touched my life profoundly:

Cissy, still the best teacher I ever had, and
Mary Anne, who took care of me when I was far from home.

There are all kinds of magic.

GILLENGARIA

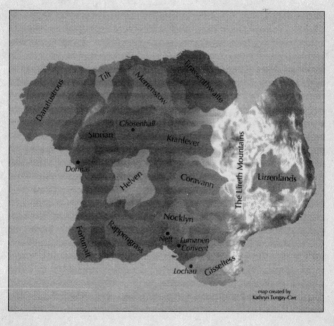

CHAPTER

I

KARDON stood at the back of the tavern, surveying the night's clientele, and smiled with a brutal satisfaction. A chilled and rainy night, so he hadn't expected many customers, and he'd been right. There were a handful of regulars playing chess in the corner or drinking at the bar and eyeing the newcomers with a speculative sideways interest. Kardon wasn't really a charitable sort, but he almost found it in him to feel sorry for the four strangers scattered throughout the long, low-beamed room. The chances were good that one or all of them would lose his money— or his life—before the night was over.

Kardon's regular customers were, to a man, thieves, cutthroats, and hired blades whose scruples had never been overnice. Honest work had been hard to come by here in the dead of winter. Who could blame them for taking advantage when good fortune presented them with a few easy purses to pick, a few unwary travelers to dispose of?

Leaning his arms on the wooden bar, Kardon glanced around the room again. There were two whose lives looked to be already forfeit. One was a slim, nervous young man who sat by himself in the farthest corner of the room and seemed to be drinking his very first glass of ale as he scarcely picked at a hearty dinner. He couldn't have been more than seventeen and did not look like he had led a particularly difficult life. Kardon guessed him to be some lord's son who had quarreled with his father and run off to seek a life of adventure. Which would tragically end tonight in this tavern or in the alley out back. So much for stupid young noblemen who didn't know where they belonged.

The other solitary visitor was also a young man, possibly in his early twenties, sandy-haired, strongly built, and a little raffish. This one, Kardon judged, had had some experience street fighting; he would not be so easily overcome, even if two or three assailants came at him at once. Still, sheer numbers would do him in. He might escape with his life but certainly without his wallet or any other valuables he might have on his person. He was drinking cautiously, nursing his second glass of ale after eating every bite of meat on his plate. Hungry, wary, and tough—but solitary. A waterfront tavern in the city of Dormas was not a place to come without friends.

More thoughtfully, Kardon examined the other two strangers, sitting together at a round table in the middle of the room and engaging in occasional conversation with the regular customers who sat close by. Seafaring folk, by their dress, probably docked overnight at the harbor a stone's throw from Kardon's place. Successful at it, too, by the cut of their clothes and their freehanded way of tossing a coin to Kardon or his servers when they brought out fresh trays of food and drink. The richest prey in the room tonight—but the hardest to pluck.

For one thing, there were two of them. For another, the man was black-haired and burly, the bulk and strength of his muscles apparent even under the winter layers of wool and leather clothing. Kardon could see the short blade at his belt and guessed he also carried a knife or two concealed in his boot or up his sleeve. The man *looked* like a fighter, even as he relaxed over dinner. One bell at the front door, one crash in the back room, and he'd be on his feet with a hilt in his hand, unless Kardon greatly missed his guess. No, this one would not go down easily, and Kardon's friends might find that his sword outweighed his wallet.

It was the man's companion that Kardon found most curious, and now he turned his eyes to the final stranger. A woman, by the Pale Lady's silver eye. A woman, whom her companion had addressed as "Captain," and who held herself so regally that even Kardon, who despised women, could understand why a man might take orders from her. She was seated now, but he had seen her when she entered. She was tall as a man, and dressed like one in leather pants and high boots and a woven vest. Her white-blond hair was cropped so short it stood out around her face in a careless aureole. He had noted her posture when she walked in, how light she was on her feet, how quick and assured her movements were. She was a fighter, too, handy with a blade and not afraid to use it, or Kardon was an idiot. She might look like easy pickings, but Kardon was willing to bet she rarely came off the worse in any encounter. Especially not with that bruiser fighting at her side. He would guess they had dispatched any number of enemies on the high seas or dry land, and wouldn't object to a little rough-and-tumble now if it came down to it.

As it would. Kardon's customers weren't nearly as discerning as the barkeeper himself. They'd see rich woman dressed as a sea captain and think they'd been delivered a bounty straight from the White Lady herself.

"A little more ale, eh, my friend?" the woman called out to him just as Kardon reached this point in his musings. "It's a nasty night to go back into, and I think I need to fortify myself against the cold."

"Take care you don't fortify yourself into a stupor, Senneth," the man beside her growled. The woman laughed and snapped the fingers of her left hand. Kardon caught a glimpse of smoky white moonstones on a bracelet circling her lifted wrist. It almost made him like her for a moment to know that she wore the badge of the Pale Mother. But even the moon goddess would not be able to protect her tonight.

"You worry too much, Tayse," she said before lifting her voice to call to Kardon again. "Another pitcher!"

Kardon nodded. "Cammon!" he shouted toward the kitchen. "Our guests need attention."

A moment later, Cammon came out through the swinging door, bearing a tray of ale and bread. He went straight toward the table with the sea folk, so he must have been spying at the door. He looked even thinner than usual under his shapeless clothes, as if he had been starving himself just out of spite. Kardon promised himself he'd find the time to give the boy a good whipping sometime in the next day or two. When the weather cleared up, when the customers cleared out, when he found a free moment.

Cammon was setting the tray on the table before the sea folk. "Ale," he said in his soft voice. "And more bread, if you want it."

The woman called Senneth, who had been arguing in a low

voice with her companion, looked up at his words. "You," she said. "You've got a funny accent. Where are you from, then? Not Gillengaria?"

Cammon shook his head, his unkempt hair falling into his eyes. "No, Captain," he said. "I've only been in this country a month or so."

"Well? Where were you before?"

He shrugged, his thin shoulders rising and falling under the fabric of his shirt. "Arberharst and Sovenfeld, mostly. We moved around a lot when I was little."

"We?" she demanded. Kardon marveled that she could actually be interested in the life story of a servant boy—an indentured one at that, with a couple of years to work off before he could consider himself a freeman. But she might be the type whose roving attention was caught by any odd detail—the type who remembered things you'd much rather she forgot. For a moment, Kardon felt sorry for the dark man with her, who no doubt hated and feared her. Capricious people were always the hardest to answer to.

Cammon glanced back at the bar to see how his master wanted him to deal with such curiosity, and Kardon shrugged. Let her talk, for now. Let her interrogate. Her mouth would be stopped up soon enough, if Kardon's friends had their way. "My parents and me. My father was a roamer, and my mother followed him wherever he went."

"And how'd you end up in Dormas working as a tavern boy and wearing a slave collar around your throat?" she asked, nodding toward the slim silver torque tight around Cammon's neck. Kardon watched him put a hand up to it and touch the moonstone on the very center of the collar. Kardon had known from the beginning that this boy could be trouble; he had taken no chances. He had bound Cammon with the Pale Mother's powerful protective jewel.

"My father died," Cammon said quietly. "We stayed in Arberharst till the money ran out. My mother's roots were back in Gillengaria, so we set sail a few months ago. She got sick on the voyage and never recovered. We landed and I—I had to pay for my passage some way. The captain bound me to Kardon."

The woman glanced over at Kardon, her eyes coolly assessing, and he felt a momentary, uncharacteristic urge to explain himself. *I paid good money for him! I needed an extra hand in the kitchen!*

I feed him hearty meals every day, except the days he won't eat them because he's such a sly and wretched boy. She looked away, back at Cammon. "Does it hurt?" she asked very softly.

He put his hand back up to the collar. "It's not really tight," he said. "It doesn't choke."

Senneth lifted her right hand, which unexpectedly held a dagger, and touched the very tip of the blade to the glowing gem. "The moonstone," she said, her voice quite low but every word precisely enunciated. "Does it hurt when it touches your skin?"

Cammon dropped his hand and stared at her. The cutthroats sitting nearest her table also turned their heads to eye her curiously. The whole room seemed to have grown still and silent, waiting for his answer.

"Yes," he said finally. "It burns."

The woman's fine eyebrows rose. Delicately, she used the flat of the blade to lift up the necklet and expose a patch of red skin under the spot where the moonstone lay. "From what I hear," she said slowly, "the only ones with anything to fear from the touch of a moonstone are mystics. Are you one of those?"

A whisper went around the room as the other occupants repeated the word. *Mystic . . . mystic . . . mystic . . . Are you one of those?* Kardon shivered, just a little. He was a plain man, mostly honest, not very subtle, and he hated and feared those who were reputed to possess magical ability. Not two months ago, he had been among the crowd that stoned an old woman to death after she was accused of magic in the marketplace, though she shrieked that she was innocent even as the rocks hit her face and stomach. He had had his suspicions of Cammon the minute the sea captain brought him through the door, because there was something about the boy's delicate face and huge, flecked eyes that radiated an otherworldly wisdom. But greed had won out over Kardon's uneasiness—a virtual chattel for a very good price—and he had been sure that he could, with force and the Mother's protection, control such a slight and contemptible creature as Cammon. So he had made the bargain and welded on the collar, and he'd had no trouble with the boy. None at all.

"He's no mystic," Kardon called, still standing behind the bar and watching. "He's just a servant. He does my bidding."

The woman called Senneth turned to look at him, and again he found her gaze unsettling. Her eyes were a crystal gray, wide and thoughtful and impossible to read. She looked like she was having no trouble at all scanning his soul. "Only a mystic," she said, "is burned by the touch of the Pale Mother's hand."

One of the regular customers gave a gruff laugh. "That right, Kardon?" he inquired. "You're piling up magicians in the back room? What, do you have them doctoring our beer so we fall asleep at our tables and you can rob us blind?"

Kardon himself felt blind with a swift surge of fury. "He's a boy. He's no mystic. And I'll thank you to remember what kind of service I've given you all these years."

Senneth had edged her knife even deeper under the collar, till the point of it rested against the soft flesh under the boy's chin. He was staring down at her, mesmerized by terror or whatever power she had in her eyes; she was smiling up at him with an expression that seemed to owe as much to rage as mirth.

"What would you do, I wonder," she murmured, "if I twisted this blade enough to break your collar? What sort of power would you show us then?"

At that exact moment, someone screamed.

Kardon's attention whipped that way. While almost everyone else had been watching the sea captain question the serving boy, another small drama had been playing itself out in the back of the room. Two of Kardon's old friends had approached the scrawny young nobleman and backed him into a corner. He now cowered against the wall, arms ineffectually raised before him, looking even more slight and helpless than before. His face was so fine and so white that Kardon imagined he'd rarely seen the countryside outdoors, let alone the rough weather in a training yard. He'd probably never held a sword in his life.

"Please," he was saying, trying to bat away the weapons pointed in his direction. "I have nothing—but my father, he'll pay you— if you don't hurt me—he's very wealthy—"

"Young handsome boy like you could be worth a lot to us," purred one of the attackers, poking at the boy's shoulder and throat with the point of his sword. "I don't like the idea of a ransom unless the stakes are awfully high, but I bet you've got more valuables on you than you even know. What about the pin on your hat here? Is that a set of rubies I see?" And he knocked the hat off with the tip of his blade.

And a cascade of golden curls came tumbling down over the young man's shoulders.

Over the young *woman's* shoulders, Kardon corrected himself.

Everyone in the bar was now staring at the events unfolding in the corner. Even dressed in a velvet jacket cut like a man's, the woman was suddenly unmistakably female, and terrified. Her face went even whiter; she crossed her arms over her chest as if to protect herself. But her attackers were chortling with unrestrained delight—what a glorious catch! what a prize with a dozen fabulous uses!—and they pressed even closer, weapons falling to their sides. One of them even lifted a hand to brush his fingers across her ivory-smooth cheek.

"Don't touch her," a cold voice said. Cursing himself for continually losing track of the other players in the room, Kardon cut his eyes over to the last remaining stranger. The sandy-haired man was on his feet, his cloak thrown over his chair, and he had a dagger in each hand. The weapon belt now revealed around his waist showed an array of other small knives tucked in well-worn sheaths. More than a street fighter—a mercenary soldier, trained for one thing only. "Leave her in peace," he added.

"*You* leave in peace before you don't have a chance to leave at all," her attacker snarled. "This isn't your fight."

"I make it mine," the mercenary said calmly. "Let her pass."

"Fight for her," the cutthroat said.

Then so many things happened at once that Kardon could not follow them all. The mercenary lunged for the cutthroat. The other assailant swung his sword at the golden-haired girl. The girl crumpled to the floor in what appeared to be a swoon—until her attacker shouted with bewilderment.

"She's gone! Where'd she go?" he cried—and then he howled in pain as something small and feral raked him across the thigh.

Kardon dashed around the edge of the bar, a blade of his own in hand, intending to join the fight. He'd only gotten two steps away from the counter when his way was blocked by the burly black-haired sailor.

"We're taking your servant boy with us," the big man said, tossing a handful of silver onto the polished wood of the bar. "This may or may not cover his purchase price."

"*What?*" Kardon screeched, but the big man shoved him back so forcefully that he lost his balance and fell heavily to the floor. Winded and dazed, he could only lie there and watch the quick,

efficient activity occurring throughout his tavern. The sea captain
had come to her feet, her knife still under Cammon's collar, and
she gave her blade one hard twist. The silver snapped in two and
fell to the boy's feet, while his hands went up in wonder to his
throat.

"Out the door," Senneth said, pushing him that way. "Wait
for us."

He stumbled out. She strode forward, knife still in hand, Tayse
at her side. They waded into the fight across the room, which now
involved every patron of the bar, so that the mercenary was totally
overmatched. Not for long; once the sea captain and her bundle of
muscle joined the fray, it was clear that these were three seasoned
warriors who had fought countless times in battles more hazardous
than this one. Their blade work was methodical and unerring, and
they beat back their would-be attackers with cold efficiency.
Within minutes, Kardon's friends had either collapsed panting to
the floor or run for the kitchen to escape.

Of the golden-haired woman there was no sign, though Kardon thought he saw a small calico wharf cat scurry across the floor
and out the front door through which Cammon had disappeared.

The sea captain glanced around once as if to make sure no
more danger lurked in the corners, then sheathed her blade in one
economical movement. "Is Kirra outside?" she asked the men who
stood beside her. Both of them were still holding their weapons in
their hands.

"I saw her go through the door," the sandy-haired young man
said.

"Good. Then we'll be off. The boy rides with you, Justin, if
Donnal hasn't managed to find another horse."

"I'll just watch this one a moment while you organize the
others," Tayse said, turning his attention to Kardon. The woman
laughed as she ushered the younger man outside.

The barkeeper stayed prone on the floor, raising one of his
hands in a gesture of submission. "I'm not doing anything," he
said. "I'm not coming after you. Just take what you want and go.
Lousy mercenaries. Thieves of the worst kind," he could not stop
himself from muttering.

The big man smiled as if he was genuinely amused. "We're not
mercenaries," he said. "We're King's Riders."

CHAPTER
2

THE hard ride down the slick, dark alleys of the city was made even less agreeable by the freezing rain that fell on them the whole way. Senneth could tell that Kirra and Cammon were absolutely wretched. The other three might have been miserable as well, but Justin and Tayse would never show it, and Donnal had ways of dealing with discomfort. The rain bothered Senneth a little more than the cold did; she was never cold. And she didn't even mind the rain, since it meant there was less chance the barkeeper or one of his friends would come after them.

Donnal pushed his horse to the lead once they broke free of the last, straggling streets of the city, taking them down the main trade road that led straight east. Numb from cold, they followed him blindly, even when he broke off and started going cross-country. He had scouted this terrain over the last couple of days while the rest of them had been in Dormas; he had picked out their next campsite against the chance of a quick departure. Senneth only hoped it was covered and dry. She wouldn't even allow herself to consider that he might have had time to lay in fuel for a fire.

Another twenty minutes down a path that only a wild creature would have been able to find, and even Senneth was beginning to tire. She heard Kirra's sharp voice—"Are we going to stop *some-time* tonight?"—and Donnal's reassuring answer.

"Just over that hill there. Old dairy house, I think. Must have been a farmhouse nearby, but I couldn't find it. Maybe it burned down."

And as he finished speaking, they crested the hill. There it was, a dark smudge against the wet darkness, holding the approximate shape of a house. They all clattered inside, still on horseback, and swung themselves out of the saddle to look around.

Little to see in the dark, but Senneth's first impression was that it was moldy enough to make her doubt its waterproofing, and not a degree warmer than the air outside. "I'll make a fire," she said, handing her reins to Kirra.

"Wood in the corner," Donnal said.

"Aahhh," she said, grinning at his shape, barely discernible in the shadows. "May the Bright Mother bless you for all your days."

She saw Cammon's head lift at the prayer, but she didn't pause just then to talk to him. Kirra and Donnal were ushering the horses to the back of the small structure, where there appeared to be some kind of stalls or gates already in place. Justin and Tayse were hauling down saddlebags, getting out blankets and food. Her own task, as usual, was to start the fire. No need to worry about the smoke escaping; this place was rickety enough to allow it all to drift outside.

In something under fifteen minutes, they had a small, dry, almost convivial camp laid out, and Senneth could feel the spirits of her companions rising.

"Good work," she said, nodding across the flames to Justin and Tayse. "He was not expecting what he got from us."

As always, Justin scowled at her, and Tayse looked merely indifferent. As she had learned during the one week they had been riding together, they neither liked nor trusted her, so her praise would not move them. Still, she would continue to express her approval when it was merited. So far, they had not failed her; she was pretty sure that pride on Justin's part and sheer damned stubbornness on Tayse's would guarantee that they never did.

Finally warm and at rest and still full of wonder, the young serving boy turned his wide eyes her way. "What did—why—who *are* you?" he stammered. "I don't know—why did you take me?"

Senneth turned to him with a smile. He was sitting between Kirra and Justin, his hands folded in his lap, waiting with a shocked patience for whatever the rest of the night might bring. She was pretty sure it would be just dinner and a well-deserved sleep, but he might worry that he had gone from one form of misery to another.

"I'm Senneth," she said. "The lady with the lovely hair is Kirra Danalustrous."

Kirra smiled in her friendly way. "Hey there."

"Justin—Tayse—Donnal. They're traveling with me on certain errands for the king. Your name, I understand it, is Cammon."

He nodded, but his attention had fixed on Kirra. Clearly he was remembering some scene from the barroom brawl. "You're—you pretended to be a boy, then you showed you were a woman, and then—did you change shapes?" he asked with some wonder. "I saw a cat where you'd been standing—"

Kirra was grinning. "It's a skill I have. I'm a shiftling," she said. "So's Donnal."

Cammon looked around at the faces ringing the fire, but Senneth thought he looked more intrigued than frightened. "So that's why you took me from the bar? All of you are mystics?"

Tayse snorted. Justin said shortly, "No. Just those three."

Cammon gave Senneth a questioning look, and she nodded. "I can't shape-shift, though. Or at least not very well. But yes, Kirra and Donnal and I are mystics—and, yes, that's why we rescued you. Because I think you're a mystic, too."

Cammon put his hand to his throat, where the red mark of the moonstone still lingered. "I don't know," he said in a low voice. "I never had any kind of magic when we lived in Arberharst."

Kirra tilted her head to one side. Any such movement always caused her glorious hair to ripple with light. Senneth grinned to see how the four men, all unwilling, turned to watch that sight. "But you're from Gillengaria, aren't you? Originally?"

Cammon nodded. "My mother was. My father—I don't know. He never talked much about his past, so I'm not sure where he came from."

Kirra shook her head. "It doesn't matter. Somewhere in your mother's family or your father's, someone was a mystic, and you've inherited the power." She glanced at Senneth. "Or so some of us think."

"Yes, she just saw you emptying a chamber pot in the alley behind the bar, and she said, 'He's a special one,'" Justin said in a mocking voice. Senneth could tell he was still furious at the detour and delay in plans, though he had no responsibility for their timetable and even less for their mission. He had played his part well, though. Give him a chance to fight somebody, and he was always willing to oblige. "So we had to stop and free you, and now I don't know what we're going to do with you."

Cammon looked apprehensive, but Senneth said, "We'll take you someplace safe. Don't worry."

"Food's ready," Tayse said briefly and began handing 'round plates. Tayse, Senneth, Kirra, and Justin had all ordered dinner at the tavern—but Senneth, at least, had been too tense to eat much, and the long, cold ride had left them all hungry again.

"We'll talk about all this after dinner," Senneth said.

Which did not take very long, since the meal was plain and there was little conversation. Donnal and Kirra were murmuring together, as they often did, and Justin got up once to check the horses, but the rest of them just forked meat into their mouths and rejoiced at how much better they began to feel. Warm, dry, fed. All a traveler could ask for.

Donnal cleaned up afterward. Tayse and Justin sat together, oiling their swords and inspecting their other weapons. Senneth cared for her own blades, but not with quite the same obsessive attention. Then again, she had to admit it: Either one of them could best her any day in hand-to-hand combat, and until she'd met these Riders, she'd considered herself a damn good fighter.

Kirra drew closer so that she and Cammon and Senneth sat in a little triangle on one of the camp blankets. "Now," Senneth said. "Let's talk a bit more about you."

Cammon shrugged again. "Like I said. I never had any magical abilities before I came to Gillengaria. I don't know that I do. It's just that—since I've been here—I've felt strange. Like thoughts and ideas are pouring in on me all the time, from everywhere. I can look at a man and know when he's lying. One day a woman came in, and I knew she was dying. I could feel this—this blackness oozing out of her. She took a room next door, and she was dead in a week. Kardon was furious, because she owed him money, and she didn't have a coin on her."

Senneth exchanged glances with Kirra. "Sensitive," the golden-haired woman said.

"Reader," Senneth added. "Did you know Kirra wasn't a man when she came in the bar dressed like one?"

Cammon frowned a moment, trying to remember. "I just got a glimpse of her before everything started to get crazy," he said. "But—yes, I did. Everyone else gasped when her hair came down. But I wasn't surprised."

"How did that barkeeper—Kardon, is that his name?—how did he know you were a mystic?" Senneth asked.

Cammon shook his head. "I don't know. He was always telling me not to be trouble, he knew my type. I think he's just suspicious of people in general, and being a mystic was the worst thing he could think of. So he gave me the moonstone." He rubbed his neck again. "I never thought—I'd never felt anything like that."

"Keep it on long enough, and it can actually kill you," Kirra said. "Poison your blood. It really is anathema to people like us."

Cammon's eyes were on the bracelet around Senneth's left wrist. "Then how can you—?"

Senneth grinned and shook her hand so the stones tinkled together. "Pretty, isn't it?"

"Are they fake jewels?"

"Oh, they're real, all right, as you'll know if you touch them," Kirra said dryly. "She's the only mystic I've ever met who can actually bear to touch moonstone."

He looked at Senneth. "But why? Doesn't it hurt you?"

Senneth shrugged. "I can feel it. Like a small fire across my skin. But I find the bracelet useful. It makes strangers fail to guess my identity. And it—" She shrugged again. "It keeps my power in check somewhat. When I was younger, I could not always control it. Now I can, but I don't mind keeping the intensity a little low."

"What exactly is your power?" Cammon asked, and then looked embarrassed, as if it was rude to ask.

From across the building, Justin raised his voice in a sardonic question. "Yes, Senneth, what exactly *is* your power? Donnal and Kirra at least have shown us what they're capable of, though I'm not so impressed at people who turn themselves into beasts, but you've never been exactly clear on what it is you can do."

Kirra half-turned to shoot her answer over her shoulder. "She *is* power, you stupid gutter boy. She can do anything. She can create heat, and light, and fire. She can heal someone better than I can. She can change shape if she wants to. She can cast darkness. She can—she can do *anything*."

Cammon's eyes were wide. "Can you?"

Senneth was laughing. "I can do a lot," she said, not caring to be too specific. "I'm particularly good with fire. And it's true I can heal you if you're hurt, but you'd be in pretty desperate straits to submit to my ministrations, especially if Kirra were nearby. Now Kirra's a talented healer."

Donnal had drifted back to join them, and he settled on the blanket next to Kirra. He was dark-haired, dark-eyed, and wore a close dark beard; a taciturn and restless man of peasant stock, he was never far from Kirra's side. Cammon glanced at him.

"Are you a healer, too?"

Donnal grinned. "Not me. One skill and one skill only—changing." He flickered into wolf form and back so quickly that it was almost possible to believe he hadn't done it. "But it's the skill I'd have picked if I'd been given a choice."

Cammon looked confused. "How do—where do your clothes go when you take animal form?"

Donnal grinned. "I can change them as easily as I change my skin. What can *you* do?"

"Cammon's a sensitive," Kirra said.

Donnal shrugged. "Don't know what that means."

Cammon laughed. "I don't either, really."

"I'm guessing you'll have to do some work to really develop your skills," Senneth said. "Most of us have known from childhood that we had some—abilities—and we worked on them."

"Or we worked on hiding them from the people around us," Kirra said. "So we wouldn't be cast from our houses and left to die."

Senneth grinned faintly. "Your father never turned against you."

"No, but it happens often enough."

"It does," Senneth agreed. She turned back to Cammon. "You may not know, if you left Gillengaria when you were young, how suspiciously most people view the mystics. Some parts of the country are very receptive to the idea of magic, and in the royal city, mystics live quite openly. And a few of the Twelve Houses tolerate them, even among their own heirs. But in many places—especially in the south—it can be worth your life to be discovered. So those of us with some power are often cautious about how we display it."

Cammon put his hand to his throat again. "This doesn't surprise me. I saw a few things in Dormas—" He shook his head.

"So, as you might guess, many of us had to train in secret—but train we did," Senneth continued. "I'm wondering where you should go to get some experience."

"We could send him to Ghosenhall," Donnal suggested.

"The royal city," Senneth explained. "We could, but he'd never make it there safely on his own."

"Too bad we're not heading toward Kianlever," Kirra said. "But if we're going to Fortunalt or Rappengrass—" She shrugged.

Senneth nodded. "Yes. There are people there I'd trust to take care of him." She glanced at Cammon. "But those are some distance away, and we tend to travel at a hard pace. You might not enjoy the journey."

"I'd rather be with you than where I was," he said instantly. "I'll go anywhere you take me."

"He'll slow us down," Justin muttered from across the room.

"He won't," Senneth said. "And even if he does, you'll just have to get used to it."

Justin grunted again and turned back to his sword. Kirra leaned forward, inspecting Cammon's face. "I want to try something," she said. "Close your eyes. No, let me blindfold you, just to make sure."

He didn't hesitate. Senneth wondered if his ability to read people made him realize that he could trust them. Kirra, at least, would never offer him harm. "All right," he said, and closed his eyes. In a moment, she had fished out a pocket handkerchief and bound it around his head.

"Every time someone snaps his fingers, I want you to tell me who's standing in front of you," she said. "Man or woman. Mystic or not. Can you do that?"

"I'll try," he said.

They all stood, and Kirra spun him around a few times, and the rest of them rearranged themselves so he wouldn't be able to identify them by memory. Kirra motioned Justin over, and, reluctantly, he joined them.

Tayse, of course, had not looked up once, or commented at all, or even seemed to notice that the rest of them were alive and in the same room.

Kirra pushed Justin in front of Cammon first and snapped her fingers together. It was clear, even through his blindfold, that Cammon was struggling to read the person before him.

"Man," he said at last. "Not mystic. Justin, I think."

Justin snorted and stalked away. Donnal took his place.

"Man. Mystic," Cammon said, speaking with a little more confidence this time.

Senneth stood before him next. He actually swayed backward a little after trying to sense her. "Senneth," he said quietly.

"Why did you do that?" Kirra demanded. "Pull away like that?"

"I can—it's like heat is pouring off her body," he said. "I didn't notice it before, and I was sitting right next to her. But now that I'm trying—it's such a strong sensation—"

Senneth laughed and stepped aside. "I'll have to learn how to disguise that."

Kirra had shifted her features while Cammon was talking and now, styled like a man, she stood in front of the sensitive and snapped her fingers. "Woman," he said without hesitation.

Kirra laughed, concentrated, and made herself into an exact replica of Tayse. Then she snapped her fingers again.

"Still Kirra," Cammon said.

"Does she seem at all different to you?" Senneth asked curiously.

"Different in what way?" he asked. "It's just—I know it's a woman, and I know it's not you. So it must be Kirra."

Senneth nodded at Donnal, who melted into the shape of a bear, features drawn back in a snarl. He lumbered over to face Cammon.

"Donnal," Cammon said.

"Are you sure?" Kirra asked. "You know it's *Donnal* and not just a male with power?"

Cammon thought about that. "Someone who's slipped in here when we weren't paying attention?" he asked with gentle irony. "No. I can tell it's Donnal, him specifically."

"Take a look," Kirra said, and pulled off the blindfold. Cammon started back at the sight of Donnal's feral visage, but recovered quickly.

"That's what he looked like when I tried to read him?" he asked.

Kirra nodded. "Seems like you have the ability to identify the essence of things even when they're in disguise," she said. "I don't know exactly how they'll train you, but it certainly seems like a useful ability to have."

"There are things you can work on, maybe, while you're traveling with us," Senneth suggested. "Differentiating a lie from truth. Trying to read passing strangers and telling us what you know about them. Paying attention to everything around you, animate and inanimate, to gauge what speaks to you and what does not. Who knows, you might be the kind of man who can look at the ground and tell if a diamond field lies below it. That could make you a rich man very quickly."

Cammon looked intrigued. "I don't think I have much ability with rocks and stones," he said, "but I'll try."

Across the room, Tayse stood up. As always, Senneth found herself noticing just how *big* the man was—tall, yes, but broad in the shoulders, massive in the thighs. He had shaved during the two days they were in Dormas, and his face looked big, too, broad cheekbones and stiff chin. Something about the darkness of his coloring added to the impression of size and menace—black hair, black eyes, weathered skin. A man you would not lightly cross.

"It's late," Tayse said, strolling closer to the fire. "If we're moving on in the morning, we'd better turn in now."

Justin turned to him for orders, as he always did, even though Senneth was nominal head of this expedition. "Post a watch?"

Tayse looked briefly undecided. Here so close to the Storian lands, Senneth knew, they'd felt safe enough to sleep unguarded. But there had been that altercation in Dormas—

Tayse nodded. "We'd better, this night. Though I don't think anyone will come looking for us in the rain."

"I'll stay awake first," Senneth volunteered.

The others claimed their hours, and then they took their places beside the fire. Within minutes, having learned by hard necessity to rest when an opportunity presented itself, they were all asleep. Even Cammon, who was probably too tired to stay awake and brood, even if that had been his nature.

Senneth listened to them breathe and watched the flames. She loved nothing so much as fire, variegated as autumn and leaping with an uncontainable vitality. To her it was the source of all beauty, all power, all creativity, all destruction. She could build a city with fire; she could bring it down. She stretched her hand out to the flames and felt the heat lick along her skin, still no hotter than her own blood. She held it there a long time, till her flesh seemed to become a wick, till the fire danced around her fingernails, red and gold and jagged. If she lifted her hand up, her skin would still be on fire.

She curled her fingers into a ball, and the flames went out.

Two more hours she sat there, unmoving, cross-legged before the blaze. She added no more fuel, and the flames never sank lower. The heat radiating from the central fire never dimmed; the whole dairy house was comfortably warm. A little before midnight, she heard a change outside—the sound of silence after the long thrum of rain—and knew the storm had broken. It would be cold in the morning, with white frost overlaying the hard ground, but once they got moving, the ride south would be refreshing in the newly washed air.

When her hours were up, she finally stirred, stretching a little and turning to look at Tayse's sleeping form. He was not asleep, of course; he always woke, unaided, a moment or two before his watch began. He lay there a few feet away from her, watching her, no expression at all to be read on his face. She could see the gleam of the fire reflected in his dark eyes and wondered, not for the first time, if he loved or hated it.

It was dark and late, and the whole world seemed to be sleeping. She spoke the thought in her head, something she rarely did. "Tayse," she said, low enough to keep from waking the others, "why do you distrust me so much?"

He rolled to a sitting position with a single easy motion. "You're a mystic," he said, as if that explained it all.

"Donnal and Kirra are mystics, and you don't distrust them," she said. "You just despise them."

She saw a smile almost make it to his face. "You're different," he said.

"Why?"

He shook his head. "Go to sleep. Dawn will come soon enough."

She pushed herself away from the flames and made herself comfortable in her blanket. But when she glanced back at him, he was still watching her. He was always watching her.

"Why?" she said again.

He didn't look away. "You have too many secrets."

CHAPTER
3

IN the cold, clear morning, they resumed their trip south. Kirra was in a festive mood, and she rode beside Donnal, teasing him. She had bound her golden hair into a braid and pinned it to her head, but there was still no disguising either her femininity or her gentility. Senneth smiled a little to see Cammon glance her way again and again. Kirra had that effect on most men.

Soon enough, though, Cammon fell back to ride beside Senneth. He really had little enough choice of companions. As was his habit, Tayse had ranged some distance ahead, scouting for trouble; Justin had lagged behind to watch the road just traveled. Donnal and Kirra were absorbed in each other.

"I realized in the night that I still know very little about you," Cammon said. "Any of you. You said you were on a mission for the king?"

Senneth nodded. "Yes. Tayse and Justin are Riders, and I am— well, I'm not a Rider, but King Baryn trusts me. I have done some work for him before."

"What's a Rider?"

"A hand-picked group of soldiers who are exceptionally devoted to the king," she said. "They train at a special facility in Ghosenhall, and they learn skills in weaponry that I am constantly amazed by. No one can be named a Rider unless another Rider recommends him and the king personally accepts him, and even then he must undergo extremely rigorous training. He swears a fealty to the king that is fanatical—that supersedes any other vow he might make to lord or wife or self. No Rider has ever deserted or betrayed his king, not for five centuries—even bad kings who should have been betrayed commanded loyal Riders. And everyone in Gillengaria who might wish to harm the king is afraid of them."

Cammon was assimilating this. "So King Baryn has asked you to do a favor for him, and he has sent some of his men with you to protect you," he said. "What is the favor? Or can you not tell me? I don't wish to be rude," he ended in a rush.

Senneth smiled. "I don't think you're rude. I'll tell you what I can. The king is growing old, and he has only one heir, his daughter Amalie. *She* is only eighteen. He remarried a few years ago, but his second bride has not produced another heir. Some of the Twelve Houses of Gillengaria think now might be a time to test the strength of the monarchy. I am riding through the countryside to see if I can discover signs of discontent."

"What are the Twelve Houses?" Cammon asked. "I'm sorry, I know I seem stupid, it's just that—"

"You're a stranger here. Which is odd, because you don't feel like a stranger," Senneth said.

"No," he admitted. "I feel like I belong. It's clear to me that this is the place I'm supposed to be. And today, this morning, waking up for the first time without the moonstone around my neck—I feel so strong. I feel like a new man woke up inside an old body."

Now Senneth laughed. "An old man," she repeated. "You can't be more than twenty."

"Nineteen."

"I am more than twice your age."

He gave her one long, slow glance of appraisal. His gold-flecked eyes were a dark brown, though his ragged hair was fair; the contrast gave him a serious look. "You're not," he said. "You might be a few years past thirty, but no older."

She raised her eyebrows. "Good," she said. "Spotted the lie and pried out the truth. In fact, I just turned thirty-four." She was silent a moment. "Though, to tell the truth, I feel older than that. Lifetimes older."

He was quiet, too, and then he sighed. "I can't do it yet," he said.

"Do what?"

"Read you. Be able to say, 'You, the mystic Senneth, were born to a gardener and his wife and studied painting when you were young.' I should be able to do that, don't you think?"

She was amused. "And I think someday you might be able to. But perhaps you should start on a more transparent subject. I am not, as anyone will tell you, so easy to read."

"Too many secrets," he agreed.

She felt a slight chill at the words, the same ones Tayse had used the night before. *Too many secrets,* she thought, *and too many tragedies.* She pointed before her. "Try Kirra," she suggested. "She shouldn't be so hard."

So Cammon gazed at the swaying back and bright gold hair, his smooth face drawn into a frown of concentration. "Rich," he said at last. "Privileged. Very much loved by—somebody. Her father, maybe. And sparkling with magic." He smiled a little. "Happy. But I didn't need to try to scan her to tell you that."

"No, and a look at her clothes and complexion could probably tell you the part about wealth and privilege," Senneth agreed. "Very good, all the same. She's the oldest daughter of Malcolm Danalustrous, one of the most powerful nobles in the country— and you're right, he loves her very much. When it was discovered that she was a mystic, he didn't expel her from the estate, as many a nobleman has upon discovering he's spawned something demonic. Instead, he imported tutors and had her taught at Danalustrous. He forced the other nobles to treat her with respect and accept her into their very rarified social circle. No other fathers from any of the Twelve Houses have been so fond, even when they didn't disown their magical children."

"You keep saying that—Twelve Houses. What does that mean?"

Kirra, who might have been pretending not to hear when they were discussing her, caught those words, at least. She reined back a little so she could fall in on the other side of Cammon, leaving Donnal to ride on ahead alone.

"Time for a history lesson," she said merrily. "But without a map and a piece of paper to write it all down on, you won't be able to keep it straight. Only those of us who have grown up studying the alliances can possibly follow who's related to whom and why it's so shocking when a boy from Merrenstow marries a girl from Gisseltess."

Senneth ignored her. "There are twelve noble Houses of Gillengaria—bloodlines and property divisions that have existed for centuries. Between them, they own virtually all the valuable land of the country, though some own acres of fertile farms, and some command the coastlines, and others own access to the mountains where gold and silver are mined. The marlords—"

"The what?" Cammon interrupted.

"Marlords," Senneth repeated. "The head of each of the Twelve Houses is called a marlord. His son would be known as a serramar and his daughter as a serramarra. His brothers and sisters also bear those titles because they're also considered direct heirs to the marlordship. So, if you wanted to be very proper about it, you would address Kirra as serra Kirra, or even serramarra Kirra, which I have always thought particularly lovely."

"Kirra will do," said the serramarra, grinning.

"Anyway, the marlords consider themselves the most elegant, sophisticated, and important men and women of the kingdom. They pretend to owe allegiance to the king, and generally they are loyal, but all of them believe that they are superior to royalty and could rule much better if the chance fell to them."

Kirra's smiled had widened. "So you can imagine the level of excitement when the royal line produces a child. Who will marry the prince or princess? Which of the Twelve Houses will gain a foothold at the royal palace?"

"What if the king and queen never have a child?" Cammon asked. "Has that ever happened?"

"A few times," Kirra said. "But not for at least a hundred years. When it does happen, all sorts of scheming goes on, as families make alliances and try to produce heirs that will be acceptable to all the Houses. Usually, of course, everyone looks first to Brassenthwaite."

"Why?" Cammon said.

Senneth smiled. "Brassenthwaite has always been considered first among Houses," she said. "The lands encompass part of the northern seacoast, a stretch of rich mountains, and some of the finest farmland in the country—in short, everything. And the Brassenthwaites have always been most fiercely loyal to the king. It is their heritage—it is what distinguishes them from all other Houses. Thus, there have been many marriages between the royal line and Brassenthwaite. And if there were no heir, Brassenthwaite would consider it had the primary claim to the throne."

Senneth glanced at Kirra before continuing. "Now, Danalustrous—"

"Danalustrous has always been just as loyal, just as strategic, and nearly as wealthy," Kirra supplied. "So a son or daughter of Danalustrous might as easily be declared ruler."

"So if King Baryn and his daughter both died suddenly," Cammon said, "who would claim the throne right now?"

"Well, Kiernan Brassenthwaite would probably step right up," Kirra said. "But a lot of people dislike marlord Kiernan."

"With some justification," Senneth murmured.

"And I don't think, say, Halchon Gisseltess would just hand him the crown," Kirra continued. "And I really believe Ariane Rappengrass and Martin Helven would rather see a Danalustrous on the throne."

"Perhaps that would be the answer, then," Cammon said. "There should be an alliance between Danalustrous and Brassenthwaite. Are their heirs of marriageable age?"

Kirra stared at him. Senneth erupted into peals of laughter.

"Yes, Kirra," she finally managed to say. "If Baryn dies, you should marry Kiernan's brother, and you and Nate Brassenthwaite can take the throne together."

"I'd rather see Halchon Gisseltess be named king," Kirra said flatly. Senneth laughed even harder.

"I suppose that wasn't such a good idea," Cammon said.

"Oh, it would be a fine idea, if Nate Brassenthwaite wasn't such a smug, pigheaded, self-important fool," Kirra snapped.

"Stupid, too," Senneth gasped out, and then started laughing again.

"Kiernan's not as bad, but he's married."

"He's *worse*," Senneth said. "Because he's mean on top of it. Just like their father."

"But he's not stupid," Kirra said.

Senneth sobered almost on the instant. "No," she agreed. "Kiernan is not stupid. And, were I Kiernan Brassenthwaite, I would be looking toward Danalustrous even now. Even if the king lives another twenty years and his daughter becomes a great queen— well, it never hurts to strengthen the northern alliances. Kiernan should be taking the long view, and that view faces straight west toward Danalustrous. If he's not thinking of a marriage between Nate and your sister, I would be greatly surprised."

Kirra made an unladylike sound. "My sister wouldn't have him."

"Would your father?" Senneth asked softly.

They rode on a few minutes in silence while Kirra appeared to think that over. "He might," she said finally. "But he would not force Casserah into a distasteful marriage, no matter how it might benefit the House. And Casserah has a mind of her own. It is very difficult to persuade her to do something she does not want to do."

Cammon seemed wholly intrigued. "This is very exciting," he said. "Tell me more. Who are the heads of the other Twelve Houses, and what are they like?"

So Senneth and Kirra obligingly went through the whole litany for him, the sonorous syllables rolling off their tongues—Brassenthwaite and Danalustrous, tiny Tilt, bustling Merrenstow, peaceful, prosperous Storian. Kianlever and Coravann to the east, Helven and Nocklyn on the southern plains. And claiming the southern coastline, rich Fortunalt, elegant Rappengrass, and ambitious Gisseltess.

"And the king thinks there is unrest now among all these Houses," Cammon said. "Do you really think it might lead to some kind of uprising?"

Kirra and Senneth again exchanged glances, and Kirra shook her head. "Surely not," she said. "The country has been peaceful for so long."

Senneth was silent awhile, watching the road ahead of them. Tayse had circled back and was riding their way; he must have thought it was time to halt for lunch. His eyes went to each of them, one by one, as if counting, as if making sure they had survived these few hours out of his immediate line of sight. "I have no idea," Senneth said softly. "That's what we're riding to find out."

THE rest of the day's journey passed uneventfully, enlivened only occasionally by conversation. Senneth thought Cammon would be willing to spend the whole day asking questions and learning answers, but she eventually grew tired of talking. Too much time alone or among strangers; she had developed the trick of silence. She could not break her habit of watchfulness even when she was among friends.

Well, some of them at least were friends. Kirra, of course; Donnal, almost certainly, though his first loyalty would always be to Kirra, to the House of Danalustrous. It was too soon to know if

Cammon would be trustworthy or not, though Senneth was inclined to like him. Such a fresh young mind, unclouded by all the calamities that had beset him early. He rode beside them like a reflecting pool, casting back their images. She was not sure she wanted to look too closely.

They were heading almost straight southeast, hoping to cross the tip of Helven lands in a day or two, and as usual, Justin and Tayse were riding behind and ahead. A few hours after the noon meal, Tayse abruptly turned back and awaited them on the road.

"Travelers ahead of us," he said shortly. Senneth nodded and brought her horse up next to his so that they rode side by side in the lead.

"Donnal to the rear—Kirra and Cammon in the middle," she called over her shoulder. Donnal was not much of a fighter, but he had a certain brute peasant strength. Kirra was hopeless with a blade, and who knew about Cammon?

The riders appeared around a bend in the road, about nine of them, dressed in Storian livery and looking friendly enough. They pulled into single file to let the other party pass, and the man on the lead horse asked, "What news of the road ahead?"

"Clear when we left it, though muddy," Tayse said. "Heavy rain the day before, at least at the coast. But no trouble."

The Storian speaker nodded. "Storms back that way, too. Some trees down across the road, but we pulled them to the side, so your way should be clear."

Tayse smiled. "We thank you. The next fine lady to pass this way in a fancy carriage thanks you."

As the Storian men laughed, Senneth found herself thinking, *See that? The man can joke and smile after all.* Not something she had witnessed much for herself. They exchanged a few more comments and continued on.

"And Justin?" Senneth asked when the Storians were out of earshot.

"He will have stepped off the road as soon as he heard horses coming. He'll be along in a few minutes."

Indeed, not long after, Justin came galloping up to make sure they were all well. "And if we had been attacked by these Storians?" Senneth asked in some impatience. "If they had not been Storians at all, but mercenaries or bandits?"

Tayse grinned. "Then he would have arrived in time to add a

fresh blade to our battle—or in time to identify and bury our corpses."

"Though I don't think a few Storian outriders would be enough to trouble Tayse," Justin said scornfully. Glancing at Senneth, he added with some reluctance, "Or even you."

Senneth gave him one quick ironic look, but the compliment warmed her for the rest of the long, cold ride. That night, after they'd made camp and eaten dinner, she stood up and nudged Justin with her toe.

"Come on," she said. "Give me a little practice."

He glanced first at Tayse as if for permission, but came to his feet willingly enough. The others hastily cleared the way, giving them one whole side of camp beside the fire.

"Long blade or short?" Justin asked.

"Whatever you think you can beat me at," she said. "I want to get better."

Justin drew his dagger, but Tayse spoke up from across the fire. "Practice blades," he said sharply.

Senneth was annoyed. "I think I can manage not to let him kill me, even if we use metal."

"Practice blades," Tayse said again, with even more emphasis. "You're both too valuable to lose in a training session."

She would have argued except it was pointless; Justin would do whatever Tayse said. So they laid aside their real weapons and pulled out the wooden ones—wicked enough, if it came down to that, to truly hurt a man. Thrust and duck and feint and lunge. Senneth was fast, but Justin was faster.

"You're dead," he said, his point against her heart.

"Again," she said.

Three times he could have killed her, twice with a blade through the heart and once by cutting her throat, but she inflicted some damage, or would have, had the fight been real. Twice she made him stop and show her some move in slow detail, reenacting it with him till she understood the flow and the mechanics. He was unexpectedly patient, Justin who was so edgy as a rule. She actually found herself liking him by the time the session was done.

"Good," he told her, taking her wooden dagger and matching it to his. "Practice every day like that for a year, and we might make a Rider of you yet."

She couldn't help grinning. "You don't want me for a Rider."

Almost, an answering smile. "If you could fight like that, I might."

Donnal's voice spoke up from the fireside. "Could I have some training some night, too? I'm good enough to get better."

Justin looked at Tayse for the answer. The big man, sitting motionless by the fire, glanced up and shrugged. "No reason not to," he said. "The boy, too, if he wants."

"Me?" Cammon exclaimed. "Yes! I've never handled a sword, though. Or a knife."

"All the more reason to start."

They all stared at Kirra, but no one made her the offer, and she seemed to not even notice that there was a great, gaping hole in the conversation. "I guess I'll be cooking, then, while the rest of you are warring," she said. "I'm glad I could bring *some* skills to this little party."

"Besides the ability to change shapes, of course," Tayse said politely.

She grinned. "You will see sometime how handy a skill that is."

He leaned forward to poke a stick back into the fire. "I look forward to that day," he replied.

CHAPTER
4

THEY encountered nothing of any interest until midmorning of the next day. Once again, Tayse rode ahead and Justin behind; the small group in the middle featured Kirra side by side with Donnal, Cammon beside Senneth, asking his endless questions. Senneth was doing her best to answer them completely and patiently, when all of a sudden he fell silent.

"What?" she said.

He pulled his horse to a stop and then turned it in a complete circle, staring with a frown at the countryside around them. They were riding through a lightly wooded area, though this particular stretch of countryside was mostly poor farmland and the occasional small community. They had passed dozens of cottages set back some distance from the road, and a hundred crop fields waiting to be tilled again in the spring.

"What?" Senneth said again.

Cammon shook his head. "Something's wrong," he said, and circled around again, as if straining to hear something or smell something on the cool, slow breeze.

Senneth barely raised her voice. "Tayse!"

Donnal and Kirra had stopped their horses and padded back. "What is it?" Donnal asked.

Senneth shook her head. "I don't know. I don't think he knows. Says there's something wrong."

Donnal slipped from the saddle and bent low to examine the fringe of dead grass that bordered the road on each side before the trees crept in. Even in human form, he was an excellent tracker, a skill developed in childhood when poaching on Danalustrous lands provided a good income.

"I don't see anything," he said. "I'll try smell."

And that quickly he was in wolf shape, sniffing along the ruts and prints of the road. It always unnerved Senneth, just a little, that he could make the transition so quickly. It unnerved her more that she could see nothing of Donnal's personality in the wolf's eyes. They were merely amber jewels set in a white face framed by a hood of black. If he came at her by night in such a guise, she would raise her dagger to kill him.

Tayse was upon them before Donnal had done more than nuzzle his way a yard into the woods. "What is it? What's happened?" he demanded, arriving at a gallop and reining up sharply.

"I don't know," Senneth said. "Cammon says there's something wrong."

She expected Tayse's face to relax to scorn at those words, but she had forgotten the heart-deep superstition of the trained warrior. As much as anything, a soldier survived on instinct, and Tayse respected that almost as much as he respected skill. "What's the shiftling see?" he asked, watching Donnal.

"Well—" Senneth began, but just then, Donnal gave a little yelp and bounded forward, following some scent or some sound.

"Kirra, Cammon—stay here," Tayse ordered. "When Justin arrives, send him after us, then draw off the road and find cover till we return."

He kneed his horse forward and went into the woods after Donnal. Senneth followed. There was no trail that she could discern, but Donnal seemed to know where he was going well enough. He loped ahead, then waited, furred mouth open in a silent pant, till they caught up. Then he trotted forward again. Easier going for him through these overhung trees, and Senneth considered dismounting, but Tayse didn't, so she didn't either.

They'd gone maybe three-quarters of a mile before they came to a small stone hut sitting by itself in a muddy clearing. Senneth instantly could see that it was accessible by a path that led away from the woods, probably to some smaller country road that they hadn't crossed. Donnal had come by a more direct route.

Tayse was out of the saddle and approaching the building in a low, crouching run, sword in one hand and dagger in the other. Senneth followed suit, straining all her senses for danger. Donnal was already nosing at the door, which was unlatched. It fell open when he pushed it aside with his head, and he sprang across the threshold.

Tayse glanced back at Senneth. "I'm guessing there's no one in there, or he'd show more caution."

"I'd like to think that," she said, and followed him inside.

Where they came upon a scene of slaughter.

Senneth stood just inside the doorway, staring around her in horror. Three—no, four—bodies strewn across the stone and rug work of the floor. Blood had sprayed across the walls, across the spare furniture, lay in dark puddles near the bodies. Very little appeared to have been disturbed except what might have been overturned during a fight. A small table in the adjoining kitchen was set for dinner, all dishes and goblets precisely placed; glassware in cases along the wall sat on their shelves untouched.

Four people killed, by whom, for what?

"Donnal," Senneth said, sheathing her blades. "Can you see how many assailants were here and who they might have been? Which direction they came from, where they went when they left, how long ago?" The wolf put his nose to the floor and began scenting, turning his shaggy head from side to side as another odor caught his attention.

Tayse had put away his weapons, too, and now he knelt by the first body. "Dead a day, maybe," he said. "Not very long. This one's a woman."

Indeed, they discovered as they made a methodical survey of the room, three were women and one was a boy, about fifteen years old. One woman appeared to be Senneth's age, and the others were older by twenty years or more.

"A mother, a son, a grandmother, and an aunt, perhaps," Tayse said in a low voice. "They would have seemed harmless enough."

But Senneth had glimpsed something under the body of the youngest woman, who had died with her face against a braided rug. "Let's turn her over," she said. "I want to see."

Death held no particular terror for Tayse; he showed no distaste as he competently turned the woman to her back. Her throat had been slashed and her face had been cut up, and blood stained every inch of her face and neck. Her hands were bound together before her with a fine rope, and twisted around the rope was a silver chain set with moonstones.

Senneth swallowed a sob. "Killed because they were mystics," she breathed, and sat down right there on the hard floor.

Tayse grunted. "All of them?"

She shook her head. "I don't know."

He went from body to body, then, hunting for clues. When he came back to crouch beside her, he balanced himself on the flats of his feet. "Moonstones on each of their bodies somewhere," he reported. "Hands or throat. Why tie them that way if they're already dead? Or did the attackers bind them with the moonstones first so they couldn't use their power to stop the blade?"

"As if any mystic had that kind of power," Senneth said in a choked voice. "Most mystics—have such small skills. They can—change themselves—or heal someone else's cut—or maybe read someone else's emotion. They can't—they can't fight with their power. They can't hurt anyone. They're—they're—there is no harm in them."

"Well, someone thought so," Tayse said. Still squatting beside her, he surveyed the room. "So, let's see, they lived here for a while—looks like the curtains are old, and the furniture's comfortable, and probably no one bothered them for years. And then, someday, something happened, someone came to mistrust them, and a party got together to deal with them." He glanced down at her. "Happening more these days, especially in the south, so I hear."

"But we're not *in* the south," she said. She had drawn her knees up to her chin and wrapped her arms around her legs. The smell of blood and the reality of what had occurred were making her feel nauseated, but she would not get sick, not in front of Tayse. "We're halfway between Storian and Helven lands! Those Houses have no grudge against mystics!"

"Today they might," Tayse said and rose to his feet.

There was a noise outside, and Tayse whipped around, knife already in hand, but it was only Justin. He stopped short on the threshold. "By the Silver Lady's hand," he said blankly. "What happened here?"

"Massacre of mystics, we're guessing," Tayse said briefly. "See anything on the road?"

Justin shook his head. "I'll go look out front."

Donnal stepped through the door in man shape. "Don't bother," he said. "They left enough tracks for even Kirra to follow."

Senneth put a palm to the floor to push upright and was surprised when Tayse reached out a hand to help her up. She took it and let him haul her to her feet before he released her. "What did you find?" she said, forcing herself to keep her voice steady.

"Shod horses, about twenty of them," Donnal said. "Military unit." She just looked at him. "Civil guard," he expanded. "They rode in fanned out for stealth, rode out in formation."

"Any idea who?" Tayse asked.

"Yes," Donnal said, and threw something across the room at Senneth. "Personal guard for one of the Twelve Houses."

She caught what he had tossed her and turned it over and over in her hands. It was a glove, finely made, soft leather lined with thin wool. On the back was embroidered a black hawk carrying a red flower in its talons. She knew that heraldry.

"Gisseltess," she whispered. "But why would Halchon Gisseltess be murdering mystics hundreds of miles outside his borders?"

"Why would anyone be murdering mystics anywhere?" Donnal demanded.

Justin looked at him. "Nobody likes them. You must know that. Everyone's afraid of them."

"Not everyone," Senneth said. Her mind felt wildly chaotic, as if too many thoughts and pictures were whirling inside her skull at once. She could not force herself to think this through, make herself understand it. "And even so—there is something different—between stoning a mystic in the marketplace and hunting one down in a quiet cottage miles from your home. What brought them here?"

Tayse looked around again. "There's nothing else we can do," he said. "Let's burn the bodies. If there's anything of value here for you," he added, addressing Senneth, "take it now."

She nodded dumbly, thinking that had been a kind gesture on his part. "Donnal," she said, "fetch the others. We'll be here a while."

THEY traveled as far from the hut as they could before making camp for the night. Even so, Senneth assumed that the others carried images all that way with them, as she did. Images of broken bodies, burning pyres, coiled silver ropes of moonstones.

Camp was quick and efficient, everyone taking his or her accustomed task, and dinner was silent. After they'd cleaned up the meal, they all just sat there, by common consent unwilling to seek bedrolls and the nightmares that might come with sleep.

"Does anyone know, do you think?" Cammon asked, the first to break the silence. The youngest, the one who found silence most unbearable, Senneth thought. "Does anyone who loves them know that they're dead?"

"Anyone who comes looking will find the blood in the house and the bonfire out back," Tayse said quietly. "They'll figure it out."

Cammon shook his head. "People should have someone to mourn them," he said. "When they die, someone should be sad."

Who will mourn you? Senneth wanted to ask, but she thought that the answer to that question was probably what had prompted him to make the observation in the first place.

Kirra leaned closer to the fire, tugging on the necklace she always wore. By firelight, it took on a muted gorgeousness, for it was a perfect, multifaceted ruby that loved nothing so much as light. "If I die on the road," she said, "take off my pendant and send it to my father in Danalustrous. You'll have to cut it off with metal, though, 'cause it's welded on."

Justin looked over at her, ready to express scorn for the nobility once he had the full story. "You wear a necklace that's been soldered on?"

She nodded, staring into the flames. "Many of the women of the Twelve Houses do. Cut to just such a length, so they fall here"—she touched a point just above her breasts—"to cover up their housemarks."

Now both Riders were staring at her. "Their what?" Justin said. "Housemarks?"

She nodded again. "Every time a legitimate child is born to one of the Twelve Houses, he or she is marked at birth with the insignia of the estate. Danalustrous is a small D. Very elegant. Gisseltess is a tiny flower. Merrenstow is a circle with a line through it, signifying—oh, something. I forget all the complicated symbols of heritage."

"Marked at birth—how, exactly?" Tayse asked.

Kirra glanced over at him. "Branded. Burned into the skin."

"And you think *I'm* barbaric," Justin said.

She smiled a little. "I know. Isn't it the strangest custom? I grew up with it, so it didn't occur to me how horrifying the ritual was, till I saw a small girl undergo it. I cried for three days."

"So you're branded at birth with the crest of your house," Tayse said. "How come I've never seen any of the aristocracy with such a mark?"

"Because we wear these pendants to cover them, of course. At least, the women do. It is considered the height of poor manners to move or dance in such a way that your necklet slips and your housemark is revealed in grand society."

"I'll never understand rich folks," Justin remarked.

Now she looked at him through the flames. "No," she said haughtily, "you probably never will."

Senneth was smiling till she caught Tayse's eyes on her. "And you," Tayse said. "If you die on the mission. How will we identify your body and to whom should we send the evidence?"

She laughed. "Oh, I don't wear anything so fancy," she said, reaching a finger under her collar to pull out a golden chain. It was hung with a worn golden disk decorated with a thin circlet of filigree. "But I haven't taken this off since it was given to me by my grandmother seventeen years ago." She kept her voice light. "Upon the occasion of my father banishing me from his house because he didn't care for witches. She said I should carry something with me that would always remind me someone loved me still. She's dead now." Leaving unsaid the corollary thought that there was no one alive who still loved her. "I suppose, if I'm slaughtered on the road, you should send this on to Malcolm Danalustrous as well. I've done some work for him, and he's always been kind to me."

Donnal was grinning. "Well, then, send word of my death on to Danalustrous, too," he said. "I suppose news of a chattel's death might mean more to the marlord than it would to the chattel's family."

"You're not a chattel. You never were," Kirra said sharply.

Donnal leaned back on his arms. "Near enough as makes no difference when you grow up on Danalustrous land and Danalustrous charity," he said, but he didn't sound aggrieved. "But your father's a grand old man. I'd work for him and fight for him even if I wasn't born to it."

This was an old argument; none of them really needed to hear it again. "How about you?" Senneth asked Justin. "Who shall we notify of your demise?"

He put a fist to his shoulder and bowed low over the fire. "Tell King Baryn, of course, that one of his Riders has been gathered to the Pale Mother's arms. And send my weapons to be divided among the Riders so that they can carry some part of me into their next skirmish."

She looked at Tayse. "Your wish as well, I suppose?"

"Tell the king, tell the Riders. My father is a Rider still," he said. "One message will inform everyone I wish to know."

Involuntarily, they all looked at Cammon, though no one was rude enough to ask the question. But he was a sensitive, and, anyway, he had started this line of questioning. "I assume I'll be with all of you if I go in the next few weeks," he said cheerfully enough. "No one else to tell."

Kirra stirred. "This is gloomy talk," she said. "Can't we discuss something else?"

"Name the topic," Tayse said.

Kirra glanced at Senneth. "Don't you find yourself wondering," she asked, "what Halchon Gisseltess thinks he's doing slaughtering innocents so near to Helven land? Don't you find yourself wondering what Martin Helven might think of such an act?"

"Yes," Senneth said. "We might find out a great deal if we were to make a visit to Martin Helven."

"How would you do that?" Tayse asked, his voice sounding interested. "Just ride up to his estates and ask him?"

"His primary residence is in Helvenhall, only a few days away," Kirra said. "Fairly large city, as cities go here in the inland properties. We could take a room at the most expensive inn in town, and I could send a message to his estate. I am, though none of you seems to appreciate it, the oldest daughter of a very wealthy man, and I can move in the most elite circles. I think he would come visit me one afternoon. And maybe he would tell me some of the things we wish to know."

Senneth sighed. "I like that part of it. The rest doesn't sound like so much fun."

Tayse turned his attention back to Senneth. "Why?"

Kirra was smiling. "She knows I'll want her to pose as my maid, since obviously a serramarra of Danalustrous would not be traveling unaccompanied." She glanced around the fire. "There are just enough of you to appear to be a respectable guard. We would have to do something about your clothes, though. You would need to be wearing proper livery."

"That'll be easy to come by hundreds of miles from your father's house," Justin sneered.

She was still smiling. "You forget," she said. "I'm a shiftling. I can change anything to look like anything else. I can make myself a ball gown out of these travel trousers, and I can dress you in the colors of Danalustrous."

"Can you make Senneth look submissive?" Tayse asked. "Because I would think that would take some pretty strong magic."

There was muffled laughter around the fire. Senneth felt her face twitching into a childish scowl.

"Senneth has enough of the shape-shifter's skills to disguise both her strength of body and strength of will," Kirra said. "I am sure she can make herself look quite dull."

"I'm willing to dress up as a nobleman's guard," Tayse said. "I think it would be interesting to see what we might learn."

Everyone else murmured an agreement. Senneth sighed again, for she knew the plan had merit. It wouldn't work in Rappengrass or Gisseltess, but Martin Helven had always been a reasonable—and not particularly observant—man. "Very well," she said. "On to Helvenhall."

CHAPTER
5

Two days later they rode into a tidy little city that rose with a self-important grandeur in the middle of the flatlands. Tayse looked around with interest, for he'd never been there. With him, it was an automatic thing to begin assessing and cataloging. Here was where the city was vulnerable to attack, here was where the back alleys lay if someone needed a quick exit. There were no gates to pass through, though there were guards lounging along the main road that led into the city. They were dressed in Helven green and gold, and they looked suitably well-trained, but they also looked as if they'd never seen a day's real combat in their lives. Tayse shared a look with Justin, knowing that they had the same thought: *We could take any five of them and win.*

The local guards didn't seem to read their expressions. Indeed, many of them gave friendly waves to fellow soldiers, since Tayse and the other men of the party were wearing sashes colored with Danalustrous gold and red. It was interesting to be greeted with such casual respect. Riders, of course, wore black embroidered with the king's gold lion when they wished to be recognized, and this generally evoked a reaction of awe bordering on fear. When they traveled incognito, they were more often mistaken for mercenaries or outlaws, and therefore treated with suspicion and caution. Rarely were they viewed as compatriots who might be good for a drink or two once the shift was ended.

Kirra swept ahead of them all like a disdainful queen. Even in travel clothes, going four days without a bath, she was a beautiful woman, but dressed like the noblewoman she was, she was literally breathtaking. She and Senneth had spent an hour braiding jewels and gold ribbon into her hair before dressing her in a red and gold gown.

"You produced that from oak leaves and meadowgrass, I suppose," Tayse had said.

Kirra had grinned over at him. Even her face looked finer, as if she had let herself gain some coarseness and weariness while they rode and now cast off those unnecessary disguises. "From buckskin and dirty linen," she said. "Do you like it? Would it make you want to confide in me?"

He had grinned back. "I don't think fine clothes would move me as much as you'd like," he replied. "But this Helven lord might be a different matter."

Senneth's transformation had been more subtle but, to Tayse, more shocking. She had stepped out from Kirra's shadow, and he had just stared at her. Her fine white-blond hair had darkened to a muddy brown, and her alert gray eyes looked washed out and tired. Even her skin, so smooth for someone who had led such an adventurous life, looked matted and ill used. Worst of all was her expression: docile, bland, and distant. "I am sure marlord Martin will respond to serra Kirra just as he should," she said in a repressive voice.

Kirra had burst out laughing, but Tayse had not been able to shake off his disbelief. "What did you do to her?" he demanded. "She doesn't look anything like—I don't know that I would recognize her."

"I didn't touch her. I told you she had enough shiftling magic in her to change her appearance."

"Does it hurt?" he found himself asking.

Senneth didn't even smile at him for the question, as he supposed serving maids never got a chance to smile. "Does what hurt? To make a transformation like this? No, but it's a little tedious and requires more of my concentration than I'd like."

"I mean—does it hurt to hold it all back? To swallow all the energy and intelligence that's usually on your face?"

For a moment she looked truly surprised, so he must have said something he did not intend. "No," she said again. "But I'm starting to think I must look even worse than I meant to."

Tayse shook his head. "I'd have sworn on any Rider's life that you had never been a servant, but right now I'd have to be rethinking that. You look the part completely."

"You're right," she said dryly. "I've never been a maid, though I've played a lot of different roles in my life."

"More roles than I can keep track of," he said.

A small smile for that. "And you don't know half of them."

"That's the trouble," he said and turned away.

He knew a few of them, though, and he reviewed them as he followed her and Kirra into the city. She had the guildmarks of half a dozen professions tattooed on her left wrist, partially covered by the moonstone bracelet. She'd worked in the gold mines, spent a summer laboring on an inland farm, been a horse trader, a fisherwoman, a blade for hire. He was still not clear on how she had hooked up with Malcolm Danalustrous, though he had finally worked out that she was one of the tutors who'd been brought in to school Kirra when she was discovered to be a mystic. And perhaps it had been Malcolm Danalustrous who had introduced her to the king, but he was not certain of that either; it could so easily have been the king who brought her to Danalustrous.

Tayse loved his king, and he would die for the man, but he was far from sure royalty had made a wise decision in trusting so much to this footloose and unpredictable woman. Her only true allegiances seemed to be to herself and to her magic, and though he knew no ill of her, he also had seen nothing to make him believe in her.

Then again, he believed wholly in no one but the king and his fellow Riders, so perhaps that was not surprising.

They rode down the broad main avenue of Helvenhall, Tayse still mentally cataloging the sights around them. A handful of taverns, all of them doing a brisk business; a number of shops that catered to a wealthy clientele; few beggars on the street. A well-run and prosperous little town, this city in the middle of Helven.

Kirra headed without hesitation down the street as if she knew exactly where she was going, and in a few moments they had turned into the courtyard of a very fancy inn indeed. It was three stories high, built of quarried stone, and looked more like a private estate than any inn Tayse had ever stayed at. Ostlers ran out of the stables to catch the reins of their horses; footmen hurried through the double doors to take charge of their woefully small pile of luggage. A thin, obsequious man—the owner himself, unless Tayse missed his guess—came straight up to Kirra and handed her down from the saddle.

"How delightful to see you, serra Kirra!" he exclaimed. "I did not know you were traveling! How may I help you? How long will you be staying? Whatever you need, we'll be happy to accommodate you—"

"Thank you," Kirra said in a languid and supercilious tone. "I would like a suite for my girl and me. And an adjoining room for my men. Unusual, I know—I'm sure you have perfectly adequate rooms closer to the stables—but I feel much safer with my own guard within call. You understand. My father is so protective of my safety."

"Yes, indeed, indeed, many of our clients prefer to have familiar swords nearby," he said. "We have just the suite of rooms to suit you—I'm sure you'll be happy there. Shall I have food brought up? Wine? Is there any other service I can do for you?"

"Indeed. If you would," Kirra said, stepping through the door that he held open for her and not even looking to see if the others were still following. "Martin Helven—I have a message for him. I wonder if he is in town?"

"Ah, marlord Helven—I will have a boy run 'round with a note. I believe he is at his estate, but I will certainly have an answer for you before nightfall."

"You're too good."

The proprietor led them up one set of stairs and down a wide, airy hall painted a gleaming white. Tayse counted doors and hallways so he could have a sense of how many people might be present to contend with if some mishap occurred; Justin, he could tell, was doing the same. Cammon looked around with barely restrained delight at the high ceilings and painted ornamentation. Tayse wanted to nudge him but didn't want to draw any attention to the boy. Of all of them, Donnal seemed least impressed by their surroundings. But then, Tayse assumed, he had seen even greater magnificence at the Danalustrous estate—where, from what Tayse had been able to piece together, he had spent some time as Kirra's playmate or fellow student in the mystic arts.

The women were ushered into a room of grand proportions and great heavy furniture; the men stood outside at strict attention. Tayse was close enough to the door to see Kirra glance around once. "Yes—very pretty," she said, still in that bored voice. "We shall be here at least two nights. Please have supper for two sent up right away. Oh, and—something for the men to eat as well."

The proprietor bowed himself out of the room. "Yes, serra Kirra. Right away."

He did pause to unlock a door down the hall that led to a much smaller but still quite attractive room with three bunk beds pushed against the walls. Tayse's eyes immediately sought the connecting door and placed where it must be situated in Kirra's room. He slipped the innkeeper a silver coin, because it never hurt to stay on the good side of your host, and the man winked at him as he pocketed it.

"I'll send up some ale with that dinner," he said. "Good stuff, too. My son makes it."

"That will be most welcome," Tayse said gravely. He waited for the other three men to file in, then shut the door behind them.

Kirra was already knocking on the door between their rooms. "I can't get this open!" she called. "Is it locked on your side?" Within moments, the two women had slipped through the door, and they had all disposed themselves on the furniture throughout the men's chamber.

"But you'd better not let him catch you socializing with your personal guard, or you're going to raise some eyebrows," Tayse warned her. "The last thing we want to do is attract attention."

Justin had climbed to one of the top bunks and was looking down at the rest of them with the air of a brooding vulture considering what to eat. "You certainly play the part to perfection," he commented.

Senneth glanced up at him. "She's not playing," she said. "Born to it."

Tayse asked, "So then is she playing when she acts our comrade on the road?"

Kirra gave him one bright, indignant look. "When I think how friendly I've been to you all this time, and how you've never been anything but hateful in return, it makes me want to spell you into a toad, it really does."

Cammon's dark eyes grew big. "Can you do that?"

"No," Kirra said with a sigh. "I can change other *things* from one shape to another, but I can't change people, except myself. It's very limiting."

Half-smiling, Tayse glanced up at Justin. "At any rate, she *says* she can't," he murmured.

Justin nodded. "I'm on my guard."

"So what next?" Donnal asked. "Except dinner."

"And a bath," Senneth added.

"And a good night's sleep on clean sheets," Justin supplied.

Kirra shrugged. "I think we wait until we hear from Martin Helven. Until then, I suppose, we just relax."

THE food was delicious; the bath, which the men took in the shed downstairs where common folk cleaned up, was hot and welcome. The relaxing came a little harder for men of action. Tayse and Justin played at card games, grudgingly allowing Senneth to join them—and then, when she asked, Kirra.

"You don't know how to play," Justin said.

"Well, at least I've got money," she said. "If I lose, you'll be all the richer."

"Deal her in," Tayse said.

Justin shuffled but didn't look happy about it. "She'll trick the cards," he said. "Her and Senneth both."

"I will not! I don't care enough about a stupid card game to go to the trouble," Kirra said.

Senneth gave Justin one long, measured look. Tayse couldn't tell if she was truly irritated or not; her unshakable calm was one of the things he found most perplexing about her. The only time he had seen her rattled was when they found those dead mystics, and even then she had not broken down and cried as so many women would have. Kirra had, when she'd arrived a few minutes later. Not Senneth.

"I wonder why it is," Senneth said now in a thoughtful voice, "that you always expect a mystic to be worse than your other comrades, instead of better."

Justin tilted his chin with habitual defiance. "Why would I think you're better?"

"Justin thinks every man has more potential for evil than good," Tayse explained. "The more powerful you are, the more likely you are to turn bad. And mystics have a certain power. Hence—"

"You could murder me in the middle of the night while I was just peacefully sleeping," Justin said.

Senneth shrugged and picked up the cards he'd dealt her. "What's to stop you from doing the same to me?"

Justin scowled. "Honor! I'd never fight someone who wasn't wide awake and facing me."

"And why can't mystics have the same sense of honor? Why wouldn't we, too, scorn to attack a man who was helpless and un-aware of danger?"

"Maybe you would," Justin muttered, "but you haven't proved it to me yet."

Tayse couldn't help grinning at the two women. Kirra was shaking her head, not even interested in arguing with someone so hopeless. Senneth merely looked thoughtful. "In fact," Tayse said, "the only people Justin truly trusts are other Riders. And unless you attain that rank and status, I'm afraid he's never going to view you with anything but suspicion."

"Then I have my life's goal before me," Senneth said. "To be-come good enough to be a king's Rider and win Justin's heart."

They all laughed, even Cammon and Donnal, lounging on their beds. Senneth laid down a card, and play resumed, and after that most of them lost interest in conversation. Kirra might have hexed the cards after all, for she won more than her share of hands, but Justin did almost as well, so he was appeased. Tayse did poorly, and Senneth won nothing.

"I hope my mistress pays me a living wage," Senneth com-mented as Tayse announced he was done for the night. "Or I won't be able to afford to play with you fellows anymore."

Which reminded Tayse to look at her face again—which was her own face, lively and untroubled. "You dropped your disguise," he said.

She nodded. "I'll resume it again tomorrow when Martin Hel-ven arrives, but it probably doesn't matter. Now that everyone considers me a serving maid, they'll see me as such, no matter what look I have on my face. But I may as well resume the veils tomorrow anyway—in case—" She shrugged.

"In case someone recognizes you," he said.

She and Kirra both laughed at that. "Yes," Senneth said, "for exactly that reason."

THE morning passed slowly, as time without activity was wont to do. Tayse sent the other three men off to run errands: procure food, take the horses for shoeing, and generally see if they could pick up any useful information in the streets of Helven. He stayed in the suite, prepared to give consequence to Kirra whenever Martin Helven arrived.

Which he did around three in the afternoon. Tayse had taken up a post at the only window in his room that overlooked the street, so he saw the expensive coach pull up, a gold-and-green crest painted on the side. He knocked on the connecting door and announced, "He's here, for those of you who need to put on your false faces," and then stationed himself in the hallway outside Kirra's room.

In a few moments, the fawning proprietor was back upstairs, the marlord of Helven at his heels. Tayse kept his hands folded on his sword and his eyes facing straight forward, but he was able to take in some details. Martin Helven appeared to be in his mid-fifties, portly and well-dressed. He was mostly bald except for a fringe of brown hair, and he was panting a little as he took the last few steps. No danger in this man, especially not with Senneth inside the room. Even Kirra could probably fend him off if he showed some inclination to attack.

"Would you be so good as to announce marlord Martin Helven to your mistress?" the proprietor asked, so Tayse rapped smartly on the door and passed the information along. Quite soon, the innkeeper had disappeared back downstairs, Martin Helven had seated himself across from Kirra on some highly decorated furniture, and Tayse was standing on the inside of the room with his back to the door. Kirra had told him the Helven man would not think it strange if he stood guard even during a private conversation, and so he had chosen to listen in—impassively, of course. Senneth sat on the window seat, appearing to embroider something. He found himself wondering if this was a skill she really had and, if so, what particular pattern she was working on. She had resumed her maid's identity and looked as plain and unmemorable as a woman could look.

"Marlord Martin. It is so good of you to come visit me upon such short notice," Kirra was saying in a warm voice. "Would you like some wine? Some tea? The innkeeper brought me these wonderful little cakes earlier today—he's really the kindest man."

The nobleman beamed at this praise. "I'm glad you find him

accommodating. I own the hotel, you know, and the man works for me. He's always seemed to do a good job, but I'm glad to hear you're pleased."

"Ah, I wasn't aware that you owned this place!" Kirra exclaimed, though Tayse was instantly certain that she had known it and had picked the establishment for that very reason. "Well, you've done a most excellent job. You've such a good head for business. My father has often remarked at how any enterprise you turn to is invariably a success."

"Well, here in Helven, we have only crops and commerce, so we do what we can," the marlord said in a voice that he tried to make sound modest. "I've long envied you your coastline and fishing ventures—but then, it is always fashionable to envy Danalustrous!"

Kirra laughed merrily. Tayse was pretty sure she was flirting with the marlord in the way that a young woman always seemed to know how to flirt with an older man—meaning nothing by it except to smooth her own way. "Danalustrous thanks you," she said. "So tell me! What's the news from the middle of the kingdom? I have been up north so long I feel I'm completely out of touch with this part of the world."

They gossiped for a good half hour, trading names and exclaiming over events that seemed so numerous and so trivial that Tayse could hardly conceal his stupefaction. Out of the corner of his eye he glanced at Senneth once or twice, to see if she was exhibiting any discreet signs of boredom, but all her attention was on her needle and thread. She never even looked out the window while Tayse watched.

Kirra, though, was subtler than Tayse had given her credit for. One name got idly tossed into the conversation, and then she hesitated for a moment, and then she said in a low voice, "But she's—didn't I hear—there was a rumor that she might be showing signs of being a mystic."

Martin Helven actually glanced around the room, but seeing only a guard and a maid—in short, nobody—he seemed to feel it was safe to speak. "Yes, and her father was quite upset about it at first, but he has tried to show forbearance. It is not—forgive me, serra Kirra—it is not what one prays for when one's daughter is born, that she will grow up to wield magical power. It makes life so hard, for the girl and all her family. And especially so these days—" His voice trailed off as he glanced around the room again.

Kirra leaned forward conspiratorially. "Yes, please, what can you tell me about the prevailing attitudes farther south? I had planned to continue my travels down toward Fortunalt and Rappengrass, but I have been starting to feel—well—less welcome than I always have. Is it my imagination, or is it my magic that is turning old friends against me?"

"I would never turn against you, serra Kirra," the marlord said solemnly, "but your instincts play you true. There have been odd reports coming out of Nocklyn and Gisseltess—tales of mystics hunted down in the middle of the night, and turned out in the streets—or worse. I don't want to upset you, but there have been—deaths—murders—terrible stories of mystics who have been found mutilated in their own homes. Even in Rappengrass— where, you know, mystics have always been tolerated—I have heard stories of men and women who have met terrible ends. It is all very distressing."

Kirra's eyes were as wide as if she hadn't witnessed such a massacre for herself only a couple of days ago. "But what is causing such animosity toward the mystics?" she cried. "Have these people done anything—said anything—to earn such enmity?"

Helven shook his head. "I believe it is all Coralinda's doing. She has a great deal of influence in these parts, you know."

Kirra fell back in astonishment against her chair. Across the room, Tayse saw Senneth look up from her embroidery and lay her glance very briefly on Martin Helven's face.

"Coralinda Gisseltess?" Kirra repeated. "But—but what—I thought she left her brother's House some twenty years ago to take vows in the Pale Mother's order."

Martin Helven nodded. "Indeed she did! She was the most illustrious member of society to join the order, and you know she brought it no little cachet. Young noblewomen in the south started becoming novices by the hundreds once Coralinda joined and made it fashionable. Then they began calling themselves the Daughters of the Pale Mother and going around proselytizing. And Coralinda herself has been named head of the order. Some fancy title—the Luster or the Lestra or some such thing."

"Yes—Daughters of the Pale Mother—that's what they used to call the converts," Kirra said in a faint voice. She was still leaning back against the chair, and all vestiges of flirtation had left her pretty face. She appeared to be thinking, and thinking hard. "There are convents up in the northern parts, too, but they only get a handful of applicants. My father has supported one for years, because he says all people need some form of faith in their lives, even if it's something they choose not to follow. Just to know it's there. Just to know there might be a power somewhere stronger than you and willing to knock you down if you don't behave."

The Helven marlord smiled primly. "That sounds very like Malcolm."

Kirra's attention returned to him. "But explain this to me! So you're saying that Coralinda Gisseltess has been named head of the Daughters of the Pale Mother—and *she* has something to do with this sudden new persecution of mystics? Why would that be?"

"Oh, well, the Pale Mother disapproves of those with magic powers," Helven said with a touch of sanctimoniousness. "Coralinda says that anyone who possesses magic is possessed by darkness. She has made it stylish—necessary, even—for members of the nobility to wear moonstones as part of their daily attire. She has been known—she, personally—to ride into a house where suspected mystics reside and expose them to the neighborhood. I have not actually seen her preside over one of those awful killings, but she—shall I say—she has seemed to feel such murders were justified to rid the world of a terrible scourge. Her views are extreme," he added, "but others in the southern Houses have taken them up. I think you will find your way difficult if you continue on much farther."

"Yes! I can see that I might!" Kirra murmured. "I cannot tell you how grateful I am that you have told me all this. Because just think what might have happened to me if I rode, all unaware, onto the prohibited streets in a Gisseltess city—"

Martin Helven nodded. "Very dangerous. Very dangerous indeed," he said seriously. "I assure you, that is not how we feel in Helvenhall—but—well—perhaps *some* of the residents of the city are beginning to echo Coralinda's words. It is very distressing to me. I have stopped such talk when it is said in the open, but there is no controlling what people whisper to each other at night."

"Indeed, there is not," Kirra said. "Once again, I must thank you for your information. Helven has always been a good friend to Danalustrous, and so it is again."

They talked a few minutes longer, but it was clear even to Martin Helven that Kirra was through with him for the day. He did offer to have her to dinner the following night—"My wife and daughters would be overjoyed to see you"—but she gave him a smiling refusal. She would be on her way again in the morning; she was very sure she would turn back to Danalustrous. But she would carry kind words about him to her father, and she sent with him all her love for the women of his family.

As soon as Tayse had saluted the Helven lord out of the room and closed the door behind him, Kirra leapt to her feet and stared at Senneth. Senneth stayed seated where she was, but she had dropped her sewing to the bench beside her, and she was staring back.

"Coralinda Gisseltess orchestrating a persecution of mystics!" Kirra exclaimed. "Senneth, did you know anything about this? How can this be happening without every mystic in the land crying out the news?"

Senneth shook her head. "The king mentioned something of the sort to me, but only in passing," she said quietly. "It was not his main concern."

Kirra was stalking back and forth across the luxurious carpets. "Well, anything that creates such a disturbance in the kingdom should be his concern!" she said. "If she has influenced the southern nobles to such an extent—what other kind of suggestions might she whisper in their ears?"

"Exactly right," Senneth said. "And Coralinda Gisseltess is a very persuasive woman."

Kirra came to an abrupt halt and gazed at Senneth. Tayse was interested to see that, as soon as Martin Helven had stepped out of the room, Senneth's face had resumed its normal contours, its usual mix of wariness and intelligence. Even her hair was its usual pale aureole.

"What do you know about her?" Kirra said more quietly. "I was a child when she joined the Daughters, and I don't remember anyone talking about her much."

"It was something of a scandal at the time," Senneth said. "Since you've been old enough to pay any attention, people have started to worship the Pale Mother again, but I remember a day when no one gave much service to any of the gods. There's a shrine in Ghosenhall that honors the whole pantheon—the Bright

Mother, the Pale Mother, the Green Keeper, the Dark Watcher—there are a dozen, if I remember correctly, but even I don't know all their names. All the gods had fallen out of favor when I was a little girl."

There was a sound, and Tayse's knife was instantly in his hand, but it was only the door opening from the connecting room. "What happened?" Justin asked. "Did he say anything interesting?"

Kirra was looking at Donnal, who walked in behind Justin. Cammon followed last. "Mystics are being murdered throughout the southern regions," Kirra said. "He thinks some of it is the work of Coralinda Gisseltess, who joined the order of the Pale Mother some twenty years ago, and now is urging nobles to cast out or destroy anyone with magical power."

Donnal's face only grew darker and more solemn at the news. Cammon looked frightened, and Justin looked unimpressed. "I told you," Justin said. "People don't like mystics."

"That doesn't mean they go around butchering them in their own houses," Donnal said.

"No," Justin said in a begrudging voice. "No—and a systematic campaign to eliminate them—" He looked over at Tayse. "What does it mean for us?"

"We were just discussing that," Tayse replied. "Senneth was giving us a lesson in religious history."

Justin looked disbelieving. Kirra sank slowly back onto her divan. "Sit down, all of you," she said. "There's plenty of food left. Let's eat, and figure out if—as Justin says—this has anything to do with us and our mission."

In a few minutes they were all eating and relaxing, even Tayse leaving his post by the door once he was sure it was locked. "Anyway," Senneth resumed. "About fifteen or twenty years ago—just as Coralinda joined the order—the Daughters of the Pale Mother began to gain some favor again. You would see people wearing moonstone neck-laces or setting up a small shrine somewhere on their property. In particular, travelers from the south would carry amulets and inquire about places of worship when they were in unfamiliar cities. People who dislike mystics were particularly drawn to their sect—because, of course, mystics can't abide the touch of moonstones. Some people started to say that the Pale Mother was returning to Gillengaria to take back her people, who had been corrupted by magic." Senneth shrugged. "You can see where two righteous and pitiless philosophies were starting to intersect. But I did not realize the sentiment had grown so strong."

Tayse chewed and swallowed an entire miniature apple, seeds and all. It was the best piece of fruit he'd ever tasted in his life. "Well, if mystics are being murdered in this part of the country, and we're traveling with mystics, what does that do to our chances of carrying out the king's commission?"

Senneth smiled at him. "But we're protected by two King's Riders," she said almost playfully. "Who would dare to do us harm?"

"That's true," Justin said in a judicious voice.

"Anyway, that may end up being what our mission is about," Senneth said. "Discovering the extent to which the Daughters are influencing the malcontents in the southern Houses."

"Besides, we don't look like mystics, do we?" Kirra demanded. "I mean, if you were to come upon us on the road, even if you were hunting out magic, you wouldn't look at the four of us who are mystics and instantly be suspicious, would you?"

"That depends," Tayse drawled. "On whether this one was turning himself into a wolf at that very moment and you were fancying yourself up in a ball gown made out of leather trousers—"

Most of the others were laughing. Cammon was not. "I'm the strange one," he said quietly. "People look at me—and they know. Kardon knew as soon as he had me indentured. Senneth, you knew the minute you saw me walking behind the tavern."

"Yes, but I'm looking for magic," she said. "I think the three of us are far more spectacular than you are, and we've been able to disguise ourselves when we wanted to. I think you can manage the same trick."

"Very well," Tayse said. "Then we press on? To Rappengrass and even Gisseltess?"

Senneth was watching him from across the room. He couldn't tell if she was smiling or not, but there was certainly a challenge on her face. "Unless *you're* afraid to travel with us," she said.

He touched his right hand to his left shoulder, the place where the royal lion would be embroidered if he was wearing his Rider livery. "My liege sends me to serve you, and serve you I will," he said. "I am not afraid of a convent of women or the message of hatred they spread."

"I am, and you should be," she said quietly. "But we will go forward nonetheless."

CHAPTER
6

THEY left the next morning, bending their route to the southwest so they could swing through Fortunalt and see how the situation stood there. "It's generally been a self-contained and rational House—no pretensions to the throne—but these days I am not so sure of anyone," Senneth said. It was her mission to command, so they rode where she directed.

The weather was colder than Tayse remembered it being when they'd arrived in Helvenhall. But that, he knew, was an illusion fostered by two days of soft living. His father had sometimes gone weeks at a time without sleeping in a bed or even inside a shelter, particularly before riding out on some demanding mission. He said he didn't want to be distracted by discomforts; he wanted to be inured to them before he took his first step on the road.

They didn't even ride as far as they could have that first day, electing to make camp while it was still full daylight and they could see to gather fuel and make dinner. Senneth said, "I'm going to look for water," and slipped away once the fire was lit. Tayse watched her go, wondering. He heard laughter and then arguing in the camp, and turned to see Justin pulling out the practice blades.

"Fine," Justin said, flipping one to Donnal. "Let me show you, then."

"Don't forget to keep an eye out for trouble while you're playing games," Tayse said.

"I'll watch," Cammon replied. "I'll know if someone's approaching camp."

Tayse grunted—because that was irritating but true—and turned away without another word. He followed the path Senneth had taken away from the road, over a hill and down through a scrawny glade of stripped trees. She'd made no particular effort to hide her passage, and so it was easy to find her, a few minutes later, sitting at the edge of an ice-encrusted brook and gazing down at her muddy boots.

"Have you come hunting mystics?" she asked without turning to look at him.

"Not this trip out," he said. He made his way closer, then dropped down to the ground a few feet away from her.

She glanced over at him. "You would, though," she said softly. "If the king told you to."

"I do whatever the king tells me," he said.

"Loyalty like that is very frightening to me," she said. "What if what the king tells you is wrong?"

"And what frightens me is someone who is entirely—unaligned," he said. "Answering only to her own voice. How can anyone be sure that voice can be trusted?"

She watched him a moment, her gray eyes giving nothing away. "It's only me you really dislike," she said. "So it can't just be that you don't trust mystics. You don't seem to mind Cammon and Donnal at all, and as for Kirra—" She shrugged. "Well, all men like Kirra."

He gave her just the edge of a smile. "I understand them and where their allegiances lie," he said. "Not Cammon, of course—he's too new to have any allegiances—but he's like some raw recruit brought into the king's guard for training. With the right guidance and the right friends, he'll be thoughtful and strong and maybe even talented. Can't tell yet how good the basic material is—but it's uncorrupted."

"And the others?"

"Well, Kirra would say she's loyal to you, but really her heart lies with Danalustrous. As long as your course doesn't jeopardize her father's realm, she'll follow you."

"Kirra has a bit more independence than you think," Senneth said. "And she has questioned her father more than once."

"My advice would still be not to put it to the test," he said.

"And the other men?"

"Oh, Justin is a Rider, heart and soul. He knows this is your expedition, but if you gave him an order and I countermanded it, he would do what I told him to. No question. Donnal's just the same as Justin, but his loyalty is to Danalustrous. He wouldn't obey you, either, if Kirra told him not to."

"I'm not accustomed to *giving orders* and *demanding obedience*," she said, her voice exasperated. "You make it sound like I'm running a battlefield."

He shrugged. "That's what any kind of mission could turn out to be. If we're set on by Gisseltess guards who somehow know you're mystics, we'll have a fight on our hands. And any time you're in combat, you want to be sure your unit is all pulling together, no loyalties divided."

"If we're under attack, I would *hope* you and Justin would be fighting for us," she exclaimed.

Again, a tiny smile warmed his mouth. "Depends on who's attacking."

She shook her head and looked down at her feet again. The way her hair was cut, so short around her head, it was easy to see every expression on her face.

"You look tired," he said abruptly. "Tough to go back on the road after two days off it."

"I am tired," she said slowly, "but that's not it. It's not the day behind me. It's—" She paused, shook her head again. "It's what lies ahead of me. It's going to be even harder than I thought."

He was silent a moment, but she did not explain. "You see," he said, "it is things like that that make me distrust you. What do you see—what are you planning—that is going to take such energy?"

She sat very still but turned her head just a little, just enough to look at him out of the corner of her eye. "I can't believe I *am* the only one who sees it," she said.

There was a rustling in the dry grass behind them. Senneth didn't bother to investigate, but Tayse turned around to see who was approaching. Justin, looking defiant.

"They need you back at camp," he said. Tayse rose to his feet, but Justin shook his head. "Not you—her."

"What happened?" Tayse asked, since Senneth didn't.

"Accident when we were fighting. My fault, but I thought—

Donnal had done reasonably well, and I tried something and he couldn't parry. It's pretty deep," he added. "Right shoulder."

Tayse glanced at Senneth, but even this news didn't bring her scrambling to her feet. "What about Kirra? I thought she was supposed to be some sort of gifted healer."

"She says Senneth is better at this kind of wound than she is," Justin replied. There was a sort of vocalized shrug in his voice. "I don't know. I've never seen anyone healed by magic, so I guess I can't set myself up to judge anyone's abilities."

Senneth finally spoke, still without turning around. "Justin," she said. "If I told you to do one thing and Tayse told you to do another, whose orders would you follow?"

"Tayse's," he said.

"Even though the king has named me head of this expedition? Even though, as King's Rider, you are bound to do what the king wants you to do?"

"The king wants me to be loyal to my fellow Riders," he said.

Now she looked at him over her shoulder. "And if Tayse woke you up in the middle of the night and told you to kill me in the morning, would you do it?"

He nodded. "You—any of them. But Donnal at least will be dead by morning if you or Kirra or somebody doesn't tend him." And with that supremely indifferent remark, he turned around and began kicking his way back through piles of brown leaves.

Senneth dropped her head to her updrawn knees. "I feel so old," she said.

Tayse was laughing. "He's even younger than he looks," he said. "But I think you're wanted back at camp."

He stepped forward to help her stand, but she was on her feet with one lithe movement that belied her earlier exhaustion. He wondered for a moment if she just didn't want him to touch her hand. Then he followed her back to camp. Only when they arrived there did he realize that neither of them had bothered to fetch water.

Donnal was stretched on a blanket before the fire. Dusk was gathering its full force by now, so the pallor of his face might be explained by the failing light—but probably not. Kirra or someone had cut open his shirt over his right shoulder and laid bare a long, deep wound.

Kirra looked up in relief when Senneth materialized before the fire. "I've done what I can but I think you—" she said, and paused. Senneth nodded and knelt down beside the hurt man.

"Donnal," she said, her voice low but sharp. "Can you hear me? Are you able to talk?"

"Yes," he whispered. "But I'm—it hurts—I don't know if I can—"

"All right. Don't bother speaking. I just wanted to let you know. The touch of my hand is going to burn. You're going to need to lie very still. It will be bad for a few moments, but then it will be much better. Do you understand me? Can you lie quiet?"

"Yes," he whispered.

Tayse gestured to Justin, and the two of them dropped to the ground on either side of the hurt man. "We'll hold him, just in case," Tayse said.

She nodded, not looking at him. When they had gripped Donnal tightly to the ground, she extended her right hand so it hovered only an inch or so above his flesh. Tayse watched her face. It was as guarded as ever, but more so—as if she had gone even deeper within herself to summon some special strength or knowledge. A moment she hesitated, and then she laid her palm along Donnal's bloody wound.

Donnal grunted with pain and shuddered against their hold, as if straining both not to scream and not to struggle. Tayse's gaze dropped to Senneth's hand, but there was nothing to see, no strange glow emanating between her fingers, nothing but skin against skin, with a layer of blood between. He watched her face again, drawn in concentration. The firelight flickered over her cheeks and danced in the white streaks of her hair. Tayse was seized by the odd belief that if he touched her, she would feel like the fire itself.

Donnal was breathing hard, his muscles still bunched against their hold, but his dark eyes were open and fixed on Senneth's face. She didn't watch him, she didn't appear to be looking anywhere, not at her hand, not at the fire, not out into the darkness. Inward, perhaps, with her eyes wide open. They all held their poses for five minutes, or ten—Tayse lost track—and then suddenly Senneth caught her breath and lifted her hand. She sat back on her heels and focused on Donnal.

Who had gone limp and boneless beneath the Riders' hands. Tayse glanced down at him, to find his face loose with relief. The wound still looked ugly and raw, but the pain, at least, seemed to have passed.

"Are you done?" Tayse asked Senneth, releasing his hold on the hurt man. She nodded.

"He'll still need a day or two to fully heal. But he should be well on his way now."

"What did you do?" He couldn't stop himself from asking.

She looked at him, nothing to read in her gray eyes. "Hard to explain," she said. "Think of it as cauterizing every muscle, every vein, and fusing them together with fire."

Donnal gasped. "That's what it felt like."

Tayse nodded, though he didn't really understand. His attention went to Justin, still kneeling on the other side of Donnal's body. Tayse said evenly, "That wound wasn't caused by a practice blade."

Justin's expression set. "He didn't want to use one."

"Rule of the camp," Tayse said. "Practice blades—unless you want to fight with me."

He caught Senneth's quick, interested look, but he kept his gaze focused on Justin. Just enough threat in his voice, his words, his expression, to make Justin back down.

"I'm sorry," Justin said, dropping his eyes. "Practice blades next time."

Tayse stood up, Justin following suit. "And there should be a next time," Tayse said. "For Donnal, Cammon, Senneth. We appear to be riding into enemy territory. We all need to keep our skills sharp."

Senneth rose also, making room for Kirra, who came over with lotions and cloths to bind the hurt man's wounds. "Though you will find, if we are ever attacked, that those of us with some magical ability can fight in our own ways," Senneth said with a touch of humor.

Tayse gave her an ironic nod. "I would be interested to see those skills deployed," he said. "It is almost enough to make me hope for combat."

By now it was dark, cold, and getting late. He went back to the little brook to fetch water while the others put a meal together. They ate in relative silence—Justin brooding, Donnal hurting, Kirra watching Donnal, Tayse watching Senneth, Senneth lost in her own thoughts, and Cammon sensitive enough to the moods of the others to keep entirely still. It was almost a relief when they all sought their beds. Tayse listened for a moment to the sounds of breathing around him, and then allowed himself to fall immediately asleep.

He woke a few hours later, as he had trained himself to do, and listened again for a few moments. Only a few night sounds—a wayfaring breeze shaking dry tree limbs together, the hoot and call of predators, the rustle of small creatures fleeing. Closer in, the sound of the fire snapping—someone else must have woken before he had and added more wood.

He slipped quietly to his feet, pulled on his boots, and soundlessly left the camp. The minute he was beyond the pale circle of firelight, he was assaulted by cold so intense that he felt the hairs inside his nose freeze up. He made the circuit anyway, a complete journey around the camp from fifty yards away, pausing every few feet to listen to the sounds of the night. He seemed to be the only alien presence in the vicinity; there was no scent or feel of danger anywhere he turned.

He returned to camp as quietly as he had left, by habit doing a visual check of the five sleeping bodies. His eyes came to rest on Senneth, to find she was awake and watching him. On impulse, he picked his way between the other motionless forms and came to a crouch beside her.

"Why are you awake?" he asked in a low voice.

"Why are you?" she replied.

He jerked his head to indicate the land around them. "Walking the perimeter."

"Do you do that every night?"

"Just about."

"I haven't noticed."

"You've been sleeping. Why not tonight?"

"I wanted to check on Donnal," she said. "But he seems fine. I suppose you didn't find any hazards in the woods beyond?"

A slight smile for that. "Cold," he said. "Much colder than it is right here. I wonder why that is."

"Well, there's the fire," she said.

He nodded slowly. "And there's you."

A real smile from her, dazzling by firelight. "It's true," she said with assumed modesty, "that I can create some heat that extends beyond the borders of my body."

"How did you do that?" he asked abruptly. "With Donnal? How can your touch cauterize a wound?"

"You haven't been paying attention," she said. "I have the gift of fire. I can cause it, I can fan it, I can control it, I can give it away. I could burn a city to the ground."

He considered. "How big a city?"

That smile again. "How big a city do you want to see burn?"

"Have you ever?"

The smile widened. "No."

"What would make you do it?"

The smile faded. "What would make *you* go to war?"

Now his eyes narrowed; he was as serious as she was. "That's what you see? War ahead of us?"

She moved her head restlessly on her flat blanket. "I see the possibility of it everywhere. I don't know if it will come to that."

"And if it does? Who will you war with? Where will you make a stand?"

"It depends on where the lines are drawn," she said softly. "But I have always been loyal to my king."

"And he trusts you, or so it seems," Tayse said. He could tell that his voice sounded hard, quietly though he spoke. "He would perhaps be glad to harness the energy that can set cities on fire."

"Or worse," she said.

He was silent a moment, still watching her, wondering what she meant by that or if it was just to goad him, wondering, as always, what her full story was. "Does it hurt?" he found himself asking.

"Does what hurt?"

"When you use that power. When you healed Donnal. When you"—he gestured—"keep the fire burning all night without adding another log to the flames."

She shook her head slowly against the blanket. "No. It is always there, that heat, pouring out of me."

"Is your skin hot to the touch?" he said curiously.

She did not answer at first. With one hand, she pulled down the collar of her soft shirt; with the other, she picked up his own hand, resting on his folded knee. He was so surprised he did not resist as she pushed his palm down right where her neck joined her shoulder. For a moment, he was just conscious of the smoothness of her skin, tender as a child's—then he was aware of the heat rising up from her body. He was enveloped in heat, drowning in heat, rich as scented bathwater and just as pleasurable. For a moment he caught himself wondering what it might feel like to lay his body the full length of hers and absorb that warmth with every inch of his own skin.

Then he pulled his hand away and abruptly rose to his feet. She was smiling as she drew her blankets back up to her chin. "Good night, Tayse," she said. "I don't think you'll be cold again."

He returned to his own bedroll, lying wakeful for a long while. But he was a soldier; he could summon sleep in the middle of a battlefield. He shut his eyes and forced himself to sleep, and he didn't wake again till morning. By then the strange experience seemed surreal enough, unlikely enough, that he was almost able to convince himself that it had been a dream. Except he was not the sort of man who dreamed.

CHAPTER
7

It was Kirra's idea to ride into Forten City and throw a party. Senneth looked at her and said, "Why did I ever invite you on this journey?"

Kirra laughed. "Because you needed entrée to all the great Houses of Gillengaria—and you wanted my irrepressible sense of adventure."

They were sitting around a campfire about a day's ride from the main city of Fortunalt, and Senneth for one was looking forward to the idea of settling into a hotel and coming to rest for a few days. She was also intent on strolling the streets of the seaport and overhearing whatever news was to be had. But she had not planned on being particularly visible during this visit.

"Why do it?" Tayse asked, as always striking straight down toward the truth. "And why not do it?"

Kirra turned to him. "We might hear gossip that we'd never hear skulking about with shop owners and blacksmiths. We wouldn't deal with the Fortunalt family this time—it would be strictly Thirteenth House."

Justin looked up from across the fire. Anything that remotely involved class distinctions instantly caught his attention. *"What?"* he demanded.

"Thirteenth House," Kirra said, tilting her nose up to take an aristocratic pose. "Nobles and gentry who don't quite have the pure bloodlines of the top families, but who possess wealth and some prestige nonetheless."

"Most of the lesser gentry are affiliated with one of the Twelve Houses," Senneth explained. "They provide some fealty to the marlords, and in return they get—favors or protection or a chance to marry their daughters into society. Whatever coin is most precious at the time."

"And if we had a party," Kirra said, "they would come and tell us everything Rayson Fortunalt is thinking and doing. We would probably learn more than if we rode onto his estates and asked *him.*"

Tayse was considering Kirra. "But why would they tell you? Particularly if they're hunting mystics in this part of the world."

"Oh, I wouldn't greet them as myself," she said airily. "I'd go as—let's see—one of my father's more indiscreet allies—"

"Erin Sohta," Donnal suggested with a laugh. He was lounging close to the fire, looking tired, but he had managed to keep up with them the past two days. Senneth was pleased to note that his wound had healed as quickly as she had expected; he had even begun practicing with Justin again.

Kirra smiled back at him. "Yes, Erin Sohta. She has quite an extensive property on the southeastern border of Danalustrous, and she considers herself one of my father's closest advisors. He can't stand her, of course," Kirra added, "but *she* doesn't know that."

"But what if Erin herself is in Fortunalt just now?" Senneth demanded. She still didn't like this idea. "It's not beyond the bounds of possibility."

"Well, it is, because my father is holding a traditional winter dinner party in about three days and none of his vassals would want to miss it," Kirra said. "Particularly Erin."

"But if that's so, what would make her come to Forten City and throw a party?" Senneth said.

"I'll think of something," Kirra promised. "It's a good idea. You'll see."

But as it happened, the necessity did not arise. They rode into Forten City the next day and checked into a small but fashionable inn to find that a social event had already been planned there for the following evening. Two young nobles were getting married, and gentry from a hundred miles around were attending.

"I wouldn't even have a room for you, since we were all booked, except someone had to leave this morning on account of her mother falling sick," the proprietor told them when Kirra and Senneth presented themselves at his desk. He looked doubtfully at the attractive Lady Erin and her less attractive but still quite genteel cousin. "Well, I've got the room for you two ladies. Your men'll have to sleep in the stables, if that's all right with you."

"They won't mind at all," Kirra said blithely, and Senneth had to hide a smile. "But what about my wolfhound? Can he stay in the room with us? I feel so much—safer—when he's near."

Wolfhound? Senneth wondered, but the innkeeper was already nodding. "Oh yes, many of our guests bring their pets in with them," he said, beaming. "We're quite partial to dogs here."

Kirra was busy signing her name on the register and counting out gold coins. "So who's getting married?" she asked casually.

"Katlin Dormer and Edwin Seiles," the proprietor replied.

Kirra looked up, pen slack in her hand. "No! But I know Katlin! She was visiting at my father's—oh, five years ago, maybe—and we were quite friendly! Oh, this is wonderful! Is there any way I can go to her mother's room and give them my congratulations? Sindra," she added, turning to Senneth, "you'll have to go out this afternoon and find a gift for me. Something very pretty—you'll know just what's right."

"Of course, Cousin," Senneth murmured.

"There!" Kirra said, signing her name with a flourish. Even her handwriting looked different, Senneth thought, while her sharp, pointed face and tangled black curls made her completely unrecognizable. "Let's go up to our room, shall we?"

Within a couple of hours, their luggage had been transferred into the small room, and both women had bathed and changed. Kirra went off to try to find Katlin Dormer's mother, while Senneth tracked down the men, who were having a beer in the tavern adjoining the inn.

"I think you're supposed to be a wolfhound," Senneth said, seating herself next to Donnal.

He grinned. Tayse looked up, interested. "That's a good idea," he said. "Since they're keeping us down in the stables."

"I appreciate your concern," Senneth said. "But I think we're safe enough inside the hotel. There are locks, and I've got weapons."

"And you'll have me," Donnal said.

"What news so far?" she asked. She eyed their beer with some longing but asked the waiter for wine when he approached. Bad enough to be fraternizing with guardsmen, but she couldn't be seen sucking down ale in the common taproom.

"City's as full as it can hold," Tayse said. "Some wedding or something tomorrow night, and gentry spilling out of every inn in town."

Senneth nodded. "Unless I miss my guess, Kirra's about to get us invited to it," she said. "This answers better than her other ideas."

"So you'll go, too, dressed as—what? Her lady in waiting?"

Senneth made as much of a mock curtsey as she could while sitting in a bar booth, a wineglass in hand. "Her cousin Sindra, thank you very much. I'm poor but respectable, and I'm grateful for every gift and kind word my rich relations bestow upon me."

"I hate the gentry," Justin remarked.

"There's a bit of news for us," she retorted.

"Do you have to change your face for these people?" Cammon asked.

She shook her head. "I wouldn't think so. No one will be paying attention to me. I'll just wear an expression of hopeful degradation, and they'll all stare right past me."

Donnal snorted and then started laughing. "I've seen these people," he said to the others. "That's exactly the way they look."

"Existing without any pride," Tayse said. "What a terrible way to live."

"There are worse ways," she said quietly. She sipped at her wine and refused to let herself think of those ways.

SHE spent most of the rest of the afternoon wandering through Forten City, shopping. To her surprise, Tayse insisted on accompanying her, though he let the other men go off on their own pursuits. She didn't actually mind knowing he was two paces behind her as she walked through the crowded streets. Forten City was a curious mix of the aristocratic and the wretched, with rows of fashionable shops only two streets over from grim little shacks that housed alehouses, prostitute quarters, and families of the very poor. Sailors strutted up and down the streets, looking for love or trouble, and the whole parade of life went by in the central district: noblemen, merchants, farmers, soldiers, laundresses, cooks, whores. No young woman walked out unaccompanied.

Though I am hardly a young woman, Senneth thought and tried not to smile.

She had decided she would buy a length of handmade lace to give to the Dormer bride; Katlin could lay it across her table or hang it from a window or ball it up and put it in the back of her closet. Senneth didn't care. But it was a reasonable gift, and it didn't have to match anything in the bride's trousseau.

Still, she went first to sweet shops and shoe shops and dress shops, just to see if she could overhear any useful conversation. For most of the day, no. Everyone seemed concerned with the weather, which was frigid, the new taxes, which were unreasonable, and the wedding, which was apparently going to be the highlight of the social season.

"Though she's not a very pretty girl, you know," one matron observed to another as they picked through silks in the fabric shop. "I'm surprised she's done as well as Edwin Seiles."

"I'm surprised anyone would take her at all!" the second woman exclaimed. "After those things that were being said about her last year—"

"No, you're confused, that was her sister," the first woman interrupted. "This one isn't a mystic. She's perfectly normal."

Senneth pulled out another bolt of lace and examined its pattern against the sample she already had in her hand.

"Oh! Well, then! Because I kept wondering—I mean, how *could* they marry off a girl like that? But if this one's not tainted, it's just fine then. Oh, I like that blue."

"But it's too thin, don't you think? For this cold weather?"

"Keep it for spring, that's my advice. What happened to her? That other girl?"

"The mystic? I don't know. I haven't heard a word about her in—I guess it's six or seven months now. Probably shipped off to relatives in Helven or Kianlever. You know how these things go."

"I know how they *should* go," the second woman said with emphasis. "People are too soft, that's what I say."

"Their own daughter," the first woman said gently. "You can't expect them to—I wouldn't, I know. I'd find a way to keep her safe."

The second woman leaned closer as if to whisper, though the pitch of her voice scarcely changed. "Mystics are born to those who consort with mystics," she said. "Those who have a magical child—well, they'd best look to their own bloodlines, that's what I say. If my daughter-in-law produced a child like that, I'd know she played my son false. And I would have no hesitation in turning both her and her child out of the house."

Senneth laid down both pieces of lace and headed straight for the shop door. Tayse was leaning against the wall, hands hooked in his belt, eyes ceaselessly watching the restless crowd.

"All done?" he asked, and then noticed her hands were empty. "I thought you were going to buy some lace."

"I've decided to get her a clock instead," Senneth said, and turned down the street to a watchmaker's shop that she had passed before.

THE wedding was an exercise in humiliation, or would have been if Senneth had been even remotely interested in the goodwill of the lesser gentry gathered to attend. The ceremony itself was brief and dull, but the reception that followed was ostentatiously lavish. She estimated that two hundred people had been crowded into a room meant to comfortably hold about half that number. The heat was intense—Senneth herself never minded the heat, but she saw more than one young woman stagger and almost faint—and the odors of perfume and sweat did not blend well with the scents of food and wine.

There was what seemed to Senneth a desperate air of gaiety, as if all these second-tier noblemen and their scheming wives were pretending to be at an elegant ball at one of the Twelve Houses. The women had dressed in remarkably fine gowns; the men wore velvet and exquisitely tanned leather. What interested Senneth was that very few of them wore diamonds or rubies or traditional jewels. Nearly everyone—from the women with their bracelets and earrings to the men with their rings and cravat pins—wore moonstones as the accessories of choice. This was particularly true for the young women whose plunging necklines and oversized pendants were meant to mimic the ball gowns of Twelfth House serramarra. The dowdy Sindra, with no pretensions to wealth or status, wore a comfortably high-necked gown and no ornament but her gold necklace, but Erin Sohta had sashayed out in a dress with daring décolletage.

"Mind your housemark," Senneth had noted as they were dressing for the event.

Kirra had lifted her pendant, which she had not bothered to alter in her own transformation. Erin Sohta would undoubtedly wear rubies in her role as Danalustrous vassal, and who in this crowd would recognize this exact piece of jewelry? Where it had lain against her skin there was only unblemished flesh. "Erin Sohta doesn't have a housemark," she retorted. "I wanted one less thing to worry about."

To Senneth, it seemed like Kirra was not worrying about a thing. As soon as the simple marriage ceremony was over, Kirra had joined the noblest of the circles available in this company and began laughing and flirting. Senneth herself slipped unobtrusively through the room, snagging a glass of wine here, a bit of cheese there, trying to listen to strangers' conversations, trying to read the mood of the city.

Taxes, weather, and weddings. This particular group didn't seem concerned with anything else.

After a couple of hours, she gave up for a bit and took a seat in an unoccupied chair in a poorly lit corner of the room. She had replaced her wine with water and continued to watch and listen to the crowd, but she was pretty sure she wouldn't be the one to garner any information this evening. If they learned anything on this outing, it would be through Kirra.

A shadow crossed her face, and then a body fell into place in the seat beside hers. She looked over in surprise at a handsome middle-aged man who wore a Fortunalt pearl in his neckcloth and a moonstone the size of a walnut on his right hand.

"I hate these affairs, don't you?" he asked in a pleasant voice. He smelled of ale and onions; he had obviously partaken fairly liberally of his host's hospitality.

She permitted herself the small smile of a woman who didn't smile often. "I don't go to that many," she said. "It's been years—" She broke off and shook her head.

"Ah, well, a chance for the wealthy to show off their wealth and the beautiful to show off their beauty," he said. "There are fewer events designed for the kind to show off their kindness and the good of heart to show off their generosity."

"My cousin Erin is kind to me every day," Senneth said in a small voice. Inside she was thinking, *What is going on here? Why is he speaking to me?* His clothes were very fine, and his skin was very good. This man was no second son, no hanger-on lordling. Not Twelfth House, because no one here was, but in the upper tiers of the Thirteenth.

His eyes scanned the crowd, picking out Kirra instantly. "Erin Sohta? Is your cousin? Yes, a charming woman. She did not mention her companion's name, though."

"I'm Sindra," she said primly.

He stretched his legs out before him with the air of a man relaxing after hard labor. "Hello, Sindra, I'm Coren Bauler," he said.

She knew the family name, high in the ranks of Fortunalt vassals, but she smiled tightly as if it meant nothing to her.

"How long do you stay in Forten City?" he asked.

"I'm not sure. My cousin determines our travel," she said.

"But you're staying here? In this inn?"

Was he hoping for an assignation with her? she wondered. He was a good-looking man, though his brown hair was streaked with gray and his face was lined with a few more years than Senneth had accumulated. Shy, bitter, lonely woman who never experienced any frivolity—yes, he might think someone like that would welcome some illicit overtures.

She could not decide if she should try to turn that idea to her advantage or go running from the room right now.

"Yes—this very inn," she said. "It's quite nice, I think."

"The rooms are small."

"Oh, I don't mind that."

He smiled at her. "Indeed, you seem like the kind of woman who puts up with much without complaining."

She allowed her smile to brighten, then cast her eyes down. "And what might you complain about, Coren Bauler?" she asked shyly. "All I've heard the other men talk about tonight is winter and taxes."

"Winter's not something we can do much about, but taxes—well, those have been a burden lately," he said thoughtfully. "Rayson Fortunalt thinks he has to increase his standing army by half, and he thinks he can only afford it by stealing gold from the coffers of his loyal houses." He shrugged. "Maybe so. But I think he could dig a little deeper into his own stores before looting from his lords."

She didn't really have to feign alarm. "Increase his army!" she exclaimed. "Why? Is it so dangerous here in Forten City? I admit, Erin and I have traveled with a very small escort of guards—"

Coren laughed. "Oh, all the southern Houses are recruiting," he said carelessly. "To hear Halchon Gisseltess talk, civil war is not so very far off—but he's a man prone to exaggeration, and he loves a good fight besides." He broke off. "Not that you could be interested in such talk."

More interested than you know, she thought grimly, while giving a small laugh. "Oh—I just don't understand such things very well," she said. "Erin tells me I should pay more attention."

"No—pretty girl like you should be paying attention to gowns and jewels and balls and men," he said, pulling his feet in and sitting up straighter in his chair. He smiled at her appraisingly.

She put a hand to the high collar of her dress and tried to force a blush. "I'm hardly a pretty girl," she said, not even sure which of the two words to emphasize. By the Bright Mother's eyes, he was not even attempting to be subtle about this.

"Pretty enough to me," he said. "Would you like to dance?"

Red hot hell! she thought. It had not even occurred to her such a possibility might arise. "I'm—I'm not very good," she said, looking down again. "I don't get many opportunities—you know—"

He stood and pulled her to her feet. She felt a sharp pain in her left hand and looked down before she realized what it must be. The touch of his moonstone against her skin. "I will hold you so close that none of your deficiencies will be noticeable," he all but breathed into her ear. And, true to his word, he wrapped her in a tight embrace and swept her onto the dance floor.

She made herself breathe slowly and tried not to react at all. It had been years since she had even attempted to dance, and the memories were not pleasant. But her body remembered the rhythms—and anyway, she had no choice but to follow Coren Bauler's lead. They did not especially disgrace themselves as they moved among the other couples, more or less to the beat of the music, and wound slowly around the room.

"Your hand is so hot," Coren murmured. "Do you have a fever? Or are you merely overheated? Would you like to go outside?"

Absolutely not. It was fairly clear what privacy with this man would lead to, no matter how cold the outdoor night might be. "I'm just—you're—no, I'm fine," she stammered, and let him interpret that answer any way he wished.

"I like dancing with you," he said. "You have much more ability than you led me to expect. I wonder what other womanly skills you hide under that severe exterior?"

"I—I can embroider—and I am a very good cook," she said somewhat wildly.

He laughed softly. "Ah, those were not the skills I was asking about."

Just as Senneth thought she might have to fake a twisted ankle or fall to the floor in a delicate swoon, hands closed on her arm, and she was yanked from Coren Bauler's arms.

"Sindra! I have been looking and looking for you!" Kirra said in the most petulant voice imaginable. "I have torn my hem, and I need you to sew it up for me!"

Coren ushered them all from the dance floor before they could cause too much of a stir. "I see there is a crisis brewing for which those womanly talents will be called into service," he said, bowing as they seated themselves on a divan to make fabric repairs. "I will take my leave now. But I hope to see you again, Sindra, before the night is over."

She really couldn't help goggling at him as he bowed again and strode away. Beside her, Kirra was giggling uncontrollably. "If I didn't think I might need you sometime in the future, I would kill you now," Senneth said, not even looking at her.

"Oh, but I rescued you!" Kirra exclaimed through her fits of laughter. "You must be grateful to me for that!"

Now Senneth did turn wrathful eyes her way. "Is this the sort of thing that always goes on among the gentry?" she demanded. "Aging cavaliers romancing wretched old spinsters at tawdry affairs such as this?"

"Oh, and the spinsters are usually quite grateful for the attention!" Kirra said. "But I could tell from the expression on your face that you were not reacting quite as Coren hoped—though I don't think he was able to read you as well as I was—"

Senneth shook her head. "How much longer must we stay here? Have you learned anything of interest?"

Kirra sobered instantly. "Yes, but not to be discussed here," she said. "Give me another thirty minutes, and I will be ready to leave. There are one or two others I wish to talk to, and then—"

Senneth came to her feet. "Very well, but I am not staying anywhere that that man might be able to find me again," she said darkly.

Kirra stood beside her, shaking out her skirts and tossing back Erin Sohta's black curls. "Can you make yourself invisible?" she inquired. "Is that one of your womanly talents?"

Senneth grinned. "I can turn away attention if I choose," she said. "It is a skill I have found very useful in the past. Signal me when you are ready to go. I do not think you will find me either if I do not wish to be noticed."

Kirra lifted her eyebrows at that but made no comment. "I will drop my wineglass to the floor," she said. "You will appear at my side and hurry me out the door to change clothes. That will get us safely out of this evening, I think."

"Very good," Senneth said. "In half an hour."

CHAPTER
8

THE events unfolded as Kirra had promised, and in less than an hour they were back in their room, where a large, lazy wolfhound lay stretched out before the fire. He raised his head when they walked in and thumped the floor with his tail a few times, but he showed no inclination to rise from his comfortable place. Kirra bent down to scratch him behind the ears, then settled beside Senneth on the room's only bed.

"Rayson Fortunalt is doubling the size of his civil guard, and not all of his nobles are in favor of it," Senneth said bluntly.

Kirra nodded. "That's because he won't tell them why. They're not sure if it means he's banding with the other southern Houses in a bid to dethrone the king—or hoping to stand against them when they rise in civil war."

"Did you get a sense of which way his vassals leaned?" Senneth asked. "Do they favor Gisseltess or Ghosenhall?"

"I'd say emotion is fairly well split," Kirra said. "But they seem to follow Gisseltess on one particular at least."

"The mystics," Senneth said. "I heard some unfavorable public sentiment this afternoon."

Kirra nodded again. "And they were all dripping in moonstones. I've never seen anything like it. They should all have been wearing the pearls of Fortunalt."

"I wonder what it is like in Rappengrass," Senneth said softly. "Ariane Rappengrass has always been an unpredictable woman."

Kirra yawned and stretched her arms. "I say we go there next," she said, "and see what we can discover."

They turned out all the lights before changing into their night-clothes, neither of them trusting to Donnal's courtesy, and climbed into the wide bed. "Ah—I shall be warm tonight," Kirra murmured, spreading her black hair across the pillow.

Senneth laughed. "Sorry—tell me if you want me to go sleep on the floor by Donnal."

"No, being warm will make a nice change," Kirra said, yawning again.

Kirra seemed to fall instantly asleep. Senneth lay awake awhile longer. She had half-wanted to detour through the stables to share their findings with Tayse, but anyone who might have been watching them would have found that odd behavior indeed. The news would have to wait till morning, when he—and the others— might have found out information of their own.

She slept lightly, reluctantly almost, as if her mind or her body or her magic did not want to shut down. She kept dreaming and waking from dreams and falling back into darkness again.

Then abruptly she was jerked from sleep altogether by a for-eign noise inside the room. Her knife was in her hand, and she was on her feet before she had even identified the sound: Donnal, up on all fours, growling softly toward the door.

Senneth gave Kirra a hard poke, and the other woman rolled to her feet as silently as Senneth had. There was very little light to see by, since the windows were shuttered against the cold, but a glance from Senneth caused the coals in the fireplace to flare to orange. Senneth crept toward the door, where she could now hear a furtive metallic scraping. Donnal and Kirra positioned them-selves for second and third assaults should a number of bodies come in through the door.

The lock fell; the handle turned slowly, and a shadow stepped inside the room. Senneth pounced and twisted the man around, so her left arm was around his neck, and her right hand was hold-ing a knife to his chest. "Be very careful, or I'll stick a blade through your heart," she hissed. "Who are you, and what do you want?"

She could smell the sweat of sudden terror overlaying the smells of alcohol and onions. "Si-Sindra?" He gulped.

"Candle," Senneth snapped, and Kirra came forward with a lighted taper in her hands. Indeed, yes, it was her newest beau, out in the wee hours to pursue his wooing. Senneth was so annoyed she almost dug the knife home just to teach him a lesson.

"Coren Bauler!" Kirra exclaimed in Erin Sohta's voice. Unlike Senneth, she had never put aside her disguise and had not forgotten she was supposed to be in one. "What in the world—why would you be coming to my door at this hour of night?"

"I—" He choked, and struggled feebly in Senneth's hold.

"Sindra, dear, please let him go. I'm sure he means us no harm," Kirra said.

Senneth complied, dropping her knife hand to her side and wondering exactly how she should play the next few minutes. Donnal had settled onto his haunches and sat there, slightly panting, watching the whole scene with canine interest. She was sure that if dogs could laugh, he would be guffawing right now.

Coren Bauler half-turned to stare at Sindra. "You are—how can you be so strong? A girl like you?"

Senneth tried to assume her submissive manner of before, aware that it might be harder to carry off this time. "I was—when the door opened—I was so frightened! I didn't know who was— what was—"

He was rubbing his torso and eyeing her with a rather ugly expression. "You could have killed me. How would a woman like you know battle tricks like that?"

"It's my fault, I'm afraid," Kirra said, coming a few steps closer. "I have always been a little—excessive—in my fears for my personal safety. I dislike traveling to strange places without protection." She gestured at Donnal, silently watching them all. "I bring my hound with me everywhere. But some years ago I insisted Sindra undergo training at weaponry and self-defense. She protested, of course, because women aren't meant to be fighters, but—"

"She seems to have learned rather too well," Coren said.

"But tell me," Kirra said. "Why have you come so clandestinely to my room? Was there trouble at the inn? Something you wanted to warn us of?"

Since he couldn't possibly admit his real motive was rape or seduction, Senneth thought cynically, Kirra was kind to offer him a plausible alternative.

"Yes—news—I thought you should know," he said, stumbling over the words and obviously trying to come up with a crisis even as he spoke. "Bandits—on the north road. A traveler rode in late to describe his encounter. I wasn't sure—Sindra had mentioned that you might be leaving in the morning. I didn't want you to ride out without knowing what dangers might lie ahead."

"Bandits!" Kirra exclaimed, her eyes wide. "In Fortunalt territory? I hope someone has ridden to tell Rayson Fortunalt the news."

"Yes—I believe—that is, I'm sure someone else has done so," Coren Bauler said. "But I thought—who knew how early you were planning to leave? You might not have gotten the news in time."

"No, you're quite right. This is absolutely information I needed to have," Kirra said. "Bandits on the north road, you say? Then perhaps we should ride out eastward, toward Rappengrass. Sindra, what do you say?"

"I am always happy to see Rappengrass again, Cousin."

"Then that's what we'll do," Kirra said decisively. "Coren, thank you so much for your warning. I don't know what we would have done without your help."

And she held her hand out so he could grasp it in both of his. And then she cried out in sudden intense pain. Her disguise flickered; her hair melted from raven to gold and back again. She snatched her hand away and nursed it to her chest.

Coren Bauler was staring at her, his hand still half-extended. "Lady Erin," he said slowly. "You—but what—"

"The lady is very tired," Senneth said briskly. "We must be up early, which means we must go back to sleep this very instant—"

He looked down at his hand, and the fat white jewel on his finger, and then back at Kirra. "You—your hair," he whispered. "And the touch of my moonstone on your flesh—"

Senneth actually put a hand to his shoulder and pushed him toward the door. "Thanks again for the warning. It's best for us if you leave now—"

He jerked away from her, and his face was dark with anger. "You're mystics," he snarled. "Both of you."

Senneth lunged, but this time he was ready for her. His own

knife was out, and he caught her blade with the flat of his, then he tried a driving thrust aimed straight for her throat. But he was drunk and stupid, and it was easy to dance out of his way. She fell into a tense fighter's crouch and watched his face.

"Mystics," he said again. "Spying on the gentry. I'll kill you both before you can set foot outside this room."

He attacked again, strong but clumsy, and Senneth parried with relative ease. All the while she was wondering, *Good time or bad time to tell him who Kirra really is?* because no one wanted to murder the daughter of Malcolm Danalustrous. She stepped forward, thrust, stepped back, thinking that she didn't want to kill him but that it might be her only choice. He swiped at her with one wild swing of his blade hand, and then went crashing to the floor with a sound of surprised horror. Donnal stood on top of him, head down and growling in the man's ear. Kirra ran up and smashed his skull with a vase of winter greenery. He lay still.

"I hope he's not dead," Senneth said, kneeling down beside him and checking for a pulse.

"Deserves to be," Kirra said, "but I hope so, too."

But there it was, a steady, unruffled heartbeat. They might not have bought themselves very much time. Senneth stood.

"Time for us to be packing up and heading out looking for bandits," she said.

Kirra said, "We should—"

And then the door swung open and another man stepped into the room. Senneth and Kirra whirled to face him, but it was Tayse, blades in both hands and stealth on his face. He saw the body on the floor and sheathed his dagger. The sword he kept ready.

"I see I'm late," he said, glancing around. "What happened here?"

Kirra turned immediately to her packing, leaving Senneth to explain. She was more conscious now than she had been during Coren's visit of the thin cotton shift she had worn to sleep in. "I met the gentleman at the wedding. He seemed to want to continue our acquaintance tonight," she said. "Donnal heard him at the door and roused us. We had a little skirmish, and then Kirra smoothed everything over. I thought we would be out of it with no trouble—"

"I was stupid," Kirra said, standing at the bed and stuffing clothes into her bags. "After I'd been so careful all night."

Tayse looked unenlightened. "Moonstone," Senneth said. "On his finger. Kirra shook his hand—and it hurt her—and she cried out—" She waggled her fingers over her head. "And then her hair did this strange rainbow change—"

Tayse finally sheathed his sword. "I take it he doesn't care for mystics."

"He thought he had better kill us," Senneth said.

Tayse crouched down, like Senneth had, to make sure the man was still alive. "I don't think he'll be out for long," he said. "We'd better tie him up before we go."

"Since obviously we have to leave right now," Kirra said.

He nodded and stood. Senneth regarded him quizzically. "And you?" she said. "Just checking on us as you make your nightly rounds?"

He gave her a small smile. "No, in fact, Cammon woke me. Said you were having some trouble."

Senneth turned to see the arrested expression on Kirra's face, matching her own. "Cammon," Senneth repeated. "He seems to be developing his skills quite nicely."

"So are Justin and Cammon ready to move out?" Kirra asked, buckling the straps of her bag.

Tayse nodded. "Or ready for whatever comes next."

Senneth smiled. "As we all should be," she said.

THEY crept out of the inn, Kirra leaving a note and a pile of gold coins on the front desk, while Senneth murmured a spell over the money to keep it safe till the proper person came along.

"Will that work?" Kirra demanded.

Senneth laughed. "I don't know. I'm not especially good at spells and curses when it comes to *things*."

Kirra sighed. "I can *change* things, but I can't get them to do what I want."

Senneth caught the look on Tayse's face, closed and suspicious. He may as well have said the words out loud, she thought: *This is why ordinary men fear and despise mystics. For just such tricks as this.* She didn't know how to reassure him, and she was not about to deny her powers. She just shrugged and made no other comment. She looked around to make sure Donnal was still with them, and found him back in human shape, though moving as soundlessly in his boots as he did on his paws.

"You're a hound with good ears, or a good nose," she said to him. "That little scene could have been much nastier."

He nodded. "I've thought about taking wolf or dog shape as we ride, or even just at night when we camp," he said. "I feel more alert then, and I'll catch things no man would ever sense."

She raised her eyebrows. "A good idea, maybe, but only if it's comfortable for you. We don't want to waste your strength."

A smile broke through his dark beard. "I'm as comfortable in the one shape as the other," he said. "It's all the same to me. Just different advantages."

Once inside the stables, they found Cammon and Justin dressed and ready. They hadn't prepared the horses yet, just in case the crisis didn't call for flight. As soon as he saw the women, Justin went straight for the saddles. Cammon hurried up to them. "Are you all right? What happened?" he demanded in a low voice. Around them, other soldiers and servants were sleeping in the straw.

Kirra kissed him on the cheek, and he blushed bright red. "That's to thank you for saving us," she said.

"They'd saved themselves, this time, but it was still good work," Tayse said, leading his horse out of the stable.

Senneth accepted her own reins from Justin's hands and followed Tayse. "We'll tell you the story as we ride," she said.

It was full dark as they took to the road; Senneth judged it wouldn't be dawn for another three hours yet. She yawned through her recital of the tale, not happy to have lost this night's sleep. She had the sense that Tayse could ride for days, snatching only a few minutes' rest here and there, or in the saddle, but she required to lay her bones down and close her eyes for several hours.

Kirra ranged beside her. "We haven't spared time to think about the repercussions of this night," she said.

"I have," Senneth replied a bit grimly. "As soon as someone finds Coren Bauler, news will be out of a party of mystics traveling through the southern regions—spying on the gentry. That will make it harder for us to try such charades as we did last night."

Tayse spoke over his shoulder. He was in the lead, the two of them right behind him; for this night journey, he had not pulled far ahead as he usually did. "Worse than that," he said. "Depending on how far and how fast the word spreads, there will be civil guards looking for parties such as ours. Small, mobile, and including two women."

Senneth pressed her lips together; he was right. "We may stay ahead of the news for a while yet," she said. "At any rate, we still have ground to cover in Rappengrass and Gisseltess. And from everything we've been hearing, Gisseltess is the place where most of the discontent is brewing."

Tayse shrugged. "I'm just telling you the stakes have been raised," he said and spurred his horse forward so that he had outdistanced them by several yards.

"Then we'll just have to be more careful," Senneth said, even though she knew he couldn't hear her.

They didn't travel far that day; they were all tired, and since they had determined they would need to keep a watch, they knew none of them would sleep well that night. So they made camp long before sunset and took turns falling instantly to sleep.

The next day was uneventful, but they rode slowly. Cammon's horse was about to throw a shoe and they didn't pass through any settlements large enough to boast a smith. They were drifting due east, heading for the northernmost boundaries of Rappengrass territory, and most of what they saw were small farms so desolate in winter they seemed almost abandoned. So they moved slowly, and took long breaks, and looked over their weaponry to see what else might need attention as long as they were going to stop at a smithy anyway.

Night came early and cold, and Senneth at least was as glad to stop as if they'd been riding hard all day. Justin went off to get water and came back with a dead rabbit in hand. He just grinned when Kirra asked him politely if he'd stabbed it with his sword. None of the mystics had ever seen him hunt before. Senneth had assumed he could, since all Riders could live off the land on long campaigns, but she was still impressed.

"I'll let you know before I leave camp if I ever plan to take the shape of game of any sort," Donnal said in mock seriousness. The men all laughed. By the look on Kirra's face, she didn't think it was funny. Senneth hid a grin and stirred up the fire.

She had the first watch that night and just sat beside the flames, brooding, until it was time to wake up Justin. Donnal had indeed taken wolf shape, but he lay motionless beside Kirra, sleeping as deeply as a man. It was clear he was no wild animal, Senneth thought as she wrapped herself back in her blankets, for he harbored no fear of fire. She willed her circling thoughts to settle and forced herself into sleep.

And woke, not an hour later, when her senses screamed a warning. She rolled to her feet, knife in hand before she'd even assessed the danger. Cammon was sitting straight up on his bedroll, looking around him as if trying to see through the dark. His eyes were wide with fright and determination. Either he or Justin had woken Tayse, because the big man was also on his feet, edging around the perimeter of the camp. Justin stalked the other side. Kirra was still sleeping. Donnal was nowhere in sight.

Tayse saw her awake and jerked a head at the fire. Senneth passed her hand over the sparkling flames, and they were instantly extinguished. Too late, though, probably; it seemed someone had already marked their location. She placed a hand gently on Kirra's arm and squeezed hard. Silent as the others, Kirra woke and sat up.

"What?" Kirra breathed in Senneth's ear.

"I don't know. Looks like something woke Cammon, though, and Donnal appears to have slunk off to investigate."

"Friends from Forten City?" Kirra asked.

"Could be. We dawdled on the road, and anyone determined to catch up would have had no trouble."

"Gets more interesting every day," Kirra said and pulled herself to her feet.

Senneth went to crouch by Cammon. "What can you tell me?" she whispered. "How many? Where?"

It was nearly impossible to see his face in the full dark, but she thought he nodded and attempted to concentrate even more closely. "I think—I think there are five of them," he said slowly. "And they're—they're coming in two directions. From there—" He pointed. "And there. They're pretty close."

Tayse had circled close enough to hear. "Looking for us? Can you tell? Looking for mystics?"

A breath of laughter from Cammon. "No idea. But they're full of violence."

"So are we," Tayse said. "Put a blade in your hand, but keep out of our way—I don't think the fight will be so desperate that you will be called upon to offer your skills. You and Kirra should stand—" He paused. "Where's Kirra?"

Senneth glanced at the shadows grouped around the remains of the fire. She could not help grinning in the dark. "Out gathering information, I would guess."

Tayse swore under his breath. "How can I protect any of you if I can't even keep track of you?"

"How about this?" Senneth shot back. "You only have to protect us when we're in direct and deadly danger. Most of the time, we can take care of ourselves."

She could hear the irritation in his voice. "Then why are Justin and I along on this excursion to begin with?"

Now she laughed soundlessly. "To give us consequence."

Cammon hissed and jerked his head to the left. Tayse whirled and flung up his blade. Three men ran out of the complete blackness of the night and were suddenly upon him, hacking savagely at his shape. He was a blur of fury and motion, and it sounded like ten men were striking blade to blade, or twenty. Senneth leapt to stand beside him, her short sword out, and engaged one of the attackers in a spirited duel.

Behind her she was aware of the rush of more bodies, the sound of Justin launched in combat. She didn't have time to turn and try to watch. Her own assailant was stronger than she was, and fiercely determined. She caught two hard blows on her sword arm, feeling the impact straight down to the bone, and she barely parried a swift thrust aimed directly at her heart.

"Bright Mother blind me," she cursed in a low voice. Her pride made her want to take him out with swordsmanship alone, but she was even more interested in ending the encounter more or less whole. She spoke a few more words, and the man before her suddenly yelped and dropped his sword. He stared at her a moment in the dark, then turned and ran back in the direction from which he'd come.

She pivoted swiftly to gauge what success the others were having. No point now in hiding the fire, so she brought it back up just enough to let them all see a little more clearly. Almost immediately, she was able to witness Tayse dispatching his second victim and go spinning around to see how the situation lay. Justin had vanquished one of his attackers and was even now pulling a sword from the man's belly. A second man lay on the ground beside him, Donnal standing over him in wolf shape with his paws on the man's shoulder. Both of them, Senneth guessed, were dead.

"Mine ran," she said to Tayse, panting a little. "Should we send Donnal after him?"

"Yes," he said without hesitation, but just then, a blood-freezing cry split the night, coming from the direction that the man had fled.

"Kirra," Senneth said with a slight smile. "He appears to be taken care of."

Tayse nodded at the ground before him, where her assailant had dropped his sword. "What did you do to make him let go of his weapon?"

"Turned the hilt hot in his hand."

He gave her an unreadable look. "You didn't think I needed such aid?"

She smiled. "I was afraid you would be angry with me for not letting you prove your skill. But if it had looked like the fight was not going your way, I would have intervened and let you rail at me all you liked later."

"Good to know," was all he said, then he stepped to the other side of camp to confer with Justin.

Senneth brought the fire up even higher to give them more light. Donnal lifted his white wolf's face and seemed to grin at her over his fallen attacker. She saluted him with the tip of her bloody blade, then knelt down beside one of Tayse's victims.

In a moment, Tayse was beside her, kneeling on the man's other side. They did a quick check for anything that might identify him—livery, jewelry, clothing, money—but they turned up very little. He wore no insignia and carried no cash. His weapons were plain but extremely well-maintained. He had a thin silver chain around his neck, but no pendant hung from it with a house-mark stamped into the metal. He didn't even wear any jewels that were affiliated with one of the Twelve Houses.

"Not much here," Tayse commented and turned to the other corpse.

Before they were finished, Justin came to crouch beside them. "Nothing," he said. "What did you find?"

"Nothing," Tayse replied.

"I wonder if—" Senneth began, but her attention was caught by a figure moving toward them from the undergrowth. Tayse and Justin were both ahead of her, on their feet with weapons in hand, but it was only Kirra. Whatever shape she had taken to hunt down tonight's prey, she had resumed her familiar body now. Donnal came up to nuzzle her hand, and she petted him absently while she glanced at the others.

"I caught one escaping," she said. "What's the story here?"

"The rest are dead," Tayse said briefly. "We've been trying to find any clues as to who they might be."

"The one I killed was wearing plain clothing and no jewelry," Kirra said.

Senneth looked at her. *The one I killed . . .* As if it was an easy thing to have done. As if she had done it every day of her life since she turned eighteen and took up a life of combat. Senneth could not be positive unless she asked, but she was almost certain this was the first life Kirra had ever taken.

She shivered a little. She was so sure this was just the beginning of blood spilled, lives lost, the most desperate gambles taken. She was sure there was much worse to come.

"So what do you think?" Justin was asking. "Were they just mercenaries? Spotted us on the road and came after us by night?"

"Coren Bauler said something about bandits," Kirra said. "I thought he was just making it up, but maybe—"

"They're not bandits. They're not mercenaries," Tayse said. "They're witch hunters. They were looking for us. For you, actually."

They all stared at him. "Why do you think that?" Senneth asked.

"Quality of their clothes. Good leather boots. Condition of their muscles and their skin. Every mercenary I've ever met possessed fine weaponry, so you can't judge by that, but these aren't men who've been camping out in near starvation, waiting for the next victim to pass. These men are funded. And as far as I can tell, what's being funded in the southern regions right now are patrols that can bring down mystics."

Kirra gave a little kick to the dead man lying closest to her. "So maybe these are some of the same ones who killed that family we saw a few days ago."

"Maybe," Tayse said. "Or maybe there are a lot of patrols like this out roaming the countryside."

"Not the same," Senneth said in a muffled voice. "The others were wearing Gisseltess colors."

Tayse glanced at her, seeming to read some of the chaos in her thoughts. "But I'm ready to wager their hands were not clean," he said softly. "Anyone who approaches a night camp by stealth, in such numbers and bearing such arms, has not come to parley. They were intending a slaughter."

"They got one," Justin said.

Kirra looked around. "So what do we do with the bodies? Can we leave them here? I have to say, it'll make it hard to sleep tonight, guarded by corpses."

"We ought to hide them," Tayse said. "Strip anything we might want from the bodies and then bury them."

Kirra was looking at Senneth. "Or burn them."

Now they all turned to gaze at her. "The less evidence left behind, the better," Tayse said, his voice unwontedly gentle. Odd that he, and not Kirra, seemed to be so aware of her distress. "A grave could be found by anyone who's looking."

She nodded. "Let me know when you're done with them," she said and went to sit beside Cammon before the fire.

The other four worked over the bodies for the next hour or so, murmuring among themselves as they came across a particularly fine knife or a leather belt that they liked. Even Donnal had resumed human shape to help check the bodies and drag them away from the fire.

Cammon was quiet at first, but she could sense his presence beside her, curiously calming. "If it helps," he said, "they really were intending to kill us. I have absolutely no doubt about that."

She smiled tightly without looking at him. Cammon she would have expected to pick up on her thoughts; Tayse, no. "I've killed men before," she said. "There was a time I thought I was good at it. There was a time I could think of a lot more men I wanted to see dead. I couldn't do it tonight, though. That will be a liability as we continue on this journey, I think."

"It's because you're afraid of how much death there is going to be," he said softly.

Now she turned her eyes toward him. He still looked so much the innocent youth, his ragged hair even more disreputable after days on the road, his clothes a sorry collection of rags. *We have to buy something better for him to wear. Very next town we come to,* she thought, letting her mind take refuge, just for a moment, in that unimportant detail. "Oh, yes," she said. "We are setting out on a long road of blood."

"Turn away now, then," he said.

She shook her head. "I can't."

"The part you play is too important."

She smiled a little. "So now you're a forecaster as well as a reader? You can see my future as well as my heart?"

"Only your heart—what little glimpses of it you ever bother to show. *You're* the one who sees some role you've been cast in."

She sighed. "And I could be wrong. This all may be—" She flicked the fingers of both hands, as if dispersing troubles. "Posturing and playing and no death dealt. It may be nothing. But I think—" She shook her head and drew nearer to the fire. She was not sure even her own considerable body heat would be enough to warm her tonight. "I think we are heading into some kind of conflagration."

He gave her a little smile. "Lucky for us, then, you are so good with fire."

W HEN they were done with the bodies, Tayse called her over. They had piled the four men like so much cordwood on the side of the road. "The less trace we leave," Tayse said again, "the better it will be."

"What about the one Kirra left on the road?" Justin asked.

Kirra shrugged. "Mauled by a wild animal. Who will be able to tell differently?"

"Good enough," Tayse said.

Senneth concentrated on the bodies, the basic materials of cloth and skin that would be most susceptible to fire. Gone the internal living flame, the raw blaze of creation; what remained now resembled nothing so much as the charred coals left behind after a bonfire sighed out. This fuel would catch fire, but it would never truly burn again.

She spoke a quiet word, and the four bodies were torched to a yellow so bright that those watching stepped hurriedly back. The flames were quick and hungry and very well-behaved. Within minutes they had burned through the stack of bodies and then subsided. When Tayse bent to touch the ground where they had been, he rubbed his fingers together and looked at her over his shoulder.

"A little black ash that will blow away by morning," he said. "The ground isn't even singed."

"Good," she said, and turned back to the fire. She knew, they all knew, they should move on from this place right now, but they were all too weary to pack up and go.

"I'll watch," Justin said.

"I'll help," Donnal replied, and resumed his wolf shape.

"We'll leave early in the morning," Tayse said. "And try to find someplace indoors to rest for a night or two. I think we could all do with a night of unbroken sleep."

Senneth nodded without answering, though it seemed she was the one he spoke to. She hunkered down in the blankets, closer to the fire. Still not warm, so she murmured to the fire itself. Hotter, stronger, higher flames. Cammon and Kirra drew back, but Senneth stayed as close as the threat of danger would allow.

CHAPTER
9

THE morning was cold, even for Senneth, and no one looked particularly rested. It was almost a relief to pack up and get back on the road, leaving this undesirable location behind. Senneth glanced around once, but they had left no overt signs of a fight behind them. Some blood in the grass, scuff marks in the dirt. A good tracker could probably read that story, but it would not be definitive. There would be proof of nothing. She turned her horse's head and followed Tayse's lead out of the camp.

A few days ago, they had left the main road that served the southern Houses, but they were still following pretty well-traveled routes that connected the smaller towns to each other. The land around them was mostly open, with occasional valleys of wild grass and brambles, and occasional stands of fairly dense woods. They only passed a few other travelers, a mix of farmers and peddlers and gentry, and rarely exchanged more than a few courteous words with any of them. None of them looked like mercenaries, even civil guards disguised as mercenaries. Neither Cammon nor Donnal showed alarm when any of them approached, and Senneth took her cues from them.

A few hours after lunch they came to a small town in unaligned territory between Fortunalt and Rappengrass lands. It seemed to be something of a local crossroads, for it boasted two inns and a number of taverns, and the stables at the far edge of town appeared large enough to hold a fair number of horses.

"Forge down that way," Tayse noted, jerking his head.

"Looks like a market town," Senneth said.

"We could stand to replenish supplies," Tayse said.

"And find something for Cammon to wear," Kirra added with a laugh.

"Who are we this time?" Justin wanted to know.

Kirra shook her head. "I don't think I should be the fine lady again, not so close to Forten City. Not even a lady from the Thirteenth House."

"But we might be some agents carrying out transactions for Malcolm Danalustrous," Senneth said. "That seems harmless enough."

"My father will be—interested—to hear how much business he and his vassals have been conducting in the southern regions lately," Kirra said.

Senneth glanced at her. "A bad idea, then, you think?"

Kirra laughed. "Well, if he doesn't like it, he can tell us so once he finds out."

"But I think we should not volunteer much information, and perhaps no one will think to ask," Senneth said. "Travelers must pass this way all the time and not share details of their journeys."

Cammon spoke for the first time. "It's a strange place, though," he said.

They all looked at him. "Strange how?" Tayse asked.

"There's—shouldn't there be more people on the street? At this hour of day? It feels like—there's fear or something here. In the houses. In the alleys."

"Fear of soldiers? Fear of retribution?" Senneth asked. "Are there Rappengrass guards here enforcing some kind of order?"

He shook his head. "I can't—I don't think so. It's just—it's strange."

"He's right. The streets are a little too empty," Tayse said. His hand had dropped automatically to his sword hilt. Justin's tiniest dagger was in his palm. "Trouble of some kind has visited this place."

"Should we ride on?" Kirra asked.

Senneth glanced around. Two women were hurrying between buildings, their arms wrapped around each other as if for warmth or support. A cluster of men stood outside a tavern, so close to the door they could dart back inside instantly if need be. Here and there, in shop windows and the upper stories of houses, faces were watching through the curtains. A man rode by on horseback, faster than it seemed he should. Even the dust behind him seemed in a hurry to float away.

"Or stay," Senneth said slowly, "and see what the trouble is."

THEY rode warily down the main street to the stables, all of them alert for any kind of attack. The big wooden door was closed, so Tayse swung down to push it open, and the rest of them rode in. Instantly they were enveloped in the warm, sharp smells of horse and manure and oiled leather. Two middle-aged men jogged over from a stall near the back.

"Room to stable six horses for a night or two?" Tayse asked.

One of the men glanced around at the new arrivals; the other turned and went back to his chores. "Room if you really want to stay," the ostler said.

"Something we should know about?" Tayse asked. His voice was gentle, but he managed to make the words sound menacing.

The man glanced around again, this time at the interior of the barn. He was heavyset but thick with muscle; his clothes were rough and dirty, as an ostler's would be, but he looked like a reasonably decent man, Senneth thought.

"There've been attacks the past two weeks or so," the man said in a low voice. "At first we thought it was a wolf, even a cougar. You know. Wild creature come too close to civilization and learning to like the easy life. But none of our hunters can catch it. We put out the usual poisons, and it won't take them. Now and then someone swears they've seen it, but it's so fast they can't make out its face or even the color of its fur. But then, the next morning, there's a body in the street."

"Human body?" Tayse asked, not sounding particularly shocked.

The ostler shrugged. "Twice. Little girl, only five years old, shouldn't have been out wandering the streets anyway, but her mama said she would get up and walk in her sleep, and what should she do, shackle her to the bed? But now she's wishing she had. And then an old man, always drunk on bad wine, you could find him sleeping in any alley come morning. Only one morning, he wasn't sleeping, he was dead. And then there have been dogs—

five or six of those. A cat. No one knows what will be attacked next."

Tayse looked straight up at Senneth, as if he thought she might understand this mystery. She didn't say anything.

"And no one knows what it might be?" Tayse asked.

The other man shook his head and lowered his voice. "Folks are saying," he said, "it might be mystic work."

"Really?" Kirra said in a sharp voice. "How would that be possible?"

The ostler gave her one quick look and returned his attention to Tayse. "Some mystics can take animal shape, you know. And they can move faster and strike harder than a real animal. Or maybe it takes the form of a different animal every time it goes out to kill, and that's why no one can say for sure what it looks like."

"Are you having trouble in these parts with mystics?" Tayse asked.

The ostler shrugged. "Not really. I mean—my mother-in-law was always a little gifted, you know—she could do small spells and was a wonder with the garden. And folks in this town never got too stirred up about mystics the way they have in the big cities. But that was before this creature came. Now—well, people are talking. And the Daughters of the Pale Mother have been by, now and then, warning us all not to let magic drift into our lives. If this animal turns out to be some kind of witch creature—well, I think you'll be seeing some angry people. I'm a little worried for my mother-in-law, to tell you the truth. I see people casting looks at her, as if she knows something she's not telling."

"Everybody knows something he doesn't tell," Tayse said with a slight smile. "But I have to say, your creature sounds real enough to me. I wouldn't be so quick to blame magic for what might be nature."

"No," the ostler said. "And the old man who got killed—he was wearing a moonstone amulet. I wouldn't think a mystical creature would be able to touch him if he was wearing a moonstone, would you?"

"I wouldn't," Tayse said.

"In any case," the ostler said, "watch yourselves while you're here."

"We will," Tayse said. "I imagine we'll be safe enough if we stay together. Any place you'd recommend we spend the night?"

"My brother runs the Golden Cup, just up the street. Pretty sure he's got a few rooms open."

"We'll try it, thanks."

In a few moments they'd paid the man in advance, unstrapped their bags, and were jostling each other as they moved in fairly close formation down the street. They only passed two others during their short walk, and both of them were moving at a near run.

"So what do you think it is?" Kirra asked Senneth.

"That was going to be my very first question," Tayse said.

She couldn't decide if she should be amused or annoyed. "Why would you think I would know?"

"You know everything," Kirra said. "Or most everything, particularly the things no one else knows."

"Well, he didn't really tell us very much," she said. "It could be anything. We'd need to know more about—" She shrugged. "How it kills, what state it leaves the bodies in, what kind of tracks it leaves behind. How often it strikes."

"I don't think it's magical," Cammon said. "I think we're the only ones in town who've brought in any abilities."

"That would be my guess," Senneth said. "I'm sure we'll find out more over dinner."

Two hours later they had settled into their rooms, washed up, and gone down to the taproom to arrange themselves around a couple of tables. Tayse and Justin sat closer to the bar, where they might hear or be included in the conversation of the local men. The mystics sat nearer the back, where travelers were more likely to congregate, so they could pick up stories of the road.

Not that there were many other customers in the taproom at all, Senneth noted. People were afraid to walk the streets alone at night, especially after they'd tipped back a few glasses of home-brewed, if there was a creature lurking in the shadows waiting to strike. And travelers were disinclined to linger anyplace that seemed marked for trouble. If this predator wasn't disposed of quickly—or if tales of its supernatural qualities became commonly believed—this little crossroads town might lose all its commerce and livelihood within a few weeks.

When the very pretty, very young waitress brought their food, Senneth tossed her a coin in payment. "Slow tonight," she commented.

The girl nodded glumly. She had a riot of brown curls and a full red mouth, and she probably did quite well in tips and favors. "Been that way for two weeks or more," she said. "Ever since—whatever that creature is—came to town."

"Ostler told us a bit about it," Donnal said. "Kills something every night, does it?"

She glanced around the table once, showed no interest in the women, and clearly decided Donnal was the best of the male prospects, for she gave him a little smile. "Not every night. Every second or third night, I guess it's been. My sister said she saw it once, running down the street with a bloody hand in its mouth."

"Did she say what color it was?" Donnal asked. "How big it was?"

She looked surprised at his interest. "Why do you want to know?"

He gave her a smile, but his face still looked serious. He was incapable of ever looking other than serious, Senneth thought. "Done some hunting in my time," he said. "I thought—maybe it was something I've come up against before—"

"Well, we've had hunters *and* hunters here," she said pessimistically. "This one used to shoot game with Ariane Rappengrass herself. This one used to track wolves for King Baryn." She shook her head. "You know how men talk. But none of them could kill the thing."

"They think it's a wolf? Is that what your sister said it looked like?"

She shrugged. "She said it was the color of a fox, but bigger. And fast as a deer. Faster. She said she's never seen anything run so fast."

"Northern harewolf, it runs fast," said a man sitting one table over. He was dressed in well-worn travel clothes, and it appeared as if it had been weeks since he washed his tangled gray hair or beard. "I've killed a few in my time, though."

The pretty girl looked over at him with even less interest than she'd showed Cammon and the women. "Have you?" she said politely.

The traveler nodded. "Any reward being offered, if this creature would be killed or captured?" he said. "It might be worth my time to try it, if the money was good enough."

"A few gold pieces," she said. "The innkeepers and tavern masters have each put up some coins. They're losing business."

The traveler looked interested. "Gold pieces," he said. "I'll have to find out how many."

The girl rolled her eyes at Donnal. "Were you wanting anything else to eat? You or your friends?"

"Thank you, no," he said, and she left.

"What do you think?" Cammon asked.

Senneth smiled. "I think no one has any idea what it looks like or how fast it is."

"You do," Cammon said.

"Not sure yet," she replied.

They sat in the bar another hour or so but didn't glean much helpful information. The four of them paid their shot and went back upstairs to their rooms. Cammon and Donnal were sharing a room across the hall with Tayse and Justin, but they came directly into the women's quarters. A few minutes later, the Riders arrived.

"Learn anything?" Tayse said, leaning against the rickety chest of drawers that was the only furniture in the room besides the bed. Senneth thought for a moment that he was so big and so heavy the chest would splinter under his weight, but it held firm.

"Fast as a deer, red as a fox, doesn't kill every night," she recited. "You?"

"It prefers to eat only sweetbreads," Tayse said. "Leaves a lot of the body to go to waste. That's why it kills so often."

"Aahhh," she said, and sank onto the bed next to Kirra. They all looked at her.

"So you do know," Kirra said.

She arched her eyebrows. "It just seems so unlikely. This far out. But it sounds like a raelynx."

Justin and Tayse looked startled; the others seemed mystified. "What's that?" Cammon asked.

"A sort of wild cat that lives to the east of us in the Lirrenlands," Senneth said. "But there are mountains between us and the Lirrens, and I've almost never heard of a raelynx crossing out of those mountains."

"I've never heard of the Lirrenlands!" Cammon exclaimed.

The others laughed. "Nobody knows much about them," Kirra assured him. "The king considers the Lirrenlands to be under his dominion, and I think they pay tithes, and they fought beside Gillengaria in the last war, but it's a strange country filled with strange people."

"And strange animals, apparently," Justin said. He was still looking at Senneth. "How is it you know so much about the creatures that can only be found there?"

She smiled a little. "I lived in the Lirrens for a few years."

Tayse shifted, and the chest of drawers protested. "Of course you did," he said in a polite voice.

"So—what—these raelynxes go prowling around the Lirrenlands, killing people off every few days? I would imagine there aren't very many people left living there, then," Justin said with some of his usual sarcasm.

Senneth spread her hands. "The Lirren people—I've often thought the whole lot of them must be rife with magic," she said. She glanced at Cammon with a smile. "I should take you with me sometime to visit there, and maybe you could tell me. Myself, I couldn't feel the magic on them, but there was no other way to explain some of their abilities. Some of them are healers with gifts that are astounding. Some of them can grow crops on land that shouldn't support a weed. And many of them seemed to have a bond with animals—particularly predators. Hunters. In any case, I never saw a raelynx attack a native-born Lirren while I lived there. They had this skill of controlling the creatures—of turning them away. At any rate, they never attacked the human communities where I lived."

"And I suppose while you lived in the Lirrens, you learned this skill of controlling wild animals as well," Tayse said in a silky voice.

She looked at him, her expression neutral. "I developed a certain aptitude for it, yes."

Kirra clapped her hands together in feigned excitement. "Oh, good! The barmaid said there was a reward for its death. Maybe we could earn a few coppers."

Senneth's smile flickered across her face. "Gold pieces, I thought she said."

"Even better."

"Seriously?" Donnal said. "You think you can kill it?"

"I think it would be hard to kill," she said, and looked at Tayse.

He grunted. "There was a raelynx up north once. Few miles from Ghosenhall. Situation much like this—small town, terrorized by the creature. The king sent a few of his Riders out to try to hunt it down." He shook his head. "We never were fast enough. I'm not a bad tracker, and I've never gone hungry in the woods, but I had no idea how to catch this thing. We never even got close."

"So what happened?" Cammon asked.

"One day it was gone," he said. "Moved on, I guess, or died in some natural accident. After a while, we just left."

"Maybe this is the same one," Cammon said. "If they never cross out of the mountains."

"My guess," said Senneth slowly, "is that this is a young one. Still growing, which is another reason it feeds so often. And too inexperienced to know it shouldn't stay long in one place."

"Makes even less sense that a baby cat could get all this way on its own," Justin objected.

She nodded. "I don't think it came on its own. I'm guessing it was orphaned when it was just a few days old and trappers picked it up. They probably were bringing it out west to ship or sell. Maybe headed to Forten City. Exotic creature like that could bring a lot in some foreign markets."

"Makes sense," Tayse said. "What happened to the trappers?"

She smiled. "An accident in the wagon, maybe, and the kit got free. Went for the men first and then started roaming."

"And you think you can stop it," Kirra said.

"I didn't say that."

"You may as well have."

"If the King's Riders can't kill such a creature," Justin said scornfully, "I don't see why you think you can."

"I didn't say I could kill it, either."

There was a moment's silence. Senneth was watching Tayse; he was watching her. "If he thought his people were endangered by such a creature," Tayse said, "the king would want us to stop the marauding, if we could."

"Even if such an act brings unwanted attention to our party?" Senneth said. "Because I think it would."

"Even then," Tayse said. He shrugged. "I'm starting to think we're destined to draw attention no matter where we go."

"There's probably truth to that," Senneth said.

Kirra was looking at her. "What do you think you can do?"

Senneth smiled. "I'll let you know when I figure it out."

IN the morning, she strolled through the town, talking idly to the few people out on the street who looked disposed to linger or gossip. Most of the stories tallied with the theory she'd developed so far, and she also discovered other bits of useful information, such as what time of night the predator was most likely to strike and where.

"Why?" asked one of the tavern keepers when he'd gotten the drift of her questions. "You think you want to try your hand at hunting it?"

"Any reason I shouldn't?"

He grimaced and wiped down his bar without answering, but his expression conveyed his opinion. Senneth grinned. "I guess you don't see too many women hunters in this area."

"Look. We've probably had twenty men through here, locals and travelers, trying to track that thing down. We've lost two people and I don't know how many animals. You can catch it, I'm happy. But I'm starting to think it's the sort of thing that can't be caught—" He paused and gave her one rather disdainful look. "Or if it can be, not by a lone woman who's not even carrying a bow."

"If I do it, I want to do it my own way," she said. "I don't want people interfering."

He spread his hands, the damp cloth dangling from his fingers. "Have at it," he said. "I don't think anyone will stop you. No one will help you, either."

"I understand there's a reward," she said.

He nodded. "Ten gold pieces. A pretty good sum."

"I hope I earn it," she said and went out.

From what she could tell, the raelynx had not struck for two days, and hadn't fed much the last time it killed, so she figured it would come out again this night or the next. It seemed to hunt sometime between midnight and dawn. She could grab a few hours of sleep before setting out after it.

She explained her plan over dinner, which the six of them ate together. The others had had a profitable day, buying a thick blue cloak for Cammon, as well as some sturdy boots, and having two of the horses reshod at the smith. In addition, Kirra had bought more supplies for the road and listened for any news that might not involve the raelynx. Only in that very last venture had she not been successful.

"So you're going out tonight?" Kirra asked. "Do you want help?"

"I don't think so."

"Will you stake out a dog or a goat for bait?" Justin wanted to know.

Senneth smiled at him. "I'm the bait."

Tayse looked at her. "I don't think you should do this alone," he said.

"If too many people are about, it might not come at all."

Tayse counted on his fingertips. "Two people and seven or eight animals dead because of this creature."

"Two rather helpless people," she amended.

He surveyed her again. "My father's one of the oldest of the King's Riders," he said. "Do you know how he lived so long, when many soldiers die before the age of thirty?" Justin was grinning. Tayse went on, "Because he was never stupid. He never went out alone, even on a task that a single man should have been able to complete."

"I would be happy to meet such a wise and skilled warrior," Senneth said gravely. "But I don't think even his talents would help much in this particular hunt."

"Good," Kirra said, yawning. "Because I want to go to bed right now and stay there till morning."

In fact, Kirra lingered downstairs with the men while Senneth went up to the room to sleep for a few hours. At midnight, she rose and dressed. Kirra was sleeping on the other side of the bed, her hair spread like amber across her pillow. She didn't stir as Senneth slipped out the door and down the deserted hallway. No one else in the whole inn, in the whole town, appeared to be awake.

She stepped outside into the star-chilled night and paused a moment to get her bearings. Only once had the raelynx struck deep within the borders of town; more often it seemed to prowl along the eastern edge, not far from a thin border of trees. Undoubtedly it had its lair somewhere in that stand of woods, but none of the local townspeople had been able to track it there.

Senneth walked through the faint moonlight to the edge of town and looked around for an old bucket or a dropped log to sit on. There was nothing. She sighed and sank cross-legged to the ground, drawing her jacket around her a little more tightly. Just a moment or two of concentration, of sensing the heat running under the surface of her skin, and she was comfortable again.

The raelynx, she thought, might be drawn as much by the warmth of her body as by her scent.

She sat there unmoving for more than an hour, relaxed as she could be while waiting for a wild animal to try to kill her. She liked the deep stillness of an untenanted night, the pervasive cold that seemed to take corporeal form and lean against her like an affectionate child. She liked the utter blackness of the sky, the stars like spilled sugar across an unswept floor. She liked being alone.

She stayed motionless but grew extremely alert as soon as her solitude ended.

She didn't pretend to have Cammon's gifts of perception, but she could sense the wild heart of the creature that was stealthily advancing on her out of the eastern woods. Its mind was a chaotic tumble of drives and hungers, impatient and lawless; its memories and impulses were all of violence. It was so single-minded and destructive that, in a way, it reminded her of fire, and that made it seem beautiful to her.

It came close enough to attack her, and it bunched its muscles to spring.

Senneth reached out with all the force of her personality and laid her will against the cat's.

Instantly she felt the roil of confusion and dissent in its brain. It loosed a furious snarl into the night, a sound to strike terror into any soul, and it jerked its whole body as if to yank free of a net. Senneth held on. She closed her mind over its mind, made her choices its choices, coerced it into obedience. It snarled again and fought her; she could feel it lay each separate velvet paw down against the ground as it attempted to back away. She clenched her fingers and tightened her mental hold. The raelynx froze in place. She made a motion with her fingers and invited it nearer.

Slowly, delicate foot by delicate foot, the raelynx minced out of the shadows and came to stand in front of Senneth where she still sat on the ground. She could sense the bewilderment and resentment in its coiled body but now, overlaying all that, curiosity, too. In its short life, it had known only one personality stronger than its own, and that had belonged to its mother, who was dead. It had not occurred to it that there might be other creatures in this chilly world with strength or subtlety to match its own.

Senneth sat very still, letting the raelynx investigate her while she examined it in turn. As the barmaid's sister had said, it was fox-colored, dappled here and there with black spots and patches of white. Its head was bigger than a cougar's, the nose longer and more pointed, the eyes dark and set wide apart. Its triangular ears seemed too big for its head, even bigger because of the black tufts of fur edging the pointed tips. Its paws were huge—this beast was going to grow to a considerable size—and also featured tufts between the divided toes. At first, Senneth thought its spine was visible through the sleek coat, and then she realized she was seeing just another ridge of bunched fur running in a straight line down the long back. A narrow, flexible tail whipped slowly from side to side, proof that the cat was alert and considering its next move. Senneth had no doubt that he would like it to be a violent one.

Involuntarily she smiled. "But I can control you," she murmured, quietly but aloud. "You are a creature of flame and hunger, and I can always bend those elements to my will. You will not kill again unless it is at my command."

She stood up, and the cat watched her, its tail lashing now, its dark eyes even wider with checked fury. "It would probably be best if we rode out tonight, but I think you are safe enough by my side," she said. "So back to the inn we go."

She took a few steps toward town, listening carefully to see if her quarry would follow her. He hissed once, more in irritation than rage, she thought, and then padded up beside her and accompanied her down the road.

They had not gone twenty paces before a shadow detached itself from an unlit doorway and approached them.

The raelynx spat and dropped to a crouch, but Senneth held it beside her. Her own knife was in hand, but it only took a few seconds before she knew she didn't need it.

"Tayse," she said. "Offering me your protection after all."

He was using the pale moonlight to stare at the raelynx, but not as if he was astounded at Senneth's audacity or power. Merely, he had never seen one before, and he was memorizing its attributes while he had the chance. "I can hardly credit it," he said, "but I'm guessing you think you're going to bring this creature along with us as we continue on our journey."

She could not help a smile. "I can scarcely let it loose to begin its depredations again."

"It seems it will stand still for you," he said. "You could hold it helpless while I cut its throat."

"There is no reason it should die," she said. "It has done nothing but try to live, given only the skills it was born with."

Tayse lifted his eyes, unfathomable in the night, to examine Senneth. "And you are not overfond of killing anything," he said.

"I am not. You think that is a weakness on my part."

"I don't think you have any weaknesses at all," he said.

She smiled again at that. "What would you do, if this creature was in your power?"

He turned his attention back to the raelynx. "I would probably destroy it. Unless I had a very good use for it. I would destroy it because I wouldn't trust that my power would control it for long."

"Are you afraid that it will slip free of me?"

He looked at her again. "Oh no," he said. "I am not afraid of that in the slightest."

"I can't think that the villagers will be so very glad that I have taken it alive and mean to leave it that way," she said. "We will have to be on our way again in the morning."

"Where will you put it for the night?"

Now her smile was irrepressible. "Why, next to my bed in my room back at the inn. It will be quite safe there, I think."

He started laughing, the sound quiet but comforting in the dark. She thought that she had not heard him laugh before. She imagined he didn't think that too much in this world was amusing. "I foresee an interesting day," he remarked, and turned his footsteps back to their hotel.

CHAPTER
10

In the morning, Senneth was woken by the sound of Kirra's scream. Half the hallway was roused by the same sound, so the next few minutes were a tumult of knocks on the doors and cries down the corridor and everyone assuring everyone that there was no trouble, everything was fine.

That whole time, the raelynx sat backed into a corner, its teeth bared, its red fur ruffled, its tail twitching, and loosed a low, menacing growl upon the world.

"You could have at least *warned* me!" Kirra exclaimed when she'd recovered her composure and all the neighbors had stopped visiting. "If I'd known you were going to bring that thing back here—though, how could I *not* have known? It is so like you! Protect all the creatures that roam under the Pale Mother's watchful eyes—"

Senneth smiled. "I wasn't sure I'd be able to hold it. But once he came close enough last night, I knew I could. I can't bring myself to kill him."

"And at night? Even while you're sleeping? You can control him then?"

Senneth smiled. "Even while you're sleeping, can you maintain a disguise? Yes."

"What do we do with it now?" Kirra asked.

"We'll take him with us some distance and then decide."

Kirra, who really feared very little, stepped a pace closer to the creature, who yowled a warning. She jumped back. "It's a he, then?"

"Well, I think so. It was dark, and I was being careful, so I didn't examine him too closely."

Kirra turned to look at her, a smile on her beautiful, aristocratic face. "Have you given him a name? For I know you, Senneth! He will become your pet, your familiar. Right now, you're thinking, well, when I have the time, I'll cross the mountains and return him to the Lirrens, where he'll be safe—but in your heart, you're already growing attached to him. You won't want to give him up."

Senneth smiled back. "I will try to do what is best for him when the time allows," she said. "Right now, we just need to move on. He is not welcome here, understandably so, and we won't be either once I emerge with the raelynx by my side."

Kirra looked thoughtful. "Maybe I'd better fetch us breakfast, then, so you can eat it in the room before we go."

"Good idea. And—if you can—something for him. He didn't feed last night, and he's hungry. He might be much more pleasant once he's fed."

Kirra grinned. "You might be the only one who's able to tell the difference. But I'll see what I can find in the kitchens." She looked doubtfully at the snarling cat. "But—if he'll only eat sweetbreads—"

"That was when he could choose his own diet," Senneth said. "He will be much less particular now."

LESS than an hour later, they were on their way—an even stranger cavalcade, Senneth thought, than they had been when they first set out. Predictably, Justin had been dismayed at the new addition to their party, but when he saw that Tayse did not protest, he more or less held his tongue. Donnal was intrigued by the raelynx and narrowed his eyes in appraisal; Senneth guessed it would not be long before he knew the form well enough to assume it for himself. Cammon seemed fascinated by the wild creature and kept twisting in his saddle to keep its russet shape in sight.

They had made quite a stir in the village when Senneth walked out of her chamber, down the hall, and through the taproom with the cat two inches from her side. She had a firm mental grip on him, for he was very edgy to appear abroad in daylight with so many people around. Almost as edgy as the people they encountered.

"May the Pale Mother blink at the Bright Mother's eye!" she heard someone swear, but most everyone else was silent with stupefaction. She moved unhurriedly, not really glancing at the other people in the hallway and open room, but aware of them all, staring, pointing, starting to heat with anger.

"You—what have you—what are you *doing*?" the innkeeper demanded just as she reached the door. "That creature—that murderer—are you taking him with you *alive*?"

Justin and Donnal appeared beside her at that juncture, Justin with his hand suggestively on his weapon belt. The others were outside with the horses. Senneth let her calm gaze rest briefly on the proprietor's face.

"I am," she said. "I have a use for him."

"But he—but we—he should be *killed*!" someone else exclaimed.

"He is mine now," Senneth said, "I will do with him what I like." She put a hand on the door, then turned back to cast one quick glance around at the staring, suspicious faces. "Be glad that he will trouble you no longer."

"But you—how can you—what power do you have that you can make him obey you like that?" the innkeeper said.

"I am skilled with animals," she said and pushed the door open.

Donnal preceded her; Justin waited for Senneth and the raelynx to step through the door first. Just before she put her foot outside, she heard someone inside mutter, "Mystic."

And another voice, a little louder. "Witch."

"*Sorceress.*"

She swung aboard her horse and spurred it forward before Justin had even mounted. "I think we'd better leave as quickly as we can," she said to Tayse, who nodded.

Kirra, of course, was laughing. "I guess you'll have to forget about your reward," she said.

Senneth smiled back. "I think I've come away with something even more valuable than their gold."

AT first they traveled at a pretty rapid rate, Justin behind them to ensure there was no pursuit. After a while, when it was clear no one had followed, they settled into a more comfortable pace. Senneth stayed primarily focused on the raelynx, so she was only peripherally aware of the other people in her party. Her hands lay lax on the reins, and she trusted her horse to stay with the others while she kept all her concentration on the immature cat.

It roved beside them, a little distance off the road, running with a fluid ease that made her, for a moment, greatly envy Donnal and Kirra and their ability to turn into such fierce, magnificent creatures. Its own energy was boundless; its attention went everywhere, to each new sound and sight that presented itself on their trip. Now and then it dashed away to chase down a rabbit or a bird, but Senneth jerked it sharply back, causing it to hiss in frustration. Later, when she was more sure of her control over it, she would allow it to hunt. For now, she did not want the thrill of adrenaline to flood its muscles and help it break free of her unwanted influence.

When they stopped for lunch, the raelynx stopped with them, sitting about five yards away with its eyes fixed unwaveringly on their small human circle. Justin kept glancing over at it with a certain nervousness, but no one else seemed worried that it would suddenly decide to make one of them its midday meal.

Senneth tossed it a chunk of cooked venison, which the raelynx ignored at first as if it was too proud to eat food provided by someone else's enterprise. But in a few minutes, it started batting at the slab of meat, playing with it, and then finally condescended to lower its sharp teeth and tear out a few bites.

Senneth grinned. She looked up to find Kirra and Donnal also smiling. Tayse looked thoughtful. He said, "You won't be able to feed it for long if your eventual plan is to release it back in the wild."

"I don't think this one will forget how to hunt for himself any time soon," Kirra said.

"Just a few days," Senneth said. "Just until he gets used to me."

Justin said, "You think that only takes a few days?"

She answered him in a neutral voice. "He has fewer reasons to distrust me."

Tayse was on his feet. "Back on the road," he said. "I'd just as soon get as many miles as we can between us and the village."

Justin was instantly standing. "I don't think they're going to send anyone after us."

"No, but they'll spread the word. Six travelers, men and women, some of them mystics. And a raelynx. Anyone trying to follow our trail will not find it difficult."

"I agree with Tayse," Senneth said. "Let's ride on."

The rest of the day was cold but uneventful, though Senneth thought she might not even have noticed if other dangers stalked them, so intent was she on holding the cat close. It was a nocturnal creature, so it grew even more lively as the afternoon faded and night drew near. She felt the tug of its will as an almost tangible cord wound tightly around her entire body and strung with tension for the whole distance between them. She increased her concentration and lost even more interest in her surroundings. The cat lunged and tested, but it did not get free.

By nightfall, she had a terrific headache. She could feel the muscles of her neck bunched with strain; heavy blood, rich with poison, thrummed through the back of her skull. She was almost startled to find the others pulling off the road and circling through the low brushy growth to find a level site for a camp. Somewhat blindly, she followed them and slid to the ground where the rest of them stood. Without being asked, Cammon stepped up and took her horse. The others fell into their customary tasks.

It didn't take much energy for Senneth to build the fire, so she did that, somewhat absently, and then began assembling food for the evening meal. Around her, she caught voices and motion, but they seemed distant and unimportant. The raelynx had dropped to its belly a few yards away and was watching them all with what attention it could spare from the sight of darting night birds and the sound of rustling wood mice.

She thought this might feel like a longer night than the one before.

Donnal squatted beside her, a container of fresh water in his hands. "Anything in particular a raelynx fears?" he asked her quietly.

She looked at him blankly for a moment before her mind was able to comprehend the question. "Natural enemies, you mean? I'm not sure. It's faster than a wolf or a bear, though either of those could probably kill an adult raelynx if it was injured. But I've had my mind wrapped around its mind all day, and it hasn't once seemed afraid. I'm not sure fear is part of its makeup."

A small, serious smile on that dark, serious face. "Maybe it wants a friend, then," Donnal said. "I'll try, after dinner. I don't think I can control it, but I think I can take some of the burden off you."

She gave him a wan smile. "That would be helpful."

As usual, the meal was quick and efficient, cleaned up afterward without much fuss. "I'll do a last check," Justin said and loped off to prowl the perimeter.

Kirra yawned and stretched. "I suppose we'd better watch tonight again," she said. "These days, it's hard to know who might be after us."

"Not Senneth," Tayse said. "She only slept half the night last night."

"And she has a headache," Cammon added.

She glanced at him but couldn't say she was surprised. "It'll be better in the morning," she said.

Tayse glanced at Kirra, as if expecting her to speak. When she didn't, he asked, "So why doesn't Kirra stop your headache with her mystical healing powers?"

"I wish I could," Kirra said regretfully. "But this is caused by magic and can't be healed by magic."

Now Tayse looked back at Senneth. "Is it?"

She nodded—carefully, though, because of the acid-laced blood in her head. "Sustained effort like this—holding to the raelynx—can cause a pain that can be pretty intense."

He lifted his brows. "Well, if you're going to be dragging the creature along with us for the next few weeks on the road, are you going to have a headache that whole time? Or a headache that gets worse?"

"I hope not," she said with a slight smile. "Usually it goes away in a day or two. It's like—" She shrugged, not thinking clearly enough to explain.

"It's like you picking up your sword and spending the day practicing a new maneuver," Kirra said. "Your muscles will be sore the next day. And the day after that, as you keep practicing. But pretty soon you'll get used to it, and the ache will go away. It's like that. Sort of."

Donnal had put down his dishes and risen to his feet. "Let me see what I can do," he said, and his body dissolved into a swirl of color. Almost immediately, it had re-formed itself into a lethal red shape of grace and power.

Tayse's breath hissed in. "I'm glad most of these creatures stay on the other side of the Lireth Mountains," he said.

Senneth nodded. As an adult raelynx, Donnal was signifi-cantly heavier and larger than the immature one, though he had the same patched and tufted fur, the same black eyes and pointed nose. The kit had been too fast and too strong for humans to catch; she thought an adult let loose in an unprotected country-side would be an absolute terror.

"Seeing you," she said slowly, "I begin to think I wouldn't have been able to hold this one if we'd come across him much older." She reached out a hand to Donnal, who nudged it aside with his nose and then took it in his mouth in a light, playful grip. She could feel the needle-sharp front teeth, the powerful back teeth.

"I thought you said you acquired this skill in the Lirrens," Tayse said.

She gave him a faint smile. "I never said I was good at it. I'm learning as I go."

Donnal released her and padded off on silent feet to where the baby cat lay. Senneth turned to watch, monitoring the encounter as much with her mind as with her eyes. At Donnal's approach, the smaller animal scrambled to its feet, mewling like a house cat. It backed off, every sinew tense, every sense straining to assess this new danger. Donnal circled it once, seeming to sniff the air between them, never getting too close. Then he sat on his haunches and merely watched the other raelynx.

"This could take a while," Kirra said, standing up and shaking out her bedroll.

"And might cause a backlash if these raelynxes aren't pack an-imals," Tayse said.

"I know," Senneth said. "I'm not letting go."

So she sat for the next thirty minutes, body loose, mind en-gaged, half-watching and half-feeling the tentative friendship rit-ual unfold between Donnal and the kit. She barely noticed Justin arriving back in camp, his footfalls almost silent, hardly realized he was holding a low conversation with Tayse. She couldn't have said what Cammon and Kirra did to prepare the camp or them-selves for oncoming night. She was concerned only with the slow, grudging trust the young raelynx offered his companion. She felt it when his muscles relaxed, when he dropped back to the ground and lay his head on his outstretched forepaws. She was so closely connected to him and his animal senses that she could almost smell what he smelled, Donnal's comforting and familiar scent. When Donnal settled his big body next to the smaller one for warmth, she almost jolted backward, so strong was her tactile impression.

She felt her own bones rumble when the raelynx started to purr.

Slowly, partially, she withdrew her magic from the raelynx's consciousness, waiting to see if he noticed, if he made a sudden bolt for freedom. Donnal could not hold the kit in check the way she could, not with sheer will, but the smaller cat seemed to have transferred some of his dependence to Donnal, seemed willing to be led by the older animal. Thus she could ease away, let up some of her fanatically close attention, relax the cramped grip of her magic.

It was strange the way the sense of the ordinary world came back to her, in one vivid rush. Suddenly, she became aware of sitting cross-legged on the ground, rocks and sticks pressing into the backs of her legs, her mouth dry with thirst, the smoke of the campfire drifting pleasantly past her cheek. The world smelled like burning wood and decaying leaves and winter. And she had the headache to end all headaches.

She put her fingers to her temples and rubbed, then massaged behind her ears and along the tops of her shoulders, but she knew this would do no good. She needed to apply pressure in places she couldn't reach, and even so, the pain was unlikely to go away. Her head felt filled with venom; her spine was a conduit of agony. She closed her eyes briefly and wondered if sleep would help at all.

When she opened her eyes again, Tayse was kneeling before her.

"I still don't understand why Kirra can't help," he said.

At the moment, she thought, it was because Kirra was already asleep. Senneth could make out three wrapped bodies lying motionless beside the fire. Tayse had apparently taken first watch. "I might ask her to, if it's no better tomorrow," she said. "But, as she said, it's not the kind of pain that usually can be eased by magic."

"You were rubbing your shoulders. Does that help? Does it help if someone else does that for you?"

She was so surprised that for a moment she didn't answer. "Yes—sometimes—a little. What really helps is a much stronger pressure than most people can bring to bear at a couple of points along my back."

"Tell me," he said.

She looked at him doubtfully for a moment. During this whole trip, he and Justin had been shaving every day or so, certainly when they had access to indoor accommodations, and he had shaved that morning; his face was entirely visible to her. Yet between the flickering of the firelight and the habitual caution of his expression, it was a face that was almost impossible to read. Strong bones, stubborn mouth, watchful black eyes. A quick intelligence, almost feral, honed by the survival skills of mistrust and combat. She was not used to expecting kindness from him. Or perhaps she did not want to come to count on it. He had been kind more than once, in a somewhat begrudging way, as they made their journey so far. She was so sure, if he chose, he could be almost unbearably brutal.

"Sit behind me," she said finally, and he moved. She could feel his hands rest lightly on her shoulder blades, waiting for the next direction.

"It is actually three places at once," she said. "Two points on the back of my neck, a little behind my ears, and then a place on the very center of my spine."

She could feel his left hand moving slowly down the knobs of her backbone, the thumb gliding first over one small lump, then the next. "There," she said, when he found the place. He pushed in a little as if to make sure. Her breath sounded almost like laughter. "Yes, that's it."

His right hand came up and hooked itself around the back of her neck. His hand seemed so big she thought he could encircle her throat with it; he had no trouble stretching it to reach the two pressure points she described.

"Yes—that's right—exactly," she said. She was on her knees, resting back on her heels; now she braced her hands on the tops of her thighs. "Apply as much pressure as you can in all three places, all at once," she said. "You'll be afraid that you might hurt me, but you won't. Unless I scream or something," she added with an attempt at humor. "But most people can't push hard enough to really make a difference."

"I probably can," he said, and she couldn't tell if he was smiling or not. "All right. Hold yourself steady."

And with no more warning than that, his fingers and thumbs gouged into the centers of pain along her body.

She had to choke back her first gasp of shock as his hands took hold. She had tried this trick once or twice before, with Kirra or other mystics whom she trusted, and she would get a moment or two of relief before the pain would come rushing back. She was not sure how it worked. It was as if her muscles or her veins or some grid of nerves paved pathways along her spine and up her neck, and troops of relentless torturers marched unimpeded along those roads. A block along any one of those routes could momentarily divert the armies, leave them milling about impotently for a minute or two, till the block was lifted or the soldiers found a way to surmount it.

Tayse's hands created dams and bulwarks; the armies of suffering came to a halt and bivouacked. Senneth took two deep breaths, savoring what was at least a temporary cessation of pain. The pressure of his hands was forcing her forward, bending her almost double. She resisted with most of her strength but still could not push herself upright against him. She could feel bruises forming where his fingers dug into her flesh.

She did not want him to lift his hands.

"Does this feel right?" Tayse asked.

"Yes," she said, gasping out the word. "It feels wonderful."

"I'm hurting you," he said. "You trade one ache for another."

"Different kind of hurt," she managed. "Better."

He said nothing more, just held his hands in place, fending off enemies. She did not know how long it would take before the armies grew sullen and wandered off, defeated. No one had ever been able to give her even this much relief in the past.

"I think—we should see—how effective that has been," she said at last, when her own body was starting to hurt from fighting the pressure of Tayse's, when she was sure his hands must be tight and sore. Slowly he eased away from her, as if lifting his hand from a wound that might start bleeding again. She heard him fold his arms across his chest.

She straightened up but did not make any other move, holding her head still, waiting for the misery to flood back. It did not. She felt odd, as if she had been dipped in fire and then battered with rocks—a few days ago—as if her body remembered such a recent pain that it did not want to move quickly to invite a new one in. And yet she did not actually hurt, not now. She just remembered hurting, and she was grateful that the pain was gone.

She turned slowly on her knees, pushing herself around with her hands in the dirt. "Thank you," she said, and even she could hear the wonder in her voice. "No one's ever managed that before."

"I have strong hands," he said. "Any time you need a task that calls for such a thing, I can help you."

"I can't tell you how good that is to know," she said.

He regarded her a moment, though her back was to the fire and her face must be in total darkness. His own showed no particular softness. "Get some sleep," he said. "You must be the most weary of all of us."

"Thank you," she said again and came somewhat creakily to her feet. Even that motion did not bring back the pain; her brain felt remarkably light. She summoned a burst of energy to check her net around the raelynx, but it was sleeping peacefully beside Donnal and showing no inclination at all to run. Picking her way carefully through the three bodies around the fire, she found her own bedroll and lay down in utter exhaustion.

CHAPTER

II

TAYSE was far in the lead the next morning when he glimpsed the riders coming toward them. In this part of the country, the road looped around curves and up and down small rises of land; he was able to make out a few individuals in the party before they vanished again. One or two wore maroon sashes across their chests or braided into their horses' bridles. They all looked well-dressed and well-fed.

He wheeled back to look for his own fellow travelers, half a mile behind him. It annoyed him that, even after weeks of riding with this group, he had the same reaction every time he rejoined them after some brief absence: *I thought there were more.* Ridiculous. There were only six of them—there had been only five until they rescued Cammon—they had always been a small party. And yet they were so varied, so strong-willed and individual, that it was like riding with twice that number, or triple.

But maybe this time he could be excused for his first quick thought. They might travel as a party of six, but there were only three of them on horseback as they headed toward him. Justin was somewhere to the rear; Donnal, he assumed, was still in raelynx shape, pacing a few feet off the road. Cammon led the extra horse.

"Riders coming toward us," Tayse said as he pulled up in front of them. "Maybe ten minutes away. Might be twenty of them."

"Soldiers?" Senneth asked.

He shook his head. "There are a few guards in the group, but it's not a fighting party. Maybe a lordling on a journey with some warriors alongside him." He glanced at Kirra, the one most familiar with aristocracy. "They're wearing the Rappengrass colors."

Kirra tilted her head to one side, and her hair rippled down her shoulder. He still wondered how she could keep herself so tidy on the road, her hair always clean and golden, her face always fresh. Magic, probably. Senneth did not seem to waste her energy on such inessentials.

"This might be good," Kirra said, "depending on who's in the party. We want to find how the political winds blow in Rappengrass, but I don't know that I want to ride up to the manor and ask Ariane to her face."

"How does she feel about mystics?" he asked.

Kirra smiled. "I'm not so sure these days. About anyone. But she has always been somewhat fond of me."

"So we encounter these travelers as a Danalustrous party," Senneth said.

Tayse nodded. "Then let's make ourselves look a little more respectable."

"Donnal!" Senneth called just as Justin came trotting up.

In a few moments, they presented a somewhat more impressive front, the serramarra Kirra Danalustrous proceeding majestically down the road, a female servant beside her, four armed guards before and behind. The whole lot of them were dressed in the Danalustrous red and gold.

Tayse spared a moment to wonder if Senneth had taken any extra precautions to contain the raelynx, who might be made even more restless when new riders approached.

In a few minutes, they swept around a curve of the road to spot the other group coming toward them at a leisurely pace. Tayse did a quick count—yes, about twenty men, a third of them soldiers of some sort, and one or two that appeared to be servants. The rest were gentry, or near-gentry—wealthy young men wearing expensive clothes and carrying fine weapons.

Tayse rather thought that the six soldiers and shape-shifters of his own party could take them all on—and win, if it came to that.

But relations did not look like they were going to be hostile. The lead rider of the oncoming party held up his hand and called for a halt, and two of the noblemen picked their way to the front of the group to investigate the travelers. Tayse and his band had already come to a stop and edged to the side of the road. As the smaller group, they would naturally give way so the others could ride on by.

But they did not want to ride on by.

"What's a Danalustrous sash doing so far south?" asked one of the noblemen in a pleasant voice. He looked to be in his late twenties, with fine chestnut hair and a smiling face.

"Taking in the sweet country air," Kirra replied, pushing her own horse forward, past Tayse and Justin.

The young man dropped his reins and broke into a wide smile. "Kirra Danalustrous! By the eye of the Pale Mother! What are you doing here so far from home?"

Kirra laughed and rode close enough to clasp his hand from the back of her horse. Tayse thought he saw the glitter of rubies buried in the tangles of her hair. "Mostly, shivering in an unexpected cold. Darryn, how good to see you! It has been ages since we last danced at a Merrenstow wedding."

A few of the other noblemen with him spurred closer then and said their hellos. She smiled kindly at all of them and spoke a few words, but Tayse was beginning to be able to hear the unspoken language of the aristocracy. These companions of the road were vassals' sons or distant relatives, and not worth Kirra's time. This Darryn was clearly Twelfth House, and therefore undoubtedly a son or brother of Ariane Rappengrass.

Worth getting to know.

"Have you had your noon meal yet? Let's stop and share lunch, shall we?" Darryn was saying eagerly. "We got an early start—I'm sure my whole group is famished. Will it delay you too much to take a break now?"

"No—I was thinking just the same thing," Kirra said. "Sindra, could you—yes, thank you very much."

In another few moments, they were off the road and had made a very sketchy camp, just enough to clear a place for the gentry to sit down while their servants put together a meal. Senneth, Tayse noticed, was very wary of the attractive Lord Darryn. She kept her face turned away from him, even though she had put it through its subtle alterations, and she did not speak loudly enough for him to hear her. He wondered at this, but only a little. It had always been clear that Senneth had a fair understanding of the aristocracy, whether she had spent her energy studying them or serving them, and he guessed that she had sold her skills to more noblemen than Malcolm Danalustrous. This young Rappengrass lord did not look particularly perceptive to Tayse, but he did not know how well Senneth might have known him—and Senneth was never one to take a stupid risk.

He thought of the raelynx, no doubt stalking the perimeter of the camp with frustration and longing. *Well, almost never,* he amended. Again, he hoped her control of the wild animal was as complete as she believed.

"But you still haven't answered, serra," Darryn said as Kirra and the noblemen ate their hastily prepared meal. "Why are you here at all? I can't think our weather is any better than it is up north, where I have had the misfortune to spend a winter or two."

Kirra glanced around, as if unsure of how much to say in front of his friends. "Oh—my father," she said, with a light laugh. "We argued, as we so often do, and I told him I would not spend another minute at his side to be insulted, and off I went."

"Ah, then," Darryn said, a world of meaning in his voice. "You are here because of your father."

She smiled at him as if pleased by his cleverness. "Yes. But I must say, I was not prepared for such an—inhospitable—welcome as I have received."

"Is it the weather or the people who have been unkind?"

She glanced around again, seemed uncertain, seemed to make up her mind to speak. "I have heard such strange tales since I have been south," she said at last. "Tales of people turning against the mystics, of the growing power wielded by the Daughters of the Pale Mother. We have our little quarrels up north, you understand, and there are plenty of people in Danalustrous and Tilt and Brassenthwaite who don't care for mystics—but I have not seen such animosity as this, anywhere else I have traveled."

Darryn sighed. "Yes, my mother is very concerned by this turn of events as well. Rappengrass has never had any cause to rue magic, and so we have never policed the mystics as they do in Nocklyn and Gisseltess. But now—there are strange stories coming from Helven and Fortunalt, and the word of the Daughters seems to be gaining more and more favor across the south. It makes my mother uneasy."

"Has she—prepared—in any way to meet trouble if it comes?"

Darryn gave her a swift, serious look. "Would your father prepare if he saw a danger building in his backyard?"

Kirra smiled. "He would."

"My mother and your father are not so unalike."

"Which has put them at each other's throats more than once," Kirra remarked. "But my father does respect Ariane."

"You might tell the marlord—when you mend your quarrel with your father and go back to Danalustrous—that this would not be a bad time to be tallying up allies," Darryn said.

"My father is always opposed to war," Kirra said. "As a matter of principle."

"That is a very fine principle as long as the people around you feel the same way," Darryn said with some grimness. "When you have Halchon Gisseltess as a near neighbor, you start thinking strategy."

"So how does Nocklyn bend in this affair?" she asked, toying with a piece of fruit. "Els Nocklyn was always a reasonably intelligent man."

"Els is sick, and his daughter has been running the estates," Darryn said. "I do not know her well, but her husband—"

"Is Halchon's cousin," Kirra finished. "I think that's our answer."

Darryn speared a piece of meat with his knife but did not lift it to his lips. "I am sure of no one at this point," he said frankly. "Your father's sense of honor is legendary—I cannot think he would ever embroil himself in any stupid uprising—so I tend to count him on the side of rationality whenever I think we might be headed to combat. And Kiernan Brassenthwaite—"

"Brassenthwaite will take the side of the crown," Kirra said. "Brassenthwaite always does."

"Yes, and Kiernan has additional incentive for hating Halchon Gisseltess," Darryn said. "There was that business with his sister fifteen years ago."

Kirra looked bewildered. "His sister?"

Darryn waved a hand. "You might have been too young to hear the story. There was a betrothal, and a scandal, and the betrothal was broken. And the girl died, you know. I am certain Kiernan blames Halchon for the whole mess. And even though it was fifteen years ago or more—well, Brassenthwaite counts time by centuries, not decades. It is not likely that Kiernan has forgotten."

"I've never really liked Kiernan or Nate," Kirra said with a little pout. Tayse thought she was trying to change the subject, put it back on a personal footing, perhaps. "They're so—hard. Unflinching."

Darryn smiled at her. He didn't mind getting personal. "Not like the friendly young heirs of the southern Houses."

She laughed. "Well, it's true I'd rather spend a day at Rappen Manor than Brassen Court."

"I like Kiernan. At any rate, I trust him," Darryn said. "I don't want him as an enemy. I don't want Halchon Gisseltess as an enemy, either, but I'm not sure I've got a choice in that. Your father, too, needs to look over the lists and see where he can trust and where he cannot."

"I will tell my father you said so," she said solemnly.

Darryn tossed back the contents of a goblet. Wine, Tayse thought. He seemed to visibly will himself into a change of mood. "And tell your father also how good I was to you when I came upon you on the road," he said, a teasing note in his voice. "Tell him I fed you, and entertained you, and offered you the protection of my sword if you agreed to travel forward with my party."

"You have offered no such thing!"

"I offer it now. I would be glad to have you travel with us."

Kirra seemed to consider it. "Where are you going?"

"To Helven, and then Coravann, and last to Ghosenhall. You would be near enough to Danalustrous, then, you could make your way home safely from there."

"I appreciate your kindness," she said. "I feel safe enough."

Darryn lifted his eyes and glanced at her small contingent of men. He looked straight at Tayse but saw only a body, not a person. Tayse spared a moment to realize that Kirra, Twelfth House though she was, never failed to mark the individual, even when she was doing such a quick assessment. "Four soldiers and a serving woman?" Darryn asked softly. "That would be enough on an ordinary day. But we are about to live in extraordinary times."

Kirra gave him her widest smile. "I have always had the power to protect myself well enough," she said. "I do appreciate your concern, though. It warms me quite through." And she put a hand to her heart with a melodramatic gesture and laughed at him.

He did not smile back. "It is that very power that puts you at risk in the southern regions," he said. "Take care, Kirra. Your father would not be the only one to mourn you if you were lost."

"Why, Darryn. I am truly touched."

The flirtation seemed to lighten the mood somewhat. "But I failed to ask," Darryn said. "How *is* your father, except disgruntled with you?"

"Well, as always. Stubborn, as always. Nothing seems to diminish Malcolm Danalustrous."

"And your sister?"

Kirra laughed. "You should swing by Danalustrous way after you visit Ghosenhall. Casserah is even more beautiful than she used to be."

"Why has your father not married her off by now?"

She laughed again. "Why has he not married *me* off? We are just as stubborn as he is. I think it is the thing he hates the most about each of us, and loves the most. But I could ask you the same thing, ser Darryn of Rappengrass. Why have you not been looking for a bride?"

He took her hand and kissed it. "Perhaps I have begun my search."

A few more idle moments like this, then both parties came to their feet and packed up to move on. Darryn renewed his offer to absorb Kirra's group into his own, but she smilingly refused again. With both hands, he helped her into the saddle, then swung up on his own horse.

"Travel safely," he said. "I think, if you get into trouble, you might apply to my mother for help."

"I will bear that in mind," Kirra replied. "I hope I encounter you again soon—in my travels."

"Count on it," he said and motioned his riders forward.

Their own smaller group pushed on in the opposite direction, east and a little south. They had ridden perhaps five minutes in silence when Senneth brought her horse alongside Kirra's. Tayse, riding just a few feet in the lead, could hear their entire conversation.

"I think somebody holds you in very high esteem," Senneth said.

Kirra's voice carried a smile. "Darryn Rappengrass flirts with all the women, even the old and ugly ones. He's charming but inconstant."

"Better hope he is not as inconstant as all that," Senneth said with a certain sharpness. "Rappengrass seems to be the only truly loyal House we've come across so far."

Kirra sighed. "And we cannot be sure he speaks for Ariane. He is the youngest of five, and her clear favorite, but he has not been named her heir."

"We should press on to Rappen Manor, then, and ask her directly where her sympathies lie."

"Yes," said Kirra, "I'm afraid we must."

A short silence followed this exchange. Tayse was about to spur his horse forward so he could watch the road ahead, when Kirra began speaking again.

"Did you hear what he said? About Halchon Gisseltess and the Brassenthwaite girl? What did you make of that?"

"There is bad blood between Gisseltess and half the Twelve Houses," Senneth said.

"Yes, but I never heard this story before, did you?" Kirra persisted.

"I must admit, I am not entirely up to date on all the gossip pertaining to the aristocracy," Senneth said in a dry voice.

"But there was an engagement between Gisseltess and Brassenthwaite? And the girl *died*? Surely you might know something about a tale like that."

"I'm not certain Darryn Rappengrass had the story entirely right," Senneth said. "I never heard about any Brassenthwaite girl who died."

"You don't want to tell me the story," Kirra said.

There was a short pause. Tayse thought he could feel Senneth's gaze lingering on his back a moment, as if she knew that he was listening to every word.

"I don't think anyone knows the whole tale," Senneth said at last. "Ask your father, when you return home. He might remember it all."

"He's married now, though," Kirra said. "Halchon is. But I can't remember his wife's lineage."

"From a minor house of Gisseltess," Senneth said.

"One of his own vassals," Kirra said in a brooding voice. "So there are not likely to be any irate in-laws if he starts making a feint for power."

"Surely a better match for Halchon than Brassenthwaite, wouldn't you say?" Senneth said. "If he was looking for complacency in his family connections."

Tayse heard Kirra sigh. "Yet we might be fabricating this all out of whispers and wind puffs. What we know is that Halchon

Gisseltess is hunting mystics on the advice of his sister, who's styled herself some kind of leader of the Daughters of the Pale Mother. That adds up to discontent but not necessarily to war."

"But we are not the only ones who are alarmed," Senneth said in a gentle voice. "And we are here, after all, to learn more about rebellion. I do not think we are so far off the mark."

"On to Rappen Manor, then," Kirra said.

NOT two hours after they'd met with Darryn Rappengrass, the skies began to fill with snow. Tayse, by now some hundred yards in the lead, slowed down when the first flakes began to fall. He sat in the saddle a few moments, gazing up, trying to determine how long the snow might last and how heavy the accumulation might be. The skies looked to be an unending white, mountains of clouds shaking bounty from their cold shoulders. He pulled on the reins and turned his horse back to rejoin the others.

Kirra had her hands outstretched to catch crystals on her gloves. "Look at this," she said happily, peering upward till flakes tangled in her lashes. "I missed the year's first snowfall at Danalustrous. Nothing is ever so beautiful."

"Beautiful and deadly," Tayse agreed. "Let's wait here till Justin catches up. I don't want us separated."

Senneth gave him an inquiring look. "The road's not even covered yet," she said.

Tayse shrugged. "Snow's one of those things I don't take chances with. It could be nothing—it could change the whole face of the world. We'll stay together."

Justin jogged up at that moment, not surprised to see them halted on the road. "I've been trying to remember," Justin said. "I don't think there are many towns directly ahead of us. No place to shelter for the night."

"It's just a little *snow*," Kirra exclaimed. "Where did you cowardly boys grow up?"

"I don't take chances with snow," Tayse repeated. "Pay attention, and if it gets worse, start looking for cover."

He glanced at Donnal, thinking that the northern man might greet his caution with the same kind of scorn Kirra was showing. But Donnal had his face tilted up, speculatively eyeing the heavens.

"I don't think it's going to stop," he said quietly. "And you can feel the wind blowing in from the west, colder. We have a hard road ahead of us."

"We'll go on for a while," Tayse said. "See how it goes."

They went forward as a party of six. Tayse still took point, and Justin still took the rear, since Justin was the only one Tayse could trust not to wander off, seduced by the beauties of nature. The snow came down more and more densely as they rode, till the air itself was thick with it, almost unbreathable. Faster than he would have believed possible, the road was obliterated. The horses were stepping with more and more caution first through one inch of snow, then two, then straining to lift their feet and set them down again in a world made of ice and white.

"This is turning into a blizzard," Tayse called back to the following riders and pulled his horse across the road to force them to stop. Through the curtain of falling white, he could still see Kirra's hair, glowing like a yellow flame at the heart of a winter campfire. Her face was hard to make out, but at least she was starting to look a little worried. "We don't want to get separated."

"Will we do better to get off the road now?" Senneth asked. "Just pull to the side and wait it out?"

"We might have to," he replied. "But I'd rather find shelter of some kind. Donnal was right. It's getting colder. If we don't find a place we can build a fire, we're going to pass a pretty chancy night."

"Surely there's a farmhouse or something along the road eventually," Kirra said in an encouraging voice. "Maybe a wayside tavern. This is a well-traveled road."

"Though you notice no one has passed us for a good hour," Justin pointed out. "Which means we're probably riding into the worst of it."

Tayse played out a length of rope, something he always kept coiled across his saddle. "Tie yourselves together one by one," he directed. "And if you somehow get lost or separated even so, call out for help."

In the few minutes it took them to loop the rope around their waists and resume their journey, the air had chilled considerably. Or else the very fact of stalling to confer on the road had brought home to them just how cold it really was. Tayse, in the lead, bent his face against the driving sleet of the storm. He felt his skin redden and then grow numb. His fingers were icy even in his gloves, and he had long ago lost much sensation in his toes. Senneth might have been right; it might be better to simply pull off the road, draw the horses in a circle, and huddle together for whatever warmth they could manufacture.

He heard a faint curse behind him and instantly wheeled around. "What? Who is it?" he demanded.

"Sorry. My hands—I lost the reins and my horse was pulling away," came Donnal's voice. He sounded faint with exhaustion. Tayse could barely see him, four riders back, a ghost in a ghostly world.

"Your hands are frozen?" Senneth asked sharply. "Here—give them to me."

Because of the rope binding them to a certain place in line, it took some maneuvering for Senneth to draw her horse alongside Donnal's. When she did, she pulled off her gloves and held out her hands to him.

"Don't be afraid," she said, a breath of humor in her voice. "Just take your gloves off and give me your hands."

He complied somewhat slowly—less from apprehension, Tayse thought, than because his fingers would not obey the dictates of his will. His hands looked cramped and white as he extended them toward Senneth. Her own fingers closed over his, and she held on for a long, quiet moment.

The strangest look crossed Donnal's face, one of bewilderment and wonder. He actually smiled so widely the expression could be seen through the broken screen of snow. "That's incredible," he said.

The others crowded a bit nearer. "What? What did she do?" Kirra demanded. "She warmed your hands up?"

"She warmed all of me up," he said, still smiling. "To my toes. I can't describe it."

Instantly, Kirra's own gloves were off. "Well, I could use a little body heat myself," she said. "If we aren't going to stop any time soon."

Smiling, Senneth took hold of Kirra's hands, and the transfer of power seemed to occur again. Kirra laughed. "You're amazing," she said. "Every time I think I know—you're just amazing."

"Do you have enough energy for me?" Cammon asked in a faint voice, and Senneth reached out for him.

"Always," she said. "I wish I'd thought to do this sooner."

Tayse's eyes sought out Justin, sitting stiff and proud in the saddle and trying very hard not to look envious. Tayse had no idea how much longer their ride in the elements would last. "Justin. You next," he ordered.

Justin looked mutinous. "I'm fine."

"My command," Tayse said gently, and Justin shrugged.

"Oh, very well," the younger Rider said, and stripped off his gloves with an ungracious snap. Tayse watched his face as Senneth closed her fingers over his, saw him try to hold back his astonishment and relief. Better than a good fire, it seemed, or a shot of new whiskey. Better than a night under clean blankets beside a warm body.

Senneth released Justin and turned toward Tayse. She was smiling. "And you, King's Rider?" she asked. "A mystic's touch to warm you on your winter ride?"

He bit back an answering smile. He had already pulled his gloves off. His hands were so cold he couldn't even tell the difference. "Whatever tool comes to hand on an afternoon such as this," he said and reached out to her.

Her fingers were warm as they closed over his, and that in itself was enough to make him feel grateful on this bitter day. But a strange thing happened as she clung to him, though her grip did not tighten and he felt no particular burning in her hands. The ice in his veins melted backward, down his wrist, past his elbow; heat flowed across his shoulders and through his spine. It was as if someone had taken a fresh coal and brushed it against his skin, up one arm and down the other, then paused to apply some warmth to his knees and ankles and toes. It was a gradual but generous heat, never fiery or uncomfortable, and he felt his mood and his body hearten as the cold was vanquished.

"Well," he said, sure that he looked as impressed and ridiculous as the others. "That *is* quite a welcome skill on a cold day."

"I think I'm strong enough to ride another four hours," Kirra said blithely.

Tayse glanced up at the sky, trying to judge the temper of the heavens, before it occurred to him to drop Senneth's hands. "I'm not sure we'll last another four hours," he said. "This may not stop till tomorrow morning."

"Can't she stop the snow?" Justin blurted out.

They all looked at him. "You mean, can *I* stop the snow?" Senneth repeated. "Why would you think that?"

Justin waved one of those recently warmed hands. "Start a fire. Shoot some heat up into the heavens. Heat up the whole world."

Senneth laughed soundlessly. "I don't think my power is strong enough to stretch to the clouds," she said. "I could melt the snow ahead of us on the road, but what a quagmire we would be riding through then! If we come to a halt for the night, I can try to keep us warm—but I can't stop the snow from falling. It might turn to rain above our heads, but I don't know that we'd be much better off."

Tayse nodded. "Not a good option," he said. "Let's ride on."

CHAPTER
12

THEY had been riding for about an hour before Senneth's little spate of magic began to wear off. Even then, Tayse thought, neither his hands nor his feet were quite as painfully cold as they had been before. But he was beginning to feel chilled throughout his body, down his back, through to his lungs—and he knew that if he, who could go on forever, was beginning to feel weary, the others must be close to dropping straight out of their saddles. They would have to stop then, in the middle of nothingness, and try to build a shelter of their own bodies. He hoped Senneth's power would be able to keep them all warm during a night that promised to be frigid as the Pale Mother's breath.

He had just lifted his hand to signal a halt when Cammon spoke up, his voice shaky and breathless. "What's that? To the left? Is that a building?"

Tayse strained his eyes but could make out nothing except the white haze of snow and the occasional desperate limb of a buried tree, waving as if to call for help. "I can't see anything," he said. The others murmured their agreement.

"There is," Cammon said stubbornly. "It's a building. I can tell it's there."

Senneth had turned to look at him. "Are there people in it?" she asked gently. "I didn't think you could sense *things*."

He shook his head. "I don't—no, I don't think so. Maybe there used to be people there." He glanced around the group, his eyes lingering on Tayse's frown. "You don't believe me."

Tayse transferred his gaze to Senneth, willing her to make the call. This was her recruit; she must judge how far to trust him. She met his eyes thoughtfully for a moment, then nodded.

"Let's see," she said. "Can you lead us there?"

Not really, no, because of the rope, but his soft, uncertain voice gave Tayse directions. Straight left—no, a little to the right of that—yes, past these two trees—even farther—right over that hill—

And there, the Mother be damned, stood a small, dilapidated building of stone and wood. The door was rotted half through, but the walls and roof were mostly intact, and the windows had been boarded up long ago. They spurred their horses forward, calling out phrases of encouragement to each other, words of praise to Cammon. It was still something of a fight to get the horses through the last few snowdrifts to the broken door, but here they were, shelter at hand at last.

Tayse pulled up hard on the reins and unknotted the rope around his waist. "Justin," he said, but Justin had already freed himself and was on the ground, dagger out, hand on the door.

"What do you—" Kirra started, but Tayse interrupted.

"No telling who or what might be in there," he said. "The two of us are going in first. Don't follow until I call you."

She rolled her eyes but settled back in her saddle. The others did not seem disposed to protest. He pulled his own weapon, then nodded at Justin, and the two of them burst simultaneously through the door.

They were instantly in a single dim room, maybe twenty feet by thirty, that smelled of disuse and dust and cold snow. It was hard to see anything in the overcast light through shuttered windows, but there seemed to be nothing in here but afternoon shadows and a few odd pieces of furniture. Nonetheless, Tayse jerked his head at Justin. He went one direction, the younger Rider went the other, feeling their way around the circumference of the room. The wall felt like broken plaster beneath his gloved fingers. The floor had once been very fine, planed wood with perfectly mortised joints. Here there was an overturned chair, ornately carved and large enough to serve as a throne. Against this wall, a cabinet with one door hanging open. Tayse glanced inside just to make sure nothing dangerous lurked behind the door. He thought he heard a mouse squealing, but nothing more menacing appeared.

"Empty," Justin said, meeting him in the middle of the room along the far wall. "What a stroke of luck to find this place."

Tayse grunted. "Luck or magic," he said. "We seem to be having the good kind and the bad kind of both."

He called to the others, and they tumbled in, bringing snow and shadows with them. Within minutes, someone had lighted torches, and they could see what they were doing as they tried to assess their find. Justin took charge of the horses and herded them all toward the back of the room, where they might or might not stay bunched up for the evening. Cammon and Kirra and Donnal strolled around the perimeter of the room, looking at hieroglyphics on the walls that were revealed by the influx of firelight.

Senneth stood by the door, waiting, until the raelynx sauntered in.

Tayse watched for a moment, his breath caught; he had actually, during the battle with the snow, forgotten about the raelynx for the afternoon. The creature looked like wildness personified, like death and beauty and remorselessness in one lithe package. It sank to its haunches just inside the door and regarded the lot of them with a close and personal attention.

Tayse made his way cautiously to Senneth's side. "Is it safe to bring that animal in with us?" he asked in a low voice. Not low enough, apparently. The raelynx turned its dark eyes his way and considered him as if for his tastiness.

"Safe as it was having him slink beside us all morning," she said, almost smiling, "and sleep not far from us last night. He is no more dangerous now than then."

"Not entirely comforting," he said. "But I trust you to know the limits of your magic."

"Thank you," she said. "I'm glad there is something about me you trust."

He tilted his head back. She was a tall woman, and it pleased him that he could still look down at her from a somewhat more lofty height. "And your headache?" he asked.

"Completely gone, thank you," she said. "I am feeling quite good, actually."

Justin crossed the room to join them, giving the raelynx one quick, disapproving glance. "I don't know if I can find any dry wood," he said. "But we're going to have to try a fire."

Senneth turned her smile on him. "Justin," she said in a mocking voice, "haven't you paid attention to *anything* that's happened since we've been on the road together?"

And, while Tayse watched her and Justin frowned at her, she stepped to the middle of the room and seemed to stop and consider. She didn't raise her hands in any kind of dramatic gesture, or move her lips to speak an incantation, and the expression on her face was simply thoughtful. If this was magic, it came without visible effort. But rapidly and thoroughly, the room temperature began to rise. In a few moments, they did not merely cease to be cold; they started to feel truly, blissfully warm.

Tayse reached up to unbutton his coat. "Well," he said to Justin, "I guess we don't need a fire."

"What if we want to cook a meal or boil a pot of water?" Justin grumbled. Tayse flicked him a look that said, clear as words, *Don't be ungrateful.*

Senneth, apparently, had overheard Justin. "Fire you shall have, then, since you are set on fire." She glanced around, picked her spot, and knelt on the dusty wood floor. More as a visual marker than as a source of fuel, Tayse thought, she swept a few twigs and dried leaves into a small pile and touched them with her finger. Instantly, a bright gold flame sprang to life and danced through the gathered debris. "Cook over it, warm your fingers, merely watch it burn," she said, coming to her feet. "It will last all night."

Justin merely scowled, since it wasn't in him to be gracious. Tayse was grinning, but before he had a chance to say anything, Kirra called out.

"Sen. Come look at this." She and the others were still standing against one of the side walls, examining marks left in the plaster.

"What is it?" Senneth asked.

"I don't have any idea."

Tayse joined Senneth as she crossed the room, and together the five of them inspected what was left of the pictures on the wall. The circles and lines meant nothing to Tayse, and he could not make out any kind of pattern in the colors, faint but still discernible in the crumbling plaster. But he could tell they meant something to Senneth. She put her fingers out almost reverently to trace a circular design that rose over a low horizon of darker figures.

"Ah," she said, and then stepped back and glanced around at the rest of the small hall, as if looking for confirmation.

"What?" Kirra demanded. "What is it?"

Senneth was nodding, and she looked strangely pleased. "I think what we've stumbled on is an old, old temple dedicated to the Bright Mother," she said.

"The Bright Mother?" Cammon repeated.

"The sun goddess," Senneth explained. "No one talks about her—or the other gods—very much these days, but a long time ago, she was worshiped much more fervently than the Pale Mother is today. Well, perhaps that's not entirely true. In Brassenthwaite and Tilt and Kianlever, you can still find some of the Bright Mother's shrines. I'm not sure if the religion ever caught on this far south." She touched the wall again, still looking happy. "Though apparently there were a few believers, even in the southern Houses."

"There's a temple not far from my father's house," Kirra said. "I've been there a few times because—" She made a face. "Because my father, of course, believes everyone should have *every* experience available to him. But it's in much better shape than this."

"Yes—well, as I said, the religion fell out of a favor a long time ago," Senneth said. "Now, those who worship at all worship the Pale Mother, the moon goddess. They've forgotten all the other gods entirely."

"You haven't," Justin said. He had drifted over casually, as if pretending he wasn't really interested. "You swear by the Bright Mother all the time."

She gave him a quick smile. "I do. My grandmother was from Kianlever. She loved the sun goddess and taught me to honor her." She tugged her circular gold pendant out from under the collar of her shirt. "See that? The filigree all around the disk? It's a sun charm. The Bright Mother protects me wherever I go."

"Well, she's certainly found a way to protect us all tonight," Tayse said practically. He didn't have much more patience with gods than he did with mystics. "We need to eat before we all drop from exhaustion."

They melted snow over Senneth's bewitched fire and made hot tea, which they sipped while they cooked their dinner. Something about the difficult travel or the unexpected refuge or the very presence of the snow itself had given them all a strange shift of mood; the entire meal had a festival air. The women laughed—Kirra flirted—taciturn Donnal made jokes—even Justin was smiling. Tayse himself felt curiously relaxed and amused, ever so slightly intoxicated with the sense of camaraderie. So he had felt sometimes after a hard campaign with trusted Riders. But only one of his companions tonight was a Rider, and the rest he did not trust.

He stayed mostly silent as, one by one, the others began telling stories around the fey and joyous fire.

"My dad was a wanderer," Donnal said. Tayse had missed the question, but he assumed someone had asked one. "He didn't own a thing in the world except two shirts and two pairs of trousers. He spent one summer working for my uncle—tenant farmer on the Danalustrous lands, a man who was never going to own more than a few changes of clothing himself. When he left, my mother was pregnant. I was her third child. None of the men in her life stayed longer than a few months."

He paused to sip at his tea. Donnal didn't talk much, but it was clear, when he felt like it, he could transform himself into a story-teller.

"I can't remember a time when I couldn't change shapes," Donnal continued. "I must have done it in the cradle—imagine that, the first time you've come in to check on the sleeping baby, and you find a cat or a rabbit or a bird in the crib. By the time I was old enough to know what a strange skill it was, the rest of my family had grown quite comfortable with my ability. My uncle even used to send me out sometimes as a mole to check the water levels under the soil—or as a hawk to see if it was safe to go poaching off Danalustrous land."

He smiled at Kirra, who shook her head and smiled back. "But I didn't think about it much," he said. "What it meant or what I might do with such a skill. It just was. It was part of my life. Till the day the young woman came riding up to my uncle's house and demanded I be sent outside so she could see me.

"Well, that caused quite a commotion, as you might imagine. My mother and I were inside, peering out the dirty windows, wondering if I was about to be taken into custody or burned for a mystic. Not that such things happened on Danalustrous land, mind you, but my father wasn't the only traveler who had happened upon my uncle's farm. We knew stories of the way the rest of the world was run. It was not always an acceptable thing to have magical powers.

"My uncle stood out front, arguing with the woman—who was

clearly an aristocrat, with her fine clothes and her haughty way of speaking. My mother and brothers and cousins and I cowered inside, trying to decide if I should change to a mouse right then and disappear out the back and never return to my uncle's farm. But we finally decided that such a cowardly action might bring even more harm to my family, if harm was to come. So I stood up bravely and tugged my shirt down and went out the front door to stand at my uncle's side."

Donnal paused to take another swallow. Tayse was irritated to find himself interested in the story, all because of the man's easy voice and calculated pauses. "I was surprised to find, when I was actually face-to-face with our noble caller, that she was only a year or two older than I was—but still just as haughty as she'd seemed from inside. 'I'm the one who can change himself to animals,' I said to her. 'Take me, then, and let my family be.'

"Well, she slid off her horse and put her hands on her hips, and she said, 'How do I know you're telling me the truth? Change yourself into something. Let's see you turn yourself into a dog.' I had been pretty afraid when she first rode up, but that made me mad, so to scare her I turned into a wolf. Big one, too, with a black face and evil eyes. She jumped back, and the guards with her raised their crossbows. I probably came as close to being killed at that moment as I ever have in my life. Well, until I joined this lot," he added, and a soft laugh went around the circle of listeners.

"But nobody shot me, and the lady came a step nearer—and then, to my utter astonishment, she melted. She just—there was no other word. She melted into a wolf shape herself. I had been a shiftling all my life, you understand, but I had never seen anyone *else* transform, and it was almost enough to send me howling across the valley. But I was too afraid to move, and when she shifted back to human state, I shifted right along beside her. And then I just stared at her.

"She looked entirely pleased with herself. 'Very well, you can come study with me,' she said. 'My father has already engaged a tutor to hone my abilities, but he thought it would be helpful if there were other students who might challenge me to try harder. So far, we haven't been able to locate anyone else with any magical ability, but then I heard some villagers talking about you.' We lived about ten miles from a small market town, and, as you might guess, everyone within fifty miles of us had heard my story by this time. I just hadn't thought they'd be repeating it to noble folk.

"She turned around and got on her horse. And then she turned to look at me like I was the stupidest man in Danalustrous. She said, 'Well? I told you you had to come with us.' And I got all mad again, and I said, 'Lady, I wouldn't come with you to study magic if you were the daughter of the village mayor himself.' And she said, 'I'm the daughter of Malcolm Danalustrous, and I think you'll do whatever I say.' And from that day on," Donnal added in a rueful voice, as the others began to laugh, "that's pretty much been the way of it. She gives the orders, and I do what she says."

"And did you really study magic with her?" Cammon asked.

"Off and on, for the next ten years," Donnal said. "It wasn't very formal, you understand. Just if some mystic or another happened to be traveling through, and Lord Malcolm heard of it, he would accost the poor soul and promise him all sorts of rewards if he'd come teach his wayward daughter and her scruffy friend. Or, who knows, maybe he promised all sorts of dire punishments if the fellow refused."

Cammon glanced at Senneth. "Were you one of their tutors?"

She nodded, her white-blond hair vivid in the soft firelight. "One of the early ones. I don't know that they learned much from me, since I don't have the temperament for teaching. And I was there selling other skills at the time."

Justin looked up at that. "Oh? What would those be?"

She grinned. "That's when I thought I could make my way as a freelance blade. I was hired as part of the lord's civil guard. I wasn't bad at it—and I must say, I learned a lot under his watch commander—but I eventually realized the life was too confining. I was not much better at following orders than I was at teaching students."

"Now, I find myself surprised," Justin said with heavy irony. Senneth merely laughed.

Cammon had turned his attention to Kirra. "What about you?" he said. "What did your father do when he discovered you were mystic?"

Kirra grimaced. "Well, first you have to understand my father. He is—he believes he is—the shepherd of Danalustrous, the living representative of all the generations of Danalustrous heirs who have gone before. That all the weight of all those centuries of Danalustrous pride sits squarely on his shoulders—and that Danalustrous itself is the most powerful, important, and precious place in this world. To somehow belong to Danalustrous is to be made holy almost—to earn the right to be protected to the death. I was mystic, but I was Danalustrous. Therefore, I was to be cherished—no matter how strange or dangerous I might turn out to be."

She brooded a moment. "My father has had three wives," she went on. "The first two were far from happy. He is a powerful, determined, and difficult man. His first wife died after ten years of marriage, and everyone said it was because she could not think what else to do to get his attention. Even that didn't do it—he remarried again within six months. His first wife had come from Tilt, an eldest daughter of a respected House. He decided his second wife should be someone with lower expectations, so he chose a woman who—while perfectly respectable—"

"Thirteenth House," Cammon said. He liked to use the phrase, Tayse had noticed; it seemed to tickle him.

Kirra smiled. "Exactly. She came from a lesser estate on the Danalustrous property, and she had not been trained in all the proprieties a true noblewoman would have understood by instinct. In fact, she was dead wild, according to everyone who knew her. Never quite appreciated the honor my father had done her. Never seemed to really enjoy the gorgeous house, the rich property, the handsome husband. I think she got bored. Two years after I was born, she left."

There was a slight pause. "Left?" Cammon said. "And didn't come back?"

"And didn't come back," Kirra repeated. "I have no idea if she's even still alive."

Senneth looked at her. "I didn't know that part," she said. "Your father always spoke of her as if she was dead."

Kirra laughed. "Well, he had her declared so, in order to marry a third time. Fortunately, his third wife turned out to be exactly what he needed—clever, self-sufficient, accomplished, and devoted to Danalustrous. She's my sister Casserah's mother, and she's been a very good stepmother to me." Kirra smiled. "She was not thrilled when I turned out to have mystical powers, you understand, but she didn't faint or shriek or demand that my father throw me out of the house. She did watch Casserah with some apprehension for a few years, because she was afraid that the taint may have come from my father, but Casserah has always been quite determinedly normal."

"How did they first show up?" Cammon asked. "Your mystical abilities."

"I was about ten. My stepmother was trying to teach me how to curtsey. She would say, 'Pretend you are curtseying to the queen,' and so I would imagine what the queen looked like—and then I would turn into the queen, or a ten-year-old's perception of the queen. You can imagine how disconcerting it was for her the first time it happened. But as I say, she handled it all quite coolly. And my father—well, it never occurred to him to turn against me. Which is why he sought tutors to train me. And he insisted I take my place as a rightful daughter of the Twelve Houses. He forced the Tilts and the Storians and the Gisseltesses and everyone else to accept me for what I was. I never suffered a single social stigma because of my magic. And, you know, there are many other children of the aristocracy who cannot say the same."

"Yes, we have all heard some of those stories," Senneth said somewhat curtly, though Tayse had not, and he wondered if the others in the room had. "How does your sister tolerate your magic? I have always found her a little hard to read."

Kirra laughed, seeming truly amused. "Casserah is—completely unaffected by anything that does not pertain absolutely, directly to her. As long as I don't turn her into a spider, or burn down the house while she's sleeping in it, Casserah doesn't really mind who or what I am. We are quite close, actually, though it is a hard relationship to explain."

"And I suppose your father and your stepmother and everyone eventually realized the tainted blood must have come from your mother, the restless one," Senneth said.

"Must it always come from somewhere?" Cammon asked. "Don't people ever just—develop magic on their own?"

Tayse looked up at that question. He couldn't say he'd ever given it much thought till recently, but in fact, that was something he would like to know as well. Where did the magic come from? Could anyone suddenly discover in himself a mystic trait, or was it a power that had to be handed down through the generations?

Senneth and Kirra were exchanging glances. "No one is quite sure," Senneth said, "but it seems to follow bloodlines. That is, Donnal's wandering father may not have been a mystic himself, but his father was, or *his* father. Many a scandal has unraveled in the aristocracy when a serramar of the house is suddenly discovered to have special skills. Generally, it turns out the mother confesses she has played the father false, because of course neither one of them could admit that magic ran in their veins from generations ago! But Kirra could sit here and name you a mystic born in one generation or another to every one of the Twelve Houses. I think the magic is inbred a lot more deeply than any of them like to believe."

"I think it was my father who was the mystic in my case," Cammon said. "Just because my mother always seemed so devoid of any—any power at all. Any strength. Surely she would have used it at some point if she'd had it." He smiled a little sadly. "Anyway, from what you say, it sounds like all mystics have a restless streak, and he certainly had that. And look at the four of us—we're all wandering. Maybe it's something in the blood."

"When did you first know you were mystic, Cammon?" Kirra asked.

He laughed. "When you pulled me out of Kardon's tavern! But I knew I was—strange—before. I could sense when something was not quite right—and I always knew when someone was lying to me. I think my father was also a sensitive. He would make these impossible deals with people—choose to trust the unlikeliest individuals you could imagine—but the crazier the scheme, the more likely it was to pay off. I think he would have been a wealthy man if he'd ever learned how to hold on to his money."

"How did he die?" Senneth said.

Cammon made a little grimace. By firelight, he looked almost ageless, Tayse thought. His face was round, sweet, unmarked by experience, but his flecked dark eyes were old and knowing. It was not hard to believe he possessed a special wisdom, that he could look into any soul and read its secrets. Tayse shifted on his blankets and cast his own eyes down.

"We were in Arberharst. We had spent almost all the money we had accumulated in order to buy passage from Sovenfeld. There was some man my father was to meet in Arberharst, someone who was going to set him up in"—Cammon shrugged—"some enterprise. I've always thought something must have gone wrong when they were making the deal. Maybe, this one time in his life, his ability to judge a man's character was wrong, and the person he was dealing with turned out to be a liar. Maybe there were others present that my father hadn't known about beforehand, and he said out loud that he didn't trust them. In any case, he didn't come home that night. His body was found the next morning, not

far from the harbor. They brought me over to identify him because
my mother was too hysterical to leave the inn. Three weeks later
we sold what we had to pay for our tickets back to Gillengaria."

Senneth was watching him. "That wasn't so long ago," she
said. "Your father died in Arberharst, and then your mother died
on the journey home, then you got sold into slavery, and now
you're wandering an unfamiliar world with people who are still
virtually strangers. Yet you seem content and not so full of woe as
I would be."

His smile was rather small and painful. "Perhaps I am just still
numb. I have come to believe there are no safe harbors. I am just
grateful when there is not a storm raging over my head at that very
moment."

Tayse glanced up at the roof, where patches of snowy starlight
filtered in through numerous holes. "There *is* a storm tonight, of a
sort," he said.

"It is not this kind of weather that bothers me," Cammon said.

Kirra reached out and gathered him to her in an easy hug.
"We'll be your family now," she said. "When this journey is over,
if we haven't found a place for you in Ghosenhall, I'll take you
back to Danalustrous, where you can be an advisor for my father.
He would like very much to have someone standing at his right
hand who could always tell him whether someone was lying or
telling the truth."

He gave her a tremulous smile. "Your father sounds a little
terrifying."

Senneth laughed. "Malcolm Danalustrous is more than a little
terrifying, but Kirra is right. That would be a very good place for
you, in the service of a great lord."

"Or the king," Justin said, as always jealous on behalf of royalty.

"Or the king," Senneth acknowledged.

Cammon looked alarmed. "I don't aspire so high!"

"If he had use for you," Justin said with great haughtiness,
"you would serve him and be glad of it."

Kirra looked over at the other Rider with a bright curiosity.
There were no end of tensions between the members of this little
group, but Tayse had always thought the animosity was greatest
between these two. Justin hated Kirra for embodying all the rank
and power of a privileged, pampered class—and Kirra scarcely
could bring herself to remember that Justin was even alive.

But she seemed to see him, at least briefly, this night. "So what's your story, Justin?" she asked. "How did you come to be part of the king's elite?"

Justin glanced quickly at Tayse, who nodded. Then he shrugged and began telling, with elaborate unconcern, the story he simply never told. Most of it, even so, he edited out. "I grew up in Ghosenhall, five miles from the palace. In the thieves' district. My mother had four children, none of whom had a father they could name. We lived in a place so filthy I cannot describe it to you." He nodded across the fire at the dark-haired man next to Kirra. "Donnal maybe might know what it's like to grow up in poverty, with absolutely nothing, but none of the rest of you would understand, no matter how long I made my story.

"My three sisters were gone before I was ten. I don't know where they went or if they still live. My mother died of a disease that started between her legs and rotted her body inch by inch. I was already spending much of my time on the streets, roving the roads and alleys with other boys just like me." He smiled, an evil smile at an evil memory. "There is a reason the very wealthy do not walk certain streets of the royal city unescorted. Boys like us would accost them in deep night or full daylight, and steal their purses and offer to take their lives. Some of us died in skirmishes with civil guards and paid escorts. Others died of starvation and sickness. The rest of us—we became very, very dangerous. I could disarm a man in twenty seconds if he chose to fight me. I could defeat three men at once. After I turned twelve, I never went a day without enough money to buy myself food and, sometimes, lodging. None of my friends went hungry."

There was a short silence. "Did you ever kill anyone?" Cammon asked.

Justin gave him one brooding look. "I don't know. Every man I fought was still alive when I left him in the streets. I don't know how well they all recovered from their wounds."

"I can hardly wait to hear the transition," Kirra said.

But Senneth was looking from Justin to Tayse; she had figured it out long ago, Tayse realized. She said nothing, though, and Justin resumed his story. "One day as I set out to rob a man of his wallet, we dueled in the street. He was better than I was—so much better that I was astonished, because no one had ever been able to stand against me longer than a minute or two. But he used a dagger like mine, and he sparred with me, and he didn't tire and he didn't give way, and I never got his purse. In fact, I was the one who slipped and fell to the cobblestones, and I lay there expecting the knife to come and end my life. But the knife didn't fall. The man knelt beside me in the street and said, 'I could use a man with skill like yours. Come with me to the palace.' "

"To the *palace*?" Kirra repeated.

Justin nodded. "It was Tayse. He brought me to the king's palace and had me train with the civil guard. It was another five years before I was found good enough to be a King's Rider. I've been a Rider now for seven years."

"I thought the Riders were the best and most faithful of the king's soldiers," Cammon said.

Tayse said, "They are."

"And so King Baryn overlooked your rough past and named you one of his own," Kirra said. "That is rather a remarkable story. And yet I believe you. The best hound my father ever owned was a stray who arrived at our estate bloody and abused, so broken that the head groom wanted to cut its throat to put it out of its misery. But something in my father made him want to keep that dog. He fed it with his own hands, and changed its bandages, and let it sleep in his own room when it was strong enough. To this day, that hound is abjectly devoted to my father. Follows him everywhere— would protect my father with his life, I truly believe. And yet it was nothing to look at when it first arrived."

Justin looked both amused and furious. "Just so," he said. "Take away the insult, and the stories are exactly the same."

Kirra seemed surprised. "I intended no insult."

Senneth was laughing. "The nobility value their dogs almost above their heirs," she said. "A compliment of the highest order."

"At any rate," Tayse said, "the king chose wisely when he admitted Justin into the ranks of the Riders."

Now Kirra's curiosity was piqued. She gave Tayse a considering look. "And you? How did you earn your grand place?"

Tayse smiled. "Oh, my story is quickly told. My father is a Rider—my grandfather was a Rider—I was born to it. It would have broken my heart to have been judged unworthy, so everything I did—from the day I was old enough to hold my first practice sword—I did in order to win my place. There was nothing else I wanted to be, nothing else I could have done. I am what I was fated to become."

Senneth was watching him, her eyes flickering to darkness and back to gray as the yellow flames postured before her. "It would have been interesting to see," she said, "what would have become of you if you could not have attained the dream. If you were turned away from your purpose and set loose on the world to forge some other way."

"As you did?" Tayse replied politely.

He had thought to discomfort her, but she merely smiled. "That is, to some extent, my story."

"Tell us that story, then," he invited. "All the rest of us have opened up our hearts."

"Some of you have," she said. "Some of you have merely recited a tale."

Now Tayse grinned, for that was surely aimed at him. "Then recite a tale for us," he said. "Tell us the story of your life."

CHAPTER
13

SENNETH seemed to deliberate a moment before she started speaking. Tayse found himself wondering how much of the truth they would learn at last, how much Senneth would still conceal. "My father never had high hopes of me, because he had no interest in daughters," she said at last. "He was far more attached to my brothers, who were numerous. He was not particularly attentive to my mother, either, though she tried very hard to be a good wife and to please him. She only failed twice, that I ever saw. Once, when she produced me. Once, when it turned out I was a mystic."

Another pause. "I try not to relive those days too often," she said, her voice very dry. "To remember my father's rage when it became apparent that I had strange abilities. In truth, I had had them since I was quite young, but my father had managed to spend very little time around me, and so he did not see my accidents with fire, the way I could make a candle gutter and go out, the way my touch could sometimes burn my mother or my nurse. I had mostly learned to control these aberrations—or so I thought—but when I was seventeen, they suddenly gathered even more force and potency. They grew past the point that I knew how to direct them."

Kirra was nodding. "That happens sometimes. It is usually between the ages of twelve and eighteen that a mystic's power grows strongest. They say that if you have exhibited no signs of power by the time you're eighteen, you never will."

"Safe, then!" Justin breathed, and they all laughed.

Senneth smiled, but she did not laugh. "So. My father learned my terrible secret, and he turned me out of the house. He would have sent me on my way without food or money, but my two youngest brothers ran after me, sobbing, pressing on me what few coins and trinkets they had. My older brothers merely watched from the windows as I was cast out into the night. My mother lay sobbing in her room. My grandmother—" Senneth smiled again. "My mother's mother turned to my father—stood beside him on the walkway that led from the front door—and cursed him to his face. Told him that he would die within three years from his own internal fires—his blood would boil, his liver would cook, his heart would burst into flames. All sorts of terrible things. Then she came running after me and gave me this pendant." Senneth tugged out the gold charm she always wore, then tucked it back into her shirt. "And away I went."

"And did he?" Cammon asked in fascination. "Die? Your father?"

Senneth nodded. "Almost exactly three years later. Yes, he did. I can't say whether his heart caught fire or any of those other dreadful things occurred, but he did die from some internal cause. He didn't get thrown by a horse or die in a brawl. His body betrayed him."

"And what happened to you? Did you ever go back home?" Cammon said.

She shook her head. "No. I haven't been back since. I took off and began my wandering." She smiled a little. "I tried my hand at almost every trade I could find, if the work seemed honest and the guild master was willing to hire a woman. I was strong, you know—I've always been. I liked working at the smith's, because I'd always been drawn to fire, and I was never afraid of the hot metal or the leaping flames. The smith and I got along famously, too, so I stayed there a year or more. But he died, and his son didn't like me—and I was restless anyway—so I moved on."

She shrugged. "I tried soldiering—took a few jobs before I signed on with Malcolm Danalustrous. I tried farming, but I found it too dull. I hired on for a while with a merchant ship, and

I liked that job just fine. The captain was a woman, and half her crew were women, and there wasn't a soft one in the bunch. But I didn't like being so far from home. I found that the farther I got from Gillengaria, the weaker I became."

"What do you mean, weaker?" Justin asked.

Senneth glanced at Cammon. "I have a theory that those of us who are born mystics really only have any true magic while we're standing in Gillengaria. That we are somehow bound to its soil. So that you, Cammon, really only had a whisper of power when you lived in places like Sovenfeld. At any rate, my magic faded while I was away from this land. My body was still strong, but my—my power was almost gone. I couldn't control fire. I couldn't summon my own heat. If I'd been trying to run away from my abilities, then I'd have stayed forever on board ship, or disembarked at Arberharst and lived there the rest of my days. But I missed that peculiar strength. I missed—being out of the ordinary. So eventually I wandered back.

"Since then it's been mostly wandering," she continued. "Though I lived for a year or two in the Lirrens, as I've mentioned, and for a while I thought I might be settled there. That whole place is strange—all those people are strange—I was not like them, and I didn't understand them, but I could live among them and feel at ease."

She smiled over at Justin. "You might fit in well with the people there. They're very fierce. They have this complex network of kin and friendship that binds them in some way to almost every family in the entire region. But they hate outsiders. They are absolutely ruthless to anyone who tries to enter their society and does not belong. Like your Rider friends."

"Why did they accept you, then?" Justin demanded.

"I did a favor for one man in one family, and he in a sense adopted me. And when I was part of his family, I was part of all families. I could go there tomorrow, and whisper a few names, and be welcomed at any household I tried. But if you did such a thing—" She lifted her hands in a half circle, a mild gesture of chaos. "You would probably be destroyed by nightfall."

She leaned forward a little, and Tayse watched how the bright fire illuminated her whole face. "This is the worst of it, if you are a Gillengaria man and you fall in love with a Lirren girl. If she agrees to marry you—which she never will—you have to prove

you are worthy of her by battling one of the men of her family—
to the death. That's right, you have to *kill* her father or her brother
or her uncle or her cousin, or you will not be given the right to
marry her. Well, as you might imagine, very few Lirren girls want
to see their family members murdered—and of course, if they
truly love some man, they don't want to see *him* die, either. So you
almost never hear of any Lirren girl running off with a man her
family has not approved. There are a few ballads—songs the
women sing when the men aren't around—and they are quite
heartbreaking to hear. Of a love so great it had to be put aside."

"I think, if I had been born a Lirren girl, I would have run off
to Gillengaria before I turned sixteen," Kirra remarked.

Senneth smiled. "Maybe. But it is quite an amazing thing to be
surrounded by a family that loves you so much it will not let you
go. I did not truly belong there, and yet there were times I would
have gladly stayed forever, just to have that sense of being enveloped and beloved. Something I lost quite early—or maybe
never really had."

"You mentioned something about them the other day," Cammon said. "You said they worshiped a different god—not the Pale
Mother everyone here talks about, and not the sun goddess, either?"

Senneth nodded. "Oh yes. In the Lirrens they're all devoted to
the Dark Watcher—the Black Mother. The goddess of night," she
explained, apparently reading the bafflement on their faces.

"I've never heard of such a goddess," Tayse said.

"No? Well, my grandmother said you used to be able to find a
shrine or two dedicated to her in any of the regions of Gillengaria," Senneth said. "Just as you could find temples to the Green
Keeper and the Wind Maker and the others. I don't think her influence was ever really very strong outside of the Lirrenlands. But
there she is quite revered. They all wear black opals on chains
around their necks, and they pray to her daily, and they believe
that many things that happen at night are sanctified because they
occur under her watchful eyes. There are a few of them who claim
to have a direct connection with her—to have spoken with her, or
to be descended from men and women who have spoken to her—
and those people are treated with great honor and considered
almost holy. And I confess, the one or two I met had really quite
marvelous abilities."

"Such as?" Kirra asked.

Senneth looked her way. "You're an excellent healer, but these women—I saw them take men back from the brink of death. More than once. And they can—hide things. Houses, people. Once I knew a woman traveling with a party of ten. They were eager not to be spotted by some others who were looking for them—a feud between families, if I remember. We had camped on the road for the night, but we heard the sounds of horses approaching in the dark. And this woman simply cloaked us in darkness. No one could see us—the dogs couldn't smell us. It was as if we were lost in the profoundest midnight imaginable. I have never felt so safe. And then there is the matter of the raelynxes—the power some of these people can exert over creatures of the night. Casually, without putting any effort into it, as we would call a dog or knock aside a moth."

"It almost sounds like magic," Kirra said. "All those things you describe."

Senneth nodded. "Yes, that's what I was telling Cammon the other day. I would like to take him to the Lirrens sometime and see if he could read the people for me, and tell me the whole lot of them are mystics."

She fell silent, but no one else spoke; it was clear she was still thinking about some part of her tale and debating whether or not to go on with it. Her eyes were fixed on the fire. Tayse wondered if she was watching some picture in those flames that no one else could see.

"In fact," she said slowly, "in fact, I sometimes wonder . . ." She glanced up at the crumbling walls around them and then back at the fire. "If the Lirrens get their power from the Dark Watcher, and they are mystics, might not all of us derive our power from some god or another? It takes no great stretch of imagination to look at me and say, 'You are a child of the Bright Mother, a descendant of the sun goddess herself. You can control flame because the Bright Mother herself is built from fire. You can will a room to fill with heat, you can create warmth from the cold bones of your own body, because you draw from that primordial source. Anything to do with flame or destruction or even creation, when it comes from the life-giving warmth of the sun, you can shape or summon with your hands.'" She looked up briefly, sending her glance around the faces in the circle, and looked back at her small fire. "I more than half believe it," she said.

Tayse stared at the fire and wanted to be shocked and wanted to be disdainful, but he found himself both unsurprised and free of scorn. It made as good an explanation as any, and he was a man who needed explanations before anything ever seemed possible to him. She was descended from a goddess; well, why not? It was true she was not an ordinary woman.

He had never had much truck with deities. Ghosenhall had been an agnostic city since Tayse was born into it, and a king's man placed the royal family above all other commitments. There might be gods, and other folk might worship them, but they did not matter much to Tayse or his fellow Riders. Truth to tell, the gods had not seemed to matter much to any of the people of Gillengaria, until the Daughters of the Pale Mother had started whispering tales of witchcraft.

Into the hushed room, Kirra's voice came, equally hushed. "If it is true all mystics derive their powers from one god or another, then what god has touched me?"

Senneth looked at her. "I think the Wild Mother watches over you and Donnal and any who can shape-shift. The Wild Mother was the one who cared for all living creatures, who made the ox strong and the hare swift. She was never revered much, my grandmother said, because people did not understand her. They couldn't determine what power she might give them—they already had dominion over animals as far as they were concerned—so they did not particularly worry about doing her honor."

"And was she a healer as well?" Kirra asked.

Senneth smiled. "Ah—well—it has occurred to me more than once that you might have a very mixed heritage. Perhaps one of your ancestors was descended from the Wild Mother, and another from the Dark Watcher. You are blessed because you have two sets of skills, and two goddesses who guard you."

"What about me?" Cammon said.

She regarded him thoughtfully. "I am not so sure about you. I am not, perhaps, conversant with all the gods. But I think you might derive your powers from the Lady of the Waters, who dwells in the riverbeds and the depths of the ocean. Water responds to every wind and every change in season—winter freezes it, spring releases it. If you blow on the surface of a pond, you send ripples in every direction. So you might call it a sensitive medium. But, as I say, I am not entirely certain."

"This is ridiculous," Justin began in a contemptuous voice, but Tayse cut a hand through the air to silence him, and he said no more.

"Are there other gods? And mystics with other powers?" Cammon asked.

"There might be. I don't know," Senneth said. "I only know the bits and pieces I have put together from tales my grandmother used to tell. And, as I say, I could be completely wrong—but it is a theory that seems to make sense to me."

"But then—why would—how did—why did the gods choose some people to bless with power, and not choose others?" Kirra asked.

Senneth smiled. "I don't know the answer to that, either! My guess is—oh, some time ago, centuries ago, the gods saw that the faith of the people was failing. And they decided to walk through Gillengaria, either together or apart, to try to reclaim their people. I don't know if they showed themselves only to the devout, or if they walked naked and terrible through every settlement and invited the villagers to look at them. I don't know if they selected one person in this town and another person in that town, and laid their hands upon the chosen, and transferred some of their own power into those bodies. I don't know if they took human lovers to produce children that were half mortal and half divine. I don't know if the whole exercise was a jealous competition to see which god or goddess could win the most converts. I don't even know if it happened. I just know that there are a handful of us in Gillengaria who appear to have been touched with an inexplicable power, and I know that the gods have all but disappeared from our land. And I cannot help but wonder if there is a connection."

"You say the gods have disappeared," Cammon said. "But the Pale Mother is all around us, at least here in the south. Does that mean she won the competition, if there was one? Does that mean her—her children have some kind of mystical power?"

"I don't know that, either," Senneth admitted. "I have never heard of one of the Daughters displaying any kind of special ability. Maybe the moon goddess has no power, and so she is the most jealous one of all. Maybe that is why she hates the descendants of her brothers and sisters with such passion—why she wants to see them all banished or murdered, because she knows they have power, and she has none. Or maybe there were never any gods, and they never walked through Gillengaria. I don't know. It is just something I have wondered."

She glanced at Cammon. "But it might explain some things—

why you could locate this building, for instance. You are sensitive to magic—or perhaps you are sensitive to divine power. This shrine is a place of divinity, and so you could perceive its existence."

"Yes, well, you can always twist a consequence to match a theory," Justin said, unable to contain himself any longer. "But to think—to hear you say—that you and your friends are *gods*—"

"I didn't say we were," Senneth said mildly. "I don't think even the gods are gods in Gillengaria anymore. I just think they left some traces of themselves behind."

"I believe it," Donnal said quietly, and the others all looked at him. He had sat so quietly this whole time, in his accustomed place beside Kirra, that it was as easy to forget he was in the room as it was to forget the raelynx. Neither of whom should be overlooked, Tayse reminded himself.

Donnal went on. "There is a temple to the Wild Mother on Danalustrous lands, which I found one day by accident. A small place, completely open to the elements after so many years of neglect. I didn't even know what it was the first time I came across it. But there was"—his hand made a half circle in the air—"a mosaic that took up an entire wall. Broken and fallen to pieces by now, of course, but you could tell it had once been beautiful. It depicted every creature that runs or flies across Gillengaria—hawk, hound, rabbit, fox, fish, cat—every one of them. As if this was the one place in the whole land all of them could be safe.

"I found that place one winter when I'd been hunting, and I'd gotten hurt, and I needed shelter for the night. And when I staggered in, and rested against that wall, I felt—I can't explain. But I knew it was a place of power. And inside it, I healed faster than I believed was possible. I woke in the morning, and my wound was almost gone. I knew it was a holy place, and I went back as often as I could after that. I did not know what kind of offerings to bring, or even what god had once sheltered there, but I would sit, and I would meditate, and I would feel myself grow stronger."

"You never took me to such a place," Kirra said.

He smiled at her. "I will take you the next time we are on your father's lands."

Justin threw his hands in the air and leaned back against his packs. "Magic and superstition!" he burst out. "Old tales and crazy notions born of a fever on a cold night!"

Donnal looked at him, his dark face neutral. "Very well, then, how do *you* explain it?" he said. "Because you have seen what we are all capable of. The fire burns without fuel—I can take any shape I desire. If we were not touched by gods, gods who are still in some sense present in this world, then how do you rationalize the things that you know we can do?"

"It might be magic, but it is not divine," Justin said flatly. "I can't explain the difference, but I know there is one."

Tayse held up a hand, bent on stopping the argument before it could properly begin. "It doesn't matter," he said to Justin quietly. "It cannot be proved or disproved, and since we have not been asked either to contain them or exorcise them, we do not have to care how they were made. Myself, I find it a story no worse than other stories—true or untrue—but it does not matter. What matters is that the king trusts them, and he has given them to our care. As long as they carry out their mission and do not betray the king, they can think what they like, and we can keep our opinions to ourselves."

"Yes, but does the king know this bit about being children of the *gods*?" Justin demanded.

Tayse turned his eyes thoughtfully toward Senneth. "I don't know. I have no idea at all what the king knows about these people, or how he came to choose Senneth for this mission."

Senneth grinned. "No, I have not shared my theories with anyone except the five of you," she said. "Certainly feel free to repeat them to King Baryn if you think they will have some bearing on how he views me."

"I am more interested right now in how he knows you at all," Justin said.

"My father had done some services for him for many years," Senneth said. "I was in and out of the royal palace more times than I could recount for you, when I was a child. The king, as you know, does not view mystics with any revulsion. He seemed intrigued to learn that I had left my father's house for such a reason."

"And how did he learn of it?" Tayse asked.

Senneth's eyes flicked to Kirra. "Malcolm Danalustrous told him, after I had spent some time tutoring his daughter. In fact, the king summoned me to his side for the first time more than ten years ago, and he asked me if I would exercise my abilities on his behalf." She shrugged. "Since then, every year or so, as my wanderings have taken me, I have made a visit to the royal palace to give my greetings to my king. I suppose he does not think it is so very bad a thing to have a mystic in his employ whom he knows and trusts. The arrangement has suited us both."

It sounded plausible enough, but, to Tayse's ears, still a little too glib. What kind of service had her father provided to the king? Nothing even remotely military, or Tayse would have known about him. Perhaps he was a farmer or a merchant trader—perhaps he dealt in fine velvets and silks, or wines imported from Arberharst and too expensive for any but the royal table. It was her right not to be specific, of course—they had all left certain details out of their stories—but still, there was something about her explanation that seemed to skirt the truth.

"I have not seen you before, on any of these many visits you made to the king," Justin said suspiciously.

"No, and I have not seen you, either," she replied. "I imagine there might be more than one visitor to the royal palace who is not brought down to the guardhouse and introduced 'round to all the men."

Kirra giggled; Justin looked furious. "Enough," Tayse said. "There is no point in baiting each other over any of this."

"Well, he couldn't make it more clear that he hates and mistrusts all of us," Kirra said. "He should at least pretend to respect us if his *king* finds us worthy of his regard."

Justin looked hot to reply, but Tayse stared him down. "I think we could all work a little harder at pretending to respect each other," Tayse said, and this time it was Senneth who stifled a laugh. "But for now, perhaps, we should call the conversation ended. Turn in for the night, work harder on our civility in the morning."

There was a moment's silence while the four mystics nodded and seemed to realize, suddenly, that they were exhausted, and while Justin struggled to contain his stirred emotions. He was a King's Rider, and a damn fine one, but there were days Justin was still a gutter boy fighting for his life and hating everyone in the world who did not have to fight equally as hard.

"Should we post a guard?" the younger man asked eventually in a cool, professional voice. "I could take first watch."

Tayse could not help a smile. "I'm not sure the sun itself will be able to find us by tomorrow morning," he said. "I think we can all sleep tonight without fear."

Senneth looked at him, and her smile was easy to read. *The sun will find us easily enough, because she will come looking for me,* her expression said. Tayse shrugged and almost smiled back, then turned to unroll his blankets and lay himself down for the night.

CHAPTER
14

In the morning, they found themselves snowed in. The storm had continued soundlessly but relentlessly throughout the night, and now there was a good five feet of snow piled up all around the small temple.

"Just as well we didn't try to camp in the open," Tayse said, peering out the door and measuring the drifts with his eyes. "We'd have been buried."

"I think we're here for another day," Senneth said. She was standing beside him, surveying the white landscape, and she did not sound overjoyed. "Or two."

Tayse nodded. "Well, we're safe—we're warm—we don't have to worry about going thirsty. I'm not sure how long our food supplies will last, though."

"Kirra and Donnal can hunt," she said so casually that for a moment he imagined them going off with traps and bows over their arms. Then he realized what she really meant, and a shiver of distaste ran down his spine.

"What about your pet raelynx?" he asked to conceal his reaction.

She smiled. "I'm not sure I trust it yet to go out killing," she said. "The longer I can keep its violent instincts in check, the more contented it will stay. I think."

He turned away from the door. "Whatever you think is best," he said, and realized it was not a very good answer.

But for the moment, their supplies were adequate, and it was so cold that neither Kirra nor Donnal expressed much interest in taking predator shape and setting out in search of game. That left six people cooped up in a small space with nothing to occupy their time.

"Get out the practice swords," Tayse said to Justin. "It's time to do a little training."

Kirra announcing that she would rather be hacked to pieces by Gisseltess men than ever attempt to learn swordplay, only the five of them spent much of the day engaging in mock combat. There weren't enough practice blades to go around, and the only ones Tayse trusted to use real weapons were the two Riders, so he and Justin used their own swords and daggers while the others feinted and parried with clumsy wooden versions. Cammon was not so hopeless as Tayse had thought he might be, and for a while Tayse paused to watch the boy as he jousted with Senneth in front of the wall with the painted sun. Senneth was better, of course— Senneth was downright good, with natural-born strength and an excellent sense of her opponent's techniques—but Cammon seemed to have an uncanny ability to dance out of her reach just before she was about to land a blow. Part of that mystical talent they claimed he had, Tayse supposed—the ability to read the thoughts and desires and plans of the people around him and somehow turn this knowledge to his advantage.

Tayse did not find the thought particularly comfortable.

They switched partners throughout the day, to expose them all to a variety of strengths and weaknesses. To Tayse's amusement, Justin spent part of the day taking on both Cammon and Donnal at once, expending his furious energy by exhorting them to come at him, don't be cowards, band together now, boys, and you might have a chance to do me in! But Justin was so very good. Even the two of them together, with their clumsy thrusts and lunges, would have no hope of disabling Justin.

"That leaves me to fight you," Tayse pointed out to Senneth, and she willingly took up her sword.

"Though I have to say," she said, "that my whole body is starting to ache. Woeful indeed will be the day I have to fight from sunup to sundown. I think my arm would fall off even before someone sliced me to ribbons."

"The more you train, the stronger you grow, and the longer you can fight in the field," he replied. Testing her while he spoke—thrust, feint, pull back, circle, strike. She was quick; her sword was before him every time, though she was not making much effort to attack.

"I cannot imagine ever training hard enough or long enough to be as good as you," she said, panting just a little.

He grinned. "You have other skills," he said. "You might combine those with your swordsmanship."

"I would," she retorted, "if my goal was to win. Right now my goal is to get better."

He dropped his sword point to the floor. "Maybe you are the one who should be training me," he said. "How to fight against magic."

She lowered her own weapon, leaning gratefully on the wooden sword as if it were a cane. "Interesting idea," she said thoughtfully. "But I only know my own magics."

"When we had that skirmish on the road," he said, "you did something to the swords of the others—turned them too hot to hold. How would I defend against that?"

She considered. "Carry a glove that can withstand great heat," she suggested. "Such as the cooks wear in the kitchen. You could still hold the hilt and wield it. The blade might be even more dangerous then," she added with a grin.

"Wait," he said, and went back to dig through his packs. He had an old pair of leather gloves, clumsy and thick; he wore them to pull down the walls of burning buildings when he wanted to get to enemies inside. He had never tried to wield a sword while wearing them.

Tucking them into his belt, he returned to the place where Senneth waited. "Now," he said. "If I am your opponent and you want to disable me, how would you fight?"

So they raised their blades again and the metal clashed against wood. Almost instantly, he felt the hilt burn against his hand, so hot a faint glow came off the metal. This was the trick—to toss the blade to his left hand, while with his right he pulled the glove free and slipped it on, all the while feeling the flesh on his other palm blister and peel. All the while parrying her advances. He was as quick as he could be, but he knew she could have done him some serious damage during that interlude if she had been really trying.

The glove on—the sword back in his right hand—awkward but not impossible to lift and swing the blade. Senneth was laughing, spinning in and out of his range, livelier now that she knew he was having some trouble adjusting. He was still stronger than she was and he parried without danger. He was starting to feel a little more confident when a sudden spark of fire against his belly and along his leg caused him to swallow a cry and glance down at his body.

The buckle of his belt glowing like a coal—the dagger in its hilt red with heat.

"Damn," he muttered. Still fending off her attack, he forced his hand into the second glove and then unbuckled his belt and let it fall. "Does this mean I can't go into battle with *any* metal anywhere near my skin?"

"If you're in combat against me," she said cheerfully. "But I have more tricks than this."

"Keep them coming," he said, and drove his hot sword straight toward her body.

Through a sudden wall of fire.

This time he did yelp and leap backward. A thin sheet of flame was suspended between them, and through its coruscating ruby surface he could see her pacing, waiting for him to make his next attack. It was as real as the fire last night; he could feel the heat against his face and throat. Behind him where the others were fighting, he heard all sounds of battle stop. Everyone must be staring in their direction.

"And how do I fight through this?" he asked.

"It depends on how greatly you fear fire," she said.

"If I leap through it to reach you—what then?"

She laughed. "Then—any number of things. If I was truly afraid and I truly wanted to stop you, I would set you ablaze."

"You can do that?" he demanded.

She nodded, or he thought he saw her nodding; it was hard to see much through the flames. "Living or dead, a man can burn at my hands," she said a little grimly.

He dropped his sword point again, and she let the fire die away. "Then I don't understand why you are so bent on acquiring poor skills like swordsmanship," he said bluntly.

She held the hilt of her wooden blade in one hand, the tip in the other. "I want to learn every skill," she said. "Anything that might defend me. Perhaps my enemy will be a mystic, one who can douse my fires as soon as I light them. One whose magic is so much stronger than mine that I will not be able to rely on sorcery. Then I want to be able to run him through the heart with a dagger." She smiled, to make the words sound less vicious. But he had the sense she was entirely serious. "I want to arm myself with every weapon I can."

Kirra had drifted over; the others, he saw from the corner of his eye, had also drawn nearer. "There cannot be many mystics with the kind of power you have," Kirra said.

Senneth looked at her. "It would only take one."

"And he would have to be your enemy," Tayse added.

Now she looked at him. "And if he is?"

"You see enemies everywhere," Justin said.

Her eyes went to him. "And a King's Rider does not?" she said softly. "Why else are you the best-trained fighters on the continent? I am the King's Mystic. I must be the best."

Tayse lifted his sword to salute her. He could feel the tip against his forehead, still hot but cooling. "You are well on your way to that distinction," he said.

They broke for lunch that Kirra, having nothing else to do, had made for them. Even with all the exercise to distract them, Tayse could tell the group was getting restless. Cammon and Donnal wrestled a bit—here was a skill Donnal was better at than all the others—while the women drew aside and giggled about something.

"We don't have a basin, though," Kirra was saying. "And I don't want to use our camp bucket—"

"I thought I saw an old pitcher over there behind the—the altar, I guess it is," Senneth said, and they went off to investigate.

Tayse glanced at Donnal, eyebrows raised in a question. "Bathing," Donnal said. "They've decided to melt snow and try to get clean."

Justin grinned. He was standing by his pack of belongings, sorting through the wooden swords to see if any of them had been nicked or splintered beyond use. "Naked women in a camp," he drawled. "It's a sight worth getting snowed in for."

So quickly Tayse barely saw him move, Donnal leapt across the room and gave Justin a ferocious shove. "You touch her, you even *look* at her, and I will kill you," the dark man said.

Justin's dagger was out, half an inch from Donnal's throat. Donnal stood unmoving, unafraid, staring him down. Behind him, Tayse could hear Kirra's exclamation, Senneth's soft footfalls. The raelynx yowled suddenly into the cold silence.

"Go ahead and try it," Justin said, "if you think you can."

Donnal's face flickered from human to bear and back again. "If I want you dead," Donnal said very softly, "you will be dead."

It was that long before Tayse could gather his wits and push himself between them, knocking Justin to one side, Donnal to the other. He didn't see Donnal shift, but he felt the bare whisper of claws along his own arm, an involuntary reaction or a hint of warning, he could not be sure. Then Senneth was there, her arm around Donnal's neck, dragging him backward with no pretense of gentleness. Tayse turned his attention to Justin, who was still smoldering, and pushed the younger man backward another step with a hard arm to the chest.

"I didn't start that," Justin said, furious, his arms up as if he would fight Tayse himself, or at least defend himself against accusation.

"You're both at fault. You're both stupid," Tayse said roughly. "We're a small group, and we can't afford to hate each other."

"I do hate them," Justin said intensely.

Tayse did not answer, merely kept his gaze, severe and cold, on the other man. After a moment, Justin dropped his eyes.

"All right," Justin said. "I won't provoke him." He looked up. "But I won't apologize."

For a moment, for no reason at all, Tayse was transported back ten or twelve days ago, to the camp where Donnal had gotten injured in practice and Senneth had healed him with a touch. To the conversation where Senneth had said to him, "I feel so old." He had laughed at her then. Now, briefly, he wanted to echo her. So much youth and bravado and undirected energy caged in one small space. He thought for a moment that there must be more important things to fight over; he was a man who had learned to conserve his strength and his hatred.

He finally said, "I don't think Donnal will apologize either. Just refrain from antagonizing him. And keep your attention on our mission."

"Which is never all that clear," Justin retorted.

Tayse gave him another icy stare, and he subsided. "Which is," Tayse said, "to serve our king."

Justin shrugged and looked down. Tayse turned to survey the rest of the room. It had emptied out since he had last paid attention.

Cammon was over by the horses, shaking out grain. Senneth was crouched by the door, practically face-to-face with the raelynx—trying to bend it to her will, he supposed, much as he had tried with Justin. Kirra and Donnal were gone.

Slowly, so as not to disturb her, Tayse approached Senneth. She rose to her feet as he got closer. The raelynx gave him one wicked look and then dropped its pointed nose to its red paws.

"I see your pet has a strong reaction to violence," Tayse said.

A hint of a smile across her face. "He's as sensitive to mood as Cammon is," she said. "Though a bit more dangerous."

"Have you calmed him?"

"I think so."

"Where are the others?"

"I sent them out. In whatever shape they chose to take, to hunt or scout or merely play in the snow, I don't care."

"I think we'll have to move on tomorrow," he said. "Impassable roads or no."

She nodded. "I think you're right."

THE others returned a couple hours later, only Kirra appearing in human form. Donnal padded through the door, a russet raelynx, and settled by the wild one as if by his only true friend. Kirra had a brace of rabbits in her hand and seemed to be in her usual sunny mood.

"Dinner," she said lightly. "Who wants to cook?"

Justin was mostly silent during the meal and afterward, but the others made an attempt to be sociable. Late in the evening, Senneth pulled out a pack of cards and did tricks with them, dealing out aces and nines seemingly at will.

"You've marked them," Kirra said in disgust.

"I haven't," Senneth said, shuffling with a cardsharp's ease. "But enough hours spent on shipboard or in a barracks with nothing else to do will give you motivation to learn all sorts of skills."

"Can *you* do tricks?" Kirra asked Tayse.

He shook his head. "I can play most gambling games, and win a handful of them, but I can't reach in and pull out a card I want."

Senneth tidied the deck and handed them over to Cammon. "Here. See what you can do with these."

He cut them a few times, but not with any particular dexterity. "What do you mean?"

"Pull out the seven of hearts," she suggested.

He concentrated, fanning the cards before him, but only shrugged. "I can't tell. They all look alike."

"I know," Kirra said. "Give us each a card."

So he shuffled again and spread the deck in his hands and let each of them choose what they would. Even Justin, a little intrigued or maybe just bored, pulled a card from the pack.

"Can you tell what we have?" Kirra asked him.

Cammon sat up straighter, looking faintly excited. "Well—concentrate a little bit," he said.

Kirra's face scrunched up as she stared at the image before her. "Queen of diamonds," Cammon said.

She laughed and turned it face outward so they could all see. Queen of diamonds, indeed.

Cammon looked at Senneth, who also focused on her card. "Six of spades," he said. Senneth sailed the card over to him, where it landed beside his boot. Right again.

"Wonder if it will work with the nonbelievers," Cammon said with a little grin, turning toward the Riders.

Tayse grinned. "Hey, I'm a believer," he said, and kept his eyes narrowed on the three of spades in his hands. He was not even remotely surprised when Cammon called it.

Cammon had more trouble with Justin, but Tayse thought that was good for both of them. It pleased Justin, anyway, that Cammon guessed the king of hearts when what he held was the jack.

"Not enough practice, or Justin is too opaque for Cammon to read?" Senneth wondered. "Try it again."

So they spent another half hour or so, alternating between trying to send Cammon mental images and trying to block them. Tayse was half convinced it was all ridiculous—and half convinced the boy had a real ability to read other's minds. He was equally divided on whether he thought such a skill was something to encourage or something to destroy with quick ruthlessness.

But he played the games, and so did Justin.

They had all begun to tire of card tricks by the time Kirra had a new idea. "Cammon—you go sit over there," she said. "One of us will do something to one of the others—hurt him, but just a little. You try to figure out who's in pain."

Cammon's eyebrows rose. "And then I get to figure out who's pulled out his dagger and stabbed someone in retaliation?"

Kirra giggled. "It won't be that bad. Come on. Try it."

So Cammon went to sit by the horses, his back to the four at the fire. Senneth held her arm out and Kirra used her fingernails to take a hard pinch of the forearm. Tayse saw Senneth mouth an exaggerated *"Ow,"* before she rubbed her skin.

"Senneth," Cammon called. "And Kirra's the one who hurt her."

"Now that's impressive," Tayse murmured. "I can see some value in a skill like this, particularly if it works over distance."

"I don't think we can manage distance tonight," Senneth said. She held her arm out to Tayse.

He found himself reluctant to harm her, even in a small way, but he took her index finger and bent it backward till her eyes widened.

"Senneth again," Cammon guessed. "By Tayse this time."

Senneth grinned at him and then, without warning, made a silent dive for Justin's throat. Tayse could see Justin force himself not to fight back as Senneth's fingers closed hard around his neck.

"Justin," Cammon called. "But he'd like to kill Senneth for trying that." They all laughed.

They had been playing this particular game for maybe ten minutes when a new contestant entered the lists. Warm breath on his cheek made Tayse whirl around, dagger in hand, to come face-to-face with the raelynx. Briefly, primeval terror held him motionless, but then he realized that this was the bigger cat, the human one in animal shape. Donnal regarded him for a moment out of dark, fathomless eyes, then pulled his mouth back in a wicked snarl.

"Who's next?" Cammon called.

"We're working on that," Kirra called back. She, for one, did not seem at all alarmed by Donnal's sudden appearance, just scooted over to sit closer to Tayse and his new companion. She appeared to be considering something—and, as soon as she had figured it out, she disappeared.

Down to the shape of a quivering white rabbit huddled beside Tayse's thigh.

The raelynx snarled again, so fiercely that Tayse wondered if this might not be the wild creature after all, and then whipped its head down to fasten its teeth in the rabbit's throat. Tayse had never known a rabbit could make a sound like that—any sound at all—but Kirra hopped away a few wobbly paces, and the raelynx sat back on its hind legs and let her go. Tayse could see no sign of blood on the snowy fur.

He happened to glance over at Senneth and saw her looking almost as shocked as he felt. Somehow, that made him feel better.

"That was Kirra being attacked by Donnal," came Cammon's voice, completely serene. "I didn't know Donnal was playing."

"And the game seems to have gone on long enough," Senneth said. "Kirra, are you at all hurt?"

More slowly than seemed usual, Kirra flowed back into her habitual shape of golden beauty. "No," she said, giving Donnal a quick look. He stayed in his cat form, watching them all. "But I think instincts might be working on all of us a little too much."

Cammon bounded back across the room to join them, smiling broadly. "That was fun," he said. "What can we try next?"

"We'll try sleeping so that we're strong enough in the morning to break through the snow and get out of here," Senneth said.

Kirra stood up, yawning and stretching. She didn't seem too upset by her near brush with death—which, most likely, had been no such thing. Just a display of power. Just a reminder, from the quietest member of the group, that he could be more dangerous than it appeared.

They were all dangerous, Tayse thought. Both Riders, all the mystics, in radically different ways. And their shifting internal loyalties made them not entirely safe even with each other. But he had to admit he felt a little better about the possibility of encountering foes on the road.

"What about that bath?" Kirra asked Senneth. "Too late?"

Senneth was also on her feet, smiling now. "Oh no. It might be midnight, but I'm getting clean tonight."

Justin was checking his weapons belt, stubbornly uninterested in the conversation that had started all the hostility in the first place. Donnal rose to his feet, twitched his tufted tail, and crossed silently to the door where the other raelynx lay sleeping.

Tayse decided he would get himself ready for bed.

Cammon was filled with the exhilaration of victory, so he chatted happily to a mostly silent Justin while the two women retired to a corner close to the horses. They seemed to have worked this out sometime when no one else was paying attention, for they quickly strung up a couple of cloaks as a curtain and ducked behind it. Not that Tayse really tried to see anything, but it was clear they had chosen their spot for shadows and privacy. Their muffled laughter drifted back, along with the sound of occasional splashing. He supposed Senneth had warmed their pitcher of water to a comfortable temperature and that the whole experience was proving quite pleasant for them.

He wouldn't have minded getting cleaned up himself, but at the moment, the effort seemed too great. He rolled himself up in his blankets, facing away from the impromptu baths, and closed his eyes. He was asleep before the others had found their own beds.

CHAPTER
15

IN the morning, they discovered that the only way out was through a carnage of snowdrifts.

Nothing had melted during their sojourn in the shrine, and wind had made some of the piles of snow almost as high as Tayse's head.

"I could melt a way through, I suppose," Senneth said in a doubtful tone of voice as they all stood by the open door, gazing out, "but I think we'd drown in mud."

"Do you suppose it will be any better once we get to the road?" Justin asked.

"*If* we get to the road," Kirra said pessimistically.

Tayse shrugged. "I'd think there would have been some traffic between towns by now. Maybe not. We can stay a day and hope conditions improve or—" He shrugged again.

"I'd rather get out, if it's at all possible," Senneth said. "We don't seem to do well confined to small spaces."

Donnal pushed to the forefront. During the night, something had impelled him to shift back to human state. He had been lying beside Kirra when Tayse woke up in the morning. "I can break a path through," he said.

"Let's saddle up and go, then," Tayse said, and headed toward their makeshift corral.

When he returned to the door, reins in hand, he saw that Donnal had already begun to make some headway. Or at least he assumed the monstrous milk-colored ox was Donnal, forcing himself at a slow but determined pace through the snow. For a moment Tayse stood and watched, wondering how long it would take them to go five miles this day, then he swung into the saddle.

"I'll bring Donnal's horse," Kirra said.

Tayse nodded, eyes still focused on the forward view. "Justin," he said, "stay with us. Doesn't seem like the kind of day we should all be separated."

Indeed, it was not much of a day at all, except a slow, weary, cold one. Once they made the arduous journey back to the main road, they found that there had indeed been some traffic in the past day, but that it hadn't done much more than trample a single-file track down the middle of the road. Donnal resumed his accustomed form and let Tayse take the lead, and they followed each other carefully down the white landscape. Twice during the day they encountered other parties heading in the opposite direction; each time Tayse led his group to the side of the road to let the others pass. It felt safer to view others riding by than to file in front of the eyes of watchful strangers.

"Do we even know where we're heading?" he asked as they made an abbreviated stop for a noon meal. They simply kicked through the snow at the side of the road and ate in their saddles.

Kirra and Senneth glanced at each other. "Rappen Manor?" Kirra said.

Senneth shrugged, not seeming too happy about it. "We may as well. If Ariane Rappengrass has thrown in her lot with Gisseltess—well, we won't need to worry about an uprising. We'll need to worry about a war."

"How far?" Justin asked.

"Day or two," Senneth said. "Or, well, maybe more on this kind of road."

"Where do you want to spend the night?" Tayse asked.

"An inn," Kirra said with heartfelt emphasis.

Senneth nodded. "It's not going to be fun to camp out for a while. If we find a town before nightfall, I'd say we take rooms for the night. If there are any rooms," she added. "Might be filled up with stranded travelers."

Tayse's eyes had gone to the raelynx, sitting a few feet away in the snow, looking bored. "What do we do about him?" he asked. "I don't know that we can bring him into any inn with us."

"I've been worrying about that a bit," she admitted. "But I think I might be able to smuggle him inside, if someone else books the room and there's a back way in. And I create a certain sense of—misdirection."

"Invisibility, you mean," Kirra retorted.

Senneth smiled. "I told you, I haven't perfected that yet. But I'm thinking I might work on it while we're riding and I've got nothing else to think about."

"How is invisibility a gift from the sun goddess?" Tayse wanted to know. "Because it would seem—if what you're good at is fire and heat and those life forces—"

"I know," Senneth said. "It seems like a contradictory skill. But I think what it will take is"—she made a gesture, as if smoothing away rough patches in the air—"turning people's attention *away* from that life force. So, for instance, if you're looking at Kirra, and I've found a way to direct your thoughts away from the heat and energy that is Kirra, you look at her but you see nothing. Because the life force is not evident."

Tayse shook his head. "I'm a soldier," he said. "All of this is mysterious to me."

Justin addressed Kirra. "Why can't you just turn the raelynx into something else?" he said. "Like a kitten or a mouse."

Kirra looked as shocked as if he'd asked her to strip naked and dance in the snow. "I can't do that!" she exclaimed. "You can't—it's forbidden—it's *impossible* to turn one creature into another!"

Justin looked both puzzled and irritated. "You change yourself into wolves and cats and I don't know what-all," he said. "Every day."

"Yes—myself, of my own volition," she said patiently. "And things—I can turn swords into butter knives and trees into rose-bushes. But I can't take another creature and turn it into another creature. I just—I can't."

Tayse found himself interested. "Can't or won't?" he asked. "You don't have the skill or—you said it was forbidden."

Kirra glanced at Senneth, who merely smiled. "It is a thing generally accepted by all mystics with the power to change shape that they will only try those tricks on themselves," Kirra said. "The tutors I had—the mystics I've talked to since—all of them, every one of them, believes that rule as a basic tenet of magic. In fact, I don't know that I *could* turn you into a toad or a warthog, much as I'd like to, but I certainly don't know the spells for changing a man into another creature. And I wouldn't do it, even if I knew how. It's—that's just—it's just wrong," she ended lamely.

Tayse glanced at Senneth. "Back to honor," he said. "When you told Justin you would not turn your talents against him in the middle of the night."

"So now you can sleep serene," she said, "knowing that when you wake up in the morning you will be a shape you recognize."

"That still doesn't solve the problem of the raelynx," Tayse said. "And even if it's possible to sneak it into a small inn in a backcountry town, I imagine you'll have trouble parading him through the city that encircles Rappen Manor."

"I know," Senneth said. "I've been thinking about that, too."

She didn't say what solution she had come to. Tayse dusted crumbs off his hands, pulled his gloves on, and pulled his horse back to the road. "If we're going to find an inn by nightfall," he said, "we'd better be moving."

They traveled onward for another three hours. It annoyed Tayse that, no matter how often he glanced backward to check on the other members of his party, sometimes they were with him and sometimes they were not. He had almost gotten used to Donnal's sudden appearances and disappearances, but today Kirra was also missing, and Senneth and Cammon were each leading one of their horses. He was not even going to bother to comment on the absences until, late in the afternoon, Senneth called a sudden sharp halt.

Tayse wheeled about, expecting trouble, but it was merely the usual strange activities of this particular crew. Kirra and Donnal had appeared from nowhere, wildness in their eyes and blood on their hands, and were crouched in the snow, feeding a pair of squirrels to the raelynx. The young cat was ripping through the mangled fur to gulp down chunks of raw flesh, then pausing every once in a while to give the humans nearby a menacing stare. Kirra wiped her hands in the snow, stood up, and walked back to her horse.

Senneth must have caught Tayse's look of disgust. "I thought it would be easier to keep him content if he'd fed well before we tried to take him to town," she explained. "Make him less likely to eat pet dogs and small children."

"A point is going to come when you're going to have to abandon him along this journey," he said shortly.

She gave him a calm and level look. "When there is a safe place to leave him, I'll do it."

Naturally, no such safe place presented itself in the next few miles—but something even more welcome appeared around the bend about half an hour later. A crossroads town, bustling even despite the recent blizzard, and looking rather picturesque with the snow laying a white piping along every steeple and eave. The streets had been fairly well cleared, and plenty of people were riding or walking through the middle of town.

"May the Pale Lady grant us an empty room for the night," Kirra prayed. She glanced sideways at Senneth. "Or the Bright Mother."

Senneth nodded. "My unfriendly pet and I will wait here on the outskirts while you go in and investigate. A small place with a back entrance would work best for us—but even then, I am not sure this will succeed. If we're booted out, I'll sleep in the woods tonight while the rest of you enjoy civilization."

Tayse frowned at her. "We all sleep safe, or none of us do."

She laughed. "Trust me, I will be perfectly safe."

But in the end, they were all able to take shelter that night under a sound roof when they found two rooms at a small, pleasant inn. Senneth and the raelynx came creeping in the back door while Tayse and Justin guarded the hallways, and they were able to leave the animal drowsing in the women's bedroom while the rest of them went down for a meal.

The inn served a hearty if not particularly flavorful dinner, their rooms were comfortable enough to encourage a good night's sleep, and they left in the morning much as they had entered the night before. One thing was immediately obvious as they set out: The temperature was considerably warmer than it had been the past few days, and the snow was already beginning to melt. Good in some respects, bad in others. In the long stretches of road that had been paved by local enterprise or royal decree, travel became easier. Where the way consisted only of hard-packed earth, mud became the enemy. Tayse made a mental note to never again travel in winter, and led the party forward.

This day, he ranged ahead of the group for a few miles, checking to see if there were any hazards along the road, then came back to ascertain whether those under his care were still unmolested. Likewise, Justin fell to the rear to make sure trouble didn't threaten from behind. They passed quite a few travelers this day, people who had been stuck longer than they expected at their last layovers and were eager to complete their journeys. In one of his forays ahead of his group, Tayse spotted a small troop of armed men who had paused for lunch beside the road. He did a quick count and turned his horse back the way he'd come.

This time, when he pulled up in front of his own party, he found three unmounted horses and Cammon talking to empty air.

"Where's Senneth?" he demanded. "Where's anybody?"

Cammon gave him a look of mild bewilderment and glanced at the horse coming to a halt beside him. Where Senneth suddenly hazed into view, slouching relaxed in the saddle. She appeared both surprised and pleased with herself.

"So you couldn't see me?" she asked. "When you rode up?"

"No," he said shortly.

She was regarding the other rider. "But Cammon could. I thought my spells weren't working, because he just kept talking to me as if I was sitting right there."

"I don't seem to be the best one to try out such skills on," Cammon apologized.

"No, it seems to be impossible to dazzle you with magic," she answered.

Tayse tried to shake off his exasperation. "What about Kirra and Donnal? There's a troop of military riders coming this way."

Her expression sharpened. "Could you tell whose?"

"Wearing maroon sashes, so I assume from Rappengrass. There were about twelve of them."

"We're probably safe if they're Ariane's men," Senneth said. "Though it might look odd to have so many empty saddles."

"Just my thought," he said somewhat acidly.

She smiled. "I don't think they've gone far. Justin's roaming, too."

He wanted to tell her that that was an entirely different thing, but perhaps in her eyes it wasn't. He thought soldiers should guard the mystics; mystics thought they should reconnoiter for themselves. Not for the first time, he wondered why the king had thought it so important to have Riders along on this journey. Senneth and her friends seemed very well able to take care of themselves.

"Maybe we should pull over a moment and regroup," he said.

But it didn't take long for Justin to catch up with them, and Kirra and Donnal came striding up from some secret hiding place just a few minutes later. "Military guard ahead," Tayse said briefly. "Looks like Rappengrass. Senneth doesn't think there's a problem, but I thought we should all ride on together."

Kirra swung into her saddle and glanced at Senneth. "And should we be anyone in particular as we pass them by?"

Senneth shook her head. "Just travelers along the way, I think."

Indeed, they could not have looked more ordinary when they encountered the Rappengrass troop a few minutes later. The head rider nodded at Tayse, recognizing an armed guard when he saw one, and appeared to quickly pick out Kirra as the wealthy member of the party who might need protection along the road. But that was automatic; any decent soldier would make those assessments almost without conscious volition. Tayse nodded back and rode on.

By midafternoon, they were starting to ride through countryside that was fairly populated—small farms here, a cluster of cottages there, then a crossroads that featured a tavern and an inn and what looked like a shop or two. Clearly they were not far from the town that called itself Rappen Manor after the major estate situated at its heart. Tayse wondered if Senneth's plan was to ride straight through to the grand house itself without calling a halt.

He asked her that when they stopped in late afternoon to take a break from riding. "No," she said. "I was hoping we could spend the night with a friend. She lives somewhere on the fringes of the city, but I haven't recognized her house yet. I suppose it's possible she's moved away."

"Her house would still be there," Tayse said, puzzled.

She grinned and glanced at Cammon. "I put that wrong," she said. "I know she's here somewhere, but I don't know where. I thought Cammon might be able to feel the pull of her magic."

He wanted to roll his eyes in a sort of mild disbelief, but he'd seen enough of their mental connections that he could not discredit what she said. Still, it made him uncomfortable.

"And if we do not find her?"

"Then I suppose we try one of these inns along the way, and use the tactics that were successful last night. But I very much hope we're able to locate Aleatha. Soon."

He resigned himself to a few dreary hours circling the

countryside, hunting up a phantom mystic, before they at last succumbed to the lure of a commercial bed. But in fact, twenty minutes after they resumed travel, Cammon jerked upright in his saddle.

"Oh!" he exclaimed, and pointed somewhere off the road to the right. "That way. Another hundred yards or so."

"Another sorceress," Tayse observed. "I can hardly wait."

THE woman named Aleatha was delighted to see her old friend Senneth. While the others waited respectfully back by the front gate, Senneth approached the house and called out a hail. Before the door opened, Tayse took note of the well kept property—winter-brown now, of course, but clearly maintained with a great deal of care. The cottage itself didn't look like it encompassed more than three rooms, but there was a sturdy barn in back and what looked like a garden beside it. He imagined that a mystic was able to keep vandals and predators at bay, and for the first time found himself thinking that magic might be an agreeable talent to possess.

Then the door opened, and the white-haired old woman gave Senneth a delighted embrace, and even Tayse could feel the welcome in the air.

Less than an hour later, the horses were stabled, the raelynx was locked in a toolshed, and the six travelers were eating an absolutely wonderful meal as they all crowded together in the small front room.

"No, Ariane has spoken out publicly against Halchon Gisseltess and his persecution of mystics. I don't think she's about to turn on us," Aleatha said as they munched on baked chicken and butter-drenched bread. "For the moment I feel safe. But Gisseltess men ride through all the southern provinces in the dead of night, and they are no respecter of boundaries. I have not heard of anyone living in Rappengrass who has been assaulted in her home. But now and then—there have been stories—of atrocities that have been visited upon mystics traveling on the roads through Rappengrass. They were not protected. Some of them have gone missing."

"Have these attacks been reported?" Kirra demanded.

Aleatha shrugged. "Not by me. And if they have been—well, what then? Is Ariane ready to start a border war with Halchon

Gisseltess over the lives of a few miserable mystics? She is not so rash. Here, Justin, is it? Would you like more of these potatoes?"

"I would, please," Justin replied, his voice a little muffled by the food still in his mouth. Tayse had to hide a smile. Justin's instinctive distrust of mystics had been trumped by their hostess's kindness and excellent cooking.

"She could tell King Baryn," Kirra said.

"And she may have. But is the king himself prepared to engage in a war over magic?"

"He might be," Senneth said, "if the war is about more than magic. If it's about power."

"And from what I can make out, that's what you're touring the countryside to discover," Aleatha said. "Tayse? Some potatoes? Maybe a little more bread? Or there's pie in the oven, if you want to wait for that."

"Bread," he decided. "*And* pie."

"It disturbs me that even on Rappengrass land, mystics aren't safe," Senneth said.

Aleatha gave her a sharp look from blue eyes that seemed not at all dimmed by the fact that she must be at least eighty years old. "Mystics have never been entirely safe," she said. "Not in Ghosenhall, not in Brassenthwaite. Not even, till young Kirra here was born, in Danalustrous. And I do not know that even Malcolm Danalustrous would shed blood to protect any of them except his own daughter. That's the truth of it."

"What of Coralinda Gisseltess?" Senneth asked. "What do you know of her?"

Aleatha soaked another piece of bread with honey and handed it to Cammon. "Only what everyone knows. She is recruiting young women to join her order. She is spreading to all the Houses her doctrine of the Pale Mother and her hatred of magic. She has not lost any of the force of her personality. I have to admit I fear her a great deal."

"Where is she basing her new evangelism?" Senneth asked. "Is she living in Gissel Plain?"

"Oh no. There's the old Lumanen Convent some miles east of here—you must know what I'm talking about—it fell into ruin a hundred years or so ago, but it was quite massive. She restored it sometime in the past few years, and they say it's quite beautiful now. All this smooth white stone that reflects back the silver light of the moon. There must be more than five hundred rooms in that place, and they say that all of them are full with Daughters of the Pale Mother who have joined the order in recent years. Filled with the Daughters—and their protectors."

Tayse looked up at that. "She has a civil guard?"

Aleatha nodded. "And not all supplied by her brother, from what I hear. Men cannot join the order, you know, but that does not mean men cannot have strong feelings of piety. They say there is a barracks of soldiers who have styled themselves an army of the goddess. They dress in silver and black livery and wear moonstone pendants around their necks."

"And perhaps some of these men have carried out the deeds that have been credited to Halchon Gisseltess's troops?" Senneth murmured.

Aleatha raised her eyebrows. "I had not considered that. But you may well be right."

"I have a lot of questions to ask Ariane Rappengrass tomorrow," Kirra said in a dark voice.

Aleatha glanced at her. "You are lucky. She is in residence. But perhaps that is not luck so much as—" She opened her hand palm up in a gesture of uncertainty. "Perhaps she feels now is not a time to travel far from her own lands."

"I have two favors to ask of you," Senneth said. "Can you keep my raelynx in your shed while Kirra and I go pose questions to Ariane Rappengrass? I do not expect you to try to control him while I am gone, but I would think a good door and a strong lock are all that are required."

"My dear Senneth, I will be happy to hold him for you! As long as I don't have to feed him or try to make him mine."

Senneth grinned. "No. Just contain him. Second—" She glanced at Cammon. "This one fell under my protection not so very long ago, and I have had no time to train him as he deserves. I don't know what your plans were for tomorrow, but if you had time—a few hours even—"

"Indeed, yes! I would be happy to see what skill and knowledge I will be able to impart in one short day," Aleatha exclaimed. "He is a reader, is he not?"

Cammon looked startled. "How did you know that?"

She smiled. "Because I am, too. A very useful talent, I have discovered. I should be able to show you a thing or two by day's end."

Cammon with an even greater ability to pick up images from other people's minds and see right through attempts at deception and illusion. Tayse could not bring himself to be sure that was a good thing.

"So!" Aleatha said, coming to her feet. "Who wants pie?"

CHAPTER
16

As it turned out, when they headed toward Rappen Manor the following day, they left behind not only Cammon and the raelynx, but Donnal besides. Senneth had decided that Tayse and Justin would ride into the city in their full Rider regalia, and Tayse was not willing to have Donnal pretend to be one of them. And Kirra, for once, seemed willing to travel a few yards without Donnal at her side. And the young man himself seemed perfectly willing to spend the whole day lounging around the mystic's house, eating rich food and dozing away the afternoon hours.

Thus only four of them rode into the city around Rappen Manor fairly early in the morning. It was a fine city, clearly enjoying its reputation for wealth and sophistication, and it was too large for Tayse to easily determine where all the roads ran and where all the trouble spots might lie. A broad scrollwork gate protected the road that led into town, and a contingent of maroon-sashed soldiers guarded the gate. But on this bright, cool morning, the metal doors were thrown back, and the soldiers themselves looked cheerful and at ease. They scrambled to attention to salute the King's Riders, and they made quick bows to serra Kirra, who rode behind them. They might have puzzled a bit over the lady's companion, who neither dressed like gentry nor behaved like a servant. Perhaps they took her for a scholar, or an advisor to Malcolm Danalustrous. In any case, she swept in behind the Riders and beside the serramarra, and managed to look both intriguing and mysterious.

Which, Tayse thought, was no more than the truth.

There was no need to ask for directions to their destination, he realized almost instantly. Rappen Manor itself sat on high ground at the center of the city, an imposing fortress of gray stone and narrow turrets, the maroon flag of Rappengrass flying at all four corners. Tayse admired the choice of location, which had to give the heirs of Rappengrass a view of all approaches to the manor. It did not look like a place that would fall easily to treachery or stealth.

"Should we send a message first, or ride straight up to the gates?" Kirra asked.

"Straight to the gates," Senneth said. "I don't think she'll turn you back unheard."

Tayse was in front of them, so he could not see Kirra's expression, but the tone of her voice was cautious. "And how do you plan to introduce yourself?"

Senneth's voice was underscored with a wry laugh. "Oh, Ariane knows me from way back. I plan just to enter the room as myself." A short silence. "But I think it is *your* name that will get us inside the walls."

Indeed, at all the checkpoints they encountered, this proved to be true—and there were quite a few checkpoints. Soldiers barred the way at yet another gate, this one set into a seven-foot-high wall that appeared to encircle the manor grounds. But Kirra's greeting and her request got them waved through with alacrity.

There were more soldiers at the outer door—more inside—and an army of servants who guarded smaller and smaller circles of sanctuary within the manor itself. Finally they were turned over to a tall, stooped, graying man who peered at them from a face of acute intelligence.

"Naturally, marlady Ariane will wish to speak with you," this individual said in a smooth voice. "But it may be a moment or two before she can free herself from other responsibilities. Will you wait here? I will have refreshments brought. Is there anything else I can do to make your wait more pleasant?"

"No, Ralf, thank you so much for your kindness," Kirra said in her warm voice. "It is good to see you again, looking so well."

He smiled and gave her a small bow. "And it is always a pleasure to see you, serra." He flicked one quick look at Senneth but did not address her by name. Perhaps he didn't know her as his mistress did. His face showed neither recognition nor puzzlement. He bowed again and went out.

"Guesses," Kirra said as soon as the door shut. "How long we'll be left here. I say two hours."

"Till nightfall," Justin said pessimistically.

Tayse shook his head. "Sooner than that," he said. "A daughter of a great House accompanied by two King's Riders? She'll be here inside the hour."

Senneth smiled. "Tayse is right."

Indeed, Ralf was back in the room before the tray of refreshments had even arrived. "The marlady is most desirous of seeing you immediately," he said. "Could you follow me?"

Kirra and Senneth stepped forward, the men at their heels. Ralf gave them a doubtful look. "I would prefer," Kirra said in a soft voice, "that they accompany us at least to the door of the room where we will meet with your mistress. I have seen things on the road that make me wish to have my friends always close about me."

Again, that small bow from Ralf. His acquiescence must mean the whole hallway was crawling with soldiers, Tayse thought— enough that Ralf believed they could overcome even two Riders who might suddenly go on a rampage. Ariane Rappengrass, it would appear, did not feel entirely safe these days.

So the four of them followed the steward—or whoever he was—down graceful stone corridors and through lovely arched doorways. Tapestries on the wall and stained glass in the window embrasures did not entirely conceal the fact that Rappen Manor had been built as a fortress. Tayse glanced out through one window that featured clear glass and found himself overlooking what appeared to be a training yard. At least fifty men were practicing maneuvers and testing each other with their swords. No, whatever trouble brewed in the kingdom, Ariane Rappengrass was not about to be caught unprepared.

They finally came to the end of a long, ornate hallway, lined with an array of weaponry and guarded by at least ten men. It ended in a wide door of dark wood and ornate brass handles. Ralf gave Tayse and Justin a cool look.

"You may wait out here," he said.

Tayse nodded, and he and Justin fell back, one to either side of the door. The guards eyed them but made no greeting or show of hostility. Ralf pulled open the door, and the women followed him inside.

The next hour passed in unrelieved tedium, though Tayse was careful to always appear entirely alert. Across from him, Justin never wavered from a watchful stance, his arms at his sides, his hands resting on the hilts of his weapons. The guards around them seemed similarly vigilant and far from bored; they did not engage in casual conversation and made no move to try such distractions with the newcomers. This was a council of war, and all the fighting men knew it. And respected it.

Finally, Tayse caught the sound of voices as people inside came close to the door. Ralf was the first one through, followed closely by Senneth. Kirra stepped across the threshold side by side with another woman, whom Tayse guessed to be the lady of the manor. She was fairly formidable looking, big-boned, tall, with thick gray hair caught back in a severe style and an expression of utter seriousness on her broad features. She did not much resemble her son, he thought.

"I am glad you came to me," she was saying, and her voice was low-pitched and strong. Tayse imagined that she could stand on the ramparts of her fortress and call out her own commands to the soldiers deployed below her, should such a need arise. "Tell Malcolm that, as always, he has my full confidence and support. Tell Baryn that as well. Rappengrass will not fail."

"I am glad to hear that," Kirra said. She paused, then enveloped the older woman in a quick embrace. "I am also glad to see you so well. Pray the Pale Lady keeps you so."

"The same prayers to you," Ariane Rappengrass said. "Where do you ride next?"

Kirra glanced at Senneth, who had come to a halt just outside the door. "Nocklyn, maybe," Senneth said. "We haven't decided."

Ariane looked grave. "Be careful in Nocklyn."

Senneth smiled. "We're careful everywhere."

Suddenly, an answering smile from Ariane Rappengrass. It transformed her severe face into one of great sweetness. "You cannot be surprised if I say I don't believe you."

Senneth laughed and came a step closer, her hand extended. Marlady Ariane shook it warmly. "It was a pleasure to see you again, Ariane," Senneth said softly. "And to receive such a welcome in Rappengrass."

Ariane did not immediately drop her hand. "I think about your father sometimes," she said. "He was a good man."

Senneth pulled her hand away. "No," she said, "he was not."

Ariane Rappengrass did not seem to feel rebuffed but continued to watch Senneth with a close attention. "When all this is done and you have come to the end of your wandering, return here if you decide you have nowhere else to go," the older woman said. "I would hear the long tale of your adventures some evening when there is nothing else more pressing to attend to."

Senneth laughed again. "Agreed," she said. "I will practice the telling of my stories."

Ariane leaned in then and kissed Senneth on the cheek. "Travel safely," she said. Then she turned on her heel and reentered the room. Ralf closed the door behind her.

"Let me see you to the front hall," he said and brushed past them.

Senneth collected Justin and Tayse with two quick looks, and the men fell in behind the women, who followed Ralf through the long hallways. The way out seemed even longer and more well-guarded than the way in, Tayse thought. It was a relief to make it finally to the front door, and then to the checkpoint where they had left their horses.

Not until they were on the road heading through the city to the outer gate did Tayse speak. "What did you learn?" he asked over his shoulder.

"That Ariane Rappengrass is preparing for war," Senneth replied.

She didn't seem disposed to share more, so the four of them traveled in virtual silence for the remainder of the ride. It was still relatively early in the afternoon when they made their way back to Aleatha's cottage.

Cammon was waiting for them at the front gate.

"I knew you were coming," he said in a voice of great excitement. "I could *feel* you. All four of you. Aleatha says if I concentrate, I'll eventually be able to pick up emotions from the people I know over great distances. I couldn't really sense you this time until you were about a quarter mile away," he added.

Senneth smiled at him and swung down. "And has she also helped you learn how to *not* sense the people whose emotions you don't want to feel?"

"She gave me some exercises to do," he said. "She said that as I get more adept at reading people, it will be harder to filter them out. I have to say, I was starting to get a headache, so I'm glad you're back."

Donnal had materialized from nowhere and was helping Kirra from the saddle. "So, did you learn anything from Ariane Rappengrass?" he asked, looking at Senneth.

"A great deal," she said. "Let me first check on the raelynx, and then we can all talk."

Twenty minutes later, they were assembled in Aleatha's front room, eating more pie and waiting for the mystics' report. Kirra seemed disposed to let Senneth do the talking, and Senneth did not seem at all eager to begin the discussion.

"So the marlady was happy to see you, was she?" Aleatha finally asked in her comfortable voice, as if unaware of the tension in the room.

"I don't know that *happy* is the word for it," Senneth said. "Willing. She seemed relieved to know that King Baryn is aware of the trouble brewing in the south—aware enough to send agents to investigate, at any rate."

"But she does not trust the king to take care of the trouble," Aleatha said in her gentle voice.

Senneth looked at her. "No. She doesn't."

Justin ruffled. "The king will shirk no responsibilities. He'll let nothing important slip through his hands."

Senneth looked at him, as if considering. "There appears to be some fear among the marlords of the southern Houses that the king is not paying attention to many important things."

Justin looked even more incensed. "The king is—whatever the king does—he knows what is vital and what is right."

Tayse spoke more calmly. "What is her specific allegation?"

Senneth turned her gaze toward him. He thought he had never seen her look so uncertain. "It seems there is some belief that, since the king married a few years ago, he has been—he has not—he has been somewhat distracted from his duties," Senneth said reluctantly.

Aleatha looked up, frowning. "You know, I can't really recall much about this bride of his. Is she from one of the great Houses?"

"No," Kirra said flatly.

"But surely she is noble," Aleatha said. Her face was creased in concentration, as if she was trying to remember something.

"That's just it," Kirra said. "No one knows much about her. He married her only a few months after his first wife died—and everyone in the Twelve Houses had been shocked at Queen Pella's death. She had been a Merrenstow girl, pretty and kind and tremendously popular. She hadn't even been sick, as far as anyone knew. But one day we received the news that she was ill—and two days later, word went out that she was dead. *Dead.* It was impossible to believe. She was barely forty years old."

"There are many fevers that will carry off a healthy woman within a day or two," Aleatha said gravely. "It is sad, of course, but it happens all the time."

"When those women have access to the best healers in the kingdom?" Senneth asked. "When no effort and no expense will be spared to save them?"

"So, as I say, her death came as quite a blow," Kirra continued. "And then, only months later, we learned that the king had remarried—in a private ceremony that no one from the Twelve Houses attended. It has been a puzzle ever since. Who is this woman? Where did she come from? Why did the king choose her? Why has he seemed so reluctant to show her off to the aristocracy?"

Tayse spoke up. He was not a member of the royal household, of course, but he lived a stone's throw from the palace and heard most of the gossip that filtered through those regal halls. "Queen Valri has presided over every public function King Baryn has held at court," he said. "She is the hostess when guests arrive and the proxy when the king is gone. How can you say he conceals her?"

Now Senneth's eyes, gray and perplexed, came to rest on him. "But she has not traveled far from Ghosenhall—or so Ariane Rappengrass claims," Senneth said. "She has not attended weddings in Brassenthwaite or balls in Kianlever. And she has not been to the southern provinces at all. It is as if she only feels safe at court. And since he has married her," she added, "the king has not showed much interest in traveling, either. It is, says Ariane, as if the two of them have holed themselves up in their castle and let the world around them be damned."

Tayse could see that Justin wanted to dispute this, but that the younger Rider was doing a quick mental review of the past eighteen months and realizing that the Riders had not been called upon more than three times to escort the king beyond the boundaries of the royal city.

"Does Ariane Rappengrass attribute this circumstance to anything in particular?" Tayse asked softly.

Senneth nodded. "Oh yes. She says she does not believe it, but that the whispers are drifting down from the other Houses. The king has been subverted. He has been enchanted. Queen Valri is a mystic."

Justin dropped his spoon. Aleatha and Cammon looked alarmed, and even Donnal's narrow face seemed troubled.

"Ariane was quick to say that *she* did not care whether or not the queen was a mystic," Kirra said. "But you can imagine how this scenario plays in Gisseltess. 'The queen is a mystic! She has ensnared the king in her spells! We must trample all mystics and depose the king, and make Gillengaria safe again!'"

"For a man who fears magic, this would be the worst news imaginable," Aleatha agreed.

"For the man who pretends to fear magic in order to devise a convenient excuse to foment rebellion," Kirra retorted.

"Still, even if she is a sorceress, unless she has evil intentions, what could it possibly matter?" Aleatha said.

"For a man who hates magic, that is not even a reasonable question," Senneth said. "He would ask instead, 'Can we leave such a woman in power? What if her children are mystics? Can we turn the throne of Gillengaria over to a mage?'"

"Princess Amalie is the next in line to inherit the crown," Tayse said swiftly.

Again, Senneth leveled that smoky gaze on him. "And when is the last time *you* have seen Princess Amalie?" she asked softly.

He could not answer that. It had been years since Riders had escorted the princess off the grounds of the palace, and what glimpses he got of Amalie and her stepmother were usually from a distance as they walked through gardens that Riders were not invited to enter. There was a story about some hazard the girl had survived in her childhood, and that had always served as explanation for why the king chose to keep her so safe, so close inside the palace confines. Tayse had never really given the matter much thought.

"So," said Kirra. "This is the situation. The king's wife dies—suddenly, under circumstances that some people considered strange even at the time. He remarries almost immediately, to a young woman no one has ever heard of. He seems so infatuated with his new bride that he rarely leaves the palace and makes no effort to integrate her into the upper reaches of society. His reclusive daughter has not been seen at all for at least five years. The new queen, one might think, would be eager to bear sons and daughters of her own. But if she is tainted by magic, and her heirs are tainted by the same magic, why should the good folk of Gillengaria be forced to see her evil progeny take over the throne? Isn't a man justified in calling together his friends and his neighbors, in ridding the kingdom of this great danger? Isn't he, in fact, almost required to do so, by the laws of honor and duty?"

"That's a powerful message," Tayse admitted. "Is that what Halchon Gisseltess has been spreading through the southern provinces?"

"Quietly, so far, so Ariane says," Senneth said. "But first he—and his sister—have laid the foundation of faith and fear, by spreading hatred of the mystics and promoting the sanctity of the Pale Mother. If the people first convert to fanaticism, it will not be so hard to convince them to turn against their ensorceled king."

"If he *is* ensorceled," Aleatha murmured.

"That appears to be the question," Tayse said, looking at Senneth and Kirra. "Both of you know the queen, I'm assuming."

Kirra nodded. "I spend so much time at Ghosenhall that I've dined with her often enough. But I wouldn't say I *know* her."

"I've met her a few times when I was at the palace," Senneth said.

"*Is* she a mystic?" Tayse asked.

The two women exchanged glances. Senneth answered. "I don't have any idea."

CHAPTER
17

THEY left Aleatha's by midmorning of the following day, their packs heavy with loaves of fresh bread and packets of dried meat. Senneth found that her heart was heavy as well, and it was all she could do to manufacture a smile as she bade farewell to the white-haired old woman standing at the gate, waving good-bye. Part of her did not want to leave at all—she was tired already of a journey that she knew was not yet half over, and she wanted a day or more to rest. Part of her was troubled at leaving Aleatha behind, knowing how uncertain life was for any mystic in the territory these days. She would have insisted Aleatha travel with them till they had come to someplace safe to leave her. But she knew there was no such safe place. Nowhere in the southern provinces—possibly nowhere in Gillengaria.

Once they were on the road, she made no attempt at all to be sociable, and after a while even Cammon gave up trying to talk to her. She didn't know why she was making this journey with so many in her party, anyway. Her first plan had been to travel absolutely alone, slipping in solitude and silence through the southern Houses, watching the unfolding activities like a troubled and diffident ghost. But one by one, companions had been added. Baryn had insisted she take two Riders for protection. Kirra had volunteered to accompany her—and, naturally, wherever Kirra went, Donnal must go. They had picked up Cammon in Dormas and the raelynx on the road. Now, riding northeast out of Rappengrass, Senneth found she had a new escort: Dread, riding beside her on a black horse, showing his face to no one but her.

Not that the others weren't alarmed. Not that they weren't thoughtful. But no one seemed to envision the future she imagined, filled with slaughter and despair. No one seemed to feel the same desperate sense of responsibility that she felt, as if an act of hers could avert disaster or invite it closer in. No one seemed to realize yet either the scale of the horrors to come—or the fact that there might yet be a chance to turn them aside.

So she rode in silence, but she was well aware that she did not ride alone.

She was surprised when Tayse called a halt for the noon meal. She was surprised, when she looked up from her cold rations, to find him watching her—though not at all surprised by the hard expression in his eyes.

"Now what have I done?" she asked.

"Nothing," he said. "I was just watching to make sure you remembered to eat. Since you don't seem to be remembering to speak."

She shrugged and returned her attention to her meal. Aleatha's cooking was too good to consume in this casual way, but she did not have the heart to savor it as she should. She swallowed her meat, took a drink from her water bottle, and was ready to move on before the rest of them had finished their meals.

"How far today?" Tayse asked. "Where do you want to stop for the night?"

Senneth looked at Kirra, to find Kirra watching her, awaiting her decision. Senneth shrugged again. "It doesn't matter. We won't make Nocklyn tonight. If we find a town that has an inn, we may as well stay."

"I'll be on the lookout," he said and swung himself into the saddle. They were on the move in three minutes.

Senneth lost herself in her thoughts again almost immediately. In her head, she kept hearing Ariane Rappengrass's accusation. "Some say the new queen is a mystic who has tangled the king in her coils."

Her first impulse had been to laugh. "And if she is a mystic?" she had wanted to say. "What is so terrible about that?"

But that was a child's question, thoughtless and irresponsible. In her unstructured wanderings, Senneth had come across more than one mystic who was not as principled as he should have been. It stood to reason that there were evil mystics, just as there were plenty of ordinary men who were bad. If Queen Valri indeed had supernatural abilities—and if she had used them to convince the king to marry her—what would she then want to do with the temporal power she had acquired? How would she work her magic on the king?

If Queen Valri was a mystic, was *she* the one who had sent Senneth on this quest? Perhaps *she* had said to the king, "I fear for my brother and sister mystics, who are mistreated throughout the south. Send someone you trust to test the temper of the Twelve Houses, and see if we might be staring down a civil war." If Queen Valri was a mystic, and her hold on King Baryn was not benign, would not the southern Houses be justified in rising up to fight her?

Senneth rubbed a hand across her forehead and wished it was possible to spend an hour without thinking. An hour without being. She remembered the game she had played with Cammon the other day—trying to make him think she was invisible—and how it had worked on everyone except Cammon. She wondered if there was a way to make herself invisible even to her own thoughts, to shut down, to go away—to cease, for a blessed moment, to exist.

A warm hand on her arm, a concerned voice in her ear. "Senneth." She jerked her head up to find Kirra riding next to her, grabbing hold of her as if to tether her to the ground. *Ah, but that was the problem, of course. Too many tethers already.*

"What?" Senneth asked, hoping her voice sounded normal. "Trouble?"

Kirra looked worried. "No. You—did you do that on purpose? Cam said you'd been practicing your invisibility trick."

Senneth felt irrationally pleased. "Oh, is that working? I can't tell around Cammon, of course."

Kirra dropped her hands. "You're acting so strangely."

Senneth thought about denying it, and then sighed. "I feel strange," she admitted. "I feel—worried. I feel like terrible forces are gathering, and storms are about to be unleashed, and it's somehow in my power to make the clouds part and blow away. But I don't know how."

Kirra gave her a serious look out of blue eyes that were rarely serious. Senneth had often thought, if she could choose to be anyone else, it would be Kirra. Who never had doubts, who never seemed unhappy, who was beautiful and golden and beloved. And who, even so, was nobody's foolish pet. Trouble had so rarely come Kirra's way; for that, Senneth envied her. But she had always thought that if trouble suddenly popped its ugly head directly in the middle of Kirra's path, the golden Danalustrous girl would trample right over it without a second's hesitation.

"If terrible things are coming, you probably cannot avert them," Kirra said softly. "And if they come, it will not be up to you alone to stop them. Why do you always think that? Why do you always believe there is no one nearby to help you?"

Senneth sighed and then gave a little laugh. "I guess because for so long there *was* no one. I have been on my own almost as long as you have been alive."

"Hardly," Kirra drawled. "You are only nine years older than I am."

This time her laugh was more genuine. "I feel a lifetime older. I have certainly lived more in my thirty-four years than most people I've met."

Kirra shrugged. "So you'll have better memories to review on your deathbed and fewer missed opportunities to regret."

Senneth was far from sure. "More memories," she said. "Not better ones. And far too many regrets."

Kirra, it seemed, was not about to let Senneth grow maudlin or slip back inside the dark boundaries of her own mind. "So tell me one of those memories now," she said. "One of the good ones. Tell me about sailing with the woman sea captain. What you saw in Arberharst. I have never been beyond the borders of Gillengaria."

Not too interested at first, Senneth dutifully began reciting the tale of her voyages on the *Fair Luck,* but she found herself warming to the tale before she was five minutes in. She had liked the adventuring—she had loved the ocean—she had even, from time to time, been relieved to lose her constant, inescapable sense of occult power. An ordinary woman, for once, just like the rest of them. No more capable, no more responsible, than anyone else on the ship. She had not had that sense of freedom and ordinariness since she—well, she had not ever had it. She had been born with the knowledge of fire curled in her hands.

Kirra's little trick worked, though; Senneth found herself growing more cheerful as she talked, as they continued down the road. She was even able to bear without much disappointment the knowledge that they were going to have to camp out that night. The past few days had spoiled her, spoiled them all. They were used to a roof over their heads and good cooking on the hearth. None of them would look forward to a cold camp on ground half made of mud and half covered in snow.

But the Bright Lady smiled on them again even as she began her elaborate preparations for night. Just as the sky began to streak with violet and pink, they rounded a curve in the road and came across a small town. It was tucked away in an overhang of trees, and it looked as though not more than fifty souls lived there all told, but there was a rickety-looking tavern with a barn out back, so there was a good chance they could find a place to stay. Even Senneth was smiling as they rode up.

"I'll ask about accommodations," Tayse said and slid from the saddle. Justin took his reins and then sat there, critically surveying the scene. There was little to consider, Senneth thought: There was only the main road running through the town, with maybe ten buildings on one side of it and half a dozen on the other. The Riders looked for danger everywhere they rode, but Senneth thought they would be disappointed here.

Her own worry was for the raelynx, who even now stalked through the undergrowth a few hundred yards from the town, snarling at the nearness of humans. She had fed him well before they left Aleatha's, and he had seemed perfectly content to pace beside them all day, not attempting to run off, even though he must have sensed her own concentration slipping. That would have been dreadful indeed—if her black mood had given the rae-lynx a quick chance for freedom, and he had taken it and disappeared somewhere into the woods of northern Rappengrass to carry on years of depredations. Ariane might not have been so happy then to welcome Senneth back to her house once her roving days were over.

Then again, Senneth did not anticipate the day all her wandering would be done.

Tayse emerged from the tavern looking philosophical. "No beds, but we can sleep in the barn, and stable our horses there, too," he said. "It's empty except for the tavern keeper's cow and the broken bits of furniture he stores there."

He was looking at Senneth as he spoke, awaiting her confirmation or rejection, so she nodded. "I'm not proud," she said. "I'll sleep in a barn. Serra Kirra?"

"I've slept in worse," Kirra said sunnily. "If there's a roof and a floor, I'm happy."

They actually rather liked the barn, which looked more like someone's old attic. It was crammed with splintered tables, chairs that were missing one leg, a bed that appeared to have given way to a man who weighed more than the joints could sustain. The smells inside were rich and varied, of stale hay, green wood, warm manure, and fresh milk. There wasn't much extra room—it appeared as though the innkeeper kept one aisle clear from the door to the stall where the cow was shut up. Furniture and kitchen clutterings took up most of the rest of the space.

"This will be a challenge," Tayse said. "I'm not sure there's even room for the horses."

"Well, let's start rearranging," Justin said.

The men began moving furniture while the women investigated. Kirra petted the cow, who did not seem particularly alarmed at the sudden onslaught of guests. No doubt she often shared her quarters with travelers, Senneth thought. The presence of the raelynx made her a little nervous, though, and she shifted under Kirra's hand as the cat padded in and greeted his new quarters with a whistling hiss.

"*You* are the real problem," Senneth told him. He was close enough to her that she could touch him, if he would let her. She willed him to hold still while she knelt beside him, but she did not quite have the nerve to put her fingers to his fur. He regarded her from malevolent eyes and seemed to wait to see what she might do next.

She could tame him, she thought. If she had the time, and no distractions, and if it had been a good idea, she could bring him to heel and even make him love her. But she could meet none of those conditions. She sighed and came to her feet.

"Senneth," Justin called—startling her a little, since he rarely addressed her directly and never by name. "There's a cage or something over here. Looks like the innkeeper may have had a dog run at some point. You might be able to keep your creature here tonight."

She went over to look, and sure enough, barricaded behind an armoire with two missing drawers was a sturdy pen about six feet by seven. It had a slatted roof and a thick door held shut by a leather belt.

"That's good," she said. "We can even leave him here while we go in for dinner.

"If you can *get* him in there," Justin observed.

She grinned. "I think I can."

The raelynx resisted, of course, snarling and spitting, but her will was still stronger than his, and he was eventually settled inside the pen. Senneth looped the belt through a couple times, set the buckle, and then breathed a spell of stability over it. The raelynx yowled once, just to prove he was not happy, and then stretched out on the old straw and shut his eyes.

Tayse came up behind her. "He secure?"

She nodded. "Let's go eat."

The tavern was dark and smelled of onions. Maybe a dozen men were seated inside, hunched over their meals and arguing over local politics or the best way to break a horse. The newcomers received a fairly thorough inspection as they entered, though their arrival could hardly have been a surprise; the tavern keeper had no doubt repeated to his clientele every word Tayse had said when he walked in asking for accommodations. Still, they were strangers, and they deserved a looking over. Not even Justin and Tayse seemed to be offended.

They found an open table at the back, and all six sat around it, choosing seats as they so often did: Senneth between Kirra and Cammon, Donnal beside Kirra, Tayse across from Senneth, and Justin between Cammon and Tayse. Everyone choosing to sit beside the ones they liked and to watch the ones they distrusted.

They were approached by a yellow-haired tavern girl wearing a low-cut dress that showed off her considerable charms. Even had they been likely to miss the full swell of her breasts, the necklace she wore pointed attention to those features. It was a silver chain hung with an obelisk of a moonstone that nestled just inside her cleavage. Senneth glanced at Kirra, to see her grinning, and at Justin, to see his eyes focused directly on the glower of the sulky gem. Tayse did not appear to have registered either the girl's jewelry or her attractions, but Senneth was sure he had noticed both. Tayse noticed everything.

"We've got beef pie and venison pie," the girl said in a bored voice, though she managed to smile at Cammon and Justin. Both were smiling at her. "Oh, and some potatoes. The greens are all gone, though. And there's beer. Also, some leftover chicken from yesterday if you want that."

"Beef pie, potatoes, and beer," Tayse said without seeming to consider at all. Justin echoed him. Cammon and Donnal opted for venison, and the women chose chicken.

The server was barely out of earshot before Cammon exclaimed, "Did you see it? Her moonstone? I wonder if the whole town's gone over to the Pale Lady."

Kirra turned marveling eyes toward Senneth. "She was wearing a moonstone necklace? I didn't notice such a thing, did you?"

"Tavern keeper had on a moonstone bracelet," Tayse said, ignoring her. "Two of the men up at the bar were wearing pendants. I'd say it's not the place to be practicing magic."

"And I was going to jump on the table, turn myself into a wolf, and go baying to the moon," Donnal said.

"Don't bother trying to impress *us*," Justin said. "We're impressed enough already."

"We're just here overnight," Senneth said peaceably. "No need to draw attention."

Tayse gave her a rather darkling look. "A good plan. We don't seem to live up to it all that often."

The food, when it arrived, was fair. The beer was excellent. Senneth imagined there wasn't much to do in this part of the country except drink, which meant the locals probably spent a lot of time perfecting their brews.

They had just finished their meals and were considering ordering a second round of drinks when the tavern door blew open, and a young girl burst in. Even Cammon seemed caught off guard by her sudden eruption into the room, and Tayse and Justin whirled around so quickly that they were almost on their feet before they realized there was probably no danger.

To them, anyway. The girl seemed hysterical. "Please, Markle, can you send your wife? My sister's having the baby, but it won't come, and she keeps screaming. I don't know what to do—and my brothers won't help—and old Hadda, who said she'd come, doesn't answer her door."

The tavern keeper shook his head regretfully. "Sorry, Sosie, but my wife's over to her sister's. Left this morning. You can take Liza, if you think she'll do you any good, but she's afraid of blood and never helped at any birthing that I know of."

Sosie released a groaning sob. "But she'll—Markle, I think the baby's breech or something. He won't come out, and I think he's ripping up her insides. She's going to die—they're both going to die—and I don't know what to do."

"Might be better that way," Markle said, polishing a glass and setting it on the wood of the bar. "You know—with your sister's troubles."

Senneth had been watching attentively anyway, but at that, she raised her eyebrows and gave Kirra one quick look. Kirra's expression matched the one she could feel on her own face.

Sosie choked with fury and then started crying. "It will not be better if she dies! You—did my father tell you to send your wife away? Did he tell you not to help me if I came to you? She's *dying*, Markle. After the baby's born, she'll leave—we'll both leave. But she's *dying*! How can a good man let such a terrible thing happen?"

Senneth was on her feet before the last sentence was even spoken. Tayse said, "We weren't going to draw attention to ourselves," but she brushed by him, Kirra at her heels. She was beside Sosie before the weeping girl even knew there was a stranger in the room. She put her hand cautiously on the girl's arm.

"We'll help you," she said softly, and Sosie whipped around to stare at her through red-rimmed eyes. "My friend is a healer, and I have a little skill in that area myself. Your sister won't die."

For a moment, an array of conflicting emotions crossed the girl's face: hope, fear, distrust, and a basic desire for honesty that almost led her to speak the secret Senneth had already guessed. Fear for her sister won out. "Can you come right now?" she whispered.

"Yes," Senneth said.

A small parade followed Sosie as she hurried out into the night, for Tayse and Justin were not about to let the women go anywhere unescorted, and the other two saw no reason to be left behind. Though Senneth fancied she saw a little relief on Donnal's face when she asked him to go back and stay with the raelynx.

"We won't need you at this task," she told him as she jogged along behind Kirra and Sosie. "And I think he'll be calmer if one of us is near."

He nodded and dropped back. Cammon hurried up to take his place beside Senneth. "What do you think it is?" he puffed. "The woman in labor is a mystic?"

Senneth nodded. "Or the baby is. Or the baby's father was, and they fear that the child will be as well. Some kind of magic is afoot, no doubt."

He grinned. "Tayse isn't going to be happy about this."

"When is Tayse ever happy?"

The way to Sosie's house was some distance off the main road through a rutted track and a tangle of scrubby trees. The house itself was unprepossessing, small and ill-built, with a few sheds and lean-tos on the back. Clearly the family members weren't farmers, so Senneth guessed they hunted or hired out for seasonal labor. Or lived off poaching and thievery; who knew? She fell in step beside Kirra and entered the dimly lit house two paces behind Sosie. The men crowded in behind them.

A quick look gave her all the particulars. They stood in a low-beamed room crammed with threadbare furniture and four people arguing. Wretched moans were issuing through a door to the left—the bedroom where the pregnant woman lay, apparently. Sosie and Kirra headed straight there without pausing, slipping inside the room before anyone else in the house had even acknowledged their presence.

Senneth waited for the inevitable explosion.

"Hey!" That came from the small, wiry, furious man whom Senneth took to be the patriarch of the family. He looked as if he wanted to run after his daughter and the unknown woman but felt compelled to confront the mass of strangers at his door. "Who are—what do you—get out of my house, whoever you are!"

Behind him, his two sons deployed; a weeping woman collapsed on a battered sofa, apparently too spent to care who entered her house or why. Senneth faced the men, speaking in her calmest and most persuasive voice.

"My name is Senneth. My friend Kirra and I have been traveling to Nocklyn on personal business. This is our escort. We were at the tavern when your daughter rushed in, asking for help. Kirra is a healer of quite remarkable skill. It seemed only humane to come as quickly as we could and offer our services to save a woman's life."

The man spat directly on the floor mere inches from Senneth's foot. She did not even flinch. It had not escaped her notice that his ragged pants were belted in place with a buckle studded with moonstones. "Better for this baby not to be born," he said.

"Surely the Pale Lady welcomes all new life to the world," she said softly.

"Not tainted life. Not evil life," he retorted.

A shriek came from the other room, followed swiftly by the

sound of Sosie's frantic weeping and Kirra's soothing voice. The woman on the sofa sobbed and buried her face in her hands.

"Don't need to worry about it, Da," one of the young men said. "She's not gonna pull through this."

"Baby'll kill her coming out," said the other. "Kill hisself, too, most like."

"Not my Annie, not my Annie," the woman on the couch moaned.

"She might die," Senneth nodded. "But between us, I believe Kirra and I can probably save them both."

"Don't want them saved!" the father said savagely. "Don't you understand plain speaking? The child's wicked! The Pale Mother is striking him down now before he can do any harm!"

She held on to her calm, but it was a struggle; fury piled like dry kindling in every vein, waiting to be ignited. "What is it you accuse him of?" she asked. "Why does such a helpless thing deserve your hatred?"

He came a step closer and practically sprayed her face with saliva. "He's a mystic's bastard, and he bears mystic powers," he said venomously. "Since he's lain in my daughter's belly, he's corrupted her with his spiteful magic—she's done things and seen things that I—" He shook his head, unable to put his disgust into words. "Maybe once he's out of her, he and his poison blood, she'll be my good Annie again, but I'm afraid he's turned her. I'm afraid she's lost to us now. The Pale Mother knows what to do with people who have been given over to magic."

"I'm sure Annie will be happy enough to leave your house once she and the child are well enough to travel," Senneth said, still speaking quietly, still behaving reasonably. Not for long, though; oh, not for long. She could feel her shoulders aching with her desire to set this man on fire. She could feel a headache lurking on the highest knob of her spine.

"They will not leave here alive!" the father roared, and lunged for the open doorway of the bedroom. His wife screamed. His sons shouted.

Senneth knocked him backward with a swipe of her fist. He cried out and put his hand to his burning shoulder. "You will not disturb the birthing bed," she said, her voice low and menacing. "You will not harm your daughter, or her child, or you yourself will not live through this night."

He came at her again, and she flung her hands before her, radiating such heat from her fingertips that he retreated, coughing and cursing and brushing at his face. Behind her, she heard the smooth metallic glide of swords being pulled from scabbards, but she did not turn to see what sort of threat Tayse and Justin were offering to the household. She was dangerous enough on her own.

"What right do you have to come into my home and give me orders?" the man panted. His sons massed uncertainly behind him, but came no closer to Senneth. His wife had stopped sobbing and now stared at the whole tableau, her mouth open in astonishment. "Who are you? What are you? Damned mystic like my daughter's son?"

She couldn't stop herself; she placed her hands on his shoulders and pushed him, hard. He screamed, and scorch marks appeared on his shirt as he tumbled backward.

"If you try to harm that baby," she said in hard, precise words, "I will burn your house down around your head. I will set your flesh on fire. No prayer to the Pale Lady, no moonstone around your waist, will save you from my magic. She is safe, do you hear me? You cannot kill her."

He was a man not used to being thwarted or threatened, and even his fear could not dampen his sudden burst of rage. He uttered a wordless yell and launched himself at her across the floor.

And then Senneth went a little mad.

She threw a fireball at him, rolling up his stomach, over his head, and down his back. She tossed sprays of red heat at his sons, who started her way and then stumbled back, batting at the air and covering their heads with their arms. She gestured at the curtains, and they burst into flames—at the scarred wooden rocker, and it burst into flames—at the central pole of the house connecting floor and ceiling, and it burst into flames. The room grew so hot it seemed as if the air itself might kindle at any moment.

"Stay where you are," she warned, as the three men stood rooted to the spot, looking about them in horror. "Nothing will be harmed if you do not approach me or your daughter's room. If you make a move in her direction, the whole house will burn. Except the room where your daughter lies laboring."

"You're a sorceress," the man whispered, half afraid and half furious. "The Pale Mother curses you."

"I'm not afraid of your paltry little goddess," Senneth said in contempt. "Or you fools who worship her. Now stay back from me."

And she turned on her heel and entered the room where the woman Annie was giving birth. She saw shadows behind her and knew that Tayse and Justin had moved to guard the door. Where Cammon was during all this she had no idea. She tried not to think about it; she tried to close her mind to every thought except what might be going on right now in this small, dark room where magic waited to be born.

CHAPTER
18

KIRRA and Sosie, positioned on either side of the bloody bed, looked up as Senneth strode in. Kirra looked very sober, Sosie terrified. The woman between them was white as death already. Her dark hair lay spread on her pillow; her eyes were closed against pain. It seemed possible at any moment that she would breathe her last.

"Can you save her?" Senneth asked baldly.

"I'm not sure," Kirra answered. "But I can save the baby."

"Please." A whisper from the laboring woman. "Please save him. Let me go."

Sosie started crying again and leaned over the bed, touching her own forehead to her sister's face. "No, Annie, no, Annie, you can't die. You can't leave me behind."

"What's the situation out there?" Kirra asked.

"No one will disturb us," Senneth replied.

"Then help me," Kirra said. "If you can stop the bleeding—"

"Oh yes," Senneth said, "I can do that."

They fought for the next two hours to bring the troublesome infant into the world. Annie struggled in and out of consciousness, laboring for her child's life even more than her own. She barely had the strength to scream when Senneth's hands cauterized her bleeding womb, but that touch seemed to improve the overall situation somewhat. At least there was a little less blood afterward.

But. "She's fading, Sen," Kirra said as that second hour crept past. "Can you—is there some way—"

"Is there a way I can hold her soul in place?" Senneth finished. "I'll do what I can."

Sosie looked up in some alarm as Senneth shifted position, moving up toward the head of the bed. Sosie herself merely sat as close to her sister as she could, clutching her hand and repeating how much she loved her. "What are you going to do?" she whispered.

"Try to detain her," Senneth said.

"Will it hurt?"

Senneth almost laughed. There was so much pain in the room already that the question seemed ridiculous. Senneth herself was dizzy with a headache that pressed in on the top of her head like a row of chisels being hammered with an axe. But her body still raged with fire; she was hot with magic. "Everything hurts," she replied, which she very well knew was not a comforting answer. "Living hurts. This is something you want her to feel."

She perched on the edge of the bed and put one hand on Annie's forehead, one hand on her chest, overlaying her heart. The woman hissed at the sudden fiery touch. "That's right," Senneth murmured. "You can feel that. You are still inside this cage of bones."

"Sen," Kirra said suddenly. "I've almost got the baby."

Senneth nodded. The baby was no longer her concern; Annie was. She could feel the ebb and flow of blood under her fingertips, the cool clamminess of the skin as Annie's will and strength failed. As her soul evaporated, insubstantial as breath. "No," Senneth murmured, "you will not escape that easily."

The heat of her own body seeped into Annie's veins and began circulating through her dormant form. Senneth could feel the woman's temperature rise, degree by degree. Still, Annie's heartbeat faltered; still, her lungs did not have the strength to fill and empty. Senneth pushed down harder, released even more warmth onto the chilled flesh. She pressed heavily on the reluctant heart, forcing it to work.

Annie sighed once and turned her head to one side. She did not breathe again.

"Annie!" Sosie screamed. "Annie!"

"No, you don't," Senneth said softly. "Not this time. Not now." And she bent down and covered Annie's cool lips with her own. She closed her eyes and breathed, imagining all her vitality, all her power, passing from her body into Annie's. She imagined her breath like a bright butterfly, skipping down the interior corridors of Annie's bones, leaving color and a sparkle of life everywhere it flew.

Annie gasped, choked, and then spasmed on the bed. Suddenly she gulped in great gusts of air, and twisted violently where she lay.

"Got him," Kirra exclaimed, and a few sounds of slickness were followed by a hiccuping cry. "A boy, just like you thought. Lady's tears, but he's a big one."

Sosie's eyes went indecisively from Annie's face to Kirra's. "Do you—do you need me?"

The boy choked once and began a long, indignant wail. "No. I can handle him," Kirra said. She rose and carried the infant across the room where water and rags were laid out.

Sosie bent over to whisper in her sister's ear, and her hair brushed Senneth's hand on Annie's forehead. "Did you hear that?" she asked. "That's your son crying. Listen to him! Hear how strong he is! But he needs you, Annie—don't let him go— stay with him—"

Annie's mouth moved, but no sound came out. From the other side of the room, Senneth could hear the infant still bawling, could catch sounds of splashing water and ripping linen, and Kirra's soft, reassuring voice. But she paid attention to none of it. All her focus was on Annie.

The woman's eyes were open, and she was staring up at Senneth as if at the Bright Mother herself, source of all life. Clinging to the image of Senneth's face, willing herself to stay alert, stay alive. Senneth shifted her hand on Annie's face and saw the red imprint of her palm on the pale forehead. Heat from her body still poured through her fingers into Annie's blood. Annie's heartbeat seemed more certain, less erratic. Her breath was more even, more determined. The wan face was brushed along the cheeks with the faintest hint of color.

From across the room, there was the sound of glass crashing to the floor.

Sosie flinched at the noise and jumped up, Annie's hand still in her grasp. "What was—did you drop something?"

Kirra was cursing. "By the Bright Mother, the Pale Lady, and all the forgotten gods! No, I didn't drop anything. *Who* was it who found your sister's bed and got this child upon her?"

Sosie stood indecisively, looking down at Annie, then over at Kirra. "I—some boy. He was with a group of peddlers who stayed at the village for a week or two. Annie said he could do amazing things—juggle plates and glasses and a cannonball—even without touching them, she said. I didn't believe her, of course."

"Well, I don't know what god would make that kind of magic, but it seems like this little one has inherited his father's skills," Kirra said. Her voice was partly amused, partly exasperated, and not a little afraid. "He just knocked over the water pitcher from three feet away."

A moment's silence. "Are you sure?" Sosie said blankly.

"Well, *I* didn't touch it," Kirra answered.

Senneth smiled down at Annie, who was still concentrating on her face with all the strength in her body. "Did you hear that?" Senneth crooned. "Your son has amazing strength. He will be a powerful man. But he needs you right now. He is so small, and he is so afraid. He will stumble and hurt himself if you aren't beside him to help him—"

"I—will help him," Annie said.

They were the first words she'd spoken for two hours. Sosie whimpered and fell to her knees beside the bed, kissing her sister's knuckles. "Annie, Annie, are you all right? Can you hear me?"

"I'm—I can hear you," Annie whispered.

Kirra came over, the wrapped infant in her arms, and stood beside Senneth. "And is she? Going to be all right?"

"I think so," Senneth said. "She's weak, of course. But she seems to have—come back to life."

"Thank you," Annie whispered.

"Hush," Sosie said. "Save your strength."

Annie moved her lips silently, her eyes now on Kirra's face. Kirra smiled and bent down, holding the fierce bundle close to her. "Can you see him? Isn't that a fine little face? I'm going to put him right up to your mouth, so you can give him a kiss, and then I'm going to take him away so you can rest."

This maneuver accomplished, Kirra crossed the room again, bouncing the baby in her arms. Sosie looked over at Senneth. "What do I do now?" she asked. "How do I take care of them?"

Yes, Senneth had realized all along that this might be an even more vexing question than how to keep mother and child alive during the labor process. "Can you trust your mother?" she asked. "Or does she do what your father tells her?"

"She's afraid of him," Sosie replied. "But I think—if Annie and the baby are alive—she'll defy him and help us."

Senneth nodded. "Good. For the short term, I'm going to put a ward on this room. A—a spell of protection. Only you and your sister and your mother will be able to leave and enter the room. Unless there's someone else you can count on who might come by at some point to help."

"Hadda," Sosie said. "She hates my father."

Senneth nodded. "It will be a while before your sister is strong enough to move. But when she is—I'm afraid you're going to have to leave here. Go someplace safer."

"I know," Sosie said. "We had planned—we were going to leave this week—but then the baby started coming—"

"It will be difficult," Senneth warned. "Not just because your sister will be weak, but because the baby is not like other babies. That pitcher he broke—that won't be the only thing he breaks. If he has the power to lift and hurl objects across the room—well—"

"How can we keep him safe?" Sosie burst out. "Or us? And if we go somewhere and people are afraid of mystics—"

"I know," said Senneth. "You're going to have to learn to control him."

Sosie stared at her. "I don't know how to control magic. I don't have a mystical bone in my body. Annie, either."

"I know," Senneth said again. "You're going to have to go someplace where someone can help you. I'm going to draw you a map to the house of a woman who lives not far from Rappen Manor. She's a mystic. She can teach your sister what she needs to know. But I don't know how long you'll be safe with Aleatha. There are—there are a lot of people these days who hate and fear us. As soon as you can, I think you should take your sister and her baby and travel to Ghosenhall. Aleatha can give you names of some friends there. So far, the king has protected mystics. You will be as safe there as you will be anywhere."

"We'll go there," Sosie whispered.

A small crashing sound came from across the room—something little tipped to the floor, Senneth guessed—and was followed by a "Damn it!" from Kirra. Senneth could not repress a smile. "What you're going to have to do," she said, "in order to even make it safely to Rappengrass, is to check the baby's power."

"How do I do that?"

"Bind him with a moonstone. Wrap it in a piece of cotton and tuck it inside his crib, or tie it around his waist. Don't let it touch his skin, or it will burn him."

Sosie's eyes dropped to the bracelet glowing diamond-white around Senneth's wrist. "You're a mystic. You're wearing moonstones, and they don't seem to burn you."

"I'm different," Senneth said.

Kirra called in a low voice, "And the sooner you get that piece of moonstone, the better. I wouldn't want him to fall asleep without it. I'm guessing his power will be even wilder when he dreams."

Senneth nodded, watching Sosie. "So, do you understand? Do you realize what you must do?"

"I think so. Give my nephew an amulet, stay here in this enchanted room till my sister is healed, then run to a mystic in Rappengrass. Then, when everyone is strong enough, go to Ghosenhall—where we might be safe, but we might not."

Senneth smiled. "How old are you, Sosie?"

The surprise showed on Sosie's face. "Seventeen."

"It's hard to have to do so much when you're so young," Senneth said. "Hard to have to be so responsible. But I can see you're strong enough. I can tell you won't fail them."

Sosie tilted her chin up. Her cheeks were streaked with dried tears, and her lips were red from the many times she had bitten them during this grueling night. "No," she said. "I won't fail them."

"Listen," Senneth said. "Do you have something—a rock, a necklace, something hard and pretty and small, something that you like? Not a moonstone," she added.

Sosie nodded, bewildered. "Yes—a stone I found down at the river one day when I was a little girl. It was washed smooth by the water, and I thought it was unusual, so I kept it."

Senneth nodded. "Is it in this room? Do you sleep here with your sister? Good. Get it now."

Sosie dropped Annie's hand and stepped away from the bed. Senneth glanced down at Annie, who was now sleeping, and laid her hand on the pale forehead. Cool, but a reasonable coolness. Her pulse felt strong and unfaltering under Senneth's touch.

Sosie was back beside her in a matter of moments, holding out an egg-sized piece of rose quartz. "Excellent," Senneth said, turning it over and over in her hands. She closed her fist around it, feeling against her palm its imperfect smoothness, marred by shallow faults and tiny pitted dimples. It had formed in the churning fire of the earth, turned to icy stone in the clutch of a stern mountain, and been tamed to a silky beauty by the relentless patting of the river's hands. It was an elemental thing with elemental energy, and Senneth woke every memory of power in its crystal veins.

She extended her hand to Sosie, whose face showed awe and wariness. "This will give you some—protection—when you need it most," Senneth said. "Carry it in your pocket, or in a bag on a cord around your neck. When you are in need of comfort, or hope, or courage, or physical strength, put your hand around it. It will not fail you."

Somewhat gingerly, Sosie picked the quartz stone from Senneth's hand. By her expression, she received a definite jolt when her fingers touched the rock, but it was not an unpleasant one. "How long will its—its power last?" she asked.

Senneth shrugged. "Years. Forever. It is not the kind of power that ever fades."

Sosie glanced down at her sleeping sister. "Can you make one for Annie as well?"

For the second or third time in this hellacious night, Senneth smiled. "Yes," she said. "I can. Give me something she cherishes that you can take with you on the road."

Kirra was watching this little enchantment with great interest, but she made no comments and asked no questions. "Is the baby asleep?" Senneth asked.

"Finally," Kirra said. "Once you're done bespelling rocks, perhaps Sosie can go hunting for a moonstone to tuck into the cradle. I don't want him to have nightmares that manage to manifest themselves."

Sosie reappeared at Senneth's side, a small chunk of fool's gold in one hand and a delicate moonstone necklace in the other. "I'll wrap this up right now and lay it by his feet," she said. "And then—and then—I don't know what then!"

"And then you'll sleep," Kirra said.

"No," said Sosie, "first I'll clean up Annie."

Sosie was still bending over the baby's bed when a small commotion at the door caused the two mystics to hurry that way. There was a small, round, white-haired woman arguing before Justin's and Tayse's crossed swords. Behind them, the main room still burned with pillars of implacable fire.

"Let me see her! I've come to help! Gone one day, one damn day of the whole month, and it's the day poor Annie needs me, and I come here to find the whole house on fire and crazy men at the door. *Let me through,* I say!"

Senneth peered around Tayse, who was so big he blocked most of the door. "Are you Hadda?" she asked.

The woman leveled hot blue eyes on her. "Yes, who are you? What are you doing in there? How's my Annie?"

"Let her in," Senneth said.

Two steps behind her came Annie's mother, deathly pale and shaking with fear. She came just to the threshold, not chancing either the drawn swords or the magic loose inside the room.

"Is she—I heard the baby cry—but is Annie—" she whispered. Her hands twisted before her, tangling in her apron.

"Annie is sleeping, but she lives," Senneth said in a gentle voice. "If you want to come in, you can. Your husband and your sons will not be allowed into this room."

The woman's face brightened. "She's—alive? She'll be— she'll be fine? She'll be my old Annie?"

Senneth held back her fresh surge of anger. "The baby is mystic," she said. "I don't know if he spilled any power into Annie's blood. She'll live, I'm fairly certain of that, especially if she has good nursing. But I can't guarantee she will ever be—the way you remember her—or the way you want her."

A little sob escaped the woman, and she stood in front of the Riders, trembling and indecisive. Senneth could actually see her shift her weight from foot to foot, as if she would come forward, as if she would back away.

"Hadda and Sosie will care for her, as much as they're able," Senneth said. "But she will need you, I think. My friends and I must leave this house in a few minutes, and we will be gone from the town by morning. We cannot help her any more than we have. She needs you."

A moment longer Annie's mother paused on the threshold. Senneth chanced a quick look around the main room but couldn't see any of the men of the household. Chased out, perhaps, by the heat of the steadily burning furnishings. Or down in the tavern even now, telling their tale and gathering a coalition of like-minded men to go hunting mystics.

From inside the bedroom, a muffled exclamation from Hadda and a short, sharp cry from Annie. "I must go to her," the woman decided, and brushed by the Riders and Senneth to hurry to her daughter's side.

Tayse kept his body facing outward, ready to absorb any hostilities that came from the main room, but he turned his head to give Senneth a look of inquiry. "Truly?" he asked, in a voice edged with disbelief. "We're leaving in a few minutes?"

She almost smiled. "There's not much more we can do here. Or, rather, there are hours of things left to do, but they are mundane chores that other women can handle. We had best leave while we can, is my thinking."

"Should we even stay the night in this town?" Justin asked.

She sighed. "I hope we can. But I don't know."

Kirra appeared at Senneth's shoulder. "I've said our good-byes," she said. "That Hadda—no one said so, but I'm guessing she's got a hint of magic in her hands. We can safely leave our patient with her."

"Then let's go," Senneth said.

She pushed between Tayse and Justin, Kirra one step behind her. Once in the main room, she paused a moment. It was tempting, but she really couldn't leave the house filled with sorcerous fire. A wave of her fingers, and the flames were doused on the curtains, on the wooden rocker, on the sturdy beam in the center of the room. A half turn, and she was facing the bedroom doorway again, mouthing new spells for a different kind of fire, safe for some, hazardous for others. She had no idea how long it would be before Annie was well enough to travel, so she bewitched the room for six months. For which period of time, neither Annie's father nor her brothers nor any neighbors except Hadda would be able to enter that room . . . and by the time the spell had faded, they might have given up trying. She shrugged a little and pivoted toward the front door.

"Time to leave," she said.

Cammon scrambled up from a seat on the floor where he had been leaning against a wall. "Trouble outside," he said.

She looked at him. Behind her, she heard Tayse and Justin draw their weapons again. "How many?"

"Fifteen men, maybe. I can hear them arguing—and boasting—
'Send the mystic out, I'll see if she frightens *me*!' Things like
that."

She nodded. "They've probably been drinking, too."

Tayse edged past her. "I'll go first."

She strode ahead of him. The fire in her blood, which had
calmed to a charcoal sludge in the last twenty minutes or so, had
sparked again to a yellow-gold heat. "Oh no," she said, yanking
the door open, "let me."

She stood in the doorway a moment, the light behind her, letting them see her, getting a quick look at them. Hard to see in the
dark, but she thought Cammon's guess was accurate: fifteen or
twenty men, grumbling, posturing, feeding off of each other's
fear and bravado, ready to fight it out with the mystic.

Well, let them try to take her on.

"That's her," said a familiar voice—Annie's father—and suddenly the mob of men was swelling toward them, voices ugly,
faces snarling, hands suddenly silver with weapons. Tayse and
Justin pressed the women between them; Cammon had his back
to Kirra's. Senneth waited until the oncoming men were almost
close enough to be slashed by the Riders' swords and then flung
her arms up over her head.

Instantly, the whole throng tripped backward as men shouted
out and cursed and rubbed their hands across their faces and fell
back even farther.

"Stand away from us," Senneth said in a commanding voice.
"We will do you no harm if you let us pass."

"We're the ones will do *you* harm," one of the bolder men
called out, and a few of the others raised their voices in agreement.

She was furious again, suddenly and violently, and fire poured
through her in a blind and painful rush. She made a pushing motion with her hands, and the mob stumbled back even farther as
the men cried out and fell to the ground and jumped up again,
hopping on the hot ground, choking on the burning air. She
pushed again, incinerating the air between them, making them
feel as if flames were licking at their feet and skin. A few of them
turned and ran then, too afraid to stay and fight; ten or so remained, even angrier, milling around as if trying to find a cool
breach in her defense, a safe place from which to launch an assault.

"Witch!" came from many throats. "Mystic! Sorceress! The Pale Lady damns you to her icy hell!"

"Get away from my house!" Annie's father shouted, coming as close as he dared till heat drove him back a pace or two. Senneth could see the sweat speckling his face. "Get away from here! Leave my daughters alone!"

She *hated* him so much that her head almost split apart. She made fists and then snapped her fingers open, spraying him with fire. He howled and danced backward; she did it again. Then she made two thin tubes of her hands, one stacked in front of the other, and blew her hot breath through them, and Annie's father stood in a living column of flame.

Everyone else in the whole clearing stood silent and unmoving as stone.

"Do—not—challenge—me," she said in a deadly voice. Annie's father screamed and jumped in his cage of fire, turning from side to side, desperate to escape. He wouldn't die—she thought—but he would be singed and drained of sweat by the time this blaze burned out. "Do not follow me. Do not enter that house and try to harm those girls or take that baby. *Stand back!*" All the men scrambled back another two or three feet. "We're sleeping tonight in the barn behind Markle's tavern. If anyone—*anyone*—attempts to disturb us, I will burn down every building in town. If anyone leaves tonight, riding for help, I will stop him before he's twenty yards away. We will be gone by morning, and you can tell what tales you wish then."

And she turned on her heel and stalked through the scrubby forest, back toward the road, toward the town. Behind her, the tower of fire still burned on no fuel but fury, as if it would burn till the end of time.

CHAPTER
19

NO one spoke to her as they made the short trip back and flung themselves inside the barn. Donnal was on his feet, looking from face to face. "What happened?" he demanded.

Only Kirra would answer. "Senneth didn't like the father's attitude and put on a display," she said. "A few townspeople came to add their voices to the protest, so she made the display even more impressive."

Donnal's eyes traveled to Senneth's face and back to Kirra's. "What about the baby?"

"Mystic-born," Kirra said, "but he'll be fine."

"What about that man?" Justin asked. "How long will he burn?"

Senneth saw the expression that crossed Donnal's face at that question. "Maybe an hour," she said shortly. "He won't be harmed. Much. How's the raelynx?"

It took Donnal a moment to realize she was addressing him. "Edgy. I think he can sense your moods."

"Tonight, I don't think you have to be a wild creature or an impressionable mystic to sense Senneth's mood," Kirra said.

It was too hot in here—too close—she couldn't breathe. "I'm going outside for a while," Senneth said, and headed for the door. Behind her she heard Justin ask, "I suppose we post a guard tonight," and Tayse reply dryly, "I suppose we do."

Outside, the frosty air was not even remotely cold enough to chill her blood. She wanted to find a river of winter ice and throw herself through the hard surface into the sluggish, frigid water below. Her skin was so hot she would turn the whole creek to steam; she would fill the whole forest with fog.

Her skin was so hot she might catch these harmless woods on fire just by brushing against a bare tree limb or setting her foot carelessly on a pile of withered leaves.

She pushed through the undergrowth, paying little attention to where she was going, trying only to put some distance between herself and the barn, herself and all living creatures. *Gods,* but her head screeched in agony; she wanted to reach up and rip it from her shoulders, toss it aside like a toxic ball. She knew from bitter experience that once the fire receded from her veins, leaving her spent and powerless, her head would feel even worse.

Hard as that was to imagine.

Suddenly, in the middle of her heedless charge away from the settlement, she was too weary to take another step. She sank to the ground right where she stood, by chance landing on a soft pile of pine needles, and pulled herself into the smallest possible shape. She hated them all, these smug, stupid, self-righteous townsfolk who dared to declare themselves better than someone else—dared to pretend their religion, their humanity, their bone structure made them right and everyone else wrong. Dared to say, "You're different, and you deserve to die." Well, she was different, and she would show them who deserved death.

She pulled her knees up and laid her cheek on the curved bones, cradling her head in her arms. But the problem was, she did not believe in exercising the power in her body to carry out such sentences. How was she any more capable of judging good and evil, of meting out punishment and reward, than these grim, fearful, and arrogant men? She hated them, but they hated her; maybe she was the canker, the witch, the atrocity they believed. And if she was not what they thought her—if she was not evil—she could not give in to evil impulses. She could not kill them all from a sense of vengeance. She could not allow herself to be guilty of such crimes. She did not want to be either as terrible as they thought her or as merciless as she thought them.

She had merely wanted to save that girl's life.

"Senneth."

Cammon's voice—Cammon who had found her without, she

was sure, a single misstep. Without looking up, she said sharply, "Don't touch me. My skin will burn you."

"We won't touch you," said a second voice, and that one did make her lift her head.

Tayse.

She stared at them, just shadows in the dark, the one solid and hulking, the other slim and fluid. "Go away," she said, but she was too tired to put any threat in her voice.

Cammon squatted down beside her, but Tayse remained standing. "You can't stay out here," Tayse said. "We need to set a watch, and we can only guard one perimeter."

She could not keep the edge from her voice. "And you really think one of them has the power to hurt me?"

"I think, when your anger fades, you're going to feel like five kinds of hell," Cammon said. "Give me your hands."

She crossed her arms, tucking her fingers next to her ribs. "No. I'm not safe to touch."

"You're safe to touch *me*," he said and held his palms out.

She gazed at him a moment, trying to read him in the dark, catching only glimpses of that smooth face and those flecked eyes. He was so young, and he didn't have any idea what the limits of his own abilities were, and she had never, in her seventeen years of wandering, encountered any mystic with a power to equal her own. But he had made so few mistakes since she had met him; he had such calm confidence. And she wanted nothing so much as to siphon off the rage and magic circling through her veins, and lay her head down, and sleep.

Cautiously, she put her hands out and let them rest, just touching his. He winced, but barely, and before she could pull back, his fingers closed over hers. He was like cold starlight on a solstice night, like frost on a limitless field of sere grass. She closed her eyes and stepped into a cave of ice and crystal. Her body radiated waves of heat and fury but could not disturb the perfect black, the eternal chill, of that lightless cavern. Her pulse slowed, and her fever burned lower—and just like that, her veins were emptied of fire.

She opened her eyes and stared at him, glad he could not see her expression in the dark. Or maybe he could—or maybe he did not need to see her face to know what it showed. "How did you do that?" she whispered.

By his voice, she could tell he was smiling. "Something Aleatha taught me," he said. "I didn't think to have a chance to use it so soon."

"And your hands?" she said. "I didn't harm you?"

He released her to show her his palms, though she could see nothing in this light. "Perfectly fine," he said.

"I'm almost cold," she said. "I'm never cold."

Cammon stood up, and Senneth rather shakily followed suit. The poison in her head sloshed from side to side, sending her momentarily off balance. Tayse caught her before she realized she might be falling.

"We'd better get you back," Cammon said, sounding worried.

"You go back," Tayse said. "We'll be there in a minute."

Senneth nodded, and Cammon turned to fight through the underbrush toward the barn. Now Senneth tried to use the patchy moonlight to read Tayse's face, but it was even harder to see than Cammon's. "Thank you," she said. "I know this was not what you wanted to do tonight."

She saw his big shoulders rise and fall in a shrug. "If I'd seen a bunch of men torturing a dog, or a boy, I'd have pulled my sword and scattered them all," he said. "Which is more or less the same thing, though my methods aren't as—spectacular—as yours."

She smiled, if he could see that, and waited for him to ask the real question. But he was silent. He wanted her to volunteer the story, she realized, and she could just as easily choose to say nothing. But he deserved to know. They all deserved it, and Kirra already knew it, and Cammon may have guessed it, because Cammon could read souls, but Tayse was the only one she would tell.

"When I was seventeen, I had a baby boy," she said, starting the story with absolutely no preamble. "My father had not known till then that I was mystic—or chose not to know it, since I so rarely came his way, and I was strong enough to control my power until that point. But the baby made me—made me careless, or made me clumsy, I don't know. And the baby himself was powerful—he came into the world so strong and so angry that the bed caught on fire as he fought from my body. I loved him," she said, her voice breaking on the words. "He was a bundle of pure rage and beauty, and I never knew that anyone could hold my heart so hard between his two small hands."

"What happened to him?" Tayse asked.

"When he was two weeks old, my father killed him. Came into the room and strangled him in his cradle."

There was a moment when she realized she had finally managed to shock the unshockable Tayse.

"It was before I knew how strong I really was, or I might have killed him in return," Senneth added. "He turned from the cradle and pulled me from my bed, and dragged me down the hall, and threw me out the door. Well, you've heard this part of the tale before. My mother hung back, and my older brothers merely watched. But my younger brothers gave me what money they had, and my grandmother gave me this pendant as I was stumbling down the walk. And then she cursed my father, and he died anyway, though not at my hands. I don't know—some days I'm glad that I didn't kill him, and some days I'm sorry. I do know that, on my blackest nights, it's a comfort to me to know he's dead."

"If we killed all the unkind people in the world, there would be scarcely anyone left alive," Tayse said.

"I know."

"But I am glad you were able to save that baby tonight," he added.

"Yes," she said. "I am, too."

She wanted to say more—she wanted to explain something to him, everything she had thought before, about good and evil and right and wrong and who truly deserved the power of vengeance— but she was so tired. She was so heavy. Her body felt like flaking limestone, solid-seeming but easy to chip apart. She had to get back to the barn, she had to lie down, she had to rest her head on a solid surface, or she would come to pieces right here.

She took a step and nearly fell. Tayse's hand was on her before she had done more than wobble. "Is it your head?" he asked sharply. "I can put pressure on your back where you showed me before."

"Yes—my head—but it's more. I'm so tired," she stammered. "I just—I have to lie down—"

Without another word, he swept her into his arms and held her to his chest tightly enough to avoid knocking her into overhanging branches as he strode back down toward the barn. She wanted to protest—she wanted to thank him—she found herself incapable of speaking at all. She rested her cheek against the rough cotton of his shirt and surrendered herself to his strength.

• • •

THEY rode out the next morning right at dawn.

No one had slept well in what few hours they had allowed themselves to rest, and they all knew that, with daylight, the townsmen would find fresh courage. So they rose early, left a few coins in payment, and were on their way before most of the town was astir.

"I'm thinking we might want to avoid all towns from here on out and sleep only in camp," Tayse said, as they trotted past the last house facing the road.

"Except that the point of our entire trip is to discover the mood of the people," Kirra said. "Hence, we must observe the people."

"The mood of the people is rabid-dog mean," Justin said. "Let's go back to Ghosenhall with our news."

Senneth smiled but didn't add much to the discussion. She was feeling odd today and having a hard time deciding if her reactions were physical or emotional. The headache was gone—and she had the clearest, most vivid memory of the feel of Tayse's hands, chasing the pain away with brute force—and she was only a little tired. But she felt awkward and almost shy, as if she had thrown a tantrum or otherwise behaved badly, and people around her might eye her askance. She covered her uncertainty with her usual stoic mask, but she didn't feel like contributing much to the conversation.

"No, I believe it's Nocklyn for us," Kirra said, "and maybe a trip to Nocklyn Towers."

"I'd like to see this place Aleatha talked about," Tayse said.

"What? The Lumanen Convent?" Kirra asked.

He nodded. "Like to judge how many fighting men have gathered under the banner of the Daughters of the Pale Mother."

Kirra seemed to ponder that. She looked sideways at Senneth, who didn't bother to voice an opinion. "It's an interesting idea," she said. "Maybe on our way down from Nocklyn."

Tayse looked at her. "And from Nocklyn we go where?"

Kirra laughed lightly. "Where else?"

He nodded. "Gisseltess."

To see Halchon Gisseltess. Senneth could hardly wait.

They rode in a tight formation this day, Tayse too worried about repercussions from last night's episode to send scouts before and behind. There were too many of them to ride all abreast, so as the hours passed they spurred forward and dropped back to fall in line next to varying companions. After an hour or two of riding, when she began to feel more normal, Senneth worked her way to the head of the column, next to Tayse. The other four rode a few yards behind.

"Let me know," she said, "when you think it is safe enough to send Donnal off hunting."

He glanced over at her, the expression on his face completely neutral. By the way he treated her, he might have been introduced to her this morning and already forgotten her name. "You think we need fresh meat?" he said. "I thought we had enough provisions to see us through another day or two."

"It's the raelynx," she said. "I think I might be able to trust it now to go off on a kill. And I can feel it getting restless—if I can let it run almost free for a few hours, I think it might grow calmer. But I'd like to have Donnal beside it when it runs just to—connect it back to me somehow. I don't know that I can explain."

He nodded. "Let's see what we encounter on the road in the next few hours."

"You think our angry villagers sent off to Nocklyn Towers for reinforcements?"

"I think we've created enough of a stir all along our journey that anyone interested in tracing our path will be able to do so."

"And I had planned to be so unobtrusive," she said in a light voice.

"Really?" he said. "And have you ever managed that?"

She laughed. "I can be most quiet when it suits my purposes," she said. "As I imagine you can. And yet, in general, a person would say you would be a hard man to overlook."

"I'm big," he said, "but I don't set things on fire. I think you're even harder to ignore than I am."

"Perhaps I won't have cause to do anything like that again."

They continued on a few moments in silence. Behind her, Senneth heard Kirra's bright voice and Donnal's rare laugh. Cammon had dropped back to ride beside Justin, who seemed to be his favorite person out of the entire party. Senneth could not imagine two people less likely to be friends, and yet Justin treated the boy with a warmth he showed to no one else, not even Tayse. Tayse he worshiped, Kirra he hated, Donnal he tolerated, and Senneth he feared. But he liked Cammon.

"What happened to your young man?" Tayse asked abruptly.

She glanced over at him, completely baffled. "What young man?"

"The one you must have known in order to have a baby."

"Oh." She thought his determination to know had outweighed any embarrassment he might feel at asking the question; there was no expression to be read on his face. As for herself, she couldn't help a tiny smile. "Him. I'm ashamed to say I never really cared about him. He was just a means to an end."

"You wanted a baby?" An edge of sarcasm there.

"I wanted—I wanted to thwart my father, who had planned to marry me off to one of his cronies' sons. I thought if I turned out to be damaged goods, as the saying goes, the marriage was less likely to go through. I miscalculated, as it turned out," she added, her voice hardening a bit. "He was still willing to marry me, though he wanted some adjustments made in the dowry to reflect my—impurity. They were still hammering out the details when my father threw me out of the house."

"So you were successful. In a way," he said.

She reflected. "In a way. But the cost was too high."

"It very often is," he replied.

"Yes," she said. "So I have learned."

"I am sorry, though," he said, surprising her. "That you would have to lose something so precious. In such a way. It's a grim tale, and I'm not surprised that you don't often tell it."

She turned her head sideways and regarded him a moment with a lurking smile. "But I am not the only one who chooses not to tell many tales of her young life," she said. "We know nothing about you except that you sprang whole from the loins of a King's Rider, sword already in hand."

He smiled back. "It was not quite that way."

"Come, then! Were you raised by a mother who made some faint, desperate effort to instill gentleness in your soul? Were your parents married? *Do* Riders marry? I can hardly credit it."

"They do marry, from time to time," Tayse said. "The women usually regret it. I know my mother did. She had three children with my father, and he was present for none of their births and very little of their lives. I remember how bitterly she would speak to my sisters about his absence and his lack of affection. When I was about ten, she and my sisters moved from the soldiers' quarters near the palace to a real house in Ghosenhall. I think she thought that would get my father's attention, but it didn't."

"I'm guessing it didn't get yours, either."

He shook his head. His smile had turned a little rueful. "I was already in training. I didn't miss her lectures and silly worries. I think I went five years without seeing her except on the days she would come to the palace just to visit me."

"Oh, I hope you were kind to her those days."

"I would like to think I was, but I doubt it. I was always very anxious for her to go, so I could get back to sword fighting or horse riding or dagger play or whatever it was we were working on for the day. I did always hug her and give her a kiss on the cheek. She requested it, you understand, but I did comply."

"And is that the typical life of a Rider's wife?"

He nodded. "From what I've observed."

"Then I can't believe that women are lining up to marry them."

He laughed. "You'd be surprised. The king holds us in high esteem, and on the streets of Ghosenhall we are practically lionized. No tavern will take our money—merchants are always pressing goods on us for free. Men like to say they have made friends with a Rider, and women—well, you might guess what women like to brag of. There are no shortage of candidates for wifehood. But I don't know many Riders who are happy in their marriages. Or, rather, they might be happy, but their women are not."

"And has this turned you against the thought of marriage? Or do you have a wife stashed away in Ghosenhall that you just have not found time to mention?"

A slight smile for that. "No time to seek one out and, so far, no inclination. I would make an even worse husband than my father."

"You could choose to do better," she said. "I have chosen to be kinder than my father and stronger than my mother. You could make the same decision."

He looked at her for a long moment, and she had time to wonder what he could possibly be thinking. "It is hard to imagine ever loving someone else so much that I would want to give her a very big part of my heart," he said at last. "If she did have so much of me, I assume my behavior would change in every respect. But I have not been particularly changeable so far in my life. It is difficult to envision what kind of force could have so much influence on my personality."

"Well," she said, "there's always magic."

He almost smiled. "These days," he answered, "I am less impervious to that than I used to think."

"Love *or* magic," she said. "No one's impervious. I would be on my guard, if I were you."

He gave her a quick, ironic nod. "I always am."

A scuffle of hoofbeats behind them and then Kirra's voice called out. "Senneth! Come settle this!"

She could have continued this particular conversation forever, and at the same time she was almost relieved to have it end. She gave Tayse a quick smile and reined back to join the others. The dispute was over the colors used on an old flag hanging in one of the hallways of Danan Hall, and Senneth told them with a laugh that she couldn't remember the flag, let alone the color scheme. But she continued to ride beside the two of them until Donnal dropped back to ask Cammon a question, and then she continued on alongside Kirra.

"Better today?" Kirra asked.

Senneth shrugged. "Tired. Worried. Wondering if Annie and Sosie are all right. Wondering what we'll find in Nocklyn. Wondering what we'll know by the time we end up back in Ghosenhall. A lot on my mind."

"Sosie and Annie will be just fine," Kirra said in a dulcet voice. "Since they have magical stones to protect them."

Senneth grinned. "Yes, I could tell you were quite impressed by my ability to turn common things into objects of power."

"But can you really? I mean, seriously? Because I'd like a stone like that, if you can find the time to cast another spell."

Senneth thought about it. "I do believe I was able to imbue those rocks with—something. Strength, courage, a little of my own power. I do think if those girls need help and they clutch those stones, they'll connect with an energy that will help them. But maybe just having something that they believe will protect them will give them courage enough to go on. I don't know. I had to do something."

Kirra lifted her eyebrows. "I mean it. I'd like a stone like that, too."

"You have enough of your own power. You don't need mine."

Kirra turned her head sideways to examine Senneth out of her blue eyes. "I don't have anything like the power that runs through you. I think you've gotten even stronger since the days you were in Danalustrous, teaching Donnal and me how to focus our minds and hone our talents."

Senneth was silent for a few paces. Finally, she said, "I think I have, too."

By the time they broke for lunch, it seemed clear they weren't being followed from behind or hunted from ahead, so Tayse permitted Senneth to send Donnal and the raelynx on an expedition. She did so with some trepidation.

"If there's trouble, don't try to control him yourself," she instructed Donnal. "Come back and get me."

"There won't be trouble," he said. "Don't worry."

She followed them with her mind as Donnal flowed from man to raelynx and the two of them took off running. She could not read thoughts—certainly not a wild creature's—but she could feel their emotions, distinguish the patterns of their moods. Donnal's were orderly and observant, a man's impressions taken through a beast's eyes.

From the raelynx she drew only the most primitive images of speed, power, rage, and hunger. She could sense his desire to outrun her, to flee this strange, troubling influence that had shackled his motions and curbed his appetite for so many days. She could feel how he reveled in the very act of racing through the scrubby brush of the countryside. For a moment she almost wished she was a shiftling like Kirra so she could run beside him, feel the earth and the stones and the fallen leaves in an elemental mosaic beneath her feet—sort through the feast of scents laden on the table of the heavy air—and hear sounds so distant and so distinct they seemed like ancient music. For a moment she felt heavy and earthbound and dull, and she wanted to release him from her own hold because she was unworthy of his beauty.

But she could set the whole countryside on fire and feel less guilty about the resulting catastrophe.

She was concentrating so closely on Donnal and the raelynx that she was not paying much attention to the road before her. She trusted that the Riders would keep her safe and that her horse would bunch with the others; thus, she left her hands loose on the reins and let her eyes lose focus. She was conscious only slightly of motion, of voices around her, the soft fall of shod hooves on a dirt road, the touch of weak sunlight on her cheek.

A shadow beside her. A voice so soft it might come from her memory. "Senneth. I don't want to disturb you."

Cammon. "Hmm?" she answered, not much interested.

"I can follow Donnal for you. You don't have to concentrate on anything but the raelynx. I can let you know if Donnal senses trouble."

Why hadn't she thought of that? "Yes—good," she said dreamily, and let Donnal's consciousness slip away from her.

Cammon might have ridden beside her for another few paces, but she had stopped noticing. All her attention now was swallowed by the raelynx. He had dropped to an absolutely motionless crouch, his belly so low to the ground the pine needles tickled his fur. Before him was a deer, thin and shaggy in the dead of winter, her sloe eyes watchful, her footsteps hesitant. But he was silent, he was still, he did not even shiver as he waited for her to come a step closer, and then another. All the world held its breath; even the wind stopped teasing.

Then a blur of motion—a burst of energy so strong that it shocked even Senneth—the pounce, the bite, the gush of blood pouring into her mouth. The sense of victory so intense, the rush of hunger so strong, the taste on her tongue so real. She jerked back, suddenly wanting to be a woman on a horse again and not a feral cat devouring a freshly killed meal. But she kept her mind hovering over the rae-lynx's, not letting him get too far from her, not letting him revel too fiercely in his freedom.

He feasted, eating very fast, and only bothering with his favorite parts of the carcass. Suddenly he looked up, alert, and licked his tongue across his face. Noises a short distance away. He dropped low again, almost to his stomach, and began crawling toward the sound of potential prey.

He was deeper into undergrowth now, almost into woods; the light came through in intermittent slants. Senneth had pulled back far enough from his mind that she could not smell what he smelled or hear what he heard; she could only catch his own narrow excitement. Some of what he saw filtered back to her in snatches—a stand of naked trees conferring in the cold, a skate of ice in a shallow ditch, a flash of red bird wing so high overhead it scarcely merited a single glance.

He crept up over a low ridge, pressed his belly to the ground, and peered down. Every muscle was strung taut, every sense strained to its fullest. Below him, half covered with leaves, lay a brown trail, winding its way around deadfalls and ruts. Deer path, Senneth assumed; there must be water somewhere nearby. By the raelynx's absolute dedication to silence, she also assumed a deer or some small animal was making its meandering way down the route toward water.

She was too disengaged from him to hear the sounds of the approaching victims or pick up from his mind the images he expected. Not until his quarry rounded the bend, stepping into view and into range, did she realize they were humans.

A boy, a girl.

The raelynx leapt.

Senneth screamed, tightening her hand so violently on the reins that her horse reared back. She was conscious of chaotic motion all around her, but her mind was nowhere near her own physical setting. She was back in the raelynx's head, directing his motions, forcing him to overleap his target and go tumbling through the underbrush along the path. The children yelled in terror and whirled around, pelting back in the direction from which they'd come. The raelynx twisted to his feet and scrambled after them, howling with rage and frustration when his feet would not obey him, when his body jerked backward against the goad of his own desires.

A moment or two he paced and screeched along the woodland path, his tail whipping back and forth, every tuft on his head and backbone stiff and straight with thwarted rage. Suddenly Donnal materialized beside him, a russet cat with black tips along his ears and paws, and began to make a sinuous circle around the younger animal. The raelynx protested, shrieking again in fury, and Donnal replied in that same strange, wailing language. Again, Donnal circled the cat, herding him back toward the main road, nudging him with his big head, batting him with one big paw. The younger raelynx hissed and lashed out, striking with teeth and claw, but he didn't connect with Donnal's body. Donnal nudged him again, then made the smooth leap from the trail to the ridge. He looked back, as if to make sure the other cat would follow. Another angry swipe of the tail, another snarling protest, and the raelynx gathered its muscles and sprang effortlessly up to the overhang beside Donnal.

The two began an indirect journey back toward the riders on the road.

Senneth drew a deep, shuddering breath and was suddenly aware of hands on her body, shaking her shoulder, patting her face. Someone was calling her name over and over. She squeezed her eyes shut and shook her head to clear it. When she looked again, she was in a circle of people, all on horseback, on a road in the middle of a desolate countryside.

"Senneth!" Kirra said sharply, her fingers slapping lightly against Senneth's face. "What are you—Senneth!"

Senneth jerked her head back before Kirra's hand could land again. "I'm all right," she said. "Sorry. I guess I screamed."

"What *happened*?" Kirra demanded. "I've never seen you—"

"The raelynx. I was letting it hunt. I let it slip my control a little more than I should have."

"And it killed something," Justin guessed.

She gave him a quick look. "A deer. That wasn't so bad. It was when he moved on to the next quarry and I didn't see them in time—"

"Men," Tayse guessed.

"Children," Senneth replied.

Kirra's eyes were huge. "And did you—what—"

"I stopped him," Senneth said. "But it was close. He's pretty angry right now."

"Excellent," Justin said. "I hope you're bringing him back to join us. Maybe he can sleep beside us at the fire tonight."

"He's calmer now," Cammon said. "He's with Donnal."

"This creature is becoming too much of a burden," Tayse said in a hard voice. "We can't drag it with us the length and breadth of Gillengaria."

She looked at him. He was angry, but she was not entirely sure why. He must have been able to see that she was about to argue, so he continued, his voice a little rough. "You can't keep trying to tame and conceal him. Your attention is split in five directions anyway. You'll have a headache every night for the rest of our journey, and how long can you continue to function with this constant drain on your strength?"

Hard as it was to believe, it seemed Tayse was angry on her behalf, anxious about her overall well-being. "You know I can't just let him go," she said, her eyes on his. "Find me a safe place to release him, and I will."

"You could cut his throat," Justin said.

"No," Senneth, Kirra, and Cammon all said in unison. "No," Senneth repeated. "I won't kill him unless I have to. He's done nothing except live according to his own instincts."

"Maybe we make a trip to the Lirrenlands after we've stopped in Gisseltess," Kirra said lightly. "At least there he'll be around people who know how to deal with him."

"Nocklyn Towers—Gisseltess—you really think you can stroll into those manors and trail a raelynx behind you?" Tayse asked. "Or do you have convenient mystical friends in every major city of Gillengaria where you can leave him behind while you pursue your mission?"

"I can handle him," came an unexpected voice. They all turned to look at Cammon. He blushed a little under his ragged hair but showed no sudden self-doubt. "I can, I think. I'll have to practice, of course, but you can work with me while we travel."

Senneth's gaze lifted briefly to Kirra's, then she looked back at Cammon. "We'll get right to work on that, starting tonight," she said. "That might be the most elegant solution yet."

Tayse still looked to be in a temper. With less than his usual poise, he tugged on the reins and set his horse in motion again. "Very well," he said. "Practice your magic on the road. We can't waste more time standing here arguing."

Justin cantered after him, and in a few moments the two of them were almost out of sight down the road. The other three fell in step behind them, moving a little less energetically.

"Well!" Kirra said in a conspiratorial tone. "*He* was certainly all in a snit over something. What could it be? Hmmm—he's a tough, cool, heartless soldier who doesn't seem to care about anyone or anything except his position as a Rider and his loyalty to his king. But—is it possible?—he's joined on the road by an exotic and powerful woman who wakes in him feelings he never knew he possessed—"

"Kirra," Senneth said in a sharp voice.

Kirra gave that golden laugh. "I don't know, my friend, I think you have an admirer."

"I don't think Tayse could bring himself to admire a mystic if she was the most beautiful and accomplished woman in the Twelve Houses."

Kirra laughed again. "Oh, it's against his will, of course, so he'll fight the attraction with every muscle of his admittedly quite muscled body. But he has a fondness for you, Senneth—against his training and against his history—and I don't think he knows quite what to do with it."

Senneth couldn't keep herself from looking at Cammon, the one person who would probably be able to tell her if Kirra was right. He could read souls, that boy; he could decipher hearts. He merely smiled at her, shaking back his shaggy hair, and said nothing.

If Cammon would not tell her and she had to wait for Tayse to volunteer the information, she would never know if the Rider cared for her or not. He was not the sort of man who would say so. Or at least, he would never say so to her.

She sighed and rode on.

CHAPTER
20

THEY camped that night for the first time in days, all of them just a little sulky about the lack of comfort. Even Tayse, who did not care about comfort—even Justin, who made it a point to never show or ask for softness. They hesitated a few moments before taking up their accustomed tasks, as if they'd forgotten who should fetch water and who should start the fire, but gradually a camp formed around them in the gathering twilight.

Senneth, naturally, built the fire. Tayse watched her lay the kindling and add the logs, as if any of these accessories were really necessary, as if she really expected them to believe any longer that she needed fuel to sustain a flame. But something about the chore seemed to please her—the feel of the wood in her hands, maybe, the rough texture of the bark, the cheerful snapping of the kindling. Maybe she just liked any object that could feed a fire the way she could, that might understand what it felt like to have a flame burning at its very core.

Still, he wondered if she had the strength to keep a fire going till dawn. She had been so exhausted the previous night that she hadn't even been able to walk under her own power; he had expected her to rise this morning looking like a troubled ghost. She had pretended to be perfectly normal, but he had observed her most of the day, wondering how much of her strength she had truly recovered, how much of her nonchalance was an act. He had seen plenty of young soldiers who refused to admit that a battle had sapped them of all will and energy, who had blundered on for another day, another week, until their bodies gave out and they collapsed in utter fatigue and were useless to themselves and their companies for the next month or more.

But the campfire lit and preened under her hands, and she seemed entirely capable of maintaining it.

It was ridiculous, he knew, but he had woken this morning with an overwhelming sense of protectiveness toward this fair-haired, contradictory, and still mysterious woman. If she had demonstrated anything at all yesterday, it had been that she had enough power to take care of herself and anyone else who happened to catch her fancy; she did not need a Rider's sword to keep her safe. Perhaps that was why he had been so moved by the vulnerability she had showed later—he would not have thought that a woman so powerful could be brought so low.

And what had she bought with her display of ferocity? The life of an infant, a bastard child of a peasant girl and a wandering trickster. Nobody—nothing. But, to her, precious enough to make her risk herself, her friends, her royal mission.

That had impressed Justin, Tayse thought, maybe more than anything Justin had ever seen. Justin had taken the first watch, while Tayse lay his hands against Senneth's pulsing head and fought down the demons in her blood. When she had finally relaxed against him and fallen asleep almost in his arms, he had laid her down and taken over the watch from the younger Rider.

Justin had still been awestruck. "I have never seen such a thing," he said more than once. "Have you? Never seen such a thing."

"Fire and fury coming from one woman's hands?" Tayse had responded in the coolest of voices. "No, never."

Justin had shaken his head. "It's just that—how often have you seen someone strong fight for someone weak? Just *because* the weak one has no other defenders? The strong take care of the powerful so that the powerful can take care of them in turn. When I was fighting in the streets of Ghosenhall, I only made alliances with others who were strong. I never protected anyone just because he needed care. I've never seen anyone do it."

Tayse had watched him meditatively in the glow of the still-smoldering fire. His whole life, his father's life, his grandfather's, had been dedicated to protecting the safety of the king. The most powerful man in Gillengaria. Now and then, Tayse had done a kind deed—interfered in a fight, pulled a child from the path of a rampaging horse, shielded a woman from an overeager suitor—but those had been chance events, easy choices to make, quickly done and quickly forgotten. His goal, his purpose, had been to guard the king.

Senneth served the king, or claimed to, but that was clearly not her overriding purpose in life. As much as anything, that was what had made Tayse distrust her from the beginning—the certainty that there was more to her agenda than seeking information for her liege. He had thought her motives might be dire or traitorous—or, at the least, opaque to him—but the events of the night before made him wonder. Perhaps she had no secret plan. Perhaps all she cared about was that the world be as right as she could make it, in whatever small part she happened to occupy, no matter what the personal cost to her might be. Nothing, after all, so sinister about that.

"No," Tayse had said, finally answering, "I've never seen anyone do it, either."

He thought, however, if he spent much more time in Senneth's company, he would see it again, and more than once.

Like the others, he had slept lightly and risen unrefreshed, but he had been happy to get out of this settlement before another alarm was raised. And now he was leading his small party to what was bound to be some new unplanned adventure, because they couldn't seem to remain inconspicuous, and he found himself unexpectedly ill tempered. That damned raelynx. Senneth's inconvenient sense of responsibility. She would wear herself out worrying about all the helpless creatures of the world, and then her vitality would be sapped at the very moment she needed it most. Had she never learned to husband her strength, guard against the hazards of the day?

Pointless to ask that question. He had already had it answered.

Well, he would just have to be ready to protect her when her own energy failed.

She did not seem particularly frail, however, as they lounged around the fire that night after eating their evening meal. She and Cammon sat with their heads close together, rarely talking, seeming to communicate with expressions and gestures. He would hardly be surprised, at this point, to learn they were speaking silently mind to mind, carrying on entire detailed conversations that the rest of them could not overhear. Senneth's face was its usual serene mask; Cammon's was furrowed in concentration, and his hands were clenched on his lap. Every once in a while he would sigh and shake his head. Now and then, he would look over at her with a grin of triumph.

This, Tayse believed, was Senneth teaching Cammon how to control the raelynx. The thought that she could transfer that knowledge was even more unnerving than the thought that she could manage the task herself. Tayse had never thought he was a stupid man, but all his power resided in his hands and his muscles; all his training focused on his body. He could only remotely imagine what it must be like to train the mind in a very different sort of combat, what kinds of exercises must be practiced, what kinds of skills might be honed.

No wonder Senneth had a headache so much of the time.

Donnal took first watch, and Tayse slept instantly and deeply. He did not even wake during the night to do his usual circle of the perimeter to make sure all was safe. He had the last watch the two hours before dawn, taking over from Cammon. After rolling out of his blankets, Tayse prowled around the edge of the camp, checking on the horses, who were quiet, and listening to the minatory sounds of the night. Outside the camp, it was bitterly cold; quietly though he moved, the ground crunched with ice under his feet. The moon was gone from overhead, and the stars seemed lost and bewildered, refusing to cohere in familiar constellations. Like his own thoughts, no longer orderly and automatically to be trusted.

He returned to camp and its sorcerous warmth, sitting with his back to the fire and his gaze toward the outward world. But all his attention was really behind him, on one dreaming form. Even in her sleep, she could control wild creatures and keep a blaze burning so hot it warmed a circle thirty feet wide. Even in her sleep, she could exert a pull on him so powerful he could not turn away. Even in her sleep, she was dangerous.

Well, he would guard her sleep for as long as it lasted.

THE next day they arrived in a good-sized market town and gazed about them as if they had drifted, all unaware, into foreign lands. Signposts gave the place the unmelodic name of Neft, and it was situated on the very edge of Nocklyn property.

At first glance, Neft looked like most of the market towns they had passed through, with a couple of major crossroads thronged with carts, horses, pedestrians, shops, and stalls. Two roads led into the town and were clogged with traffic, but a labyrinth of narrow streets and back alleys offered alternate routes to anyone familiar with the layout. Fanning out from the market center was a network of houses and public buildings, growing progressively smaller and shabbier the farther they were from the main square.

"Cute little place," Kirra said, reining up behind Tayse. "Looks like there are a lot of merchants. We can stock up on provisions."

Tayse looked back at Senneth. "Where's your cat?"

She grinned. "I was just going to ask you. I want to send Cammon ahead, outside the town limits, to sit with the raelynx and wait for us there. Any reason you can think of not to?"

"The fact that he's not strong enough to control it?"

She raised her eyebrows. "I'm still controlling it. Cammon's reinforcing. But there's a lot going on here, and I might get distracted. I was just asking you if—"

He turned away. "Fine. Send them ahead. Probably better."

He caught the look she gave Kirra and the shrug she directed at Cammon. The boy was grinning as he turned back, intending to make a wide circle around the outer borders of the town. Of the raelynx, of course, there was no sign. Tayse wondered just how far the wild creature could go before its human overseers lost contact with it. A mile? Five miles? How far away was it now?

And then Justin, the least sensitive of the lot, said abruptly, "There's something odd about this place."

Senneth gave him a sharp look. "Maybe you saw it when we rode in."

"Saw what?"

"The shrine."

She glanced back the way they'd come, and that was when they all noticed it. It was a small stone statue, no higher than a man's waist, carved from a glowing white stone that seemed phosphorescent here in the weak winter sunlight. Its shape was simple, of a woman in a loose robe, holding a heavy ball before her in both of her hands. The expression on her face was one of worship and ecstasy. At her feet were scattered inexpensive trinkets and a few glittering stones and a handful of pressed flowers. Someone had made a wreath of winter holly and laid it like a crown upon her head.

"The Pale Mother?" Kirra asked in a low voice.

Senneth nodded. "And a much-heeded one. You can tell the offerings are fresh."

Donnal was glancing around. "The place feels tense."

Tayse could sense it, too, and it was clear Justin had already picked up on the emotions. "Like a barracks yard," Tayse said, "the day before a unit rides off to war."

"Maybe we'd better be more careful than usual," Kirra said.

Senneth was watching Tayse. "Maybe we need to be more obvious."

He gave her an inquiring look. "You think we should wear our insignia? It will call attention to us."

"But we're less likely to be harassed."

Kirra seemed undecided. "I would say, let's see the mood of the town first. Perhaps there's no reason to be alarmed." She smiled. "And even if they're not wearing the king's gold lions, Tayse and Justin can defend us if trouble arises."

Senneth nodded. "All right. Let's see what's here. But let's go dressed appropriately."

One by one, except for Senneth, they edged their horses over to Kirra so she could touch some object on their wrists or throats and make it appear to be a moonstone. Senneth pushed back her own sleeves so her heavy bracelet seemed to drip from her hand. Not for the first time, Tayse found himself wondering what kind of effect that bauble had on Senneth's power. Most mystics seemed genuinely wary of the opalescent stone, and he had seen them start back in pain if one of the gems came too close to their skin, but Senneth seemed completely oblivious to any discomfort from the ring of white jewels.

But then, even among mystics, Senneth seemed unique.

They rode slowly forward into the press of people, looking around them with cautious curiosity. What Tayse noticed first was that everyone seemed to be wearing some mark of the Pale Mother—a moonstone collar, a moonstone ring, a cloak embroidered with the silver phases of the moon. The people of Neft didn't just set up a shrine to the Pale Mother; they embraced her in their daily lives.

"Good thing we don't plan to spend the night here," Kirra observed. Tayse glanced around, wondering what had prompted the remark, but it was still a moment before he noticed. And then he saw, hanging above the doorway in a nearby tavern: a huge round

rock of a moonstone, dangling just about at head height. A man
would have to duck to avoid brushing it as he stepped inside for a
drink.

And a man who ducked away from the touch of the goddess?
He might be considered suspect.

Tayse lifted his gaze to inspect the other shops and houses lining this crowded boulevard. Not every establishment boasted a
moonstone over the threshold, but many private homes had them
hanging in the windows, just inside the lace of the curtains. More
than one house featured its own tiny shrine out front, and a few
public buildings flew three flags from their brass poles: the lion-
splashed standard of Gillengaria, the pennant of Nocklyn with its
spray of wheat against an ocher field, and the flag of the Pale
Mother, a black background with a silver moon.

"We're very close to the Lumanen Convent here," Kirra said.
"No wonder there is so much sentiment in favor of the Silver Lady."

"And look," Senneth said in a cool voice, "some of her converts are visiting for the day."

And, indeed, before them they suddenly saw the reason that
the streets of Neft were so crowded. There were maybe a dozen
young girls, all dressed in pristine white robes, standing in the
middle of the road, blocking the way of travelers in all directions.
None of them looked to be more than seventeen or eighteen, and
on their sweet, half-formed faces were expressions of passionate
purity. They approached each individual rider or driver, hands up-
held, offering the blessing of the goddess on this fine winter day.
As Tayse watched, two or three riders jerked their horses away
from those uplifted hands and rode around, but most stopped, and
held out their hands, and stayed a moment, palm to palm, with
these messengers of the Pale Mother.

Each of the young women wore a moonstone ring that touched
the flesh of every person she blessed.

"Senneth," Kirra said softly.

"Can you stand the contact for a moment?" Senneth replied in
an equally quiet voice. "Knowing it is coming, and not wince
away?"

"I don't think I can," Donnal said.

Tayse had spotted something else, so carefully placed that until now it had eluded his notice. A contingent of guards ringing
the whole market square—two or three here, three or four there—
closely scrutinizing everyone who traveled through. "Now is not

the time to appear afraid of the Pale Lady," Tayse said. "Unless I miss my guess, those are some of her champions lying in wait, watching to see who pulls back in pain at the touch of the goddess's hand."

"Witch hunt," Kirra said. "We rode right into it."

"All right," Senneth said. "I'll go in the lead. Kirra and Donnal in the middle. Tayse and Justin to either side of them. Kirra, Donnal, pull your hoods up to cover your faces. If I say something that gives you some direction, you might change your features to match my words. Nobody else speak."

They deployed as she had commanded and followed her as she made her way slowly forward through the bunched crowd. They had only traveled another twenty yards or so before they were approached by a duo of the young girls in white. Tayse supposed they were recent converts to the goddess who as part of their training went out into the public towns to proclaim their faith.

They stopped, one on either side of Senneth, their eyes shining, their hands upraised. "Joyous morning to you, fair sister," one of them greeted Senneth in an exuberant voice. "May we share with you today the blessing of our most gracious lady?"

"A pleasant morning to you as well," Senneth said. "Who are you, can you tell me? I've not seen women dressed like you in any of the towns I've visited."

"We're novices at the Lumanen Convent, studying the ways of the Pale Mother and carrying her glad news throughout Gillengaria," one of the girls said.

"Daughters of the Pale Mother," Senneth said, her voice admiring. "And you live at some convent? Is it nearby? I've never heard of such a place."

"It has been open just a few years after nearly a century of neglect," said the other girl. Their voices were nearly indistinguishable to Tayse, dreamy and soft; he could only tell who spoke by watching the motion of their mouths. "It is a beautiful place. You are welcome to come visit."

"Really? Well, I would be curious to see it, I admit. How many of you live there?"

The girls exchanged glances. "Hundreds," the first one replied. "I don't know the number."

"And you learn—what?"

"The ways of the goddess," the second one said. "Of her great bounty and her great power and how to do her will."

"She lights the stars and guards the night and sees into the hearts of all men and women," the second one intoned.

Tayse wasn't much impressed by the philosophy, but he was deeply impressed by the light of fanaticism on their faces. Someone who believed in a cause could be just as dangerous as someone with a weapon—and these believers were backed by swordsmen. Trying not to be obvious about it, he glanced around him again to see how many of the guards were close to them and if any were paying attention to his small group.

Two. And yes.

"How often do you leave your convent to spread word of the Pale Mother's goodness?" Senneth was asking.

"We have just begun to proselytize, and we have not gone far from our home," said the second girl. "But soon the Daughters will go north and east and west, to all corners of Gillengaria, to tell the news."

"I fear you may have your work cut out for you in Kianlever and Brassenthwaite and Danalustrous," Senneth said. "In those parts, they don't seem to think a great deal about the Silver Lady."

"They will," the first one said tranquilly. "Very soon."

Senneth gathered her reins tighter in her hand. "Well, I'll think of your words as I travel," she said, and made as if to ride on.

But the girls, appearing all innocent, blocked her way. The first one said, "Won't you please give me your hand so I can share the blessing of the Pale Mother with you?" Her hand was already up, palm toward Senneth. Tayse thought the nearest soldiers looked even more interested.

Not hesitating at all, Senneth leaned from the saddle and pressed her hand against the Daughter's. Her moonstone bracelet slid forward on her wrist and brushed against the novice's arm.

"Your skin is so hot," the girl observed, her voice concerned. "Are you ill? Should you perhaps pull over for a day and rest?"

Tayse straightened in his saddle and waited for Senneth's response.

"Am I warm?" Senneth said, just a shade of worry in her voice. "I hope I have not caught the fever."

"The fever?" one of the girls said.

Senneth motioned with her head. "My two companions. They have been sick for days. I am trying to get them home where they can be cared for, and there have been many delays on the road."

Now the novices' attention turned to the others in their group. "Ah," said one, "we wondered why they were wrapped so closely on such a sunny day. Let us give them, too, the blessing of the goddess, and offer them her healing strength."

"No," said Senneth sharply. "I do not know how contagious this fever is, and I will not be responsible for introducing illness into a convent of several hundred women. You cannot touch them—it is not safe."

"The Silver Lady fears no fever," one girl said softly.

"But I do, and it is my conscience that must be answered to," Senneth said. "My guards would happily take your blessings, however, and my friends would be grateful for your prayers."

"May we see their faces?" one of the girls asked. "So we know for whom we pray?"

"Certainly," Senneth replied, and turned in her saddle to nod at the two riding behind her.

Kirra reached up a shaky hand and pulled the hood back from her head. Tayse had to admire her handiwork. Her face was pallid and dull, her eyes watery and red, and her glorious hair hung limp and brown to her shoulders. She put a hand across her mouth before speaking, as if to keep from breathing infection on her well-wishers.

"Please," she croaked. "Do not get too close."

"The Pale Mother spreads you with her benediction," one of the girls said solemnly. "We will pray that you will soon be well."

"Thank you," Kirra whispered.

Donnal also tugged off his hood to reveal a face as ravaged as Kirra's. He did not even try to speak, just made an effort to control his labored breathing, and nodded as they spoke their words over him. Then both of them rewrapped their faces.

"Thank you for your concern," Senneth said gravely.

The women moved over a few paces, one turning toward Tayse, one to Justin. "The blessings of the Pale Mother upon you," they murmured, holding up their hands. Tayse pressed his palm against the novice closest to him and saw Justin do the same.

"Many thanks," Tayse said.

"Much appreciated," Justin added.

"We must ride on," Senneth said. "May the Silver Lady guard you both."

And, in no apparent hurry, she nudged her horse forward again and began to pick through the crowd. Once clear of the knot of Daughters, they were able to move more rapidly. Tayse was ready to draw a breath of relief as they reached the edge of the market square.

Where three guards were blocking their way.

Senneth pulled to an abrupt halt, her horse snorting and dancing under her. Tayse moved up alongside her, and Justin came up on Tayse's other side. Tayse quickly took in details of the men before them. All appeared to be in their early thirties or forties, clean-shaven, well-muscled, intensely serious. They had as many weapons strapped to their waists and saddles as the Riders had, and they were dressed in the black and silver colors of the Pale Mother.

All three of them looked as much like zealots as the novices bestowing blessings on chance wayfarers.

"Greetings, travelers," said the middle guard in a civil voice. He looked to be the oldest of the three. His dark hair was worn short, and there was a battle scar across his chin. Holding his black cloak to his shoulder was an ornately wrought silver clasp of a falcon holding a flower in its talons.

The Gisseltess crest.

"Greetings," Senneth replied in a neutral voice. "Is there some reason you will not let us pass?"

"You talked for some time with the Daughters in the market square," he replied. "And yet you ride on in apparent haste with two members of your party hiding their faces. I was wondering what tale you told them and what trouble makes you move so fast?"

"The two who hide their faces are ill, and we are in a hurry to get them home," Senneth said, her voice just a shade combative. "Does this somehow fail to meet your approval?"

"If they're ill, perhaps they should stay in town and be tended by healers or the Daughters themselves," the guard suggested.

"I would not want to risk the contagion," Senneth said. "And they will be more comfortable in their own beds."

"Anyone so ill perhaps should not risk spreading disease through the whole countryside," the guard said. "I wonder what sickness they have that worries you—but only worries you so much."

"I wonder what right you have to question me," she replied.

He gave her a short, hard nod. "The right of any concerned citizen to keep his neighbors and himself safe."

"Ah—and you live here?" Senneth said. "In this town? You guard its gates and its people?"

Tayse could tell she had vexed the guard. He was fairly certain they were about to make their visit to this town memorable. Even now, bystanders were gathering on the corners of the street, watching them and whispering to each other. Travelers passed them on either side, glancing over at what was clearly a confrontation, and hurrying on before they got ensnared in the quarrel.

"Nearby," the guard said stiffly. "Close enough to have some concerns for the residents of this city."

"Well, I have some concern as well, and that is to keep from spreading fever through these streets," she said. "So if you will let us pass, we will be on our way."

"I think I should take you first to see my captain," the guard replied.

Senneth's voice was very soft. "I think you will be sorry if you try to detain us," she said. "We travel on royal business—my friends are friends of the king—and, sick or well, they have a duty they must perform on his behalf. Stand out of our way."

"Prove your affiliation," the guard demanded.

With one hand, Tayse scraped his sword from its scabbard; with the other, he pulled back the front of his coat to reveal the golden lion embroidered on the sash beneath. Beside him, in perfect synchronization, Justin did the same. Neither of them spoke, but their faces offered expressions of cold menace.

The guard and his companions reined back a pace or two, looking both nervous and alarmed. One of them whispered an oath and pulled back even farther. The guard who had addressed them forced his horse forward again as if he felt no uneasiness.

"That is no proof," he said. "Anyone may wear a vest of any design he chooses."

Tayse effortlessly swung his sword upright, holding it motionless right before his face. "I shall offer you any proof you choose," he said. "But perhaps you would prefer not to suffer a massacre here on the market streets."

"It would be no massacre," the guard said.

"Yes," Tayse replied, "it would. We are King's Riders, these travelers are under our protection, and we will not sit here longer and bandy words with you. Move aside and let us pass."

He wasn't sure what it was—the absolute assurance of his voice, his unyielding expression, or the fact that this guard really had no rights here and knew it—but the Pale Mother's soldiers slowly and reluctantly backed their horses from the road. Not sheathing their weapons, Tayse and Justin escorted their companions forward. It seemed as if they, as if the whole town, had been enveloped in a waiting silence, holding a deep collective breath as the standoff unfolded. The whole world seemed to be watching, wordless and uncertain, as the five of them trotted down to the edge of town and then continued onto the outer road. No one shouted after them; no one followed. Yet neither Tayse nor Justin put away their swords as they continued to ride, shifting to a canter as they got farther from the city.

"All the great goddesses defend me," Tayse heard Kirra's voice, for naturally she was the first one to feel the need to break the silence. "We barely got out of there without a battle."

"That would have been disastrous," Senneth said. "This was bad enough."

"I'm almost dumbfounded," Tayse said. "I'd expect soldiers from one of the Twelve Houses to have that sort of nerve, but a personal guard? From what amounts to a single manor? What kind of power do they think they have behind them to be able to question private citizens that way?"

"He wasn't even frightened at the sight of your lions," Senneth said. "When's the last time that's ever happened to you?"

Justin glanced over at her. "Never."

"Well, if we ever thought we were riding incognito through the southern provinces, we can rid ourselves of that notion," Kirra said. "Coralinda Gisseltess will learn very soon that Riders are investigating the mood of the southern towns. And if she pieces together all the stories about us, she will be able to figure out that Riders are guarding mystics. What will she make of that tale, I wonder?"

"Do we care what she thinks?" Justin asked.

Senneth was the one to answer. "Oh yes," she replied. "Coralinda Gisseltess is greatly to be feared."

Tayse said nothing more. His eyes were scanning the way before them; his ears were straining to hear any sounds of pursuit from behind. He finally judged it safe to replace his sword, but he kept his hand upon the hilt. He was relieved when they came around a bend in the road to find Cammon awaiting them, already mounted and ready to travel. He had expected to find the boy sitting somewhere off to the side, plucking winter grass and languishing in boredom, but he had forgotten: Cammon never mis-read the moods of his companions, even from a distance. He had probably been in the saddle and ready to ride while they were still arguing back in the city.

They didn't even have to break stride as Cammon swept his mount around and fell in beside the others. "I suppose we didn't have a chance to buy supplies," he observed.

A laugh from Kirra. "Why, no. Somehow in all the excitement, we forgot."

"How's the raelynx?" Senneth asked.

"Calm," Cammon replied. "Tell me the details. All I could tell was trouble."

"Trouble about sums it up," Justin said, and launched into the tale.

"I'm guessing we're going to find all of Nocklyn given over to the Silver Lady," Senneth said when he was finished. "We may find it impossible to stop at any of the small towns with the hope of spending the night."

"Maybe the mystics can detour around the settlements and the Riders can pick up provisions," Cammon suggested.

"Even at Nocklyn Towers?" Kirra said, her voice faintly mocking.

"Nocklyn Towers will be a different story," Senneth said. "I think Cammon is right—we should skirt the towns along the way. But we'll have to ride into the city. We'll have to see just exactly what Els Nocklyn has gotten himself into."

CHAPTER
21

IT was two and a half more days before they made it to Nocklyn Towers. Along the way, they were actually successful at being circumspect. As Cammon had suggested, they mostly boycotted the small towns, though Tayse and Justin did ride in for supplies once while the others waited a reasonable distance down the road. All the towns they passed through were, like Neft, festooned with evidence of the Silver Lady's presence: moonstones in the windows, flags over the doors, shrines in the squares. A young shopgirl handed Tayse a few coppers in change, accidentally brushing his palm with a heavy moonstone charm hung from her silver bracelet. He found himself wondering what it would be like if that cool touch brought a searing pain instead of the faintest sensation of glasslike smoothness.

He wondered what it would be like to fear such a touch, which could occur randomly and expose a dangerous secret. He was not used to either secrecy or fear. But his imagination did not entirely fail him in this instance.

During the days, while they rode, and during the nights, while they sat around the campfire, Senneth and Cammon practiced various skills. To judge by the bits of conversation Tayse could overhear, Cammon was becoming rapidly more adept at handling the raelynx, so much so that Senneth felt comfortable giving him entire control of the creature for several hours at a time. None of the rest of them were quite so comfortable. Particularly not after that first night on the road, when Kirra had looked up from the fire and screamed.

The raelynx crouched just outside the circle of firelight, watching them all with a hungry attention.

"Mother defend me," Senneth swore—and then did something, and the raelynx slunk away. Tayse didn't even have to look to know that Justin had drawn his dagger for close fighting, as he himself had. But he had no illusions that either of them was fast enough to kill the creature before it killed one of them.

"Sorry, sorry, sorry," Cammon apologized. He didn't seem too upset about the incident, so Tayse guessed that his control had been holding well enough to prevent an actual attack—or at least Cammon thought so.

Even Donnal looked a little unnerved. "I didn't sense it anywhere near us," he said. "Usually I'm more attuned to the wild creatures."

Kirra had a hand to her heart, though with her it was hard to tell if that was drama or genuine hysteria. "I feel faint," she said. "I feel the way a little rabbit must feel upon looking up and seeing the hawk's wings overhead."

Tayse looked at Senneth. "How exactly did that happen?"

She met his eyes, complete tranquillity in hers. "A little slip. Everything's fine."

"Once we leave Nocklyn," he said, "we have to seriously consider detouring to the Lirrens."

"We'd hardly make it through the mountains this time of year," Senneth said. "But maybe spring will be closer by the time we're on our way back from Gisseltess. Though—by then—we may be in a hurry."

No one asked why they might be in a rush. They all worried about what they might find at the end of their journey, in the heart of Gisseltess. They already had plenty of disturbing news for the king; it was clear Senneth was expecting more.

"I won't slip again," Cammon said. "You'll see. I know what I did wrong this time."

Justin sheathed his dagger. "We'll see if we aren't dead," he said with his usual sarcasm, though he softened his tone a little for Cammon's sake.

Cammon grinned at him. "Well, I think the creature *is* hungry. Maybe if he eats one of us, he'll be better behaved."

"Maybe we'll let him hunt tomorrow," Senneth said. "Though we're in pretty populated territory. I don't know."

"Let's just kill something ourselves and throw it to him," Justin said. "*I'll* go out and bring down some game. Anything to keep him from turning his eyes my way."

But Tayse didn't want to lose Justin's sword arm, so the next day they sent Donnal off in search of fresh meat. He returned with enough to satiate the wild creature and add some variety to their own cook pot, and even Justin congratulated him on his success.

They were still sitting around the campfire, having finished their meal, when Senneth said, "All right. All of you watch me for a moment. Cammon, don't say anything. The rest of you just tell me—well, you'll know."

So they all shifted position to stare at her across the low flames. Not for the first time, Tayse had the odd impression that she herself was like a fire—or rather, a long, sturdy candle, her white-blond hair like a lit wick around her face. She shut her eyes and appeared to meditate for a moment, and then she vanished.

"Hey!" Kirra cried, and the rest of them also offered some exclamation of amazement.

Except Cammon, of course, who looked around in bewilderment. "What? What did she do? Did she turn herself into something else?"

"She disappeared, you halfwit," Justin said in exasperation. "It's worse than being around a blind man—being around a man who sees things that aren't really there."

"She *is* really there," Cammon said.

Sounding completely normal, which made it even eerier, Senneth's voice emerged from the vacant space above her bedroll. "So no one can see me but Cammon?"

"Obviously not," Tayse said.

"Can you hold the illusion if someone touches you?" Donnal asked.

"Ah, there's a good question," said the disembodied voice. "Let's see—"

A little yelp from Kirra, who rubbed her arm and looked in what was surely feigned apprehension at Senneth's empty blanket. "You *pinched* me! This is very spooky."

"But you didn't materialize," Donnal said. "We didn't see you even when you put your hand on Kirra. That's good."

"*I* saw her," Cammon said.

"How long can you stay invisible?" Kirra asked.

"I'm not sure. I might practice tomorrow on the road. But now I want to try something else." Suddenly she was sitting among them again, looking entirely relaxed and more than a little pleased with herself. "Who wants to volunteer?"

There were, for a moment, no takers.

"I will," Cammon said.

"Not you. Donnal?"

The dark man nodded. "Sure. What do you want me to do?"

"Just sit there. Everyone look at Donnal."

Tayse obediently bent his eyes in the required direction. He was not entirely surprised when Donnal suddenly seemed to wink out of existence. From the rest came low murmurs of approval or uncertainty.

"I can't see myself," Donnal said.

"I can see you," Cammon said.

With an effort, Tayse restrained himself from telling Cammon to shut up. By the look on Kirra's face, she was making the same effort.

"Do you have any unpleasant sensations? Do you feel strange?" Senneth asked.

"No, I feel fine. But I have to say it's a little odd." Almost on the words, he was corporeal again. He looked down at his body as if to check that no parts were missing. "I wonder how many people you can enchant at a time and how long you can hold it," he said.

Justin was nodding. "That would be a damn useful skill to have on a battlefield."

"So far, I don't think I can work the magic on more than one or two people at a time," Senneth said regretfully. "And I wouldn't think I could hold the spell for very long. But I'm convinced it will still come in handy from time to time."

"But what about your code of honor and all that?" Justin asked. "You know, can't turn someone else into a wolf, those things Kirra said before."

Tayse saw the women exchange glances filled with a bit of humor and a bit of rue. "He's right," Kirra said. "Though it's not exactly the same thing, since you didn't really change him."

"Now I suppose I'll have to examine my conscience before I try such tricks again," Senneth said, but she was laughing. Tayse thought, not for the first time, that her sense of honor was strong but probably a bit adaptable—and that she was not afraid to break rules if the incentives were desperate enough.

"Isn't all this experimenting giving you a headache?" Tayse asked.

She was laughing again. "No, I think that last time my headache was more a product of fury than magic. Besides, this sort of spell isn't particularly draining. It's just—complicated."

"I wonder if I could learn it," Cammon said.

Tayse was sure he was not the only one thinking, *You need to learn the spell that strikes you silent,* but no one said it. Senneth grinned at him. "Once you entirely master the trick of subduing the raelynx," she said, "we'll work on this one."

Kirra snapped a stick and tossed it into the fire. "So we'll be in Nocklyn Towers by tomorrow evening," she said. "Have you figured out what approach we should take?"

"How well do you know Els Nocklyn?" Senneth asked. "Will he see you if you try to make an appointment?"

Kirra shook her head. "I know him well enough to be able to make conversation if we're seated next to each other at the dinner table," she replied. "But I would think—if I said I was in town—well, he would hardly turn me away. He would imagine I come on my father's behalf."

Senneth was pursing her lips. "But Darryn Rappengrass said he's been sick and that his daughter is doing much of the day-to-day governing," she said thoughtfully. "Will *she* see you? And do you suppose she's in residence at Nocklyn Towers?"

"Mayva Nocklyn," Kirra said. "Oh, yes. She considers herself a friend."

THE problem, as Tayse had foreseen all along, was the raelynx. Nocklyn Towers was a bustling city of many thousand souls, and there was no way to attempt to smuggle the cat through the guarded gates and onto the crowded streets. Senneth did not seem entirely certain that Cammon's hold on the animal was strong enough to endure for more than an hour or two, but their foray into the city was likely to take a full day or even longer. And she was not willing to let Kirra attempt the interview with the Nocklyn family alone.

"I'll be fine," Cammon said more than once, as they halted that afternoon within sight of the city gates. "We'll pull off the road a half mile or so, and I'll just hold him as tight as I can."

"So many temptations," Senneth said, her voice worried. "Hundreds of people use this road every day. It might be more than he can stand, seeing so much prey stroll by."

"I'll stay with them," Donnal said. "I'll hunt every few hours—bring him back a bird or a squirrel or something. I'll keep him so full he won't even want to move."

"Sounds like our best option," Tayse said. Senneth reluctantly agreed. They made quick plans for where Cammon should camp and how they should get in touch again if something went awry.

"I'll be able to tell," Cammon said.

Senneth nodded. "Send Donnal into the city to find us if something happens. Hawk, jay, some kind of bird shape. One of us will be at the western gates. But I don't think anything will go wrong here."

Justin snorted in disbelief, so Tayse didn't have to.

"We'll be at the Nockworth Hotel," Kirra added. When the others gave her questioning looks, she said in a haughty voice, "A Danalustrous *always* stays at the Nockworth when visiting in Nocklyn Towers."

"Come to the gate first if anything goes wrong," Senneth instructed Donnal. "And then the Nockworth. But come to the hotel in human form."

Donnal grinned. "I think I would have figured that out on my own."

Tayse was getting impatient. Dark was almost upon them, and he wanted to get inside the city while it was still light enough to look around. "Are we ready? Good. See you both in a couple of days."

They separated, the two mystic men heading off the road, the other four riding forward toward the city. In a few minutes, they had reached the gate and were passed through with only a cursory inspection.

Tayse looked about him with interest as they entered the city. He had been here before, more than once, when escorting King Baryn to some function or another. He remembered it as a prosperous, well-kept place, and it still was—perhaps even more so. There appeared to be many new buildings crowding next to old ones at several intersections, and the streets were thronged with people. The traffic was heavy, even at this time of day, and the profusion of carts and carriages made it difficult for the horses to travel down the streets. All sorts of people could be seen, all at once: rich matrons in their textured silk, Nocklyn soldiers in their formal uniforms, farmers with their wagons, beggars with their bound eyes and truncated limbs, schoolgirls, errand boys, dreamy lovers, angry friends. The city embraced a profusion of humanity and swirled them all together.

"Do you know where this hotel is?" Senneth called to Kirra over the constant rattling and shouting in the streets.

Kirra nodded.

"Then you take the lead."

It was nearly an hour later, and close to full dark, by the time they had navigated the streets to Kirra's destination. It had been clear for several blocks now that they were in the most elegant part of town, with broad avenues lined with spacious houses and discreet shops. The hotel Kirra had selected was charming, offering a wide stone sweep of a driveway for carriages to pull through and an ornate fountain before the triple doors. The weather was too cold to allow for running water, of course, so instead the bowl of the fountain was filled with ice sculptures, all of them starting to look a little mushy at the end of a sunny day. Tayse wondered if the hotel proprietors commissioned and installed new ones every morning. He could hardly imagine anything more ridiculous.

He had been paying too much attention to their progress through the streets to give much notice to his companions, but he was not surprised to find both Kirra and Senneth transformed by the time they pulled up in front of the Nockworth. Kirra wore a fine red riding cloak and had her hair held back with ruby clasps. Senneth looked dull but respectable in her ordinary riding clothes and her assumed submissive demeanor. Tayse found himself wondering by what unnoticeable increments they had managed to change their clothes and their features as they made their slow parade through the city.

"Two rooms. One for myself and my companion, one for my guards," Kirra greeted the man who had come rushing through the doors to welcome her. It was always something of a shock to hear the unpretentious Kirra assume the tone and manner of a titled lady. "And dinner sent to us. Immediately. We have had a very long, very trying day."

"Yes, of course, my lady," the footman said, first bowing and then reaching up to help Kirra from her saddle. An ostler had appeared from somewhere behind the hotel to take the reins of her horse. "Do you have—is there a packhorse behind you with more of your luggage?"

Senneth slid from her saddle under her own power, keeping her face so set it was almost mournful. Kirra was already stalking toward the door. "No," Kirra said over her shoulder. "The absence of luggage is part of what has made this a very unfortunate day."

Tayse swung down from his own horse and handed the reins to the groom. He couldn't keep himself from glancing over at Justin for a second and sharing a grin. The servants were already pitying them for having to ride with such a shrew. If they came down later and wanted to buy a pint of ale, they'd probably get an extra portion just out of sympathy. At times like these, Tayse thought that even Justin could appreciate Kirra.

They were led across expensive rugs and through high corridors to a set of rooms on the second floor. Kirra inspected hers for a moment as if she was not sure it would be good enough, and then she sighed and said, "Fine. Send wine with our meal." And she shut the door in the footman's face.

Grinning, Tayse let himself and Justin into their own quarters, adjacent but not nearly so spacious. "Fine as well," he said. "I find I am not nearly as picky as our mistress."

Justin laughed and threw his saddlebags to one of the narrow beds. "Day like this, a man can be glad he's not a mystic," he observed. "We get to sleep inside on clean linen while Cam and Donnal huddle under the stars. No magical fire to keep them warm all night, no aristocrat ordering them meals."

"And we don't have to worry about being eaten in our sleep," Tayse said. "But even without those incentives, most days I'm glad I'm not a mystic."

And to Tayse's surprise, Justin merely looked thoughtful, and nodded, and did not add another word.

SHE had sent a note to the manor house of Nocklyn Towers, Kirra informed them over the dinner they shared, and now there was nothing to do but wait. "I wouldn't think we'd hear back before morning," she added.

"What do you want to do tonight?" Tayse asked.

Senneth looked at him. "Sleep."

He grinned and gestured. "Whole town out there. Some entertainment you haven't been offered while on the road. You might enjoy an evening in civilization."

"You go," Senneth said. "You and Justin. Carouse. I'm sure the king won't mind. Kirra and I will be just fine here at the hotel, helpless females prey to all sorts of unsavory types who might have designs on our purses—or our virtue."

Kirra was choking on her giggles, and even Justin was grinning. Tayse managed to keep a serious expression on his face as he examined her. "When was the last time you were ever actually helpless?" he inquired. "Or afraid?"

She seemed to debate. "I can't remember."

"Then, if you don't mind, we'll go out. To test the mood of the town, if nothing else."

She nodded. "Actually, I was hoping you would. You'll get inside some places that might not let us in."

"Tayse and I don't go to places like that," Justin said in a virtuous tone of voice.

Kirra turned her bright blue eyes on him. "Well, this just might be your chance."

So they left the hotel as soon as they'd eaten and had an opportunity to change clothes. Even though he knew that the women were safe—in such a place, and with their own powers of protection—it bothered Tayse just a little to leave them behind. His directive was to protect them, and he had scarcely been more than fifty yards from either of them since they started out on this journey. It was not through his neglect that they would come to harm.

Still, it was hard to worry for long with all the distractions around them. Justin's mood was good, and the city was pulsing with excitement. Certain sections of Nocklyn Towers came alive at night, even on a night as cold as this one. They strolled through expensive districts where rich young men spilled out of fancy clubs and held dainty duels in the street. They went farther afield, to the rougher parts of town, where the liquor was higher proof and the fights in the alley were for blood. They were neutrally dressed; they could not enter the exclusive clubs, of course, but they could walk into any of the fancy pubs as well as the workingmen's establishments, and not raise eyebrows.

Accordingly, they stopped first at a tavern that seemed to cater to merchants and businessmen, some there with their wives or other companions—a respectable place with a long list of beers to choose from. They didn't make any attempt to mingle, and didn't speak much to each other either as they sat there, nursing their glasses and listening to the conversation around them.

Talk of money. Talk of trade. Grumbling about new taxes and a son or two who'd signed up with the expanded civil guard.

"Well, so, my boy goes off to join the soldiers, and my girl goes off to join the Daughters," one man said with a careless laugh. "If I can get my wife to run off with the theater troupe, I'll have the whole house to myself! But she says she doesn't like to travel and that I'm stuck with her."

Other voices chimed in with their own stories. What Tayse noticed was that none of them sounded too disgruntled. These men might be irate at a new tax, but they were able to afford it, and they didn't disagree with how it was being spent. And they seemed proud rather than alarmed that their sons and daughters were finding places in the barracks yard and the convent. He finished his beer and nodded at Justin, and they went back out into the night.

The story was much the same at the other taverns they tried, though the tale was told in a rowdier fashion the farther down they went on the scale of civility. More sons had gone to be soldiers than daughters had gone to be novices, from what Tayse could tell, but everywhere were the accouterments of both professions: swords and moonstones. In one rather disreputable pub situated next to a brothel, there was a large contingent of fighting men gathered at most of the tables. Tayse and Justin, who normally would have felt at home in such a crowd, found seats for themselves near the bar, away from the action, and surreptitiously watched the gaming and quarreling going on among the other patrons. Soon it was clear that there were two main factions, and they were competing over a variety of skills: the ability to drink, the ability to throw a dagger with accuracy over a short distance, the ability to turn up an advantageous card. More than one crash of glass and shouted oath attested to the fact that the drinking did not do much to aid in the accuracy of throwing a knife.

"Sweet and silver hell," the barkeeper swore once when he happened to be standing in front of the Riders as yet another glass went smashing to the floor. "It'll take me all day tomorrow to clean this place up."

Tayse nodded for another beer and reflected that it had better be his last one. "Who are they?" he asked. "Can't you throw them out?"

The barkeeper gave a short laugh. "Well, half of them are Nocklyn men, so, no, I can't. And the other half are convent guards, and around here it's considered bad luck to treat them with discourtesy."

Tayse lifted his eyebrows and sipped from the glass. He could taste the smoothness of the southern grains; nothing like Nocklyn beer. "Bad luck because you offend the Pale Mother or bad luck because you offend the guards?" he asked softly.

A twist of the mouth and the barkeeper looked down at the counter, swiping it with a dirty towel. He wore a small moonstone ring on his thumb. "Both," he said, "though I think the Pale Mother is not as easily offended as her servants."

"There seem to be a lot of them," Justin said.

"Oh yes. And on best of terms with the Nocklyn guard. Some folks here don't like it—too many soldiers make people uneasy— but I like them well enough before they start drinking." He shrugged. "A city needs a strong guard, and friends who have their own strong guards. No harm in that. Makes people respect you if you can put some force behind your words."

Tayse nodded. "I believe that myself, friend."

"Soldiers yourselves. I can tell that by how your carry yourselves," the barkeeper said. "That last drink's on me."

"Appreciate it," Justin said and toasted their host with his glass before draining it.

Tayse did the same and slipped to his feet. "Thanks for the ale. I've never tasted better than Nocklyn's."

The man behind the counter grinned. "No, and you never will, not if you travel from here to Ghosenhall or even farther."

Tayse laughed. "And some days, you know, I think I might."

They were back on the street in a few moments, hunching their shoulders against the chill of a bitter wind. They were far enough from the hotel that they would be good and cold by the time they made it back.

"Nocklyn guards on the best of terms with convent soldiers," Justin said once they were a few yards away. "Senneth won't like that."

"No," Tayse agreed. He was thinking that Justin should have said, *The king won't like that*—but he was thinking that he, too, would have phrased it exactly as Justin had if he'd been the one to speak first.

CHAPTER
22

THE next day opened with a headache from all the beer consumed the night before. "Acquired in the interests of obtaining information for *you*," Tayse mumbled when Senneth laughed at them in the morning. "I don't normally drink much at all, so I wasn't prepared for the backlash."

Kirra was more sympathetic. "Here," she said, and came to stand beside him where he sat slumped on her very expensive sofa. He was not sure what would happen when she laid her delicate hands on either side of his face. For a moment he was conscious of nothing except the thought that aristocrats had the smoothest skin imaginable; no working woman had palms like that. And then he was aware of a strange, delicious sensation. His headache eased and evaporated; his knotted stomach relaxed. The low sense of malaise that had greeted him when he awoke transformed into a warm sense of well-being.

He looked up at her in astonishment. "How did you do that?"

She laughed and lifted her hands. "It's magic. I'm a healer."

"I think I want to be sick again."

"Do that for me," Justin demanded. "Whatever you did."

Looking a little less delighted, because she didn't like Justin any more than he liked her, Kirra rested her hands on the young Rider's head. Tayse watched his face as the miracle occurred, and wondered if he had looked quite so foolishly pleased.

"*Now* I'm hungry," Justin said with relish. "Pass me that tray."

So they ate, and the Riders told stories of their night before, but the women had no news. Then there was nothing to do for the rest of the day but wait. Justin and Tayse cleaned their weapons and practiced a little swordplay, dancing through the furniture of their bedroom like they might sidestep bodies on a battlefield. The women didn't want to leave, in case word arrived from Els Nocklyn, so the men went out a couple of times to pick up supplies and see if they could absorb any more information. Then they returned to the room again for more waiting.

It was almost dinnertime when a messenger knocked on Kirra's door with news that a visitor was below. Kirra looked bored.

"Did this—visitor—bother to announce who he was?"

The footman was bowing. "No, my lady. But it's—it's—I recognized the crest on her cloak."

"Yes? And?"

The footman glanced over his shoulder, well aware he should not be gossiping about any member of nobility, particularly not this one. "She's a serramarra of Nocklyn, my lady," he whispered. "Come to pay you a visit."

"Ah," said Kirra. "Well, please show her up."

The footman disappeared; the four of them disposed themselves around Kirra's room. "We stay?" Tayse asked.

"You stay," Kirra confirmed. "She'll have her own guards with her. The room will begin to seem quite crowded—except that all of you, of course, will be invisible."

He couldn't help grinning. "Senneth could see to that."

"I didn't mean *literally*," Kirra said. "Merely, that Mayva will not realize you exist."

Indeed, a few minutes later when the small entourage entered, it was clear that, for the serramarra of Nocklyn, there were only two people in the room: herself and Kirra. This despite the fact that she was accompanied by a maid, a groom, and two guards. The men ranged themselves against the wall; the maid took up a seat close to Senneth, who had done as much as she could to make herself disappear without actually invoking the spell.

"Mayva," Kirra cooed, coming forward to kiss the young woman on both cheeks. "I am so glad to see you! I know I arrived completely without notice and I was so sure you wouldn't have time to see me—how kind of you to come by like this!"

Mayva Nocklyn was small and sophisticated, with very dark hair pulled back in a severe style. But even that didn't serve to give much maturity to the round, childish features or counteract the sulky expression that seemed habitual to her face. "Oh, well, I am famished for news of the world, and I was simply delighted when your note came yesterday. But I just couldn't get away till now, what with one thing or another. You would not *believe* how much there is to do now that Papa is sick and Lowell and I are responsible for everything."

Kirra pulled the young woman down to a seat next to her on the silken sofa. "Yes, I was so sorry to hear about your father! Will he be better soon, do you think?"

Mayva Nocklyn shrugged. "Well, I wish he would be! But he just lies there, and doesn't get better and doesn't get worse, and isn't interested in anything, and so all the work falls to us. Lowell likes it, I think," she added, "but I find it very tiresome. Taxes and trade bills and who's loyal and who isn't. I mean, it's so dull."

With every word the woman spoke, Tayse was mentally subtracting a few years from the age he had originally put her at. He was guessing she had to be in her late twenties, but she sounded as petulant as someone nearly ten years younger. Kirra showed no surprise, however, and indeed was nodding vigorously.

"Oh, I know what you mean. Now and then my father will call me and Casserah into a room and tell us something that he swears is *very important*, so of course we nod and listen, but I almost never understand what he's talking about," she said. "I suppose someday we'll have to pay more attention, so we can take over when—when we must, but for now—" She waved a hand. "I don't want to bother."

"Oh, you won't have to bother even when you become marlady," Mayva said carelessly. "Your husband will handle everything."

Not Kirra's husband, Tayse thought, and he saw Senneth's eyes lift oh so quickly to his. She wasn't smiling, but she may as well have been.

"Well, I'm not sure Casserah or I will ever be married," Kirra said merrily. "Casserah is too stubborn, and I'm too flighty. Or so my father says. So we might have to learn about taxes and crop rotation after all."

"I very much like being married," Mayva said. "Maybe I should help you find a husband."

"Do you have anyone in mind?" Kirra said. "I warn you, I can be very picky."

Mayva seemed to be thinking. "Let's see . . . Lowell has a cousin who's handsome and very easygoing. You might like him. He's Thirteenth House, but he has very fine property in Gisseltess."

"But I can't marry a Gisseltess man," Kirra objected. "You could hardly get farther from Danalustrous, and I will want to spend much of my time at home."

"Maybe someone from Kianlever or Coravann," Mayva said. "Kianlever is close to Ghosenhall, you know, so you'd be going to the royal palace all the time. You'd like that. But, again, the only ones I can think of are Thirteenth House, and you might not care to marry so far from your station."

"Well, my mother was Thirteenth House, so I don't know that I can be too particular on that score," Kirra replied.

Mayva was still mulling over bloodlines. "In fact, there are so few marriageable men among the Twelve Houses—well, Darryn Rappengrass, but he—" Mayva shrugged.

"Now, I like ser Darryn," Kirra said, failing to mention she'd encountered him on the road a couple of weeks ago. "A little frivolous, perhaps, but he seems like a pleasant man to be around."

"Yes, but to have Ariane as a mother-in-law—" Mayva shuddered. "She controls him completely. You'd end up doing whatever *she* wanted, and, well, frankly, her politics don't always please me."

"You mean, they don't please *Lowell*," Kirra said coyly.

Mayva laughed. "Well, you're right! He hates Ariane Rappengrass, says she absolutely cannot be trusted. I always liked her well enough before, but I do understand what he's saying. I mean, politics are so much more important than personality, don't you think?"

"Sometimes personality predicts politics," Kirra said. Tayse was fairly certain the subtlety was lost on their visitor.

"Let's see, who else . . . well, of course, there are several young men to choose from among the Brassenthwaites, but you could never marry there," Mayva said.

"Why not? Brassenthwaite and Danalustrous have ties that go back a long way."

Mayva gave an artificial laugh. "Kirra! My dear! Nate

Brassenthwaite is an utter *boor,* but that's not the worst of it! His brother Kiernan has been posturing all up and down Gillengaria, claiming to be from the only House truly loyal to the king. Lowell *hates* all the men of Brassenthwaite, *hates* them, says if there's ever civil war between Houses he will choose whatever side Brassenthwaite does not."

"But Mayva," Kirra said, all wide-eyed, "why would there be civil war? What have you heard?"

Mayva responded with an elaborate shrug, rolling her shoulders, spreading her hands, and casting her eyes upward. "All they talk about," she said, "at my father's house, *all* they talk about is war. The king won't do this so they refuse to do that. The southern Houses don't like that, so they're going to do this instead. I don't understand it. I always thought everybody liked King Baryn. But Lowell keeps saying the power is slipping through his fingers— that he's not strong enough to hold on to it much longer. I don't know. Everywhere I look, I see soldiers. I thought maybe it was the same in the northern Houses. But you look so astonished that I suppose it isn't."

Kirra seemed to pull herself together with an effort. "If it is, my father didn't mention it. And I didn't notice it. When I return, I'll have to ask my father—"

Mayva leaned forward and interrupted. "Ask your father to remember his past friendships with Nocklyn and Gisseltess," she said earnestly. "Lowell told me to mention that as soon as he heard I was coming to see you. Nocklyn has always been good to Danalustrous. We will need allies among the northern Houses."

He probably hoped you would phrase that a bit more cleverly, Tayse thought, for the sentiment could hardly have been more baldly offered. But perhaps this Lowell thought Kirra was just as dim-witted as his wife, and so he didn't think to school her in how to speak.

Kirra was still managing the wide-eyed and ingenuous act. "Do you know—for I'm sure my father will ask me—who else is allied with Nocklyn and Gisseltess?"

Mayva waved a hand. "Fortunalt. Lowell seems very sure of Rayson. I think he is hopeful about Coravann but not so certain of Kianlever. Well, it sits so close to Brassenthwaite, he says—that would be the first House Kiernan would look to if he were trying to crush a rebellion."

"I still don't understand," Kirra complained. "A rebellion? Over what? As you said, I thought everybody liked the king."

"It's the succession," Mayva said. "The king is old, and his daughter is—well—where is she? If she was fit to rule, wouldn't we have seen something of her by now? And if she is not fit to rule, has the king married this strange young woman in order to have another heir? But what if he dies a year from now? Are we to wait for a baby to grow up and be ruler to us all? Lowell says no." Mayva shrugged again. "I don't know."

Kirra appeared to be thinking hard. "Say the new queen had a baby and the king died a year later. Couldn't he appoint a regent? Isn't there someone all the Houses could agree on?"

"I don't know," Mayva said again. "Who?"

"Say Princess Amalie *is* fit to rule," Kirra said, obviously still thinking through it. "She's only seventeen now, isn't she? There would still probably be a regent if the king were to die. He must have thought of that already—he must have someone in mind."

"Well, I've never heard Lowell talk about that," Mayva said doubtfully. "I don't think he likes the idea of regents."

"And the king may live another twenty years," Kirra added. "To be planning for his death like this—well—I don't like the way that sounds, Mayva, I have to be honest. It smacks of—disloyalty."

A risky comment to make, Tayse thought. Mayva's dark brows drew down in a frown, and her full mouth turned even more sulky. "You can't think that Lowell would do anything *traitorous*," Mayva said. "All he cares about is the well-being of the kingdom. We can't let an old king fail to provide for our future."

"But we can't assume he hasn't made those provisions," Kirra said. With every word she seemed to be throwing off her simpering mask and assuming more of her true personality. Tayse could only suppose that she figured she had already learned anything Mayva might have to impart and did not feel like keeping up the pretense any longer. "It seems to me that instead of puffing themselves up on war talk, the southern Houses ought to send a delegation to Ghosenhall and ask the king some of these very questions. Why is that so unreasonable?"

"Oh, and I suppose that's what your father will do," Mayva said.

"Would do, if he was worried about the succession," Kirra said flatly.

Mayva was gathering up her gloves and hat and other small

items she'd carried in with her. "Then I suppose I won't have good news for Lowell after all when I get home," she said. "Danalustrous *won't* side with the southern Houses if there is war."

Kirra came to her feet just as the Nocklyn woman did. "Mayva," Kirra said, her voice very serious. "I hope with all my heart there *isn't* war. I can think of nothing more terrible for the southern Houses *or* the northern ones. I can't tell you what side my father would take because no one can ever predict what my father will do. But you can tell Lowell that Danalustrous will always remember its past friendship with Nocklyn, and that we hope that friendship always remains strong. We have no wish to see a rift between our Houses. I hope there is no war that could bring such a calamity about."

The words had the effect of melting Mayva's pout and causing her to throw herself into Kirra's arms. "No—no—you and I shall be friends forever," she promised, laying her dark hair against the gold. "But I am very uneasy, Kirra. I think sometimes men make plans that women don't understand and can't undo."

Kirra hugged her for a moment, then released her and stepped back. Her eyes were shadowed. "Sometimes women nurse dark secrets as well," she said. "I will not say that men are the only villains."

Mayva laughed and pulled on her gloves. "No! And what Lowell would say if he thought I'd called him a villain! I'm so glad you stopped by, Kirra—even though this conversation has been so strange. I hope I will see you again sometime—when things make more sense."

"Yes," Kirra said softly, "and may that day come soon."

She said nothing else as Mayva made her way to the door, which her groom opened for her, or as the small party filed out into the hallway. Justin closed the door behind them, and they all listened in silence to the sound of their progress down the hall.

Then Kirra pivoted slowly to look at Senneth, still sitting by the window with her eyes downcast. It was not her habitual pose; Tayse wondered why she would not have thrown off the docile disguise the instant Mayva Nocklyn stepped into the corridor.

"Well?" Kirra demanded. "Nothing new, of course, but chilling nonetheless."

"She's the stupidest woman I've ever seen," Justin commented.

"She's average for her rank and station," Kirra shot back at him over her shoulder. She was still watching Senneth.

Justin made a small, ironic bow toward Kirra, who couldn't see him. "Then you must be extraordinary," he said.

"Sen?" Kirra said. "What do you think?"

When Senneth finally lifted her face, she showed an absolutely masklike expression. "I think Justin's right," she said. "You're extraordinary."

Kirra stamped her foot. "That's not what I meant."

Senneth shook her head. "I think Mayva said it best. Men are making plans that none of us will be able to undo. And you said it well: Why are they not seeking a council with the king? We need to go back to Ghosenhall with some speed and lay that proposition before Baryn."

Kirra looked uncertain. "Before going on to Gisseltess?"

"I hardly think we will learn anything in Gisseltess that we don't already know," Senneth said, sounding unutterably weary, "but somehow I think we have to take a look at Halchon Gisseltess for ourselves to be able to make a full report."

"Then," said Tayse, "let's start for the south tonight. Waste no more time here."

Senneth glanced his way. "Yes. Let's pack and be gone within the hour."

The proprietor was astonished at their abrupt departure, begging to be told it was not the accommodations that were inadequate, but Kirra told him in the coolest possible voice that everything had been exactly to her specifications. "But I have received news," she said in a firm voice. "And I cannot linger. I will see you again, I hope, when I return this way."

Justin fetched their horses, and they pushed out into the press of traffic. They hadn't gone more than half a mile when Kirra said, with almost as much petulance as Mayva might be able to muster, "Damn it, I'm hungry. We should have stayed for dinner."

"There are vendors along the way," Justin said with a grin. "We can eat as we ride."

"Oh, yes, *that* suits my notions of elegance," Kirra said. But when Justin plunged off the street to pick up four roasted chickens on wooden skewers, she ate happily along with the rest of them and even praised the quality of the cooking.

"It'll be dark soon," Tayse observed. "We won't get far."

"We won't get anywhere if we have to hunt for Donnal and Cammon," Justin said.

Tayse looked over at him with a grin. "How much would you

like to wager that they're loitering in the road, half a mile from the gate, waiting for us already?"

Justin laughed. "Not a copper, thank you. But it will be interesting to see if they are."

They were. Tayse collected them with a wave, and then the whole party turned south into the gathering dusk, on the well-traveled road to Gisseltess.

CHAPTER

23

Gisseltess was not like other Houses, Kirra explained the next day as they rode. "Each House has its own personality that seems to hold fast through generations," she said. "As, for instance, the Brassenthwaite tradition of loyalty. Even though Kiernan is such an unlikable man, everyone knows he is unswervingly loyal to the king. Even Mayva knows he won't rise up in rebellion. She would never have asked Kiernan or his brothers to join in a plot against the throne. Danalustrous has a reputation for being just—for listening to all sides of an argument and then making a fair disposition. Other Houses have come to my father when they needed mediation—and to my grandfather and my great-grandmother. Those of the Danalustrous line are level-headed. Tilt is sneaky, Merrenstow is charming—those are the sorts of traits that get associated with a House and then seem to stick. And stick because they're *true,*" she added. "But Gisseltess—"

"It has a checkered history," Senneth said. "Sometimes the leader of the House is faithful, sometimes he's faithless, other times he's so tricky you can't tell which way the wind will blow him. In some generations the people of the House are known for their ruthlessness—in other generations, for their calm. It is as if they are always atoning for the sins of their ancestors, so that the sons and daughters of this generation must be as different as possible from their mothers and fathers."

"So?" asked Tayse. "How would you describe Halchon Gisseltess's father?"

Kirra and Senneth exchanged glances. "Absolutely dependable," Kirra said.

Senneth nodded. "A man who would never break his word, though it cost him his fortune and his life. Stubborn, and often unpleasant, and not a man I'd want to spend much time with—but you could trust him."

"Ah," said Tayse. "Then we do have a challenge."

"What about his sister?" Justin asked. "The leader of the Daughters? What's she like?"

Kirra shook her head. "I never met her. She was a recluse by the time I was going out in society. And I never heard people talk about her much, so I think she must have been a bit withdrawn even when she was attending balls and parties." She glanced at Senneth. "Did you ever have any dealings with her?"

Senneth was quiet a moment, as if considering her answer. Tayse instantly suspected that the answer was yes, and that the story would be very interesting if Senneth chose to tell it.

"My father knew her," she said finally, seeming to choose her words with care. "I think he admired her—but then, my father always had a soft spot for fanatics. It made them so easy to understand."

"Was she always a fanatic, then?" Kirra asked.

"A religious fanatic, you mean? She was always dressed in silver and black, any time I saw her, and dripping with moonstones, so, yes, I suppose she's been devoted to the Pale Mother most of her life. But—I meant it in more ways than that. She always seemed to be a person who was completely committed to any cause, any belief, that she happened to take up. She always wore the same colors. She always ate the same foods. If she hated someone, she hated him with all her heart. Not much subtlety to Coralinda Gisseltess."

"What did she think of you?" Tayse asked.

The look she turned his way was full of humor. "Why would she have any reason to think of me?"

"Well, if she knew your father—" Justin said impatiently.

"Let me put it this way. I'm sure, once she learned he had banished me from his house for being a mystic, she congratulated him for having acted with all propriety. I wasn't there, of course, so I don't know for sure." She glanced at Kirra. "And I would be willing to bet she deeply condemns *your* father for not taking a similar course of action when you proved to be tainted with magic."

"That will be interesting, you know," Kirra remarked. "Once all the Houses start taking sides. Those who go courting my father will have to decide how they feel about me."

"Maybe your father will have to decide how he feels about you," Justin said.

Tayse waited for the explosion to come, but Kirra only laughed. Senneth said, "That would be an astute observation if you were talking about any House but Danalustrous. Or even any Danalustrous except Malcolm himself."

"My father would declare war against all other eleven Houses rather than give me up," Kirra said.

Tayse could not keep the soberness from his voice. "I hope you're right. Many an heir has lost his father's preference over something more minor than magic."

"But is that what the war is really about? Magic?" Cammon asked, entering the conversation unexpectedly. He had pulled up close enough to listen to the other four talking, whereas Donnal still followed a few paces behind, not entirely interested. "Or is it about the succession?"

Tayse looked over at Senneth, to see her looking at Kirra. "Well?" Senneth said softly. "What *is* the root cause of the war? If there is a war?"

"I'm unclear," Kirra admitted. "But I think they're intertwined."

"Let us say, for argument's sake, the Houses align according to who can tolerate mystics and who cannot," Tayse said. "Where would the alliances fall?"

Kirra bit her lip. "Well, first, you must determine the king's position, because that determines where Brassenthwaite will go."

"The king seems fond of mystics," Tayse said, glancing sideways at Senneth.

She laughed. "Yes—and if he's married to one, as Aleatha suggested—we will say the crown favors magic."

"Thus Danalustrous will favor the crown," Tayse said. "And we already know Brassenthwaite will follow the king—"

"How does Kiernan Brassenthwaite feel about mystics?" Justin asked. "And could that outweigh his loyalty to the king?"

Again, Tayse caught that quick exchange of glances between Senneth and Kirra. "Kiernan has spoken out harshly against mystics in the past," Kirra admitted. "I don't think he's gone so far as to have them hunted down, like Halchon has, but he—he might be troubled to find himself defending them."

"Then Brassenthwaite is a question mark," Justin said.

Senneth shook her head. "No. Not if the king declares for magic. Brassenthwaite *will not* betray the king."

"I agree," Kirra said.

Justin still looked doubtful, but Tayse pressed on. "All right, then. We'll say Brassenthwaite and Danalustrous stand with the king. What about the other northern Houses?"

"Merrenstow will be loyal," Kirra said. "The king's first wife came from Merrenstow—it is her daughter they would be fighting for."

"And if his daughter is unfit to rule? And a new child of Queen Valri's is the one fighting for the throne?" Tayse asked.

Kirra looked worried. "I don't know."

It turned out they didn't know about most of the Houses. They were pretty quick to put Gisseltess, Nocklyn, and Fortunalt on the list of potential enemies, with Helven likely to ally with other southern leaders, despite Martin Helven's generally peaceable outlook. The women both liked Ariane Rappengrass and felt certain she would not side with Gisseltess—but admitted that she was badly placed, as she was completely ringed around by potential rebels. Coravann, Kianlever, and Storian could have incentives both ways—and Tilt, they said, was impossible to predict.

"Though I can tell you one thing," Kirra said darkly. "Whatever side wins the war will believe Tilt was its ally."

"What about the Lirrenlands?" Tayse asked.

They all looked at Senneth for the answer to that. She thought it over for a moment, then shook her head. "I don't believe the Lirrens will fight," she said. "Unless they are attacked or in some way threatened. They don't seem to care much for the concerns of the rest of Gillengaria. If they are left in peace, I think they will merely watch from behind the mountains."

"Even if the Lirrens stay neutral, your numbers are not good," Tayse said. "You have more solidly against the king than for him, and too many who might bend either way."

"That might be the information we'll need to bring back to the king," Senneth said soberly. "It is time for him to strengthen his alliances now. Make concessions where he must, and make friends where he can."

"And decide," Kirra said slowly, "if he can afford to keep his sorcerous friends. For if he decides not to declare for magic, all the alliances change."

"If the war is about magic," Cammon said.

Tayse narrowed his eyes and looked at Kirra. "If the war is about the succession instead, and no one opposes mystics, what side would your father take? If Princess Amalie is unfit—or dead—and Queen Valri produces no heir? Who would your father back then?"

Kirra looked troubled. "I don't know. It is very hard to say with any certainty what my father will do—unless a member of his family is involved. If it is merely politics—well. I have no idea where he would cast his vote."

"Has he even thought about the succession?" Justin asked.

Kirra gave a little laugh. "My father thinks about everything."

They rode on a few moments in silence. "I foresee an interesting year," Tayse said at last.

Senneth made a sound that might have been a laugh and might have been something more despairing. "Interesting—and bloody," she replied. No one else added a word.

THAT night when they camped, it seemed a good idea to practice swordplay again. Donnal and Cammon were willing, but Senneth merely shook her head when Tayse offered her a practice sword. A few weeks ago, he would have insisted, but he had witnessed what she was capable of; he realized she could defend herself perfectly well without any additional training in blade work.

Thus he and Justin gave their full attention to the other two men, switching opponents halfway through the session. Donnal was competent and, with consistent practice, might eventually become good, but he would never rise to a higher level than that of ordinary civil guard in the service of some minor noble. Cammon—who had neither the upper body strength nor the experience to be a really gifted swordsman—surprised Tayse now and then with his quickness. In particular, he was excellent at predicting and blocking his adversary's next moves, so that Tayse rarely broke through his defenses and landed a blow. The few times he did, of course, he could have killed Cammon with ease—but he was impressed by how rarely he managed the feat.

"You're using your magic, aren't you?" Tayse asked once, as

they dropped their points to the ground and rested a moment. "You're reading me to see where I'll strike next."

"I have to," Cammon admitted. "Or I'd be dead by now. I'm not sure if I can stop even if you tell me to."

Tayse grinned and shook his head. "Use every advantage you have, especially if you're in a fight to the death," he said. "Your enemy won't know why you're so good at evading him. But you'll have to learn how to land a killing blow now and then or the fight will never end."

Even while he talked with Cammon, Tayse surreptitiously watched the women, who were huddled together on Senneth's blanket and talking very quietly but with much animation. Tayse was very sure that whatever they were discussing was more interesting than his own conversation and probably had more bearing on the ultimate outcome of this mission. He glanced at Cammon, wondering if the young man could catch actual words of distant conversations or merely the emotions and intentions communicated by the people around him.

He was fairly certain that even if Cammon could hear what Senneth was saying, he wouldn't repeat it to Tayse, and so he didn't even ask.

They all turned in early, Justin taking first watch and handing it over to Tayse after midnight. Tayse made his usual prowling circle around the perimeter, inspecting the horses, pausing every few yards to merely stand and listen to the noises of the night. The ground was hard beneath his feet and, once he passed outside the light of the campfire, the air was bitterly cold. But the weak breeze that fingered his cheek left cool, moist fingerprints against his skin, and that touch spoke of the green promise of spring. If he breathed deeply, he could almost smell the signs—the unclenching of the earth, the unspiraling tendrils of seeds beneath the soil. Not long now. Winter would finally be over.

He returned to camp, still feeling restless, and made his habitual check of each quiet sleeper. Justin rested on his back, one hand lax upon his dagger. Kirra lay on one side, Donnal curled around her, dark as her own shadow and mimicking her shape just so. Senneth slept with her blankets tossed to either side of her, only her day clothes to protect her from the chill, yet Tayse could feel a pulse of heat rising from her body.

Cammon stirred and started upright as Tayse leaned over to look at him. "Sorry," Tayse whispered, straightening. "It's just me."

Cammon shook his head, his eyes wide with concentration. "No—it's something," he breathed. "Travelers, I think."

"Justin," Tayse snapped in a low voice, and the other Rider moved smoothly from sleep to a combat crouch almost before the syllables of his name had finished sounding. Cammon leaned over to shake Donnal awake. Donnal gathered himself on all fours, glanced around to see Tayse and Justin arming themselves, and slid into wolf shape even as the others watched.

They all listened in absolute silence except for the sound of the women breathing. For a second—for an infinitesimal fraction of an unguarded moment—Tayse wanted to leave them sleeping, undisturbed, while he and the other men vanquished whatever danger was headed their way. And then, in the morning, they could point with pride to whatever had menaced them and been disarmed in the night, and say, "See how we have protected you? See how your preciousness is safe with us?"

Ridiculous. If they had a true fight on their hands, they would need the skills that Senneth and Kirra could contribute.

He became aware of Donnal's low growl, of his stiff-legged stance. The heavy black head swung back and forth as he sniffed the air, then he froze, and bared his teeth, and stared fixedly in one direction.

To the north. Back behind them on the trail.

"How far?" Tayse whispered to Cammon.

"Not far. A hundred yards, maybe."

"We have to wake the women."

But Donnal had already dropped his cold nose and was nuzzling Kirra's cheek. She gasped but made no other sound as she rolled to a seated position. Tayse stepped carefully between the blankets to kneel by Senneth's side and lifted a hand to shake her shoulder.

She opened her eyes before he had touched her and looked straight up at him in the half-light of the fire. For a moment he just regarded her, the unreadable eyes, the tousled white hair, the expression on her face that could have been secretive and could have been merely the lingering effects of dreaming. For a moment, he forgot to speak at all.

"Trouble?" she asked in a very low voice.

"Riders up the road. From Nocklyn Towers, maybe."

She nodded, and the world went dark. That suddenly, the fire disappeared and the cold of the night descended on them all.

Briefly, Tayse was blinded; he could not even make out the shapes of his companions around him. He could hear the sounds of Senneth moving, pushing herself first to a crouch and then to her feet, and around him the others made quiet noises. Gradually he could make out their shadows against the blackness of the night.

"Are they looking for us?" Cammon whispered.

"Hard to know," Tayse replied, breathing the words. "We've drawn some attention along the way, and we might have made a few enemies. But I'd prefer not to get into a fight."

Senneth spoke, her voice as quiet as his. "Cammon. Go keep the horses quiet. Kirra—Donnal. Predator shape, on the other side of the road. Tayse, Justin—stand beside me."

"You'll keep us all invisible?" Justin said, even his whisper managing to sound mocking. "They'll smell the fire."

"Not this fire," she said.

It was true, Tayse realized. He had not given it much thought before. Since she could generate heat without benefit of fuel, the usual scents of burning pine and cedar did not hang over their campsite. The horses were down in a small gully, where the travelers had found a circle of winter grass that had served their mounts for a meal. If Cammon could keep them silent—if Donnal and Kirra could disguise themselves as night creatures—if Senneth could conceal the rest of them—the riders might actually pass this camp without noticing it.

Hushed sounds drifted to his ears as Cammon crept down toward the horses, and Kirra and Donnal padded across the road. Tayse had missed the moment when Kirra transformed herself, but he thought she had taken the shape of a large cat. Not a raelynx, because he didn't see the characteristic tufts on the ears and backbone. Perhaps the majestic royal lion, the golden beast that served as the king's emblem, though it hadn't been seen in Ghosenhall for centuries. Kirra was certainly not above the poetic gesture, even at such a desperate juncture.

Tayse couldn't help but smile.

The smile faded instantly, though, as he caught the sound of oncoming riders. First the quiet clop of shod hooves, then the jingle of bridles, then the occasional whuffle and snort of the horses themselves. It was true; a man on foot could travel much more noiselessly than a man on horseback. But this group was proceeding at an exceedingly stealthy pace. They moved slowly, as if looking for something hidden on either side of the road, and not as if they were in such a hurry to get home that they had made the dangerous decision to travel by night. There was no banter between riders, no random curses or smothered laughs. This was a group of riders on the hunt.

Tayse felt Senneth's hand wrap around his wrist and tug him closer. On her other side, Justin crowded nearer as well. Tayse splayed the fingers of his free hand and stared down at them as best he could in the unhelpful moonlight. While he looked at them, they disappeared.

A few moments later and the riders were passing before them, closely bunched on the road and moving as cautiously as if they expected to fall over a precipice if they took one unwary step. Trying not to breathe, Tayse counted the shapes he could discern in the dark. At least twenty—maybe thirty. There was no way to tell what colors they wore, but their clothes seemed as dark as if they were dressed all in black.

The lead riders were safely down the road and the back riders were just passing the camp when suddenly a low-voiced halt was called, and the whole column stopped. The nearest horses sidled and stamped their feet. Tayse could hear the riders slapping their hands reassuringly against their horses' arched necks, but none of the men spoke a word.

Then a quiet voice carried back from the front ranks. "Wasn't it here? Just about? Isn't this where we spotted that campfire?"

"I would have thought so, but—" A shrug in the voice. "There's nothing here."

"Maybe around the next bend."

"That's what you said fifty yards back."

"I would have thought it was here."

"Do you want us to break up and comb the sides of the road? Maybe they heard us coming and put out the fire."

"I don't smell a fire."

"I thought it was here."

The voices went on in a hushed argument. The men in the back ranks sat patiently on their horses, reins dropped, shoulders slumped a little with weariness. Tayse kept his eyes on the nearest soldiers, moving his gaze from one to the next. They were the closest; they would be the first to inflict damage.

Suddenly, one of the rear soldiers jerked upright in the saddle and yanked on the reins. His horse whinnied with protest and danced backward. The men around him stirred uneasily, one or two admonishing him to be quiet.

"What was that?" the first soldier demanded. "Did you see that?"

"No. What? Too dark to see anything. Stop spooking everyone like that."

"Over there. Eyes. I swear I saw a wolf's eyes."

"Well, maybe you did. Plenty of wolves out this time of year. But they won't attack a party this big, so stop fretting everyone."

"It's too close! If it's not going to attack, why would it get this close to the road?"

"Well, maybe it's—"

"It's rabid, that's what! It's crazed! It'll attack anything, 'cause it doesn't care if it lives or dies!"

"Will you shut up? There's no wolf—there's no attack—and if we aren't quiet, there'll be trouble for all of us—"

"It's just that I saw something—"

"Be quiet! Listen for a minute. I'm sure there's nothing there."

Absolute silence fell again over the soldiers' ranks. They all seemed to be holding their breaths—the soldiers, Tayse, Justin, even Senneth, completely motionless beside him.

And then out of the profound darkness came the most eerie and disturbing wail that Tayse had ever heard. It started like a woman's moan and then rose to a high-pitched keen that was suddenly and decisively strangled. Tayse felt every inch of his skin prickle with primitive fear.

The horses on the road snorted and pawed in a nervous panic. Now the riders lost all hope of silence as they had to calm their mounts and call out cries of "What was *that*?" to each other. One of the horses bolted forward, and his rider shouted out as he tried to wrestle the animal back in position. A commander from the front of the ranks came trotting back, issuing orders in a furious undervoice. "Silence! Control your mounts! Back in formation and no more commotion from back here!"

"Sir!" one of the soldiers called out. "Did you hear that? Do you know what it was?"

"A night predator—probably a cat of some sort," the officer said in disdain. "Certainly not something that should provoke you all into behaving like the rawest recruits."

"That was no ordinary wild cat," one of the soldiers said positively. "I grew up in Coravann, and my daddy and I hunted in the Lireth mountains, and I've heard that sound before."

"What was it, then?" someone asked.

"Raelynx."

His companions reacted with various degrees of horror, shock, and bewilderment—depending, Tayse supposed, on whether or not they'd ever heard of such a creature and had any idea what it could do. The officer was contemptuous.

"Nonsense. There are no raelynxes in this part of the country. Now get back in formation and be ready to move on out." He spurred his horse forward, and his shadowy form was quickly lost from view.

"Guess if anyone was camped here, we've scared them off by now," one of the soldiers said with a flash of humor.

"Or they got eaten by this—raelynx." A soft laugh all around.

"I don't think there were any riders, anyway. I never saw any campfire. Carles said he could see light, but we were half a mile back. Who could see anything that far?"

"Lady's tears, just let me be home and sleeping in a warm bed some night this week," one of the soldiers begged.

A barked command from the head of the line made them all fall silent again. Tayse agreed with the soldier. If there *had* been any campers sleeping along the roadside, they would have woken up by now and scurried off to safety. He could almost breathe freely again. Surely this troop would move on soon.

He felt Senneth's hand tighten on his wrist, and then the night was haunted for a second time by that unearthly, disturbing cry. The moan, the shriek, the whole thing abruptly cut off with a garbled choke. Tayse hoped Cammon was having better luck with their own horses because the ones on the road in front of them were drenched in fear. There was a confusion of neighing and rearing—riders' shouts, horses' wild grunts—and then four or five animals took off at once, running flat-out for freedom. Moments later it was a stampede as the rest of the horses joined them, and the road became a tangled coil of twisting bodies and pounding hooves. But all the chaos was moving away from them, southward. Five minutes after the revolt started, the road before them was clear. Tayse could still catch echoes of cries and whinnies, but the sounds seemed to be coming from a great distance down the road.

Cautiously, their own group reassembled. Senneth released her grip on his wrist—and, Tayse supposed, on Justin's—and Cammon came creeping up from the gully. Kirra and Donnal appeared in human shape, darting across the road. They huddled together before the blackened campfire and spoke in whispers.

"They were looking for us," Tayse said.

"Us? Or just someone camped around a fire?" Donnal asked.

"Us. I'd guess they were guards for the Daughters or else they were men of Gisseltess. We've drawn the attention of both in the past weeks."

"It was too dark to see standards," Senneth said. "I couldn't tell who they were, either."

"Guards for the Daughters," Donnal said. "I could see moons embroidered on their sashes."

"Does that make it better or worse?" Cammon asked.

Senneth shook her head. "I don't know."

Kirra nodded toward Cammon. "Good job with our horses. They didn't panic at all."

Tayse saw him grin in the dark. "Thank you."

Now Kirra was looking at Senneth and laughing. "And most excellent job with the raelynx. Donnal and I had just been wondering if it might be appropriate to raise a howl or two, but that was more effective than anything we would have managed."

Senneth was smiling. "And a Coravann man in the troop to identify the sound! I never thought we would be so lucky."

"I have to admit, it's the first time I've been glad we have that creature along with us," Justin said.

"What now?" Donnal said. "Can we risk going back to sleep?"

Tayse nodded. "We have to sleep sometime. We'll just pull farther off the road—and light no more fires."

A swift smile from Senneth. "I can bring us some warmth even without a flame."

"And you two," Tayse continued, looking at Cammon and Donnal, "you'll have to take turns standing guard for the rest of the night."

Cammon grinned; Donnal merely nodded. "Yes," said the dark-haired Danalustrous man. "I think we're the best watchers you have."

THEY made a cold camp down in the gully, merely finding a relatively flat place on the ground and clearing out the most uncomfortable of the rocks and branches before laying down their bedrolls.

They were all exhausted, but their nerves jangled with adrenaline, so it was hard to sleep. Tayse lay awake a few moments, wondering how long they could continue to travel like this, expecting an attack at any time, day or night, relying on the heightened senses of two of their members to warn them of danger, which might approach from any direction.

They would need all their wits about them as they penetrated into Gisseltess country; it would not do to waste all their energy merely trying to stay alive.

He slept poorly and woke early, starting a fire before the others were up. Senneth's magic had kept them warm enough during the night, but he thought they could risk a fire in daylight this far from the road, and he longed for the taste of hot food. Justin was the next to wake, then the women. Cammon had fallen asleep when he saw Tayse's eyes open; Donnal was still snoring faintly, having taken much of the night watch.

"This will be too hard on them over too many nights," Senneth said, accepting a mug of hot tea from Tayse's hands.

Kirra shook her head. "I should have taken a watch last night. I can take predator shape and listen as well as they can."

Senneth gave her a droll smile. "Why is it I think Donnal's wolf is more alert than your hawk or mountain cat?"

Kirra tossed her gold hair back and laughed. "Because you, like so many others, make the mistake of thinking I am beautiful and frivolous."

"Frivolous, certainly," Justin muttered.

She ignored him. "But I assure you, my senses are every bit as sharp as Donnal's."

"Good, then," Tayse said. "You can relieve them tomorrow night."

Justin looked doubtfully at the sleeping forms. "Should we delay departure this morning? Give them a chance to rest?"

Kirra glanced up at the gloomy sky. "Is it going to snow again? Don't you think we've been on the road for years already as it is?"

"The serramarra appears to be voting against delay," Senneth said. "I would say, let them rest an hour and then be on the move again."

Tayse nodded and rose. "I want to check those tracks. See how many passed by last night and try to gauge how much farther they went. If they're camped ahead of us, waiting for us to ride by, we're no better off than if they find us sleeping in the night."

Justin came to his feet, too. "I'll come with you."

Tayse shook his head. "Stay here with them—in case. And you might look for water nearby. We're low."

"There's a pond down that way," Kirra said, pointing away from the road. "Donnal found it in his wanderings. Frozen over, though."

"Good enough," Tayse said, buckling on his sword belt. "I'll be back within the hour, then we'll head out."

He was on the road a few minutes later, bending from the saddle to try to read the marks left in the dirt and mud. Here was where the whole troop had halted on the road, arguing over where their quarry might be; here were the hoofprints from panicked horses racing at a dead run down the unlit road. Tayse jogged along at a slow rate, eyes on the ground. Looked like the horses had bolted a good two miles before the riders had been able to pull them up. Even then, the ground was churned with hoofprints, indicating that the riders had had a hard time holding their mounts once they'd slowed them. Tayse doubted they'd really been able to quiet the horses for another mile or two, so they'd probably kept going another hour or more until both men and beasts were so exhausted they practically dropped to the ground to make camp.

He halted in the middle of the road, squinting forward, as if he could see a few miles ahead of him to that imagined camp. They would be as tired as the members of his own small group; would they choose to stay a day, or at least linger late, before pushing on southward? And was this the only convent troop out searching the roads for Senneth and her friends? If Tayse and his party cut through the backwoods and took an indirect route south toward Gisseltess, would they be safe, or would they find soldiers awaiting them at every crossroads?

He shook his head. Surely not. Surely no one could think they were that important. No one even knew who they were for certain, and there must be thousands of travelers who crossed this territory every week. The Daughters of the Pale Mother must have many more errands on which to send out their soldiers—other boundaries to guard, other nonbelievers to track. Tayse and his party would go cross-country toward Gisseltess, which would slow them down even more, but at least they would be safe enough from the Silver Lady's soldiers.

He tugged the reins and turned his horse back in the direction from which he'd come.

Blocking his way were four soldiers dressed in silver and black.

He jerked the reins so sharply his horse reared backward, almost pitching him from the saddle. Soldiers behind him now, too—soldiers creeping out of the woods—half of them armed with drawn swords, half with leveled crossbows. He had fallen into a trap, and he was surrounded.

CHAPTER
24

SENNETH went for water, and Justin went with her. "I think you're supposed to watch the camp," she said.

"You're the one who's supposed to be guarded," Justin said. "Tayse doesn't even like to leave you alone in a hotel room."

Is Tayse so dedicated to every person he's commanded to protect? she wanted to ask, but she knew it was a stupid question. Most often, Tayse rode in defense of the king, for whom he would willingly give his life. Even if Justin could detail for Senneth other protective missions Tayse had undertaken, he still would not give her the answer she wanted. Even if he understood why she was asking.

She herself wasn't clear on what she wanted to know.

"This way," Senneth said, skidding a little down an ice-slick trail. "When exactly did Donnal have time to go looking for water last night? That's what I want to know. I think he made this up."

Justin was grinning. "I think he prowled around in wolf shape while the rest of us were sleeping."

"Unfortunately, that still doesn't make me feel safe about sleeping."

"That one could have been bad," Justin admitted. "There were a lot of them."

"Night battle, the advantage would always go to us," Senneth said, reaching more level ground and spotting ahead of her a smooth circle of ice barely as wide as she was tall. "But I'm just as glad it didn't come to bloodshed."

Justin knelt by the frozen pond and began hacking at it with his knife, not waiting for Senneth to offer to melt it with a touch. "It will, soon enough."

She had no answer for that except a sigh.

They broke through several inches of ice to find extremely cold water below, and they filled all their containers. Senneth cupped her hand and scooped up a measure of water, warming it on her palm till it was almost as hot as tea, then sipping it as the steam rose from her fingers. Justin sat back on his heels and watched her without speaking.

She smiled. "I know. You hate my magic."

He rose to his feet. "Not as much as I used to."

She knelt there a moment longer, glancing around to see if there was anything else here they might be able to turn to good account. For a moment, foolishly, she wished it was spring. Or she wished they were going to stay in one spot long enough that she could force spring on one small patch of land. She could do it, she was sure—warm the ground with her hands, coax a few buds from the dormant shrubs, grow flowers and fruits in the dead of winter. If she had the patch of land. If she had the time. If, for more than a day or a week or a month at a time, she ever stayed in one place.

"What's wrong?" Justin asked.

She shook her head and stood up, brushing the cold mud from her knees. "Nothing."

Cammon and Donnal were still sleeping when they got back, but Kirra had breakfast ready, and the three of them ate quickly. It was strange not to have Tayse nearby, his big bulk both a threat and a reassurance, his watchfulness something to count on, to lean against, like the bole of an enormous tree.

"Have you thought about what you're going to *say* to Halchon Gisseltess?" Kirra demanded without preamble. "What you're going to ask him? Will he even see you?"

Senneth's lips twisted. "Will he even see me . . . oh, I think so. By now he must have heard reports of our whole party. He might not have pieced together who we are, but once he hears your name and mine—"

"*Your* name," Kirra said.

Senneth caught Justin's quick look and smiled at him. "Halchon dislikes mystics," she said lightly. "And he has long been familiar with my story."

"I would think that might put you in more danger, then," Justin said. "If you ask to meet him and go to his house—what's to stop him from keeping you?"

Kirra said, "Oh, I don't know—let's see—the fact that he won't want his manor burned down?"

"I can think of places a man could keep a mystic that wouldn't catch fire so easily," Justin said. "A stone dungeon, perhaps, with iron bars."

"It's not entirely safe," Senneth admitted. "Which, I think, is why the king insisted I bring two Riders with me. Surely, even if he was moved to offer violence to *me,* Halchon would not be fool-hardy enough to offer violence to a Rider."

"He might be," Justin said, "if he was already planning a war against the king."

Senneth knew her face looked troubled. "In which case, none of us is safe, in any House, on any road."

Kirra looked around her, as if watching for oncoming foes. "How long has Tayse been gone?" she asked. "He said he'd be back within the hour."

Justin rose to his feet. "I'll go look for him."

Senneth also stood. "Oh no. He wants you with us."

"We'll all go," Kirra said, and leaned over to wake the sleeping men. "Hey, you two. Donnal. Cam. Come on, we know you're tired, but we all are."

Donnal came awake quickly and completely. Cammon moved more groggily, as if coming back from the brink of death. He had guarded the camp for half the night, Senneth thought; it was a wonder he could force himself to open his eyes at all. Her attention shifted to Justin, pacing back and forth between the camp and the road. His uneasiness unsettled her, even though she knew Justin could be volatile. But Tayse was not, and Tayse should have been back by now. It was just that she had gotten so used to rely-ing on Cammon to sound the alarm in the face of any real danger—

Her gaze went back to Cammon, just now taking advantage of a huge yawn to shove a square of bread into his mouth. But Cam-mon, of course, had been sleeping so soundly—

He caught her eyes on him, or the worry in the forefront of her mind. His mouth snapped shut and he glanced around the camp. "Where's Tayse?"

Justin spun to look at him. "We don't know. Scouting. He's supposed to be—"

Cammon scrambled to his feet, a wild expression on his face, and cast about like a hunting dog. Donnal and Kirra rose more slowly, alarm in their eyes. Without warning, Justin flew across the camp and grabbed Cammon by the arms, giving him a hard shake.

"What is it?" the Rider demanded. "What do you see? What happened to him?"

Cammon looked small and frightened in Justin's menacing hold. His eyes went over Justin's shoulder and sought out Senneth. "I think someone's taken him," he said.

THEY were too far behind to do much good—an hour, at least, Justin estimated by the tracks. It was Donnal who had led him to this exact spot, taking the shape of a bloodhound and sniffing his way down the southern road. The scents were fresh, and they had a pretty fair idea of what had happened, so he loped along at a good clip, nose down, ears flopping beside his long face. He had come to a churned-up section of the road and paused there a few moments, snuffling the mud and crossing the road multiple times as if to follow four or five different trails.

Justin had crouched on the side of the road and seemed to be trying to count the hoofprints. When Donnal flowed back into human shape, the Rider came to his feet and they all clustered together in the middle of the road.

"Here," Donnal said quietly. "I'd say there were at least ten soldiers surrounding him. Laid a trap, obviously—probably hoped they'd catch the whole lot of us."

"Did he fight?" Senneth asked.

Justin gave her a quick look, full of morbid humor. "No blood," he said. "No bodies. He didn't fight."

"Where are they taking him?" Kirra asked.

"Depends on who has him," Senneth said. "If it's Gisseltess men—"

"I saw moons on their cloaks last night," Donnal said.

She nodded. "Then—to the convent, I would guess. For—interrogation?"

"For ransom?" Kirra asked doubtfully.

For execution? No one wanted to say the words out loud, but they hovered at the back of Senneth's mind. It was as Justin had said, not an hour ago. A man—or a woman—intent on declaring war against the king could make no stronger statement than to assault a Rider."

"He's still alive," Cammon said. "But I can't tell much else."

"Maybe unconscious," Donnal said.

Senneth shrugged. "He was never easy for Cammon to read."

Cammon rubbed the heels of his hands across his eyes. "I'm sorry," he said in a subdued voice. "I'm so sorry. If I hadn't been sleeping—I would have felt something—even sleeping, I should have felt something—maybe I did, maybe I was too tired to realize it—"

Senneth put a hand on his shoulder. "It's not your fault," she said gently. "Tayse is the last one who would have said *you* had to protect *him*."

Justin flung something violently into the road—a rock, Senneth thought—and strode back for his horse. "Enough talking! We ride to find him *now*!"

Senneth hurried to catch up with him, grabbing one of his arms and pulling him around to face her. He turned so fast she thought he was going to swing his fist and hit her, but he restrained his impulse. His face was wild with fury and fear, and he wrenched free of her with one hard tug.

"Let go of me!" he cried. "He is—Tayse is—I have to go to him! Stay here if you want—all of you—but I must find him! He is—he is—"

And he stood there in the middle of the road, that sneering, cynical boy, and began to weep with grief.

"Justin—Justin," Senneth exclaimed, pulling him back to her with one hand on his arm, putting her other hand up to his cheek, his forehead, pushing some of her own heat and strength into him. "Justin, listen to me, we will get him back. Justin, do you hear me? We will go to him. I will go after him. I will not abandon him, Justin, I swear to you."

He tried desperately to stop his crying and made an effort to turn away from her, humiliated and terrified and paralyzed with helplessness. "You can't—you won't," he sobbed. "You would save Kirra or Cammon, but you won't go after Tayse—you hate him, he's not important to you—"

"Justin," she said, catching his arm again, pulling his face around so he must look in her direction even if he refused to look at her. "I would go after any of you. The Riders, the mystics. I would save you—I will save Tayse. Look at me, Justin. Tell me you believe me. Tell me you trust me. I will not let him fall."

He sniffled and drew his sleeve across his face, trying to clean it, trying to hide it. "It's Tayse," he whispered.

"It's Tayse," she agreed. "We will go after him. But we have to have a plan. Are you with me, Justin? Will you trust me? I can do this. But you have to help."

Finally he looked at her, his eyes swollen, his face blotched with tears and terror. For a moment she saw the boy Tayse must have seen so long ago on the streets of Ghosenhall—fighting for his life, knowing it was such an easy thing to lose. She put her hands again to both sides of his face and drew him closer so that his forehead rested against hers. "I trust you," he whispered. "What do you want me to do?"

FOR the thousandth time, as they cantered down the tricky road, Tayse wondered if he should have fought to what surely would have been his death back there at the ambush. Had he had even one Rider next to him—Justin, or any of them—he would have risked it, because he knew that he could have accounted for at least five of them, and there had only been twelve arrayed against him. But alone he could not have taken them all on. And if their orders had been to fetch him alive, they would not have dared to kill him outright, but they would have injured him seriously to avenge the deaths of their companions. And injured, he would have less chance to escape, less ability to plan.

But it had gone sorely against the grain to remove his hand from his sword hilt and lift both arms into the air and meekly surrender.

Now his hands were tied before him, and he rode in the center of the entire troop, all twenty-five of them. That their leader was delighted with their catch was obvious, for he hadn't been able to hold back a smile when the smaller party came riding in with the hostage. But he hadn't said much, hadn't let any careless words fall, and the whole group was too well-trained to talk a lot during the journey south. Tayse overheard scraps of conversation but nothing that really helped him, nothing that told him for certain who these people were and where they were going.

Although he knew.

As Donnal had reported, they all wore the black and silver of the Pale Mother. Most were young—in their early twenties, he thought—though a few appeared to be more seasoned. He was guessing that the youngest ones were third and fourth sons who could easily be spared from the lower ranks of the gentry, while the veterans were probably lifelong soldiers who had shifted allegiances to a cause that seemed to them more meaningful than merely guarding a noble or a town. Indeed, here and there, Tayse caught glimpses of a pair of gloves embroidered with the Nocklyn crest or a cloak pin ringed 'round with the pearls of Fortunalt. They were believers, most of them, or so Tayse would guess; and that made them, if not as skilled as the Riders themselves, in many other ways just as dangerous.

They stopped only once, to give everyone a chance to take care of personal needs, and were back on the road in less than fifteen minutes. They ate on the run, someone handing Tayse utilitarian rations without comment. He drank from his own water bottle, using his bound hands to lift it to his mouth. He was not sure how far they were from their destination, but he was fairly certain this group didn't plan to stop for the night. And that despite the fact that the whole lot of them had to be even more exhausted than Tayse's small party, since they couldn't possibly have gotten much more sleep.

When they reached an east-west intersection, they turned to the right. West. Then Tayse had been correct: They were heading to the convent that housed the Daughters of the Pale Mother. Well, he had said he wanted to see it. Looked like he would get his chance.

It was close to dusk, and Tayse could feel his own weariness reflected in all the men around him, when he took the chance to speak to one of the men riding nearest him. The recruit looked young—maybe not even twenty—with short brown hair and an eager expression. Tayse could spot no colors on him except for the ubiquitous black and silver, and wondered if the boy might be a merchant's son, or a farmer's. No one important. Not likely to rise in the ranks. Maybe a touch indiscreet.

Tayse leaned over and caught the young man's eye. "How much farther?" he asked.

"Another hour," the soldier replied. A pause, while he apparently determined whether or not he should actually be having a conversation with the prisoner, and then he added, "That's a good horse."

Tayse nodded. "I think he'd last longer than I would. And I'm a heavy burden."

"Big man," the soldier acknowledged. "But strong, I bet. Impressive reach with your sword."

Tayse almost smiled. "So they tell me."

The young man hesitated, then the words burst out of him. "Are you really a Rider?"

Are you really a traitor? Tayse wanted to ask in return, but he knew better than to antagonize the first person who had showed him the slightest sign of friendliness. "I don't think I should be discussing who I am until I'm talking with someone—a little more official."

"Oh! Right! Yes, and I—stupid," the soldier said and seemed to blush. He must not have been with this outfit for long, Tayse thought. His skills probably weren't very good, either. Something to keep in mind if Tayse had a chance to try to hack his way to freedom. Go for the young ones, the inexperienced ones. They would fall faster to his sword.

"Where's your home?" Tayse asked, trying to put the young man at ease again. "Originally, I mean."

"Helven. Fellows here from all over, though."

"Even the northern counties?"

"Not so many of those. But one or two."

"How'd you hear about it? The Daughters—this place."

The young man shrugged. "Some soldiers came to town, talking about it. Well, we'd all heard about the convent and a couple of women from town, they went to join. I didn't think there was a place for men. But my ma, she's always had a little shrine out in the woods—gone to it since her grandmother's day. Took me there when I was a little boy." He looked earnestly over at Tayse. "There are plenty who don't follow the Pale Mother—who don't understand her. But I've felt her presence since I was a kid—I always knew she was real, that she was with me. So when the chance came to serve—I don't know who wanted to pack me up the fastest, my ma or me. I never cared for woodworking anyway. It's not like I was leaving anything behind."

"They train you? In swordfighting, other soldier skills?"

"Yes," the young man said proudly. "And I'm good. Or I will be good. And I get better every day."

"How many of you are there?"

The soldier opened his mouth to answer, and then stopped and considered that he was speaking to an enemy. He blushed again, deep red this time. "Plenty of us," he said stiffly. "And more every day."

Tayse tried to think of something else innocuous to ask, just to keep the conversation going, but it was clear his young informant was not about to accidentally let slip any more facts. The soldier nodded at him, just to be polite, then spurred his horse forward and rejoined the ranks of his fellow guards.

No one else spoke to Tayse for the rest of the ride.

Finally, just before full dark, Tayse got his first glimpse of the building that housed the Daughters of the Pale Mother. The sight would have brought him to a dead halt if he hadn't been swept along by the other riders. They were in deep forest now, and the path ahead was more often than not obscured by heavy growth and the solid bulk of ancient trees. There was a flash of luminescent white—then a turn in the trail hid it from view. Another quarter mile and the block of white became bigger, more lustrous, but still hard to make out—and then the winding of the path put it out of sight once more. Finally they broke free of the forest and into a monstrous clearing—and sitting at the heart of the open space was one of the prettiest sights Tayse had ever seen.

Before him lay what looked like a castle made of lacy stone architecture, with tiny turrets at a dozen points along the roof. It was built entirely of white stone and graced with a hundred windows, and in each window burned a candle with a still, white flame. Tayse could not immediately gauge its scale or how many stories it might encompass, but he thought it might be four or five levels high and big enough to hold twenty or thirty rooms on every floor. Behind it to either side he could make out lesser structures—both smaller and not as ornate—and he supposed these were the barracks for the soldiers as well as stables and other working buildings. The entire compound was enclosed by a wall higher than Tayse's head and set with a grilled gate that looked strong enough to withstand even a determined battering. He was guessing that the convent had its own water supply—a deep well or perhaps even the upsurge of an underground stream—and probably a vegetable garden and some livestock on hand as well. The entire compound was about the size of a small farm and no doubt could be self-sufficient for an extended period of time.

If anyone was thinking of laying siege to it. If anyone had reason to.

Tayse's escort closed around him as the heavy metal gates swung open. He counted ten men at the gate and spotted more dotting the far perimeter of the wall. No doubt there were also soldiers stationed on the roof of the castle, and even more guards now off duty in the barracks. Still looking, still counting, he followed his escort and rode in.

It was hard to take in much during their brief ride up to the castle. It was almost dark, and he was surrounded by bodies. But he caught a glimpse of a fountain here, a stand of decorative trees there, a statue or two, and a carpet of faded brown grass that would no doubt turn lush and green come spring. A lovely place, obviously, designed for graciousness. A serene site for losing oneself in contemplation of the Pale Mother's many blessings.

Though he imagined that serenity was harder to come by when it was intruded on by troops of armed men riding out to scour the countryside.

Flambeaux flung wavering light onto the long stone pathway leading up to the massive door of the castle, and more soldiers guarded the entrance. Tayse became aware that most of the other riders in his group had turned off the path to head toward the outbuildings, whereas he and a small escort kept proceeding forward. The commander of the riding party was already out of the saddle and standing beside his horse, awaiting him near the entrance. Tayse came abreast of him and pulled to a stop.

"Dismount," the officer said. Awkwardly, because of his bound hands, Tayse slid from his horse. "I have a knife at your back," the officer said—and, indeed, Tayse felt the point prickle against his neck. "And there are guards everywhere. You would be wise to just go straight forward and enter the manor without resisting."

"You've taken all my weapons," Tayse said calmly. "I have nothing with which to resist."

A small grunt for that and a nudge with the knife tip. Tayse walked forward, mounted the broad stone stairs, and stepped through the great doors.

He had entered an anteroom big enough to serve as the king's audience chamber. The ceiling was groined with delicate woven arch work; huge circular chandeliers threw brilliant light onto the flagged floor and the embroidered curtains hanging on the distant walls. Several hundred people could fit in here at once and not feel crowded; a troop of mounted soldiers could wait here for an assault on the door.

At the moment, there were only a handful of people in the hall, most of them young women crossing the room from one doorway to another and casting quick, curious glances at Tayse and his guard. There were, of course, additional soldiers inside, and two of these hurried over as soon as Tayse and his escort stepped through the doors.

"So this is the Rider," one of them said, but the other silenced him with a sharp gesture.

"A room has been prepared for him," the second guard said, which made Tayse realize that someone must have ridden ahead with the great news of his capture. "And the Lestra wants to speak with him."

Tayse's guard made a quick half bow, clearly a gesture of respect for a senior officer. "I'll leave him in your hands, then."

"Good work," the other said. "The Lestra will be pleased."

Tayse's guard touched the first two fingers of his right hand to the embroidered moon over his heart. "Praise the Lady," he said quietly, nodded again, and smartly stepped away.

The senior soldier turned to Tayse. He looked older than Tayse, dark hair graying to silver, hard face starting to lose some of its shape to the pull of old age. The green eyes were cold. "So, Rider," he said in an even colder voice, "do you have a name?"

No need to conceal it. If word returned to Ghosenhall that a King's Rider had been taken in the southern provinces, Baryn would know instantly which Rider it was. "Tayse."

"Where are your friends, Tayse?"

"We got separated on the road."

"Are they likely to follow you?"

Tayse lifted his eyes and glanced expressively around the room. "Here? To what end?"

A wintry smile from the veteran. "To negotiate your release?"

"It would seem," Tayse said carefully, "that they might have better luck continuing their own journey and meeting their original goals."

"They will return to Ghosenhall, then?"

"Eventually."

"I don't know that you will be joining them there."

Tayse met the frosty eyes with a cold look of his own. "I expect not. Will the king be told where I am?"

"That's up to the Lestra. I'm sure in time the king will learn what's happened to you."

That was pretty plain, Tayse thought: They did not expect him to ever leave this place. Could it be they truly planned to kill him? It seemed impossible—with no war declared, no overt enmity at all between the king and any of the southern factions—but as an opening salvo in a planned rebellion, it was sure to get attention. Tayse tried not to shiver. A lifelong soldier, he had always lived intimately with the shadow of his own death; he did not particularly fear it. He would fear it less if he was allowed to face it with a sword in his hand and the prospect of bringing some of his opponents along with him. But that seemed unlikely to be his destiny. More likely a fairly public execution, though he would like to think a religious order would balk at torture. Hanging, then, or beheading, or burning.

He had to suppress another shiver.

"This way," the soldier said and turned into one of the many doorways that opened off the grand hall. Tayse followed him, and another guard fell in step behind him.

What Tayse saw of the rest of the convent was as impressive as its exterior. The white stone walls gave every hallway a sweet, glowing beauty; the proportions of the arches and doorways and occasional niches were exceptionally pleasing to the eye. Now and then they passed some of the inhabitants of the convent—mostly young girls in the white robes of novices but some in darker colors of green and blue—though his guards spoke to none of them and the women did not even look their way. Tayse paid close attention to the turnings they took and was pretty sure he'd be able to retrace his steps—less sure that he'd ever have a chance.

They eventually made their way into a small, more dimly lit corridor lined with dark wood doors, and the guard unlocked the one at the very end. The room revealed was small and featured spare furniture: a narrow bed, a straight-backed chair, a nightstand and pitcher, a chamber pot. There was a meager fire burning in a tiny grate, though it did very little to chase the chill from the room.

In the single window, small and high, a solitary candle burned. Iron rods eliminated any thought of escape through that opening.

A long chain had been shackled to one of the window bars, and as soon as they entered, the senior guard attached the other end to Tayse's left wrist. Then he slit the rope tying Tayse's hands together. The manacle was heavy; the weight of the entire chain would quickly become tedious if Tayse tried to do much pacing.

The guard gave Tayse a curious look as he stepped back toward the door. "You're tame, for a Rider," he said, a note of contempt in his voice.

Now—when he was utterly powerless, when he could not for a moment inspire in anyone a desire to kill him for an implied threat—Tayse gave him back a slow, dangerous smile. "You only think I am," he said.

The guard actually looked taken aback—almost alarmed—but he recovered immediately. "The Lestra will be by to see you shortly. Food will be brought to you. Do not speak to any of the women—they are pure. Do not—" He shrugged. "Do not do anything foolish."

I already have. I have let myself get taken by your men, Tayse thought. "Is there anything you can tell me about my probable fate?" he asked coolly.

The soldier hesitated and then shrugged. "Much depends on the king himself and answers he gives to questions the Lestra poses. But you are a rich prize, as you must know. The best you can hope for is a long captivity. I do not think it will be made unduly unpleasant, no matter how your king responds."

Tayse nodded. "What I would expect, then. It will be interesting to speak with the woman who heads your order."

"If you are wise, you would be respectful."

Tayse shrugged. "I'm a Rider," he said, and left it to the other to determine whether that meant habit would compel him to graciousness or arrogance would lead him to disdain.

The soldier nodded and left the room without another word. Tayse heard the lock fall in place seconds after the door shut.

He stood there a moment, glancing from side to side, but there was little else to see, nothing to assess that he had not noticed when he first walked in. No way to escape, no chance of getting word to his king or his companions. He was here until they killed him off or decided to set him free.

He moved closer to the window, gauging its height. He missed on his first try, but the second time he leapt up, he was able to knock the candle from the sill. It rolled to the stone floor, its flame instantly extinguished.

One empty window looking out over the convent walls. It was an exceptionally minor victory, but it pleased Tayse nonetheless. Dragging the chain, he crossed the room and relit the candle at the hearth fire, then stepped across the room to seat himself cross-legged on the bed.

Nothing left to do now but wait for Senneth to find him.

CHAPTER
25

TAYSE had been in his room maybe two hours when the lock clicked back, and the door was opened. He was sitting on his bed and made no effort to stand as the two white-robed novices entered. One carried a tray of food, the other a fresh pitcher of water. Neither of them looked at him, and he did not attempt to speak. He was a little surprised that there weren't servants to do such work, but then he supposed that there might be some clause of humility in their order that led them to care for themselves or take turns caring for each other. Clearly no one considered him a threat so great that young girls could not risk exposure to him. It made him want to roar and shake the shackle, but he did not.

Once they were gone, he ate the food, since poison didn't seem to be among the hazards he would have to face here. Boredom might be, but he had the effective antidote to that, for the moment, anyway: exhaustion. He stretched himself out on the narrow bed and slept.

It might have been midnight when there was another sound at the door. Trained to sleep lightly, especially in perilous circumstances, Tayse came instantly awake and scrambled to his feet. Automatically, he bunched his hand around a coil of chain. Not much of a weapon, but it made him feel as if he might have something to strike with after all if someone came in intending him harm.

Two women entered, dressed in dark violet robes. He guessed the color signified some status, since both of them were older than the novices he'd seen so far. One looked patrician enough to at least be Thirteenth House; the other looked more rugged, like a peasant or a farmer. The patrician one spoke.

"The Lestra has come to speak with you. You will stand unless she gives you permission to sit. You will address her always as 'my lady.' You will speak in quiet and respectful terms. Guards wait outside the door to enforce your cooperation."

"I will be happy to meet under those conditions," he said.

The women nodded and backed out.

A moment later, the Lestra marched in.

Despite the very real danger of his circumstances, Tayse's strongest emotion was curiosity as he looked over the woman who had organized the Daughters of the Pale Mother. She was not exceptionally tall—maybe five and a half feet—but she was so solidly built and filled with such assurance that she had an instant presence. Her thick hair was a streaky gray and hung in a braid all the way to her knees, though wisps of it curled around her face as though to soften its strong, square contours. She was dressed in a black silk robe embroidered so heavily with silver thread that the darker color was hard to see. Tayse thought immediately of a winter sky at night, so laden with stars that it was possible to forget there was a sky beneath all the glitter.

It was clear she considered herself the incarnation of the Silver Lady herself.

In one hand she carried a lamp, held almost face high. Its globe was round and glowed with a rich golden light that set all her finery to twinkling but emphasized the harshness of her face. Tayse had a quick thought that this lamp was meant to symbolize the moon, and that the Lestra believed she was the Pale Mother, holding the night beacon in her hands.

Tayse had even less reason than before to believe that she might be amenable to rational argument.

She set the lamp down on the floor and drew up the single high-backed chair to face him where he stood. She had not seemed to calculate her movements, but he was quite sure she sat just outside the reach of his hand should he suddenly try to leap to the length of the chain. Her eyes, which she now turned in his direction, were wide-set and large. In the uncertain light of the chamber, they looked to be dead black.

"So," she said, and her voice was low and curiously musical. "They tell me you are a Rider named Tayse."

He nodded. "I am."

Her eyes moved expressively from the end of the chain attached to the window grill and down to the manacle on his hand. "Forgive our makeshift measures at holding you in check," she said. "We are not used to accommodating prisoners here at Lumanen Convent."

"If you intend to take many more of them, perhaps you'll need to invest in more traditional cells," he replied.

Her nostrils flared to indicate dislike of his impertinence, but she did not respond to him directly. "Tell me, Tayse, what are you doing on the road between Nocklyn and Gisseltess at such an inhospitable time of year?"

"Carrying out the commission of my king."

She cocked her head to one side. "And what is this commission?"

"I believe the king would prefer I not share his private business with you. Or anyone."

She nodded; it was a perfectly legitimate response. "You have been traveling for some weeks now in the company of several others, have you not?"

"There are six in our party."

"Who are your companions?"

He was silent.

"I believe I can guess at some of their roles," she pursued. "Two of them at least are mystics, for their antics have been described to me by those who have witnessed some of their more spectacular displays. Two of the others appear to be additional guards of some sort, though not Riders. The last one is, like yourself, in service to the king."

Tayse nodded again. "Most of that is accurate."

She leaned forward. "I am most interested in the identities of the women who are mystics."

"I wonder why that would be," he replied.

"It is always good to know the names and the faces of the people who are ranged against you," she said with composure. "And these two, I think, are women with whom I am somewhat familiar."

"Oh?"

Her fingers toyed briefly with the strands of her braid. "A

golden-haired woman of noble birth with the skill of healing in her hands," she said. "There are not so many mystics born to the Twelve Houses, and only one I can think of who fits that description. Kirra Danalustrous."

"A pretty name," Tayse commented.

She smiled. "And her traveling companion. Some years older than Kirra, with hair as white as a candle flame and the ability to start a fire with her touch. The only one I knew of with such power I thought had died some years back. But perhaps this is another woman."

Tayse shrugged. "I don't know who you know and who you don't."

"So you will not tell me their names."

"I am enjoined by the king to tell as little as possible."

She fixed those dark eyes on him. "I admit I am interested to know why your king—"

"Your king as well," he interrupted.

She narrowed her eyes but did not bother to reprimand him. "Why he would send mystics on the road in company with Riders on a mission they are not eager to discuss."

Once again, Tayse declined to answer.

"You do not look to be a stupid man, Tayse," she said. "I will have to assume you made some observations during your trek through the southern provinces."

"I have noticed that the Daughters of the Pale Mother have achieved some influence with the southern Houses. There are not so many shrines and moonstones to be found up near Ghosenhall."

"More shame to the king and the northern Houses, then. For the Pale Mother is all present. Her eye looks everywhere; her light falls to the farthest corners of the world."

He shrugged. "Not that I've seen."

She smiled, a rather grim expression. "You will yet be amazed at what you see, Tayse."

That seeming to require no answer, he gave none.

She shifted in her chair. "As I said, you do not seem like a stupid man, but I am thinking you are perhaps untaught. You do not know certain things. You are not evil so much as uneducated."

"Evil?" he repeated before he could stop himself.

She nodded. "The mystics are evil, Tayse, and those who worship them are evil as well."

"I don't worship mystics. I don't worship anyone. I am loyal to my king. I am faithful to my fellow men. Those are the only covenants I strike."

She lifted a finger as if in admonition. "Ah! So your soul is as yet unclaimed by either the sweet light or the bitter darkness. Yet you are in danger, Tayse, great danger, for you have consorted with sorceresses and you are tainted down to the last drop of your blood."

Again, he spoke before he really took the time to review his words. "I feel like I'm in more danger here in your presence than I ever was while I traveled on the road with mystics."

She gave him that chilling smile again. "But then, you are unenlightened, and you do not understand the difference between physical and mortal danger."

He smiled back. "I understand death," he said. "Are you dealing in that? The mystics did not, while I was with them."

"They could kill your soul, Tayse. They could blacken it with sorcerous fumes till it turned so dark you would never get it clean again. A mystic's touch is degrading. It may, for a time, exhilarate the flesh, but it ultimately eats away every living organ beneath the skin. Have you been consorting with mystics, Tayse? Have they corrupted you? Is the flesh even now barely binding together a heart that is veined with ill intent and blood that runs black as tar?"

He was almost speechless. Both her venom and her imagery made his skin crawl with distaste, and every one of his warning senses screamed danger. But there was practically no defense to make. "I consider myself an honest man," he managed to say. "I believe myself corrupted by no one."

The Lestra leaned back in her chair. "I hope for your sake that is true, Tayse," she said. He wished she would stop using his name. "But your king has already fallen prey to magic."

For a moment, he stopped breathing. "What do you mean?"

She lifted her arms in an uncertain gesture, as if the boundaries of good and evil were so amorphous she could not describe them with a single arc of her hands. "He has allowed himself to be tainted, Tayse. He has gone into the embrace of unhallowed women. He has allied himself with enchanters. He will bring ruin to his whole country."

"He is a good king," Tayse said.

"He must be destroyed," she replied.

If he had not been standing already, he would have leapt to his feet. He could not even say he was surprised, but shock lanced through him in a single pulse of fury. He managed to refrain from speaking until the spell of darkness passed. "And you would consider yourself the agent of his destruction?"

"It is the task the Pale Mother has given me," she said simply.

"Then yours is the heart that is black," he said in a quiet voice. "For you will bring death and bloodshed to the Twelve Houses of Gillengaria."

She nodded. "There are those who will see it that way. So it always is for those few who have the insight and the strength to wrench a country away from its headlong, disastrous course. I am prepared to be despised because I know I am righteous. I will eventually be honored. So is the course of every savior."

"How do I fit into your plans?" he asked.

She considered him, as if she had just now noticed him. "It is unclear. I am sure your king has a great interest in recovering you, which makes you very precious to me. If I harm you, he will wish to harm me in return. I am not prepared yet to open hostilities. Thus, for the moment, you serve me better alive. But now that I look at you, I have to wonder: Is there not a way I can serve you as well?"

She was a raving lunatic. He kept his voice neutral as he said, "What could you possibly mean by that?"

She leaned forward again. "You are a man hovering between influences, Tayse. I feel it so clearly. You have long been your king's most loyal vassal—a good man, according to your lights, and I respect your dedication, your commitment to a cause. But lately—I can sense this, I can feel the disturbance in your heart and your mind—lately you have begun to waver. You have begun to fall under the spell of one of these mystics—these enchanters. You are so close to being consumed by magic. Your white heart is on the brink of turning to cinder and ash. *I* can rescue you from this fate. *I* can turn your heart back to the light, back to the way of silver. *I* can make you a soldier in the Pale Mother's army, which is the path to certain glory. I can save you—and you in turn can pour your strength into my cause."

For a moment, he absolutely did not know what to say. It was seriously disturbing that she had picked up on his divided loyalties, for he had no doubt that part of her could read his growing obsession with Senneth, though she had not correctly divined the nature of that attachment. But the last person he would go to for aid or salvation was this ranting fanatic caught up in her own austere rapture. Yet he was not in a position to alienate her entirely. He could neither laugh in her face nor brush past her and walk out.

"I—I don't know how to answer you, my lady," he said at last.

She nodded. "Yes. You are conflicted. You are bound deeply by old vows. I would not expect you to suddenly swear fealty to me. I could not trust a man who could so blithely cast off old associations. But I will work with you. I think you have promise. I think you could be a brave knight to our most gracious Silver Lady."

He bowed his head and judged it safe to say nothing. He heard the rustle of fabric as she came to her feet. "Tayse," she said, and he looked up. She tossed a small gleaming object his way, and he caught it by instinct. It felt cool as glass in his hand. He opened his fingers to see what he was holding.

A moonstone the size of a bird's egg. When he looked back at her, she was smiling.

"It does not burn your skin," she said. "It does not make you cry out in pain. You are not so far gone as you think, Tayse. You are still open to the influence of the goddess."

"Does this mean that you can trust me?" he asked.

She laughed, a sound so merry that it was almost bizarre, in this place, under these circumstances. "Oh, Tayse. It will be weeks and weeks before I can trust you. But it means that you are not hopeless. It means you have not given your soul to evil. Would you like to keep the stone?"

Why not? "If I may," he said.

She nodded. "I will be happy to leave it with you. I hope the goddess sends you peaceful dreams."

This seemed to be a benediction and farewell. "I would wish the same for you, my lady," he replied gravely.

She paused with her hand on the door. "We will talk again," she promised. "I am looking forward to it."

He nodded so deeply she could take his response as a bow, but he did not speak again as she opened the door and went out.

He very much doubted his dreams would be peaceful. He very much doubted he would sleep at all.

SENNETH and her companions traveled slowly down the path that Tayse's captors had followed, trying to avoid the hazards of the road. Indeed, they were so careful that, from time to time, Senneth thought their greatest danger lay in driving Justin mad. The young Rider was trying very hard to tamp down his impatience and his fear, but their cautious progress south and then west clearly made him want to run them all through with a sword.

They ignored him as best they could, which was easy enough as they were all preoccupied by different tasks.

Kirra had taken hawk shape and flown ahead to scout out the road, making sure no soldiers lay in ambush. Cammon gave most of his attention to controlling the raelynx. Donnal remained in dog form, following Tayse's scent, though Senneth was pretty sure where the trail would lead them: to the Lumanen Convent in the unclaimed land between Nocklyn and Gisseltess.

Senneth was wholly absorbed by planning what she would do when they arrived at the gates to the convent. She could already feel a faint headache building at the back of her skull, a warning to hold her fury in check. So she made an effort to keep her shoulders relaxed, her mind clear, her thoughts orderly. She would not be much use to anyone if she practically destroyed herself every time she lashed out with magic.

"They can't hurt him. A King's Rider? That would be stupid," Justin was saying. He had continued this litany more or less continuously since they had set out from the site of the ambush this morning. "I mean, if they kill him, the king will send his troops to the convent to destroy them. What have they gained then? They're all dead."

Unless Gisseltess guards and Nocklyn soldiers were massed before the convent awaiting the assault. Unless the very thing the southern rebels wanted was a pretext to go to war. Senneth did not offer these observations.

"I mean, killing a King's Rider would be like assassinating the marlord of one of the Houses," Justin went on. "It would be suicide."

Cammon looked at Senneth as if she was the only one beside him on the road. "Are we going to ride straight through or stop for the night?" he asked.

"Ride straight through," Justin said.

Senneth shook her head. "Stop for the night."

Justin was incensed. "What? And leave him there—leave him unprotected for another eight or ten hours? No, no, you don't leave a fellow Rider in danger that long. We go straight to the convent."

Senneth looked at him, willing him, for just a moment, to shut up. "Coralinda Gisseltess is the handmaiden of the moon goddess," Senneth said softly. "She is strongest at night. I want to take her on when we have some chance of defeating her."

"But Tayse—"

"I don't think she will act so soon," Senneth interrupted. "He is too rich a prize to throw away on a whim."

"She would be a fool to harm a Rider," Justin said.

"Yes," Senneth said, "she would."

It was not quite nightfall when Kirra returned to the riding party and resumed the shape of a woman. Even at such a critical time, Senneth was fascinated to watch her transformation. Donnal's shifts between human and animal shape tended to be swift, melting exchanges that were impossible for the eye to follow or the senses to absorb. But Kirra altered shape more slowly, metamorphosing in discrete stages. The hawk landed practically at their horses' hooves in the middle of the road, then craned its neck, which stretched and stretched to a ludicrous length. The spread wings rolled into slender shapes and brightened from feather dark to skin light; the thin, taloned feet grew plump and pink. The transmogrification still took no more than a minute or two, but it was so deliberate that Senneth was sure Kirra was thinking through every single stage. Donnal, she thought, operated purely on instinct as he flicked from being to being. Though Donnal sat quietly panting in the middle of the road and showed no inclination to become human at all.

"How far is the convent?" Senneth asked when Kirra was done.

"About three miles down this road. We can be there very quickly in the morning."

"We could be there in less than an hour *now*," Justin said.

Senneth gave him a long, careful look. If he was going to try to storm the convent on his own, they would all be lost—Justin, Tayse, all of them. He fidgeted a little under her gaze but stared back defiantly. "Justin," she said. "We will save him. We will not do it tonight."

"But the Daughters of the Pale Mother—"

"I am a Daughter of the Bright Mother. Do you know what that means?" she interrupted. "Have you listened as I've talked during this trip? Have you seen the power I can conjure with my hands? I am a creature spawned by the sun. My strength is at its greatest during daylight. You cannot get him back without me, and I say we move tomorrow. Do you understand? Do you agree? Because I swear to you, I will strike you silent here, in this place, to await us until we return tomorrow with Tayse safely in our hands, if you will not give me your pledge now."

She spoke coolly but with great emphasis, and she meant every word. He stared at her, looking so young, so helpless, yet still so dangerous, and she was afraid to let herself blink or turn away. So she held his gaze, as she would have held the raelynx's gaze, and she did not relent or drop her eyes. Finally he took a quick gasp of air, dropped his head, and nodded.

"Say it," she said.

"I will trust you, Senneth," he said in a low voice. "I will do what you want."

"All right. We camp here for the night. But I don't imagine that we'll get much sleep."

They traveled some distance off the main road to make an entirely uncomfortable—though, they hoped, invisible—camp within the edges of the forest that guarded the convent. The ground was damp, though Senneth used her hands to heat the soil to the point where the mud grew cracked and dry. She was also able to encase them in a small bubble of acceptable warmth, but they ate their food cold and washed it down with what water they had left in their supplies.

"Three watches," Senneth said as they sat together finishing their meals. "Cammon first. Then Kirra in the middle night, Donnal in the early morning. Kirra—"

"I know," she said. "Animal shape. So my senses are sharpest."

"I can watch some part of the night," Justin said.

Senneth shook her head. "You and I don't have the skills they have, so we cannot really help. Rest while you can—if you can."

He nodded. "It's one of the things the old soldiers try to teach the new ones. Sometimes the only thing you can do that's of any use is keep yourself strong. It's the hardest thing to learn."

"When we leave the convent tomorrow—when we have freed Tayse," Senneth went on, as if that was a foregone conclusion, as if she didn't fear that they would all lose their lives or their freedom in this wild gamble, "we will go south again. To Gisseltess."

"Is that safe?" Kirra asked.

"Oh, I doubt it. My plan is to send one of you—Kirra or Donnal—ahead with a message to Halchon. We will have him

meet us in some neutral place. I think he will agree to it, just out
of curiosity."

"But Sen," Kirra said, her voice urgent, "what can we learn
from speaking to him directly that we don't already know? Why
don't we just take Tayse and head straight back for Ghosenhall?"

Why indeed? Senneth made a fist of her hand and rested her
chin upon it. "Because I, too, have a curiosity," she said at last. "I
want to hear what he has to say."

She half expected someone—Justin, most likely—to grumble
Fine reason to get us all killed, but no one said anything. It was
her mission, after all; they were all here to support her. And she
was convinced they had to see Halchon Gisseltess to put all the
pieces together.

"Well, if we're all going to be up for part of the night, we'd
better sleep now while we can," Cammon said, breaking the silence at last. "Or—well—the rest of you lie down. I will stay up
and watch."

Within a few moments, the others had arranged themselves as
well as they could. Kirra and Donnal appeared to fall instantly
asleep; Senneth could tell that Justin lay awake for a long time,
though he held his body very still. If she'd been thinking about it,
she would have had Kirra brush her hand across his forehead before she curled up on her bedroll, for the healer's touch could
sometimes soothe a man into dreaming. But perhaps not Kirra's
touch on Justin's head, and perhaps not this night.

Senneth knew she should sleep while she could, but for a
while she let her mind drift with the mind of the raelynx, prowling through the undergrowth about fifty yards from their camp. It
was hungry and restless, but she would not allow it to feed, merely
let it scent the rich odors of the night and occasionally hiss with
frustrated desire. Briefly she wished that she had the ability to
shape-shift, so she could take raelynx form herself, run like sup-
ple sunlight through the forest, exist on nothing except hunger
and menace and power.

But she would not trade her own fiery skills for the ability to
transmogrify. She had power and menace enough as it was.

Eventually she dozed for a few hours, rousing again as Cammon shook Kirra awake and the serramarra slipped into the shape
of a lion. Seeing Senneth's eyes open, Cammon turned to her and
whispered, "I can take the raelynx back while you sleep."

She shook her head. "I want to keep him now and through the morning. I want you free to concentrate on danger, even while you sleep."

"Do you think they're looking for us? Do you think they really expect us to approach them tomorrow?"

She smiled at him in the dark. "I don't think the Daughters do, but I would guess that Tayse knows we're coming."

"Will we free him?" Cammon asked.

Yes, or all become prisoners. "We'll free him," she said. "Now lie down, and let's go to sleep."

CHAPTER
26

Morning came swiftly, and they were all tired. They'd been tired for a long time, and Senneth couldn't imagine things would get any less exhausting as they traveled into Gisseltess. Maybe Kirra was right, and they should just head straight back to Ghosenhall.

Maybe not.

They ate quickly, then mounted and set off along the forested road. Donnal was in wolf shape now, though Senneth had told him she wanted him human and on horseback as they approached the convent. Still, even for these last few miles it seemed prudent to have animal senses scenting the road for danger. Once he snarled and circled back to them, and they hastily moved off the road to allow a party of soldiers to pass. They encountered no one else until they came within sight of the convent.

"It's bigger than I thought it would be," Kirra said, as they pulled off into the woods again to eye their target. "It's *huge.*"

"If they're provisioned, they could last months under a siege," Justin observed.

"Good thing we don't plan to wait them out, then," Senneth said. She glanced around at her four companions, all sitting easily in their saddles and awaiting her word with complete confidence. "Ready then? As we discussed."

And they moved back onto the road and arranged themselves for travel. Senneth was in the center of the group, in the lead. Kirra and Donnal flanked her, half a horse to the rear, and Cammon and Justin were just behind them. In this arrow formation, they trotted up to the very gates of Lumanen Convent.

None of the guards lounging before the gate saw them until Senneth and her party were only a few yards away. Then there was a sudden scramble and call for reinforcements and quick maneuvering until the five of them were surrounded by at least twenty soldiers.

"Halt! Who are you? What do you want?" one of them demanded, clearly unsettled by their sudden appearance.

Senneth looked down at him coolly. Her head was perfectly clear, but she could feel a dangerous tingling in her fingertips. "We wish to speak to the head of your order."

"The Lestra does not speak with random trash who ride up to the gate unannounced," the guard snarled back.

"Oh, she'll very much wish to meet with us," Senneth replied. "Tell her there are mystics at the gate. Describe us. I think she'll be happy to hear what we have to say."

The guard stared at her in narrow-eyed uncertainty for a moment before turning to one of his underlings and issuing curt orders. All of them must know by now of the prisoner in their midst and of the mystics who had traveled with the Rider throughout the southern provinces. Even the lowest-ranked guards in the barracks must be able to figure out who sat before them now.

"Will you open the gates for us?" she asked pleasantly.

He gave a nasty laugh. "The Lestra herself must invite you in."

Senneth nodded. "Then we will wait."

She had warned her companions that the wait might be long, for she assumed that Coralinda did not like to stir early in the day. So she held herself relaxed in the saddle and hoped that the other four did as well. Justin particularly. He did not wear his gold lions growling across his chest, but he wouldn't have to. Anyone who knew there was a Rider in their party would look at the group and instantly be able to pick him out.

They had been sitting there maybe twenty minutes when the massive doors to the convent were flung back and about a hundred women streamed out into the winter sunshine.

Most of them were dressed in white robes, though here and

there Senneth spotted clothes of darker hues, indicative of greater levels of devotion, she supposed. In the middle of the pale flood paced a lone figure dressed in silver and black. She moved in a measured, stately fashion, and it seemed to take an hour for her to cross the long distance from the building to the gate. As she walked, the young women fanned around her, a silent, sweet-faced choir of acolytes. They formed a random audience on the inside of the high wall, peering out through the scrolled gate at the heathens come to call.

The woman in black came to a halt when she was just on the other side of the gate. She tilted back her head, so that her gray braid slid across the silk of her gown, and she stared at the mystics with fierce black eyes. She said nothing. The hundred novices, the scattered guards, the party of mystics all waited in silence.

Senneth smiled. "Good morning, Coralinda."

There was a beat of soundless astonishment across all the people gathered inside the convent, but Coralinda did not flinch or recoil. "Senneth," she said, in a low, beautiful voice. "I thought it must be you."

"I'm sure you hoped it wasn't."

"I'm hardly afraid of you, if that's what you mean."

"Excellent," Senneth said. "For I am not afraid of you either. Will you let us in? We have something to discuss."

"Oh, please," Coralinda said, "step inside." She nodded to the guards, and two of them instantly went to pull open the gates. Senneth and her companions spurred their horses forward.

"I would welcome you," Coralinda said in that melodious voice, "but I am not sure you will find your stay very pleasant."

"It will be brief," Senneth said. "You have something of mine, and I have come to retrieve it. As soon as it is back in my hands, we will be on our way."

"As soon as the gates close behind you, you will be prisoners along with the Rider whom we captured yesterday. In fact, I think you will be my guests for some time."

Senneth smiled. "Do you really think you can hold mystics inside your walls?"

"Do you really think mystics can operate in the compound of the goddess? Even now, you must feel how weak your power grows, as the moonstones seeded into the very earth leach away your sorcerous strength."

"An odd thing," Senneth remarked, lifting her arm and shaking her jeweled bracelet. "I am rife with power even when I wear the Pale Mother's charm around my wrist."

Coralinda smiled back. "Yet I feel that even a woman made of fire will find little to burn in a small room made of stone."

"If you harm me," Senneth said, "everyone in your convent will die within a matter of weeks."

"Oh come now, Senneth," Coralinda said in an impatient voice. "Let's not be melodramatic."

"I thought I was being practical," Senneth replied. "I brought with me a most effective weapon, you see."

And she pulled her horse a little to one side and lifted the veil of obscurity she had dropped down, so that Coralinda and everyone in the compound could see the feral red creature crouched on the ground beside her. Its tufted tail flicked with barely controlled ferocity, and its ears were laid flat against its head. Its hot eyes were fixed on Coralinda's face.

There was a collective gasp and a few small whimpers, and many of the hundred Daughters scurried backward. A few looked puzzled, a few looked terrified. Coralinda herself appeared to be furious.

"What have you brought to the Pale Lady's house, Senneth?"

"A raelynx. Do you know much about its kind? A full-grown one might kill a man every two days to feed. This one's only about six months old, and very hungry. It feeds as often as it can."

Her voice scarcely raised at all, Coralinda said, "Kill it." From five directions at once, crossbow arrows drove into the ground where the raelynx had been standing. It had darted away, almost seeming to disappear for a moment; then suddenly it materialized again between Kirra's and Cammon's horses.

"Curiously," Senneth said in a conversational voice, "a raelynx is very hard to kill. It avoids traps, it won't eat poison, and I've never heard of an instance where one was brought down by a hunter. Don't you know any of the tales, Coralinda? Living so close to the Lirrens, I'd have thought you'd have come across a raelynx or two by now."

The Lestra's black eyes were filled with hate as she lifted them to Senneth's face. "Remove this creature from my sanctuary."

"No," Senneth said. "This is its new home. Your novices will be its flesh and its fowl. He will be safe and happy here."

Coralinda lifted her hand in some prearranged gesture, and

another volley of arrows curved through the air. Kirra's horse shied and whinnied, for the weapons landed very near its hooves, but the raelynx was miraculously unharmed. He had shimmied away at a pace too quick to watch.

Now he was advancing at a slow, predatory crawl toward some of the white-clad girls. They shrieked and tripped over each other to get away from him. A few of them ran back toward the house itself; some raced toward the ornamental trees as if to take shelter in their branches.

"He can climb," Senneth called out to them. "That's really not safe." Two of the girls screamed and ran on toward the fortress.

Coralinda's fury was obviously growing hotter and darker by the second. Her black eyes bored into Senneth's face as she snapped, "You control that creature with mystical power, do you not?"

"To some extent," Senneth said. "But as he grows older, he grows stronger, and I do not know how much longer he'll respond to my commands."

"Take him and leave this place. Immediately."

"Not until you release the Rider you hold."

"He is mine."

Senneth shrugged. "Then your girls start dying."

Coralinda glared. "Oh, no, Senneth, you are not hard enough to make war on innocents. You would not let him feed on my novices."

"Yes," Senneth said, "I would. Would you like a demonstration? Tell me, and I'll release him now from my influence."

The two women stared at each other, Coralinda bristling with black rage, Senneth showing a countenance that was serene and unruffled. More crossbows creaked and snapped; more arrows flew. The raelynx continued his eager prowling, wholly unhurt.

"He is not real," Coralinda breathed, still staring at Senneth. "You have devised a most clever illusion to trick me."

Senneth shrugged. Suddenly, there was an unholy scream, and Coralinda whirled to see one of her novices writhing on the ground, blood streaking her white robe. Other girls clustered around her, kneeling or standing, looking fearfully over their shoulders.

The raelynx crouched a few feet away, licking one paw and then snarling in frustration. Abruptly it let out that disquieting wail, choked off at the end. More arrows fell harmlessly around it.

"No illusion," Senneth said. "Hesitate much longer, Coralinda, and I swear to you, someone will be dead."

"Fetch the Rider," Coralinda snapped over her shoulder, and two soldiers ran with alacrity toward the manor.

"And his horse," Senneth added.

Coralinda nodded, and another man sped toward the stables.

"If you follow us, if you attempt to harass us on the road, we will kill all the men you send after us," Senneth said, her voice exceptionally cold. "I can see you want war, Coralinda, and I think you even more of a fool than I always did. But if you attack me and mine, I will slaughter any force you send against us. You are not a soft or sentimental woman. Don't make the mistake of thinking I am."

"You are an abomination in the eyes of the goddess," Coralinda spat out.

Senneth laughed. "Which goddess? There is a whole pantheon, Coralinda, and they do not all love your mistress."

"Only the Silver Lady has any power in Gillengaria."

Senneth's attention was fixed on Coralinda, but she could see movement on the periphery of her vision. A horse being led from the stables, a man being led from the manor. "The Silver Lady is restless and vain, and she seeks worship and glory, but she is not the only one with any power," Senneth replied. "The Bright Mother has put her hand on me, and she is not content to watch her sister overrun the land."

"I will see you destroyed, Senneth, you and all foul mystics who profane this country."

"Strange," Senneth said, "I was going to say much the same thing to you."

Into the harsh silence of the confrontation came the sound of footfalls and hoofbeats as Tayse and his horse arrived at the same time. The beast was saddled and ready to ride; Tayse's weapon belts were draped over the pommel. From the corner of her eye, Senneth could see that Tayse's hands were tied before him, but he looked essentially unharmed—no visible marks on his face, at least. He appeared not to have offered resistance, and the guards seemed to have treated him with some courtesy.

"Release him and let him mount," Coralinda said. In a moment, Tayse had flung himself into the saddle with as much grace as a bound man could manage. The guards fell back a few paces.

Senneth did not turn to look behind her. "Open the gates," she said, "and order all your men inside the compound."

Coralinda looked contemptuous. "We will not attempt to impede your exit."

"Open the gates," Senneth repeated, "and bring all your soldiers inside."

"Do it," Coralinda directed, and the closest commander bawled out orders. Behind her, Senneth could hear the barred gates swing open and the slow tramp of booted feet cross into the enclosed space.

"Back away—all of you—toward the house and the stables," Senneth said. "Give us some space."

"I said that we will not—" Coralinda began, but a disturbing keen rose from near the back of the compound. Coralinda flung her hands into the air. "As she says," the Lestra ordered with heavy sarcasm, "retreat. Everyone step back till we stand alongside the manor."

There were a few grumbles, but the guards and what brave novices remained trudged in a sloppy group back across the lawn, away from the gate. Senneth briefly watched them, then returned her gaze to Coralinda, who had retreated along with the novices.

"Cammon," she said softly. "Are there any guards left outside?"

"No. They're all in here."

"Justin. When you judge them safely back, lead the others out. Head east and then south. Travel quickly but stop before sundown. I'll catch up with you as soon as I can—within a few hours."

"You leave with us," Tayse said sharply.

Five minutes out of captivity and he's already resumed his usual autocratic manner, Senneth thought. "No," she said. "They won't be able to harm me. You go. Justin, take charge."

She heard the sound of horses turning in a circle. "Pull out," Justin said. "Donnal, animal shape in the lead. Tayse, take the rear. Let me cut your ropes first."

"I think Donnal should stay with Senneth," Kirra said.

"No," Justin replied. "Ride out!"

She listened to their hoofbeats pounding down the road until the sound was so distant she could not distinguish it at all. And still she waited, sitting solitary between the gates, watching the novices and guards grow restless and begin to disperse. The raelynx paced back and forth on the thin, invisible line that Senneth had drawn for him, maybe ten yards away from the front door. Now and then he leapt and whirled, inches in front of another arrow or thrown dagger. Senneth didn't even bother to protest the attempts to kill him.

"Leave now, Senneth, or do you plan to hold us hostage in our own house for the rest of the day?" Coralinda called out across the broad lawn.

"I am just waiting for my companions to get safely away."

"I have told you, I have no plans to send my men in pursuit."

"I feel so reassured," Senneth said. "Would you like me to take my raelynx with me or leave him behind?"

The silence was eloquent with fury. Senneth laughed. She closed her attention over the seething mind of the raelynx and forced the creature to turn with a wailed protest away from the spread of humanity. It hissed at her and lifted its paws as if to bat away at an annoying insect, then bounded forward, passed her with two leaps, and headed out to the road.

Senneth backed her horse through the gate, moving slowly, never taking her eyes off Coralinda and her assembled companions. None of them moved, even after she was past the metal scrollwork. She kept backing up, judging her distance, judging her power.

When she was about fifteen yards outside of the compound, Coralinda must have given a sign. Some of the guards broke for the gate at a dead run. Others ran for the stables. So much for promises to leave the mystics unmolested.

Senneth flung her arms in the air and felt heat scatter through her fingertips. Fire leapt up on top of the high stone wall and traveled like a runner along the entire perimeter. She clenched and released her fingers, and another sheet of flame created a shimmering and deadly barrier across the entire opening of the gate. She heard cries of alarm and terror as men tried to dash through and then skidded back. Maybe none of them had believed that magic would burn as hotly as fire.

She wheeled her horse around and pounded down the road, in fast pursuit of her fleeing companions.

IT was an hour or so past noon before Senneth and the raelynx caught up with the others. She had started out at a dead run but knew the horse could not sustain that pace for long, so as soon as she felt she was out of immediate danger, she slowed to an easier gait. The fire she had left at Lumanen Convent would burn for a day, she thought, though there was always the chance a few of the hardier soldiers would be able to nerve themselves to dart through the flames. She didn't think they'd convince any horses to break through, though, so she hoped they were safe from immediate pursuit.

Though safety, it would seem, was not something this small group was really destined to enjoy.

Once she'd been traveling for nearly four hours, she spotted the hawk circling above and then angling down as if to make a landing some distance ahead of her. Kirra, she suspected, and so she was not surprised when she rounded another curve and came upon her five companions drawn up on the side of the road. Justin's face broke into a smile of elation when he saw her. He spurred forward to meet her, catching her hands in both of his and seeming as if he actually wanted to lean over both saddles to embrace her.

"Senneth! Amazing! You were so—I've never seen anything like that! She was afraid of you!" he exclaimed.

Senneth laughed and dropped his hands. "Not really. But I had her at a momentary disadvantage. How's Tayse?"

Justin turned back to the other Rider, who was trotting up. So were the others; she was in the middle of a small, grinning group of friends. Well, Donnal only appeared to be grinning as he sat in wolf shape, panting on the side of the road. And Tayse did not have anything even remotely resembling a smile on his face.

"Unhurt," Tayse said tersely. "But while I was there, she boldly threatened war with the king."

"In a private interview with you?" she asked.

He nodded.

She continued. "Did she give her reasons?"

"His soul is corrupted by magic, and she's the savior of Gillengaria. Standard fanatical rhetoric, but she strikes me as dangerous."

"Very dangerous," Senneth said. "Did she try to recruit you?"

A flash of surprise in his eyes, quickly hidden behind a neutral expression. "How did you guess?"

She smiled. "Standard fanatical rhetoric."

"She gave me a moonstone and told me she could reclaim me."

"And where's the moonstone now?"

He smiled grimly. "I left it on the pillow of my bed."

"Is it safe for us to be standing in the road talking?" Justin interrupted. "Do you think she'll send soldiers after us?"

Senneth turned her smile on him, and he actually smiled back. She might have done it, she thought; she might have found the way to win over Justin. Save Tayse's life. "Well, I think she will eventually," she drawled. "But when I left, there was a ring of fire around the whole compound, so I don't think anyone will be leaving soon."

General laughter at that. "So we've got, what, a head start of a full day?" Kirra asked.

Senneth nodded. "Probably."

"Then we can all sleep the night through without setting a watch?" Cammon asked.

She laughed. "Well, I'm not sure Coralinda's men are the only ones looking for us. She may have gotten a message off to her brother after they captured Tayse. 'Mystics on the loose, headed south.' And who knows what else he's heard about our escapades to date? I don't know how far we can relax."

"Oh, to sleep in a bed again for just one night," Kirra groaned. "To bathe. To eat a meal that someone else has cooked."

"Not just yet," Senneth said. She glanced over at Tayse, who still seemed remote and far more unfriendly than someone who had just been rescued should seem. "But when we stop tonight, Tayse will have to tell us all the details of his stay."

He nodded. "I think it might prove to be valuable for me to have gleaned what information I did about the workings of the convent."

Justin pulled on his reins, turning his horse back in a southerly direction. "Let's move on, then."

"Senneth." Cammon's voice stopped her from following immediately in Justin's wake. All of them lingered to hear what he had to say, made curious by the troubled sound of his voice.

"What?" she asked.

"Back there. At the convent. There was something—" He stopped, looking uncertain. "Someone there is a mystic," he said.

Senneth felt her eyebrows stretch as high as they would go. "Are you sure?"

He nodded. "It was very faint. And she seemed—fairly young. I would guess she has no idea she has any power."

Senneth glanced at Kirra, who looked as wide-eyed as Senneth felt. "So—not a spy gone gamely to the enemy camp," Senneth said.

"There's someone who will come to grief if she ever starts exercising her abilities," Kirra commented.

"Maybe they're so buried they'll never surface," Senneth said. "But that's the last place I'd want to be if I was infused with latent power."

"It was the last place I wanted to be at all, and I don't have a speck of magic," Tayse said.

They all laughed. Justin, still taking very seriously his duties as temporary leader, kneed his horse forward. "Move out," he said, sweeping his left arm forward. "We can cover a lot of ground before nightfall."

With a little sigh, Senneth silently relinquished to him all immediate responsibility for command. She settled back in her saddle, watching the others dispose themselves for travel. With Justin in the lead, Tayse fell back to take the rear. Donnal trotted ahead of Justin and then disappeared off into the undergrowth. Cammon and Kirra arrayed themselves on either side of Senneth, Cammon leading Donnal's horse.

"How's Tayse really?" Senneth asked quietly. "He seems—withdrawn. Did something happen?"

Kirra smothered a giggle. "I think he's just miffed that he was careless enough to get taken on the road. I think he also wishes he'd fought back—even though it's clear that he would have been dead if he'd lifted his sword." She glanced at Senneth. "And maybe he thinks it's embarrassing that you had to rescue him."

"I don't think it's embarrassment," Cammon said thoughtfully, and then looked alarmed and refused to elaborate when they both demanded to know what that meant. Finally he said, "It's just that—Senneth, you know. She's so powerful. She puts everyone in awe."

Senneth felt her mouth twist. "I don't think he looks on me with awe. Maybe he thinks we're stupid to be going on to Gisseltess."

"Maybe he's mad because Justin's acting all serious and in charge," Kirra said.

"Give him a night to recover," Cammon said. "And he'll be in charge again."

"I think this is *my* mission and *I'm* the leader," Senneth said.

When they laughed, she allowed herself to smile. "Some of the time, anyway."

"I wouldn't worry about Tayse," Kirra said.

Cammon's smile was secretive and hard to read. "Or you could just ask him," he said. "What's on his mind."

After that they rode on in silence for a while. Senneth thought that if the day ever came where she could lie down in safety, she would sleep a week through. As dusk drifted down, Justin called a halt, and they pulled off the road to try to find a level place to camp. Donnal stood on all fours for a moment, sniffing the air, then bounded off to seek out game or water or whatever he was focused on at the moment. Senneth dropped her bedroll to the ground and expended a small quotient of energy to warm the air around them.

"Ah," she said in a light voice, "so good to be home."

CHAPTER
27

TAYSE knew he was being surly and that only Senneth cared, and she was the last person in Gillengaria he wanted to offend. Yet he could not shake off his strange sense of oppression and behave in a normal fashion. He had been so sure she would come for him that he had not even been surprised when the breathless guard burst into his room and demanded that the Rider leave with him instantly. He had not known precisely how she would accomplish the rescue until he saw the pacing raelynx, the phalanx of mystics, Senneth at the absolute center of every pair of eyes in the courtyard. Her star-white hair made a halo around her face, and her expression was one of pure serenity. She might be the focus of the whole world, he thought; she had that much strength of purpose, that much force of will. The royal court and the Twelve Houses and the merchants and the farmers and the laborers would all gladly revolve around her.

Or maybe he was the only one who felt her presence so powerfully, who had made her the sun for his own small world.

Something he did not want to do.

She had scarcely glanced at him as she sprang him from his trap. All her attention had been on the Lestra. Tayse had climbed into the saddle, followed Justin and the others through the gates, and ridden away as fast as their horses could take them, and all the while his body had been clenched in mute protest. They could not leave her behind, solitary and undefended! Yet it was clear she had planned this whole escape, down to the final tongue of fire, and that the only part any of them could play had already been scripted by her.

So they had ridden out—and he had strained every sense to catch the sound of her horse cantering up behind them—and interminable hours had passed before Kirra brought the welcome news that she was just a few minutes behind them. He had waited as gladly as the rest of them for her to ride up, relaxed and smiling, but he had not been able to show his emotions on his face.

Something had changed.

He could not define it; he had no words for it; he did not even want to understand it. He would almost rather still be a prisoner inside Lumanen Convent than to feel this crushing weight upon his chest and not have the first idea how to dislodge it.

He was as weary as the rest of them, but it was no particular relief to stop for the night. He felt the quick bloom of warmth as Senneth did something to ward off the chill, and all of the others fell gratefully to the ground.

"Can we just stay here?" Kirra said drowsily. "Forever? Do we actually have to get back on the horses tomorrow and ride?"

Tayse handed his reins to Cammon, who was collecting the horses. "I'll look for water," he said.

Kirra pointed. "Donnal went that way. That usually means that's the first direction to go." She tossed him her water bottle. "Thanks."

Tayse gathered the other containers, then headed out the way she'd indicated. Sure enough, within a quarter of a mile he practically stumbled across a slim, mossy stream. It was so covered with leaves and fallen branches that it was easy to miss, but it was moving swiftly enough that there were only margins of ice showing white along its narrow banks. He knelt down and filled the containers one by one, first emptying and rinsing them of their stale contents.

He rose to his feet but found he was in no particular hurry to get back to camp. Looking around, he saw the stump of a tree, neatly sheered off below waist height. He settled onto it as if it was a tall barroom stool, and for a moment he wished he had a glass of ale to accompany the illusion. After the events of the past two days, he thought he deserved a drink or two. Too bad the forest yielded no taverns.

He heard a rustling in the undergrowth, coming from the direction of camp. He leaned his fists on his knees and waited. It was entirely without surprise that he saw Senneth break cover and make her way slowly to where he sat. It was not quite full dark, but she was still a shadowy shape, her face lit faintly by the glow of her hair. She approached him slowly, as if uncertain of a welcome.

"The others assure me that you're just fine, but you've been so quiet," she said in a low voice. "I find myself wondering if you were subjected to torture and just haven't wanted to say so. Kirra can cure most hurts, you know, if you're hiding wounds beneath your vest."

That did make him smile, just a little. "No. A wound to my pride, perhaps, that I let myself be ambushed. But the Lestra offered me no torture, only her views on the world and a chance at salvation."

"And some strictures about the dangers of consorting with mystics."

He was able to smile. "Ah. I was already aware of those."

"Justin was so afraid for you," she said. "He actually let me comfort him. I think I would have felt I had betrayed him even more than I had betrayed you if we had not been able to free you."

The smile was easier this time. "With the result that he has now transferred his allegiance to you."

"Oh no," she said. "You will always be his hero. It's just that he doesn't quite despise me now. Which makes for a pleasant change."

He couldn't exactly dispute that, so he introduced a new subject. "How's your head?" he asked. "After your conjuring of fire this morning."

She smiled. "Very well, thank you. I think it is not the fire so much as the fury that puts me in such pain. I knew I had to stay very, very calm, or I would lose control of the raelynx—and I wouldn't be able to face down Coralinda. And I was able to manage it. Though, I don't know—all the horror may come rushing in on me tomorrow, and I'll be paralyzed with pain."

"Well," he said. "Let me know. I will do what I can to ease it."

"It eases me just to know you are among us again and safe,"

she said quietly. "I was sure—I thought—it seemed she would not have the nerve to harm you, and yet—"

"I knew you would come for me," he said. "I was not afraid."

She came a step closer, close enough that her knees almost brushed his. While he remained perched on the tree stump, their heads were at almost exactly the same height; he could look straight into her gray eyes. As always, her face was guarded and serene, but the expression in her eyes was neither.

Her next words were unexpected. "Does nothing ever break you?" she asked in a soft voice.

His breath caught. "Why should I break?"

A slight shrug. "Capture—threat of death—daring rescue. But you're not moved to any emotion. Not fear, not fawning gratitude."

"I was not afraid, and I am indeed grateful," he said. The cadence of his voice sounded formal, even to him; that was the result of holding great emotion in check. "I don't know how it is you want me to present myself."

She put her bare hands on either side of his face, silencing him completely. Her skin was so warm it was as if summer had come to visit him, rich with fertile possibilities. He felt heat skim through his bones to every extremity of his body. He sat utterly still.

"Maybe I expect too much of you," she said, her voice almost a murmur, directed, perhaps, at herself and not him. "Maybe you are, after all, a King's Rider and nothing more, with room for no one else in your heart. Not friend, not lover. Or maybe it is only me you have barred your heart against. Maybe it is only me you do not trust."

"I trusted you to save me," he said. It was hard to speak the words.

"I suppose that's something," she said, and leaned in and kissed him.

Shock went through him like a poison-tipped arrow. Her hands pressed against his cheekbones, her lips pressed against his mouth, and heat raged through him and flushed his whole body. He moved all at once, his arms sweeping her against his chest as he rose to his feet. He held her crushed against him, her feet dangling off the ground, her body a part of his, his mouth devouring hers. He felt broken open then, as if a finely honed axe had split him like kindling, cleft him right in half. He felt the ache down the middle of his chest, a pressure so intense that even holding Senneth more tightly could not assuage the pain.

He set her on the ground and dropped his arms and stared down at her, his face entirely somber.

She stared back up at him. Her eyes had gone so dark they looked like ash-flecked coals at the edge of a fading fire. Her mouth was reddened by his rough treatment, but even that did not give her a look of uncertainty or discomposure. Nothing at all was to be read in the smooth contours of her face.

"And I still don't know," she said. She watched him another moment, then she shook her head. "And neither do you."

And turning on her heel, she headed back for the camp without another word.

She was wrong, of course. He knew; he just did not want to know. He sat back on the tree stump and waited till the pounding of his heart slowed, till the flush receded from his face and body. He waited till Cammon came looking for him with the news that the meal was ready.

"All right," Tayse said, standing up. He thought his voice sounded normal. But Cammon looked at him curiously and then glanced away, as if he'd accidentally peered into a lady's diary or a man's bedroom. Tayse felt a crooked smile cross his face, and he shook his head. "Do you think it gets worse than this?" he found himself asking.

Cammon glanced back at him, his expression full of both hope and rue. "I don't know much about it," he said, "but I think so."

Tayse nodded. "That's what I was afraid of."

THE next two days were exactly the same, down to the wistful conversations about clean sheets and warm baths, except for the kiss. That didn't occur again. Tayse went off alone each night to fetch water or fuel, but Senneth didn't come after him. No one did.

She seemed completely unchanged, day after day, laughing and talking with her usual ease to the others, even to him. She did not stir in the middle of the night during the hours when Tayse took the watch, and sit up on her bedroll, and survey him. She neither looked for opportunities to talk to him nor avoided him if the motion of the party brought her horse alongside his. She was completely herself.

So he must seem to her, he thought. The day after the rescue, he had just naturally resumed command from Justin, giving directions for the day, checking on the status of everyone's health and strength. He had never been particularly talkative, so he did not suddenly start babbling to everyone in his party, but he made some effort not to appear unduly taciturn, either. In the evenings, he fenced with Justin or proceeded with training Cammon and Donnal. Senneth declined to participate—but then, that was not unprecedented, either. Nothing was different.

Everything was different.

The evening of the second day of travel, Senneth and Kirra sat by the fire while the others battled, arguing over the best way to approach Halchon Gisseltess.

"I don't want to go to Gissel Plain," Senneth said, for what Tayse was sure was the third or fourth time. "He could sweep us up so fast we wouldn't even know we'd been captured till we were rolled into the dungeons."

"He's not going to imprison us—not when he knows you come on a mission for the king."

"He doesn't like me," Senneth said gloomily. "And he'll like me even less once he hears about how I bested his sister. He's just the sort of man who would throw us into a dark cell first, and then later start thinking about the consequences."

"I can't believe this," Kirra said. "You're afraid of him. You're not afraid of anybody."

"I'm not afraid of him," Senneth said instantly, but her voice lacked conviction.

Kirra shrugged. "We don't have to go to Gisseltess at all. We can turn around right now and head back for Ghosenhall."

Senneth sighed. "Yes. We could. But I don't think we should. So I guess what we need is an alternative to Gissel Plain."

"Lochau is right on the coast," Kirra suggested. "He's there fairly often, because it's a port, and he runs a lot of shipping businesses. It's a big enough city that it offers some amenities—and there would be lots of places for us to run and hide if you really think we're going to be in danger. Maybe he'd meet us in Lochau. It's only a day's ride from Gissel Plain."

Senneth tilted her head to one side. "That's a good idea," she approved. "And maybe we could book passage out on a commercial ship. Get back to Ghosenhall faster."

Kirra grinned. "Probably Danalustrous ships in port even as

we speak. They'd be only too willing to take me wherever I asked to go."

"Good. Then we'll send a message to Halchon and ask him to meet us in Lochau in a few days."

Kirra grimaced. "And I suppose you want me to take this message to Gissel Plain. I can take hawk shape and fly there and back in—I don't know—a couple days."

"I'd rather have Donnal go," Senneth said slowly. "Halchon knows you, and if something went amiss—if someone spotted you in Gissel Plain—well, that's even worse than all of us getting locked in dungeons."

"You have a most morbid attitude about Gissel Plain and its dungeons," Kirra exclaimed. "I've never even *heard* of any dungeons there! Let alone anyone being locked in one."

"My morbid fears just reflect my attitude about Halchon Gisseltess," Senneth said in a moody voice. "I think he's capable of—anything."

"All right. So we send Donnal tomorrow or the next day. And let's say Halchon agrees to meet us in Lochau. And then?"

"And then—well, I guess, then we'll see."

IN the morning, they were back on the road. They were far enough south now that Tayse could feel the difference in the air: lighter, sweeter, noticeably warmer. If they stayed here any length of time, they would get the first pastel glimpse of spring long before it deigned to show its pretty face in Ghosenhall and other northern regions. Almost, Tayse thought, the incentive was enough. It had seemed like a very long winter.

They were still on secondary roads, but traffic was heavier than he would have expected. Then again, Gisseltess was a powerful and prosperous province; it enjoyed a healthy level of trade. Donnal had continued to rove ahead of them, taking various animal shapes, and Tayse had to trust him to be an advance scout. He didn't feel any of them were safe separated by more than a few horse lengths, and he and Justin had both stayed with the group these past few days.

Twice they saw Gisseltess soldiers, once riding into the region, once riding out, but neither time did their own small party occasion any particular interest. More frequently they passed small merchant caravans or farmers driving loaded wagons; now and then they encountered trappers with a season's worth of furs strapped to their backs. Tayse always hoped Donnal was wise enough to stay out of sight of such hunters—or to take a less appealing form if he caught their eyes.

They had determined they would send Donnal out that afternoon. Tayse was not wild about the idea; he was starting to think this group needed every soldier it had, and Donnal could be formidable in certain forms. Still, Kirra could as easily serve as advance guard, and obviously someone would have to be dispatched to send the message. Like Kirra, Tayse was half inclined to say, *Let us head back to Ghosenhall without making this swing through Gisseltess. We know already what we need to know.*

But once they were back in Ghosenhall, Tayse would rejoin the Riders, and Senneth would resume her wandering, and he would never see her again. So they might as well ride into Gisseltess and extend the journey by another five days, or another ten. He would offer no resistance.

They stopped around noon to take a break for food. "I am so very tired of sitting in the saddle," Senneth complained when she dismounted, putting her hands on her hips and stretching backward. "Have I become bowlegged? I know I look weather-beaten and scruffy, and I am resigned to that, but I just can't stand it if I'm bowlegged."

"Riders are all bowlegged," Justin informed her, taking an exaggerated stance that showed his legs irredeemably malformed. "You can come back to Ghosenhall and be one of us."

"A King's Rider! Can that really be the next step in my career?" Senneth said. "I know you do have some women in your ranks—but not many, I'd guess."

"Half a dozen," Justin said. "But they're very, very good."

"Are you implying—"

He grinned. "You'd have to practice a little more on the road. Your strength is impressive, but your skills aren't as ferocious as they might be. You're willing to rely on other abilities," he ended up, his smile broadening.

"Yes, well, I might rely on other abilities to turn you into a torch," she said grumpily. "Tayse! I saw a glint of water down that way, not more than a quarter mile from here. I'm going to refill my water bottle."

"Take Donnal with you," he said.

She smiled very sweetly. "And I might wash some of the travel grime from my body," she said. "I think I'd rather make the trek alone."

He wanted to repeat his order, but it was hard for him to tell these days how much of his fear for her safety was real and how much was just heightened awareness of her existence. "We move out in thirty minutes," he said. "Make it fast."

Senneth sent a questioning glance at Kirra, who waved a languid hand. "I just want to be still for a moment," the other woman said. "I'll bathe—sometime. In Lochau."

"Sooner than Lochau, I hope," Cammon said, and Kirra threw a half-eaten crust of bread at him. Senneth grinned, slung all the containers over her shoulder, and hiked down a sloping hill. Within five minutes, she disappeared behind a small stand of trees that had grown up by the pond or stream or whatever water source she'd found.

Donnal's head lifted, and his whole body stiffened, then he bounded off after some prey invisible to the rest of them. Kirra watched him for a moment, then sighed. "Guess we won't have to feed *him* lunch," she said, and began digging through one of her packs for food.

"So he really eats raw meat when he's in animal form?" Justin asked, sounding as if he was fighting not to gag.

She nodded. "So do I. It's quite handy when civilized food is scarce and you find yourself hungry."

"But then—when you change back—and it's in your stomach—"

She looked up, grinning. "Speaking for myself, I take care not to change back till I've completed my digestion."

"Do you ever think you might forget how to change back?" Tayse asked. "If you've stayed in animal shape too long?"

She seemed to be thinking it over. "I tend not to hold a shape more than a few days, so I never forget who I really am. But Donnal—it's occurred to me once or twice he might spend a whole season with the wolves or the falcons, and lose the memory of his true self. I've seen him come back sometimes with such a strange look in his eyes—" She shook her head. "He's wilder than I am, that's for certain."

"I'd like to spend a season with the wolves," Cammon said wistfully. "What a strange and wonderful time that would be!"

Kirra laughed. "Well, we'll take you to Ghosenhall and you can spend a season with the human predators at court," she said in a comforting voice. "You'll find that a strange but not so wonderful experience, I think."

Justin sat on a fallen log, rested an elbow on his knee, and planted his chin on his fist. "What exactly *are* we going to do with Cammon when this adventure is done?" he asked.

"I want to stay with all of you," the boy answered quickly.

Justin shook his head. "'All of us' won't be staying together," he said. "Tayse and I will be back with the Riders till we're sent off on some other mission. Kirra and Donnal will go back to Danalustrous. Senneth—well, who knows what Senneth will do next?"

"You might sign up to train with the King's Guard," Tayse suggested, since Cammon looked so forlorn. "Justin and I would vouch for you. You're not good enough to be a Rider, but you'll make a decent soldier with a little more work."

"Or come back with me to my father's estate," Kirra said. "We'd find a place for you somewhere."

Cammon sighed. "Senneth thinks I should find another mystic and learn to handle my magic," he said. "But I just—I didn't think—it will be so strange not to be with all of *you*."

"Well, if you're in Ghosenhall, Tayse and I will be nearby," Justin said in a bracing voice. "We'll take you out to taverns now and then and teach you how to brawl. And consort with women."

"I'm sure you know how to brawl, but I wouldn't want Cammon to learn about women from you," Kirra said.

Justin was grinning. Tayse knew he was only teasing Kirra; Justin had no taste for brothels. "*You've* already taught him what he needs to know about consorting with ladies," Justin said. "Now it's our turn to teach him something a little more useful in general life."

"I don't think—" Cammon started to say, and then he stopped, a look of uncertainty crossing his face.

Kirra was addressing Justin. "The things that you consider useful—" but Tayse flung up a hand.

"Be quiet," he said, watching Cammon. "What is it? What are you listening to?"

Cammon shook his head, his face creased in puzzlement. "It's like—but I can't tell—I think—"

"Here's Donnal," Kirra said in a strained voice, and Tayse glanced over his shoulder to see Donnal racing up, sleek and low to the ground.

"Cammon," Tayse said. "What's—"

And just then Cammon screamed. *"Senneth!"*

CHAPTER
28

"SENNETH!" Cammon cried again. "She's been hurt—Tayse, Justin, I think she's been—there must be soldiers, I think some-one's put an arrow through her—she's in agony—"

Tayse only heard a few of Cammon's words. He had flung himself on his horse after the first broken phrases and pelted at a dead run down to the stand of trees where Senneth had gone to look for water. Behind him, he could hear the sound of Justin leaping onto his own mount and following him closely down the incline. A streak of black vaulted past him—Donnal. A streak of gold—Kirra. He was only seconds behind them as the four of them plunged into the scraggly wood.

Instantly, they were in the midst of a white-hot battle. Tayse had time to register very little except the black and silver of their livery before he was set upon by two soldiers wielding deter-mined swords. His own weapons were out; the roar of rage in his ears almost drowned the metallic clamor of blade against blade, the grunts and screams and curses that were part of combat. He was aware only of the bodies around him—Justin beside him, swinging his sword in a berserker frenzy, the convent guards ar-rayed against them, falling back a pace or two at the maniacal en-ergy of the Riders.

He did not see Senneth. Where was Senneth?

A black wolf sailed through the air and knocked a soldier from his saddle. The cry of terror and pain was truly horrifying, but abruptly silenced. Tayse thrust his sword straight through the heart of a soldier attacking him, yanked the blade free, and twisted in his saddle to meet another assault.

He saw the wolf strike again, heard another heart-stopping yell. Out of the corner of his eye he saw a mountain lion make a sinuous leap from the ground to horseback, and literally claw a man to death. The big cat leapt straight from this kill to land on the back of another soldier, raking her bloody paws down the side of his face while he tried frantically to wheel in his saddle and defend himself. No time to watch the end of this contest—a sword was slamming through the air directly for Tayse's head. He lifted his own blade and felt the impact all the way down his shoulders and ribs into his hip.

He slid his sword free, parried the man's next thrust, and lunged forward in the saddle. His opponent fell to the ground, sliced in half.

Where was Senneth? Pale Lady, Bright Mother, Dark Watcher, any god who might be listening, *where was Senneth?*

A break in the action gave him a chance to look wildly around, but he still could not spot Senneth anywhere in the woods or near the water. At least eight bodies lay on the ground, all dressed in black and silver, all covered with copious amounts of blood. Justin was still battling with one of Coralinda's soldiers, but it was clear who was going to win that fight, and quickly. Donnal and Kirra were circling another soldier, who had apparently been knocked from the saddle but managed to scramble to his feet. He crouched before them, waving his knife and looking desperately afraid. Another contest that was already effectively decided. Tayse wrenched his eyes away.

His attention was caught by motion through the trees, maybe twenty yards distant: a soldier bent over the saddle, racing back up the road toward the convent. "Kirra!" he shouted, and her golden head snapped around—but there was no need for her to go hunting this particular prey. Even as Tayse watched, there was a sublimely beautiful explosion of red as the raelynx leapt through the air and tore the soldier from the horse. Man and beast somersaulted in a tangled curl onto the road and disappeared from view.

Tayse did not wonder who would survive that encounter, either.

His eyes darted around the small plot of trees, looking for

more attackers, bracing himself for the next round of trouble. But there appeared to be none immediately lurking. Justin was pulling his blade from the breast of the last soldier he'd faced; Donnal was glancing up from the mangled throat of his own final victim. Kirra stood there in human form, wiping the blood from her mouth with the sleeve of her filthy shirt.

"Where's Senneth?" Tayse demanded. "Do you see her?"

Kirra shook her head, and her eyes were as wide and as frightened as Tayse thought his own must be. "No—I think—she might have turned herself invisible as soon as the arrow hit home. It had to be an arrow—a crossbow—they couldn't possibly have gotten near enough to harm her with swords."

Tayse slid from his horse's back, a terrible fear rising up in his chest, pressing against his constricted ribs, making his muscles loose and unhelpful. "Then she—somewhere here on the ground— if I have to crawl on my hands and knees and cover every square inch—"

Kirra shook her head. "Donnal," she said and he trotted over. "Where's Senneth? Can you find her?"

But when Donnal's head swung over to sniff the breeze, it was clear his tracking skills would not be needed. They all followed his yellow gaze down to the side of the stream, where Cammon knelt beside a patch of winter grass and appeared to be trying to resuscitate formless air.

"He can see her," Kirra whispered, her hand to her throat.

"We will all need to be able to see her," Tayse said, striding forward, "if we are to save her."

The other three hurried after him, though Donnal made it to Cammon's side the quickest. Kirra pushed the wolf away and knelt beside Cammon, her hands shaping themselves over an unseen body. Tayse could hear Cammon's voice, low and anxious.

"The arrow went straight through. I've done what I can to stanch the bleeding, but I'm not sure she's conscious. Can you help her?"

"Cammon—I can't see her," Kirra said, her voice strained. "Can you—what can you do? Can you reach into her mind? Make her respond to you? I have to bind her wounds, but I can't *see* her—"

Justin and Tayse hovered one step back, staring down at nothing, at Kirra's hands patting the invisible, unconscious figure. Tayse had never felt so cold in his life, and he didn't think it was just fear. He suspected he had grown so used to the waves of heat pouring from Senneth's body that when that heat was shut down, he felt the loss all the way through to his bones.

Cammon leaned forward and appeared to be whispering to a rock on the ground. Justin crowded closer to Tayse. "Do you think we can move her?" the younger Rider asked.

Kirra looked up, her face exceptionally grim. "No," she said. "I think we have to build the camp around her body."

Tayse nodded. "What can we do?"

"At the moment, nothing. Except fetch my packs and build a fire. The biggest fire you can keep going through the night."

Justin glanced around. The stream was at the bottom of a small hill, the woods to one side of it, open land in three directions. It was clear what he was thinking: This was not an ideal site to set up camp. Then there were all the bodies nearby, sure to attract predators, sure to begin giving off an unpleasant odor within a very short period of time.

"We're not very protected here," Tayse said. "In case more of them come."

"We'll just have to set up better guards," Kirra said.

Tayse was gazing down at Cammon, still appearing to murmur to the earth. "We've grown too accustomed to relying on heightened senses," he said. "We've grown careless."

"I wonder why he didn't know those soldiers were coming," Justin said. None of them asked Cammon, not wanting to distract him from the more critical task at hand. "He's picked up riders from much farther away than that."

Kirra glanced up swiftly. "They were wearing moonstone clips on their hats," she said. "At least, the ones I killed were. Probably something to do with the moonstones so close to their heads—Cammon couldn't sense what they were thinking." She looked back down at where Senneth should be. "I don't know. I'm just guessing."

Tayse spared an instant to marvel at how flatly she referred to the men she had killed. Not the sort of cold unsentimentality you would expect from a serramerra of the Twelve Houses. But she had not flinched. If a fresh hazard pounded up from around the bend right now, she would take animal shape and fight again. He was fairly certain Kirra was sophisticated enough to realize that a death she caused while in lion shape was still a death at her hands. He was fairly certain she felt not the slightest remorse.

"Ah," Kirra gasped just a second before Tayse saw Senneth's shape waver into being. For a moment she seemed faint, insubstantial, as if she would wink back out of sight, but Cammon whispered something else in her ear, and she grew more solid.

Though seeing her was suddenly no comfort at all. She looked near death, her face so white that even her hair seemed densely colorful by contrast. She was unnaturally still; if she breathed, the movement was so faint it was undetectable. Kirra caught her own breath on a small sob.

Tayse leaned over, trying to trace the source of the wound that had left her entire shirt bloody. "Where did the arrow strike?"

"Her lung," Kirra whispered. She sat motionless for a moment, then jerked her head up, the expression on her face angry. "Don't just stand there! Get water! Get wood! Build a fire! Help me—"

They all leapt to their tasks, but the next hour passed in such emotional agony that Tayse, at least, was almost unaware of the physical exertions of his body. He and Justin combed the area to find fallen branches to drag back and break into smaller pieces; they eventually had enough to last for two days of straight burning. Donnal, who had resumed his human form, built the fire and set water on to boil, fetching whatever supplies Kirra asked for. Cammon knelt beside Senneth, across from Kirra, and put his hands where Kirra directed him, and seemed to engage from time to time in some silent communication with the unconscious woman.

The raelynx came and sat just outside the circle of the fire and watched them all with a fixed and sober attention. Its tufted ears were tilted forward, and its restless tail was wrapped unmoving around its body. Tayse found it in him to wonder what kept it so near them this day—Senneth's plight, Cammon's will, or the potential to make a few easy kills as these frail humans grew lax with worry and exhaustion.

But he was willing to believe it was the first possibility—that the raelynx, like the rest of them, had come to love this strange and powerful woman and did not want to stir more than a few steps from the place where she lay in such fearful danger.

"How is she?" he couldn't keep himself from asking every time the completion of his chores brought him back within a few feet.

Each time, Kirra compressed her lips and shook her head. "I don't know. She's so cold. But she's still alive."

Justin was dropping another branch on their pile of logs

during one of these exchanges. "I thought you were supposed to be such a fabulous healer," the younger Rider said in a hard voice. "I thought you had such magic in your hands—"

Donnal scrambled up and punched Justin in the shoulder. Justin made a fist and swung back, and suddenly the two of them were scuffling, inches away from the prone body. Cammon strangled a shout and jumped to his feet, shoving himself between them. Tayse reached them seconds later, wrapping his arms around Justin's waist and hauling him away from the fire. He hesitated to try such tactics with Donnal, who might turn into a beast and maul him.

"Stop it! Both of you!" he commanded in a rough voice. "We're all afraid. Stop it."

Justin shook himself free and stalked off into the woods. Donnal said nothing, just dropped back down in a crouch beside Kirra. Tayse knelt beside Cammon.

"Is there anything I can do?" he asked, hearing the urgency in his voice even as he tried to keep it gentle. "Hold her? If there's another body next to hers to give her some warmth—"

Kirra nodded. "Yes—maybe—a little later. First I want to stop the bleeding. It's as if she—as if all the heat in her body has already run out, and there's this cold river of power just leaking from her fingertips—"

"Her hands are never cold," Tayse said, and could not stop himself from reaching out and taking her left hand in his. Just to see, just to prove to himself that there was some heat remaining in her body.

The bloody sleeve fell back from her arm and showed the moonstone bracelet glowing white against her skin.

With an oath, Tayse ripped the circlet off her hand, flinging it into the river. The fire beside him leapt six inches and crackled with a sudden heat. A wash of fever burned through the fingers wrapped in Tayse's hand.

Kirra caught her breath on a sob. "The bracelet," she whispered. "The *bracelet*—"

Tayse found himself crushing those frail fingers in his hand as if he could force some of his own heat into her flesh—or as if he would reassure himself that there was a fugitive warmth in her own skin. Carefully he eased the pressure and laid her arm next to her body. He stood. "Does that make a difference?" he asked, his voice constricted. "Can you tell?"

Kirra was nodding, her hands fluttering over Senneth's ribs, her forehead, her wrists. "Yes—I think I can—yes, already she is more responsive—" She drew in a long, ragged breath. "Bright Mother of the morning skies, help me now—"

Tayse waited a moment, but there was no more conversation, just Kirra's intent face and healing hands. He pivoted and went off in search of Justin, whom he could hear tramping through the stand of trees. When he found the other Rider, he was tying one of the convent horses to a sapling. He looked up when Tayse appeared.

"Sorry," he said, and sounded sorry, though it didn't appear he was willing to dredge up any more words.

Tayse nodded. "What are we going to do about their horses?" he asked. Justin, he saw, had already secured most of them; two more had drifted outside of the shelter of the woods and were cropping at unsatisfying brown grass.

Justin shook his head. "I don't know. Too many for us to bring with us, though we could probably use a spare mount or two. That dapple gray looks big enough to carry you, and the bay is the finest of the lot. But we don't need eleven or twelve more horses. That would raise all kinds of suspicion on the road."

"I suppose we strip them and set them loose, once we're ready to leave," Tayse said. "I'd guess most of them will make it back to the convent—but not for a few days. We'd be safe in Lochau by then."

Justin gave him a swift look, almost humorous. "We don't seem to be safe anywhere."

"True," Tayse agreed. He came close enough to stroke the dapple gray on the nose. It was deep-chested and sturdily built, calm even in the presence of so much carnage. An excellent battle horse. Tayse would no doubt need another one of those. "I suppose if we release them, there's enough grass and bark that they can forage on to survive the trip back to the convent."

Justin shrugged. "Or some other travelers using the road will round them up and add them to their own caravans. Not asking too many questions about where they came from."

Tayse glanced around at the scattered corpses, already starting to rime with frost. If the weather stayed cold enough, they might not start to smell so quickly. "I don't think I have the strength to bury them all," he said.

"Gather and burn them," Justin suggested.

"Or let the Lestra's other men find them when they come out to see why their fellows didn't ride back."

"Should we search the bodies?" Justin asked.

Tayse shook his head. "No reason. We know who they are. I suppose if you see a knife you particularly want, you can take it, but half of them probably have moonstone hilts. And I want to carry no part of the Pale Mother with me when we ride out from here."

Justin nodded, looked down at the ground, looked back up at Tayse. "Is she going to die?"

Tayse felt the pain in his chest clench tighter. "No," he said.

Justin nodded again. "I'll start stripping the horses."

Tayse stepped out of the woods again and surveyed the scene around him. Impossible that it could still be only early afternoon—it seemed like hours had passed, if not whole days. But the sun was still at a comfortable level in the sky, pouring down golden light. It wouldn't be night again for another few hours.

He had no idea how they could possibly defend this camp if more soldiers came riding down the trail looking for them.

Stepping carefully through debris, undergrowth, and the occasional body, he made his way back to the place where Senneth lay. Cammon was still kneeling beside Kirra; Donnal hovered nearby, waiting to be pressed into service. Tayse gestured to Cammon. The young man rose, and Donnal took his place. Cammon followed Tayse a few yards away from the fire.

"I'm so sorry," Cammon said. He looked almost as pale as Senneth, but terror and guilt kept his features tense, whereas hers were loose and empty. "It's my fault—I didn't feel them coming. I don't know why—Kirra mentioned the moonstone pins in their hats—maybe. I don't know—but I should have, I should have known something was—"

Tayse laid his heavy hands on the boy's shoulders, and Cammon fell silent. "You are not wholly responsible for our safety," he said. "All six of us have been trained to take care of ourselves. Senneth is the last person who would tell you that you had to protect her."

"But I should have," Cammon whispered. His eyes appeared wet, as if with any encouragement at all he would weep.

Tayse tightened his hold for a moment. "And perhaps next time you will be able to," he said. "For I expect the Lestra will send more guards after us if these fail to return. We must determine how they were able to escape your notice and what you can do in the future to detect them. What was it that first caught your attention this time?"

"Senneth's pain. I felt it when the arrow hit her."

Tayse shook his head. "No. Before the arrow struck, you could sense something—you looked as if you were listening to noises none of the rest of us could hear. What were those noises?"

Cammon frowned, trying to concentrate. The effort of reconstructing memory had at least had the effect of drying his tears. "I didn't *hear* anything," he said at last. "I could tell horses were coming. A lot of them." He focused on Tayse's face. "I guess I didn't think—but of course a party of horses would be carrying men."

Tayse gave Cammon's shoulders a friendly squeeze, then dropped his arms. "Yes. Good. Then that's something you're going to have to teach yourself to look for—listen for—whatever. I don't know if there's any way for you to practice that, but—"

Cammon still seemed to be thinking hard. "I don't pay much attention to the wild animals we pass in the forest. But now and then I can sense that they're nearby. I suppose I could—I could start listening for them, trying to distinguish a rabbit from a squirrel, for instance. A hawk from a crow." He lifted his eyes to Tayse's. "Would that work?"

Bright Mother, now he was training mystics to hone their craft. "I think it would," he said gravely. "Maybe Senneth will have some ideas when she—after she—"

Cammon nodded. "When she's better," he said. "Yes."

CHAPTER
29

THEY returned to the small patch of ground that held all their hopes, all their terrors, to find very little changed. Tayse crouched down across from Kirra and put his hand briefly against Senneth's cheek. Cool, too cool, but not bone cold. Some flicker of life still beneath the skin.

"How is she?" he could not stop himself from asking.

"I don't know," Kirra mumbled. She looked even worse than Cammon, though where Cammon was pale, she was disheveled and flushed. She had tied her long hair back with a dirty strip of leather, but there were smears of blood and mud across her face and down the front of her shirt. Tayse wondered if she had acquired the bloodstains from tending Senneth or—

"Is any of that blood yours?" he asked.

Donnal answered. "No. I already asked."

Of course; that Tayse should have known already. Kirra, Cammon, Tayse, Justin—all of them were poised to do anything possible to save Senneth. Donnal was prepared to care for Kirra. It gave Tayse an odd sense of relief; he need not feel guilty, then, for thinking of no one but Senneth. Some of the others had their own protectors.

"What can I do?" Tayse asked.

Kirra shook her head. "Nothing, now, I think. She seems to be stable, finally—the bleeding has stopped, anyway. But I'm worried about what happens when the sun goes down."

He was confused. "Why?"

She glanced at him, and her eyes looked almost feverish. "She is the child of the Bright Mother," Kirra said quietly. "The Red Lady loves her. See? We should be in shadow even now, but sunlight falls on Senneth's face. As long as the sun is in the sky, I believe Senneth will gain some strength from the goddess. But when the sun goes down and the Pale Lady rises—I don't know. I don't know what happens then."

Tayse felt his fear flare up again, as if fresh fuel had been tossed on a slumbering coal. "She—but then she—what can we do? How can we protect her?"

Kirra nodded to the flames leaping nearby. "Fire will help. We have to keep it burning all night. Maybe a ring of candles as close to her body as we dare."

Tayse's mind was racing. "What about—are there amulets that the Bright Mother prizes? If the moonstones give power to the Daughters of the Pale Mother, what would give power to Senneth?"

Kirra looked thoughtful. "I don't know—I know so little about the Bright Mother—about any of the gods except the Silver Lady. Senneth wears that golden charm, you know—does it lend her any power? I don't know. It might."

Tayse rose to his feet. "Gold, then. Let us see what we can find."

It was a reason to go through the bodies, after all, though Tayse suspected few of the soldiers would bedeck themselves with a metal antithetical to their goddess. Still, as he'd hoped, a couple of them wore small gold rings—wedding bands or House signets— and a few of them carried gold coins in their pockets. One of them had a sword hilt wrapped in gold, but it was overlaid with a filigree of silver and set with moonstones, so there was no point in bringing that back to lay at Senneth's side. Justin found one fallen soldier with a belt buckle cast in gold; Tayse found another with a thin gold chain around his neck. It was hung with a tiny charm that looked like a flower—a gift from a lady friend, no doubt.

"Will this be enough, do you think?" Justin asked, looking at their paltry haul.

"It will have to be," Tayse said, "unless you are concealing any gold jewelry on your own person. I can't think Cammon is, since he has no possessions at all, and Kirra and Donnal would have spoken up by now."

Justin laughed. "No," he said. "I do not own a single gem, a single rope of jewelry. It never seemed worth the investment."

Tayse had stood, but now he was surveying the plundered bodies nearest to him. "I wonder," he said, "how far the influence of the moonstones extends. Perhaps if we gather all the moonstones and carry them a mile or so from camp—perhaps that would do some good."

"We may as well," Justin said. "We have to do something."

Since there was nothing else to do but wait.

Kirra accepted the gift of gold somewhat gingerly, but wasted no time wrapping the gold chain around Senneth's wrist and tucking gold coins into the tops of her socks. Tayse watched to see if the fire would shoot up again, but it remained unmoved by Senneth's new bounty. Perhaps the talismans would do no good at all. But Tayse felt heartened by making the effort.

"What can I do now?" he asked.

Kirra shook her head. "Sleep."

"I don't think I can. Ever again."

A half smile for that. "You will have to. Sometime. And I think I'll need you in the night. So you should sleep now so that you're strong enough to help later."

Bitter advice, but absolutely realistic. He had given the same orders to young recruits out on difficult missions. "How shall we split the watches tonight?" he asked. "Two to guard, two to sleep, I suppose. Cammon and Donnal obviously must serve in opposite shifts, and so must Justin and I."

"Cammon is exhausted," she said. "He should sleep now, too, so he can take the midnight watch with you."

He tried to make a joke of it. "Justin and Donnal are not best suited for a partnership."

"Justin and Donnal will be fine," she said. She was so tired she didn't even smile.

"When will you sleep?" he asked.

"When I can no longer keep my eyes open."

Tayse's gaze went to the other side of the stream, where the raelynx lay motionless. "What happens to that creature while Cammon is dreaming?" he asked. "Can he control it in his sleep?"

Kirra gave a hollow laugh. "Let us hope so," she said. "Senneth could."

"He's not Senneth."

She spread her hands. "I don't think we have any other options."

Reluctantly he nodded. "Is there anything I can do for you now?"

"No. Just rest so you can help me later."

He fetched Cammon, who protested at first, but who finally agreed to rest while he could. When Tayse asked if he could monitor the raelynx in his sleep, Cammon said, "Of course," in an absent voice. Tayse figured there was nothing he could do about it if Cammon's self-confidence was misplaced. The two of them ate a cold and hasty meal, then rolled themselves into their blankets on the other side of the fire from where Kirra sat with Senneth.

It was an old campaigner's trick, the ability to fall asleep at any time, under any circumstances. Tayse had learned it long ago, but he was not sure he would be able to force his body, this time, to comply with his wishes. To let himself sleep while Senneth lay a few feet away, fighting for her life—it seemed criminal, it seemed obscene.

Even more unforgivable would be to find himself so exhausted he could not aid her if the need arose. He closed his eyes and willed his mind to shut down, his breathing to slow. He summoned darkness, and darkness came.

It was full night when he woke again, suddenly and completely, assessing before he even sat up what time it was, how the situation lay around him. Probably an hour or so before midnight; the air seemed dense with cold, and the stars had progressed only so far in their journey across the sky. Someone was bending over the campfire, prodding at a log. Justin, keeping the fire burning.

Tayse stood and prowled immediately to the other side of the fire. Senneth lay stretched in front of it so that her face, her torso, the whole front of her body were exposed to the flames. Donnal lay against her back, a woolly bear whose body heat had to be considerable. He lifted his black head from his outstretched paws as Tayse came around the fire. Kirra sat cross-legged at Senneth's feet, her elbows resting on her knees, her chin on her fists. She appeared to be dozing, but she opened her eyes when Tayse stepped closer.

"How is she?" he asked.

"No different. No worse, anyway. She seems to be sleeping."

"Time for you to sleep, then."

She nodded. "Donnal can stay beside her to keep her warm."

"I'll do that," Tayse said.

She nodded again, too weary to argue. "I'll wake Cammon."

In a few moments, the camp had redistributed itself. Justin appeared to fall instantly asleep on the blankets still warm from Tayse's body. Kirra lay a few feet away from him, Donnal curled up next to her, still in the guise of a bear. Cammon sat with his back to the fire, his eyes fixed on the road leading toward the convent.

Tayse lay on the blanket spread beneath Senneth and brought his big body in close to hers. He slid one arm oh-so-gently beneath her head, then brought it up to cross her chest; he draped the other across her hip. The bend of her knees fit over the bend of his. He could feel the heat of his body pouring itself into her—or else he was willing the transfer so mightily that he simply imagined the sensation of strength streaming from his body and filling her empty veins with his own life and vigor.

During the next six hours, there was very little movement in the camp. Cammon rose every half hour or so to patrol the perimeter—a trick he had to have picked up from watching Tayse take his turn at watch. The others shifted position now and then, and twice, when Kirra woke, she sat up to gaze across the fire.

"How's Senneth?" she asked each time.

"The same. Her breathing is a little ragged, but steady. She doesn't seem quite so cold. But she has moved very little, and she hasn't spoken at all."

"Wake me if there's a change."

"I will."

But when the change came, he didn't.

It was very late in the night, so late it was almost dawn, and Cammon was off on one of his periodic excursions. Tayse was lying with his body absolutely relaxed, but his mind completely engaged, imagining—as he so often did—what moves he would make, what weapons he would use, if enemies suddenly came charging at him. His sword was inches away from him on the ground, sheathed; he had a knife tucked inside each boot. He would make a good accounting of himself even if he was on foot and his opponents were on horseback. He could disable the horses, of course—he hated to do that, but it might become necessary—

And then Senneth stirred in his arms.

His whole body tensed, but he did not speak, in case this was just some sleeper's unthinking stretch. But then she moved again, seeming to roll her shoulders in an experimental shrug. He felt her hands lift and fasten themselves on his own arm, laid like a bar across her chest.

"Tayse?" she said, her voice very faint.

There was no way she could see him, could tell by any of her human senses who pressed against her, feeding her warmth. He felt his spine tingle with disquiet even as his arms tightened around her. "Yes," he whispered. "How are you feeling?"

"Awful," was the reply. "But—I think, not fatally awful."

"We've been very worried."

She seemed to think a minute, perhaps trying to reconstruct what had happened to put her in this plight. "Are the soldiers dead?" she asked next. Clearly she remembered most of it.

"Yes. And all of us—but you—unharmed."

"She said she wouldn't send anyone after us. She lied."

"I imagine she often does."

"Where are we?"

"Near the streambed where you fell."

A wince for that, as if she wanted to start upright but didn't have the strength. "We can't be safe here."

"When you're strong enough, we'll move."

"Has Donnal left for Gisseltess?"

He couldn't stop a very small laugh. "No, we thought we'd wait to see if you lived before we set up meetings in Lochau."

"I was careless."

"We were all careless. Cammon is blaming himself—I am bitterly certain I am the one at fault—"

"Not you," she said, and her voice was so drowsy it was clear she would not be able to sustain this burst of energy much longer. "You have always taken such good care of me."

"I was commanded to do so by my king," he said, his voice rough.

If she had had the strength, the sound she made then would have been a laugh. "That's not why you do it," she breathed.

He had no reply to make to that, and she was silent for so long that he thought she had fallen back to sleep. Then he felt a shiver of movement run through her muscles again. "Tayse," she whispered.

"Yes."

"Don't leave me."

As if he would. As if the thought would cross his mind for an instant. As if he could. "No," he said. "I'll stay right here."

After that, almost instantly, she did fall asleep. He could feel her ribs expand and contract, ever so slightly, with her regular breathing. Cammon returned from his circuit and came to crouch beside him, just inside the circle of firelight.

"She woke up, didn't she?" Cammon asked. "How is she?"

Impossible to try to conceal things from this young man. Tayse pitied the woman who ever fell in love with him and then tried to deceive him. "Lucid. But weak."

"That's a good sign, though, isn't it? That she could talk?"

"Could you actually hear what we said?" Tayse demanded, keeping his voice very low but unable to completely hide his irritation.

Cammon was grinning. "Not the words. I could just tell that she was conscious. And speaking. But that's good, isn't it?"

"We'll see come dawn," Tayse replied. "But I think it's good."

KIRRA was the first one awake in the morning, stepping over the sleeping bodies to make it to Senneth's side. "How is she?" she asked, kneeling.

Those were the only words any of them seemed able to utter, Tayse thought. "Stable, I think. Sleeping. She woke up in the middle of the night and spoke a few words."

"She did? Wonderful!" Kirra exclaimed.

"But she's sleeping now."

"When she wakes up again, we'll have to see if we can get her to eat something."

"And maybe get her out of these bloody clothes," Tayse suggested.

Kirra grimaced. "Yes. I should have done that yesterday."

Before any of them could say more, Donnal and Justin stirred, and Cammon reappeared from making his last sweep around the perimeter. The next thirty minutes consisted of everyone asking about Senneth, comparing notes, eating a quick meal, and rearranging themselves for the next six-hour shift. Cammon lay down and was almost instantly asleep. Justin was across the river, investigating the possibility of setting a trap or two. Donnal, now in wolf shape, was sitting by the fire, mouth half open, watching Kirra.

"You should be sleeping, too," she said to Tayse.

"I will. In a few minutes. I just want to see if there's anything I can do to help you with Senneth."

Kirra glanced at Donnal, so close, and Justin, too far away to hear. "If you'll prop her up for me while I change her clothes—you have to promise to be a gentleman, though, and not look—I'll make Donnal go sit somewhere else—"

In spite of everything, Tayse found himself grinning. "From what I've seen of the men of the Twelve Houses, being a gentleman doesn't necessarily mean displaying great honor," he said. "But I will turn my eyes away while you undress her."

Donnal's broad mouth widened into what had to be a lupine smile, but he rose to his four feet and trotted away from the fire. Kirra poured water into a pan and added a rag to soak. Then she leaned down and put her hands on either side of Senneth's face.

"Sen. Are you awake? Sen? I want to clean you up a little, so we're going to be moving you. If it gets too painful, let me know, and we'll stop."

"I'm—awake," the whisper came back faintly.

Kirra's face lit with delight. She clasped her hands to her chest like a little girl excited over a gift. "How are you feeling? Are you stronger? Do you hurt?"

"I feel—pretty bad," Senneth replied. "My chest hurts."

"That's from the arrow," Kirra said dryly.

"But—better than last night. A little."

"Good. We're going to clean you up, and then I'm going to try to feed you. All right?"

"All—right."

"Tayse is going to help," Kirra added inconsequentially.

Senneth turned her head slightly so she could see Tayse's face, but she didn't say anything. Kirra was quickly all business. "Tayse—if you'll lift her up and brace her so that I can get this shirt off—good—"

It was a delicate and awkward maneuver, Tayse found, to strip a woman of her bloody clothing, and wipe her flesh clean, and bind a new bandage around her chest. He did only what Kirra told him, supporting Senneth's weight against his chest, lifting her when instructed and then letting her settle back against him.

Senneth remained more or less awake the entire time, for she gave little moans of pain now and then, and once whispered, "Thank you," but she mostly kept her eyes closed and did not speak. Kirra moved swiftly and competently, leading Tayse to wonder how many of her nursing skills were magical and how many had been learned through training. Soon enough Senneth was in a fresh bandage and a clean shirt, lying against Tayse's chest and taking slow, ragged breaths.

"Good. You're still awake," Kirra said, though Tayse could not see Senneth's face to judge if her eyes were open. "Can you eat something? Some broth? At least drink some water?"

"I think so," Senneth breathed.

Kirra leaned toward the fire to fetch a metal mug that had been heating all this time. "Just a little, just at first," she said. "We'll see how well you do."

Also awkward was the act of feeding an invalid, because some of the soup sloshed from the spoon straight onto the clean shirt, and some of it dribbled down Senneth's chin. But most of it went in her mouth, and Tayse could tell by Kirra's expression that she was pleased.

"Now have some water and then we'll let you lie down again," she said, holding a container to Senneth's mouth.

Tayse picked up one of the cleaner rags that Kirra had used to remove the blood from Senneth's body. As soon as Kirra lowered the bottle, he started wiping at Senneth's mouth and throat, chasing the droplets of broth down her neck and into the V of the fresh shirt. He had to push aside her gold amulet to clean the hollow of her throat. He could see a darker stain just below the top button, and he dabbed at it ineffectually, trying to reach it without compromising Senneth's dignity.

"Did I leave a bloodstain?" Kirra asked, returning her attention to him. "Here—let me unbutton the shirt a little—"

And she did, and Tayse swiped at the blot again, but again it would not come off on the damp rag. He leaned closer to see what it might be—another wound, perhaps, that they had missed because of their focus on the arrow's path—and saw a small, raised patch of reddish skin. It was positioned just above and perfectly between her breasts, exactly where a pendant might fall if Senneth were wearing jewelry for a formal ball.

It was a brand.

A housemark.

Tayse kept his eyes on the symbol of power and prestige while the world rocked around him like a shaken toy. He could feel Senneth's weight against his shoulder, could feel the texture of the wet cloth in his hand. He knew that Kirra's gaze had lifted from the housemark to his face and that Senneth's own eyes were probably closed with resignation. But he could not move. He could not speak. He could not take it in.

A housemark. The brand of one of the Twelve Houses. She was one of the highest-ranking noblewomen in the country. He loved her and he did not want to love her, but it did not matter if he did or if he did not: She was not for him, never would have been, had he declared himself that night she kissed him or last night when she woke in his arms or at some point farther down the road when he was no longer able to keep his secret to himself.

He made himself lift his head and look at Kirra, whose face was a study in wretchedness and compassion. He found a moment to wonder why Senneth had bothered to lie about her heritage at all, though he supposed she'd had her reasons, but it was clear Kirra had known all along. Well, of course she would. Kirra, too, was a serramarra. They might have known each other since the day Kirra was born.

"Which House?" he managed to ask, his voice a rasp.

Kirra glanced down at Senneth, so Tayse followed her gaze. Senneth had twisted her head enough so that she could look up at him through her lashes. Her skin was absolutely white; her gray eyes showed only the faintest wash of color.

"Which House?" he repeated.

Senneth answered. "Brassenthwaite."

CHAPTER
30

TAYSE slept heavily till noon. He had thought, of course, that he would never sleep again—or else he would sleep forever, lie down on this crumpled blanket and close his eyes and then give over his spirit to whichever of the jealous gods chose to claim him. But, like any ordinary man, he slept for a few hours and then woke. He could not say that he felt any better for it. His body moved with the sluggishness that might come after secret poisoning. His heart beat with a listless rhythm, and his limbs responded with protest to his commands.

He had heard of men who were laid low by despair or grief, men who let bitter emotions rob their bodies of all strength. He had thought of them with some contempt, for who would ever be weak enough to be ruled by the passions of the heart? But he understood them all now. For the first time he believed that a man could be wounded even if no sword cut his chest, even if no arrow pierced his throat. He realized there were wounds to the soul that could fell even the strongest soldier.

He forced himself to his feet and walked around the fire to where Kirra sat and Donnal lay beside Senneth. "How is she?" he asked, and even to himself his voice sounded choked.

Kirra looked up at him. "Sleeping. But she ate some more a few hours ago, and I can feel the heat building up in her body. She's getting stronger. She'll recover fast, I think."

He nodded. "What about you? I think you need to sleep, too."

She nodded. "I will. After she wakes again and I feed her again."

Justin came up from the land beyond the stream, a dead rabbit dangling from his hand. "Dinner," he said with a grin. "Who needs wolves and raelynxes when he can set a trap?"

Tayse nodded at him. "Good. Now you sleep awhile. I'm up." He glanced at the wolf, who had lifted his head from his paws and was regarding Tayse with a meditative stare. "You, too. Sleep."

On the other side of the fire, Cammon was sitting up and yawning. "How's Senneth?" he called.

"Better," Tayse replied. "Time for our watch."

Kirra waited till Donnal and Justin were settled and Cammon had trotted down to the river to wash up. Then she said to Tayse, "You can't be angry with her for not telling you who she is."

He shrugged, tired and in pain and not wanting to talk about it. "She owes me nothing. It is her right to tell me the story of her life, or not. How can it matter to me?"

"She was seventeen," Kirra said in a hard, rapid voice. "Her father killed her son and threw her from the house. Because she was a mystic. My father would have taken her in—her mother's relatives in Kianlever would have taken her in—Ariane Rappengrass offered her a home. But she wouldn't stay. She just wandered off and—and—had that strange life she's had. You've heard some of her stories. She doesn't consider herself a Brassenthwaite anymore. She doesn't claim to be from the Twelve Houses."

"But she is," Tayse said.

"No," Kirra said. "She is Senneth. She is the greatest living mystic in Gillengaria. She has a wild power that she has brought under fierce control, and she has offered that power to the king. She is someone you can trust absolutely. Tayse, you've traveled at her side for six weeks. You know who she is. She hasn't changed."

He looked down at Senneth's face, peaceful in sleep, brushed just now with the faintest blush of color. A good sign, that the fire was building again in her veins. "I never knew who she was," he said. "And I haven't changed either."

THE next two days followed the same unvarying routine of sleeping and watching and tending to an invalid. Tayse took his turns acting as guard, tramping off to look for fuel, fetching water, cooking the meals. But there was no longer any need to help

Kirra with Senneth, because Senneth was well enough now to sit on her own, feed herself, change her clothes if she needed to. Her temperature had risen back almost to its normal pitch, so not even Donnal needed to lie beside her at night to keep her body warm. Indeed, it would be only a day or two, Tayse guessed, before she would again command such reserves of heat that she would be able to light fires with her fingers and create whole temperate zones with her physical presence.

She didn't need any of them, though only Tayse seemed to realize that. The others hovered around her, solicitous and affectionate by turns, made ridiculous with relief. There was a great deal of laughter around the campfire those two days, though Tayse himself did not laugh much. He was fairly certain there was no laughter left for him in the world.

The evening of that second day Senneth insisted on standing, and walking a small circle around the campfire, and then taking even more halting steps down to the edge of the stream. "I started out four days ago, hoping to get clean," she said stubbornly, "and clean I will be. You men—go somewhere else. Kirra will help me."

So he and Justin and Cammon and Donnal withdrew some distance, going up to the road to see if there had been much traffic recently. Cammon and Donnal faced in the direction of the convent, as if to sense or smell trouble that might come from that route, but neither of them had any observations to offer. Tayse's own attention was fixed behind them, on the water, in case there should be a cry for help from a weak woman or a drowning one. But no voices called them back, and when they returned to the fire, Senneth and Kirra were sitting before it, damp and smiling.

"I think we should ride out tomorrow," Senneth said.

"No," Kirra replied.

"The day after, then," Senneth said.

Kirra narrowed her eyes and looked at Senneth, as if considering. "Maybe. But we'd have to go slow."

"We'll set out the day after tomorrow," Senneth repeated, and it was clear they would not be able to dissuade her. "So, Donnal, you should leave in the morning for Gisseltess to carry a message to Halchon. We can probably be in Lochau four or five days from now. Perhaps he can meet us then, or soon thereafter."

Donnal nodded. "Will he come, do you think?"

Senneth stared somewhat moodily into the fire. "Yes. I think so."

"Then I'll be on my way in the morning."

They had no paper with them, no writing implements—but Kirra was never at a loss in such situations. A broad, dry, winter leaf became a sheet of pressed paper; in her hands, a twig and a cup of water transformed to pen and ink. Frowning and writing very slowly, Senneth composed a letter to Halchon Gisseltess, then threw it in the fire.

"I need more paper," she said.

Kirra gave her a look of exasperation, then produced a whole sheaf of pages. "Let me know when you're about to ruin all these," she said.

Senneth laughed. "I think it will only take me a few more tries."

In the end, she produced a message that seemed acceptable to her, though she did not appear delighted with it. She folded the paper, fastened it with a royal seal she borrowed from Tayse, and handed it to Donnal. "I would prefer that you give it directly into Halchon's hands," she said. "Though you may not be allowed so close. If you find that the king's seal does not get you very far, use my name. It may open some doors."

Donnal nodded and tucked the paper inside his pocket. "Should I meet you in Lochau or somewhere on the road?"

Senneth shrugged. "Start in Lochau, maybe, and if we're not there, come look for us. We'll be staying—" She looked at Kirra.

"The Dalian Inn, by the harbor," Kirra said. "It's where my father stays in Lochau."

"And you'll be under your own names?" Donnal asked.

Senneth laughed and did not answer. Kirra was grinning. "We'll use Danalustrous," Kirra said. "It may do us some good in that particular city."

None of them had breathed the name *Brassenthwaite* since that morning two days ago. Tayse was not even sure that Justin and Donnal and Cammon knew it. Well, Donnal, surely. Cammon perhaps. And Cammon might have confided what he knew to Justin. For such a small group, they had an amazing number of individual connections. But no one had said the name again in Tayse's hearing.

He would be just as happy if no one ever did.

• • •

DONNAL was gone before the rest of them were up. Cammon assumed a quiet air of responsibility, since he was now the only person in the camp with heightened sensibilities as long as Kirra remained in human form. The rest of them spent the day getting ready for travel: repacking clothes, organizing their remaining food, refilling water containers, taking a last chance to get thoroughly clean as long as they were so close to water. Tayse checked and rechecked his weapons. Senneth alternated between taking long naps to refresh her body and taking long walks to strengthen it. Tayse had to admit she looked more hearty than he would have expected, only five days after a potentially fatal wound. Her own magic or Kirra's, he could not be sure, but magic nonetheless.

In the morning, they were on their way almost at the first sign of dawn. Tayse paused to release most of the convent horses from their tethers. He kept the bay and the dapple gray that Justin had praised so highly, herding them along with Donnal's horse as their party headed for the road. The weather was crisp but clear and not unduly cold. A few more weeks, a few more weeks— spring might actually arrive.

They rode at a steady but not particularly demanding pace, halting frequently to give Senneth a chance to rest. During the morning, she indignantly declared that she was just fine, they should stop worrying about her, but by late afternoon, it was obvious she was weary. Tayse pulled off the road while there were still a couple hours of daylight left, insisting they make an early camp.

"I'm *fine*," Senneth said, scowling.

"Glad to hear it," he responded. "*I'm* tired. We camp now."

She was stronger in the morning, though, and they covered a greater distance by day's end. Traffic on the road was brisk, and they saw plenty of Gisseltess soldiers riding to or from the region, though no convent guards passed them. The raelynx, who had stayed very visible during their last few days at the river camp, now melted into the countryside again, not even showing up as they stopped for the night.

"Is it still with us?" Tayse asked Cammon that second night.

Cammon nodded. "Not far away."

"What are we going to do about him in Lochau?" Justin asked.

Senneth grimaced. "I've been worrying about that. We can hardly bring him into the Dalian Inn with us, even if I conceal him. Lochau is too big a city to be parading wild animals down the streets."

Kirra appeared to be thinking. "Well," she said at last, "if one of my father's ships is in the harbor, we can crate him and put him on board. They must have accommodations for animals if we're going to bring the horses."

Senneth looked at her. "And who exactly will put the raelynx *in* the crate?" she asked.

Kirra grinned. "You, I thought."

"I'll do it," Cammon said.

They all switched their attention to him. He reddened a little, then shrugged. "I think it will be calm for me. I'll wait with it outside the city limits while Kirra makes arrangements with the ship captain, and then I'll box it up and ride back with it to the ship. I'm sure I can handle it."

Justin was nodding. "Sounds workable. *If* we can find a Danalustrous ship, *if* it's big enough to take us all north. *If* the captain is willing to ferry wild animals in his hold."

Tayse shook his head. "I cannot believe we have traveled all this way and found no safe place to leave that creature behind."

Senneth looked at him, something she had rarely done these past few days. She was smiling, but her eyes were unreadable. "But Tayse, that creature is what got you rescued from Lumanen Convent," she said. "Surely you would not abandon it now?"

You are the one who rescued me, he wanted to reply. *Are you asking if I would abandon you after all our adventures together?* "It is a wild thing," he said deliberately. "We cannot ever truly know what it thinks or what it wants. It belongs to a world outside of ours, and we cannot bring it inside our own. It will always be more exotic than we wish."

Kirra raised her eyebrows and divided a look between Tayse and Senneth. Cammon looked down at his plate. Justin seemed oblivious. "Well," the other Rider said, "I think we owe it safe passage. And I kind of like having it prowl along beside us, nobody but us knowing it's there or what it can do. It makes me feel—" He stopped and spread his hands. "Well, I just like it," he said.

Senneth was smiling more warmly now. "Yes," she said, "it's become one of us, whether we wanted it to or not. No turning back now or casting it aside, even if we tried. No matter how strange or dangerous it is to our peace of mind."

To Tayse's intense irritation, Kirra was trying to smother a giggle, and Cammon was grinning into the fire. Justin was nodding. "Exactly," Justin said. "So I hope we can find a way to get it back to Ghosenhall. The king might enjoy seeing it."

"The king," said Senneth softly, "will be delighted."

TAYSE had the middle watch that night, taking over from Cammon. By habit, he first checked all the sleepers to verify that they were still breathing, then stepped away from the circle of firelight to make a slow tour of the perimeter. They were only half a day's ride from Lochau now; he would not have been surprised to find other travelers settled nearby. Indeed, he could see a few campfires in the distance, because most of the countryside here was hilly but open, undulating away from the road in gentle brown waves. None of the other campfires was close enough to be in hailing distance, however, and Tayse felt relatively secure. Though he would not truly feel they were all safe till they were back in the barracks at Ghosenhall—and some of them would not be safe even then.

What would Senneth do after she made her report to the king? Set off on her random wandering again, or pursue a more specific mission for the court? What would the king do? Call up his loyal armies and prepare for war, or assemble his councilors and make plans for peace? Whom would Tayse himself follow and protect, if he were given a choice? He could not bring himself to answer the question. He tramped on in a widening circle around the camp, intent on providing what sanctuary he could for those currently under his protection. He could not, at the moment, do better than that.

When he turned to make his way back to the campfire, he was brought up short by a dark silhouette standing in his path. His body tensed, and his hand went automatically to his knife hilt. But the figure moved until it caught the faint starlight, and its outline was entirely familiar. He knew by the color of her hair, the shape of her shoulders, the response of his own body, who had come to find him in the dead of night.

"You should be sleeping," he said.

"I was restless."

"Are you still in pain?"

A shadow of a shrug in the starlight. "Now and then. Less every day. If I lie on my left side, pain is what wakes me."

"Kirra might have something for that."

"I'm always fine by morning."

He came a few steps closer, and Senneth fell in step beside him. Much more slowly than was necessary, they made their circular way back toward camp. "Are you worried about this meeting with Halchon Gisseltess?" he asked.

"A little," she said. "He's powerful, he's unpredictable, and I don't know what he wants. Is there any way to turn him from an enemy to a friend? And will I be able to discover that way? These questions keep me awake much longer than pain does."

"You should try harder to sleep when you can," was all he could think to say in response.

He was looking straight before him, but he caught her quick sideways glance. "What keeps you awake at night, Tayse?" she asked softly. "For you look grim and exhausted every morning."

He found himself unable to reply.

"You should at least make to my face the accusations you have been making to me silently," she went on.

"Is your own name an accusation, then?" he said heavily. "Senneth Brassenthwaite. You tell me."

"I have not gone by the name Brassenthwaite since I was seventeen," she said. "I have not been in my father's House since that time—I have not made any claim on my heritage or my blood. There is nothing Brassenthwaite about me except the brand on my skin."

"Brassenthwaite is branded into your soul."

She stopped and twisted around to face him; by her quick movements, he knew she was suddenly flushed with anger. "Magic is branded into my soul," she said in a hard voice. "Magic is what shapes and defines me, and magic is why you distrusted me from the very beginning. Now you find that I bear a noble name and come from a haughty lineage, and you despise me even more. Tell me, Tayse, what would I have to be—who would I have to be—for you to allow yourself to love me?"

"Riders allow themselves to love no one but their king."

"You could at least do me the favor of not lying to me."

"You could do me the favor of unenchanting me," he whispered.

She made a small sound of exasperation and looked away. He could tell by her stance, by her profile, that she was still furious. "If I had that kind of magic, do you think I would bring it to bear on you?" she asked. "Do you think I would try to cast a spell that brought you misery and grief? I might wish for you to love me, but I would trust to older magic than any I possess to make that happen. I have not ensorceled you, Tayse. I have only made you unhappy. Surely you would not think that is something I would try to do with witchcraft."

"No," he said, "but I thought you might be able to undo it if you wanted to."

"I would make you stop hurting, if I could," she said. "I can't honestly say I would cast a spell that would keep you from loving me."

"Why did you lie to me?" he said. "Why did you not tell me who you are?"

"I didn't lie," she said. "You know who I am."

"No," he said. "I have discovered you, bit by bit. You are a woman made up of many parts, all of them concealed. As the truth has been forced from you, you have reluctantly showed one side of yourself, and then another. I have assembled you in pieces."

"And have you truly hated all of those pieces?"

"I have hated none of them," he said. "But none of them has put you within my reach."

"None of them has put me outside your reach, either," she said.

"You were always too rare for me," he said. "So many days I have felt like Donnal, a mute dog following at the heels of a glorious mistress. But I am not fashioned like Donnal is. I am just as loyal, but not nearly so humble. You asked once before what it might take to break me. That would do it, I think—to be around you so long, and be so despairing. That would tear me right in half."

She came a step nearer then, so near he could feel the heat radiating off her skin. All her anger seemed to have flown, but he could see the intensity on her face, the thoughtful, considering expression. "You are too strong for that, Tayse," she said in a soft voice. "Even love will not break you. Even magic you would withstand." She lifted a hand and touched a finger lightly to his lips, enjoining silence. Not that he was capable of speech anyway.

"I cannot heal you, not of this particular grief, but I can give you something else to consume your thoughts. And it is this: I love you, Tayse. If I were to fashion a man I would want to see riding at my side, I would fashion him just like you. He would look like you, he would fight like you, he would be just as wary and hard to convince. He would *be* you. But he would learn, no matter how slowly, that he need not put love aside. He would come to understand that I am lonely, that I am frightened, that I am a woman building fires to ward off the dark.

"I am so used to being solitary and strong. I do not like being worried and weak. But I feel safe when you are near me and troubled when you are gone, and these are not feelings, I think, that will easily pass. You say I have the power to break you—well, you have changed me, and I did not think I was capable of changing again. I only hope you will not abandon me, so altered and strange to myself, because you think I am too proud to accept your love. I would hate for my life to go on like that, empty of you. I think I would be the one to finally break after that."

And while he stood there, numb and dumbstruck, she dropped her hand, arched to her tiptoes, and kissed him softly on the mouth. When she pulled away, he could tell she was smiling.

"And now let us see if either of us sleeps for the remainder of the night," she said.

He made no reply, and she slipped away in the dark. He watched her make her way directly back to camp and roll herself into her blankets before he took another step, staying on his previous circuitous route. It was a wonder to him that he could move at all, for every bone felt weighted with gold, every vein felt charged with fire. He stumbled twice more around the camp, narrowing his spiral till he was back before the cheerful fire.

His watch might end in two hours, but she had been right about one thing: He would not sleep again this night. He was not sure he would ever sleep again.

CHAPTER
31

LOCHAU was a port town down to its very bones. Senneth thought it was possible that the frame of every house, every tavern, had been built from discarded mainmasts, that the timber from old hulls had been reused to construct the buildings and furnish the wood for the painted signs that hung over every establishment. You could not take a breath without inhaling the scents of salt and fish; you could not speak without having to raise your voice over the cry of the gulls. Even on a day as bright as this one, the cobblestoned streets felt wet with the accumulated moisture in the air, and the wind never stopped blowing off the sea.

"Lochau," Kirra said, running a hand through her long gold curls. "My hair feels gritty already."

"Let's get settled," Senneth said. "No telling how quickly Halchon may be arriving. If he arrives."

Kirra sighed. "And we have much to do."

They found the Dalian Inn with no trouble. It was an old hotel, a little weather-beaten, but maintaining its dignity with a fresh coat of whitewash over all three stories. Senneth and Kirra left the men to deal with the ostlers and went inside to check for accommodations.

"Let's say Danalustrous only," Senneth murmured as the smiling clerk approached them.

Kirra nodded, then stepped forward to greet the man with her own smile. In this place, she opted for charm, not hauteur, and soon enough she had secured two adjoining rooms on the second floor.

"We are expecting—we are hoping—to be joined in a day or so by Halchon Gisseltess," she said very solemnly. "I have sent him a message under a different name. If he comes, could you direct him to my quarters? It is very important that I speak to him."

"Yes, serramarra Kirra. Most certainly, serramarra Kirra. How long will you be staying with us?"

Kirra waved a hand. "All depends on the outcome of my conversation with the marlord. You understand."

"Naturally."

"Do you know if any of my father's ships are in harbor?" she asked next.

"Indeed, there were three flying the red-and-gold standard as I came to work this morning."

"Excellent," she said. "I need to see a captain about travel arrangements."

They followed the clerk to their room, which smelled slightly musty but looked clean, and Senneth allowed herself to tumble headfirst onto one of the beds. "Fabulous," she murmured. "Such softness! Such a sweet cushion for my maltreated bones!"

Kirra grinned down at her. She was braiding her hair back with a length of red ribbon she had conjured from nowhere, and she was already dressed in a pretty scarlet gown suitable for walking. "Why don't you sleep awhile? I don't need you for this particular transaction."

"Oh—well—maybe," Senneth said, finding herself almost unable to force herself from the bed. "Take Justin or Tayse with you."

"I suppose it will have to be Justin," Kirra said wickedly, "since Tayse will not leave your side."

Senneth wanted to throw a pillow at her, but she didn't have the energy. "Tayse will be happy enough to leave my side when we're back in Ghosenhall."

"Will he? I think our dour Rider will find himself very torn between the two halves of his heart."

Senneth turned over on her side, away from Kirra. She could hear Tayse and Justin talking in the hall. "Wake me if Donnal arrives," she said drowsily, "or if Halchon shows up."

"I will," Kirra said. If she added anything else, Senneth didn't hear it; she was already asleep.

She guessed it was a couple of hours later that she woke. She lay there a few moments, trying to determine what time it was and what might be going on around her. Sunlight was still filtering in through the stiff white curtains, but it was weak enough to indicate day was almost over. She could hear no voices from the rooms next door, so her friends were undoubtedly out on their own pursuits: canvassing the harbor for ships, stopping by some of the local shops for specialty foods or new items of clothing, drinking a glass or two of ale in a tavern nearby. Clearly they had all decided that she was better off sleeping than being informed of their movements.

She turned to her other side, feeling the protest in all her bones as she did so. The ache in her left side was much better than it had been a few days ago, but it was a constant, nagging presence; if she moved too swiftly or injudiciously, it reacted with a fierce contraction. She would have thought magic would have been more efficacious than this. She had truly expected to be fully recovered by now, all through Kirra's spells and her own force of will.

She supposed she should be grateful she was still alive, since once the wound had been described to her, she had realized she very well could have died. But gratitude was hard to come by when the mere act of sitting up in bed made her grunt with pain. And when she was so anxious—about the Daughters of the Pale Mother, about Coralinda Gisseltess, about Halchon Gisseltess, about the potential for war, about everything.

About Tayse.

Stupid to say those things to him the other night—stupid even though they were true, stupid because he had set himself against her, and she didn't have the graces or the wiles to win him over. Kirra, now—Kirra had charm and beauty and a knack with men. If Kirra had set her heart on Tayse—or on Justin, even, who mistrusted Kirra as much as Tayse mistrusted Senneth—she would have been able to secure him. She would have seduced him with her soft laugh, her bright hair, her sidelong smile. She would have fascinated him, and he would have followed her anywhere, helplessly drawn to her color and beauty.

Kirra would not have chased a man down on a night watch and baldly declared her love for him, and then turned and walked away.

And he would not have regarded Kirra the next morning with a face utterly unchanged except for having grown more remote.

Even if she could claw off the Brassenthwaite brand, even if there was no visible taint left on her skin, Tayse would not forgive her. She could not seem to make him understand that she had not set out to be deceptive. It was not a lie to fail to mention a past that no longer applied. Justin did not forever go on prattling about his life as a street urchin, robbing rich men and dueling in the streets. Cammon had shared his own story once, and then seemed to forget he had a former life. Donnal could hardly be brought to talk about himself at all. Yet she was supposed to pause every three sentences and say, "By the way, I was born a Brassenthwaite, you know." That wasn't fair in the least.

But it didn't matter. Even if he would be able to accept that she had not lied to him, he would not be able to accept that she came from noble blood. She could say it was unimportant to her, but it was clearly important to him. He would as soon let himself fall in love with Princess Amalie.

She sighed and wondered if perhaps she just shouldn't bother to get up at all. The sun would be down soon enough. She could just close her eyes and pretend it was night already, and sleep straight through until morning.

She had no chance to put this admirable plan into action, because at that moment, Kirra swept into the room. "Oh! Are you still asleep? Sorry. I'll leave—"

Senneth yawned and sat up. "No, no, I'm awake. What's the situation here?"

"Everything in train," Kirra said, plopping down on the other bed. "Found a ship—cargo transport, loads of room, *and* I know the captain. They were going to pull out tomorrow, but the captain's graciously agreed to wait upon our convenience and set us down in Dormas, even though it's not a scheduled stop." She grinned. "He feels certain such a kindness to me will endear him to my father, though he did not phrase it quite that way. But he's right, of course—I'll make sure he's rewarded."

Senneth yawned again. "What about the raelynx?"

"Being brought aboard even as we speak. Well, I didn't wait to observe the whole maneuver. I imagine it'll take some time to get the animal lured into the crate and then hauled back on the gig we hired, but Cammon seemed quite convinced that he could take care of the whole operation. Captain Abernot was not *thrilled* by the idea of carrying wild animals on board, but he did admit he was curious to actually see a live raelynx. Since, I suppose, they've never wandered too far west of the Lirrens and lived."

"I wonder if your father would like a raelynx," Senneth said. "We could leave it with—Captain Abernot, you say?—and let him take it all the way to Danalustrous. Your father's a resource-ful man. He'd be able to think of something to do with it."

Kirra grinned. "My father's a practical man. He'd have it slain and its coat turned into a red fur collar for Casserah. No, I don't think you'll be able to palm this trial off on anyone till you get to the Lirrens."

Senneth sighed. "And I suppose that's where I'll be going once we leave Ghosenhall."

Kirra tilted her head. "But you could come to Danalustrous once you completed your journey. My father would love to see you again."

"I don't know where I'll be headed after that," Senneth said lightly. "Perhaps the king will have more work for me. I'll have to see."

"Aren't you tired of wandering yet?" Kirra asked quietly.

Senneth covered her expression by pretending to yawn again. Sharp, stupid stab of pain for that question. She didn't even know how to answer it. "I expect to be wandering most of my days," she replied and made herself stand up. She actually felt better once she was on her feet. "Do they have any kind of baths here? I could soak for a week."

CLEAN, rested, and in a rather better mood, Senneth joined her traveling companions for dinner a couple of hours later. All six of them were present for the meal, since Donnal had arrived while she and Kirra were bathing. His news was good, she supposed: Halchon had agreed to come to Lochau as soon as he could gather a party and ride. It was what she wanted, of course, though she could not bring herself to look forward to the meeting.

Nonetheless, like the rest of them, she was able to summon a hearty appetite for the meal. The dining hall at the Dalian was nothing like the taprooms of most of the small hotels they'd stayed at along the way. It was elegant and formal, though its white paint was peeling a little from the onslaught of incessant humidity, and a few of its ceiling beams looked warped from the same cause. They had their choice of several entrées, and all the food looked tasty.

"Have I mentioned this? I'm never eating rabbit again," Kirra said.

Donnal grinned. "At least not cooked rabbit," he said with rare humor. "But if you're traveling in hawk shape, and you get hungry—"

Kirra shuddered and bit into a forkful of chicken that had been grilled in some kind of wine-based sauce. "At the moment, I can't ever imagine being so hungry again."

"I like rabbit," Cammon said. "But this is good, too."

"I like rabbit well enough, but I like it better if I get to vary the diet now and then," Senneth chimed in. "You know, perhaps deer meat one night, and grouse the next—"

"Well, considering that I'm the one who caught us the last few rabbits we ate, and all of you seemed pretty damn happy to eat them at the time, I just want to say you're a bunch of ungrateful wretches," Justin said.

"Not ungrateful," Kirra said. "It's just that it's so clear that *these* elegant surroundings are really what suit me best."

Conversation went that way for the entire meal, all of them seeming relaxed and happy for the first time in days. Senneth supposed there was no guarantee that Halchon's men wouldn't burst into the inn and suddenly take them all hostage, though she thought it was less likely now that Danalustrous men would be aware of the outrage and take word instantly back to Kirra's father. So she abandoned her own habitual wariness, and she could tell that the others did, too, and the resulting sense of freedom made them all a little silly.

Except Tayse, of course. He did not seem relaxed at all. He sat with his back to the wall, his eyes on the door, and he put his attention on each individual waiter and customer who entered the big room. He ate hungrily enough, laughed when the conversation called for it, and even added a comment or two—but only, Senneth thought, so no one would remark on his quietness. She wondered if he would relax even once he was back in the Riders' barracks behind the palace in Ghosenhall.

She probably would never know.

"So!" Justin said, pushing his plate aside and glancing around the table. "What shall we do tonight? Anyone up for—entertainment?"

"I am," Cammon said.

"I might be," Kirra said cautiously. "Depending on what you had in mind."

Donnal nodded.

Tayse said nothing, but his eyes lifted to Senneth's face. "My idea of entertainment right now is dreaming," Senneth said. "I'm going back to bed as soon as we finish the meal. But have fun without me. Keep in mind that not everyone in Lochau is your friend."

"Yes, but they can't *all* hate us," Justin said. "Tayse? You in?"

Tayse shook his head. "Not tonight."

Senneth caught Kirra's quick glance but refused to look in that direction. *Tayse will not leave your side,* Kirra had said. Senneth had to believe that if she had agreed to join the others, Tayse would have accompanied them as well. But he had a charge to keep her safe, and he was not about to fail now. His stubborn shadowing of her meant nothing more than that.

"Tell me the truth," Kirra was saying. "Will it inhibit your revels if I come along with you?"

"Oh, you'll be welcome at the brothels, never fear," Justin said, grinning. "Glad to have you."

Senneth gave him a pained look. "I don't think I've ever seen you in such a rollicking mood," she said.

He laughed. "Too many days under too much strain," he said. "Everybody feels a little crazy."

"Careful about just how crazy you get tonight," Tayse warned. "Limit your drinking. And never forget you're in hostile country."

Justin nodded, instantly sobering. "We won't go if you think we shouldn't."

"Go," Tayse replied. "But go carefully."

Justin's glinting grin came again. "Or at least go well-armed."

They all returned to their rooms to dress for the night, Kirra putting on black trousers and a black jacket and covering her braided hair with a soft black cap. As Senneth watched, she subtly shaded her features so that they were neither so patrician nor so feminine.

"You want to look like a boy," Senneth observed.

Kirra laughed. "Never been inside a brothel."

"You wouldn't really—"

"Well, no, probably not. But I would be tempted, I admit."

Senneth shook her head. "You're a hoyden."

Kirra laughed again. "Always was."

Senneth stretched out on the bed, sinking gratefully into the yielding mattress. "Strange, when you can be so elegant. Even when I was living in my father's house, I couldn't attain the same degree of refinement that comes so naturally to you."

Kirra checked herself in the mirror. Her chin grew harder and firmer, and the shape of her nose more bulbous. "Oh, no, that's simply acting," she said. "That's me trying to imagine how Casserah would behave. I'm really just as undomesticated as your raelynx." Her eyes met Senneth's in the glass. "You can't do it because it's impossible for you to be anything but totally honest. You could never have been a shiftling. You can't pretend to be something you're not. It's too hard for you to lie."

"Some people would dispute that," Senneth said with a sigh.

Kirra grinned and turned from the mirror. "And some people absolutely cannot tear themselves away from you, even for a night of pleasure," she said. "Now, what are you going to do about that?"

Senneth scowled at her. "What do you mean?"

Kirra gestured. "Our room—his room—empty except for the two of you. Surely you can think of ways to mend your differences."

Senneth groaned and slid down on the bed, pulling one of the pillows over her face. "Go. Out. Leave before I set you on fire."

"Other people you could be enflaming tonight," Kirra said, and hastily departed. The cushion Senneth threw at her bounced harmlessly off the door.

In truth, Senneth fell asleep again before she could seriously consider acting upon Kirra's suggestion. Her body had been sapped of strength by too many demands; she was not prepared to add to its litany of stresses another unfruitful argument with Tayse. The idea that this time the argument might end differently did force her eyes open again for a moment, but tonight she didn't have the kind of energy that she would want to bring to any kind of physical encounter. No—and, anyway, Tayse hardly seemed ready to relent and love her. He would not welcome one more bold advance from the deceptive noble mystic. She closed her eyes again, and she slept.

• • •

IN the morning, Kirra and the young men were full of secrets and laughter, leading Senneth to suppose their evening of merriment had gone extremely well. "What exactly did you *do* last night?" Senneth finally asked over breakfast.

"Are you sure you want to know?" Kirra replied.

Senneth looked around at the grinning faces, then glanced at Tayse. Smiling faintly, he shook his head. "I guess not," she said.

"But you can come with us tonight, if you like," Cammon said.

"Sure. We'll find something else to do," Justin added.

They all laughed again, shared guilty looks, then broke into fresh giggles. "You're very annoying," Senneth said.

"They're very young," Tayse said.

Senneth sighed. "I was never that young."

"Come on," Kirra said. "I'll take you shopping."

"No. I want to be here in case Halchon arrives."

"He probably won't get here for another day," Donnal said.

"Still," Senneth said. "Just in case. That means that some of you have to be with me at all times." She let her gaze flick quickly around the table. "Kirra—Tayse—Justin. Don't go far."

Tayse nodded. "We'll be here. No matter when he arrives."

CHAPTER
32

IN fact, Halchon Gisseltess and his entourage pulled into the courtyard of the Dalian Inn shortly after noon. All six of them were sitting in the men's chamber, playing a game of cards for money, and all of them were losing pretty handily to Donnal.

"I think he's cheating," Justin said at last. "I think he's changing the cards as he holds them in his hands."

"That's what *I'm* doing, but it doesn't seem to be doing me any good," Kirra said.

They were all still laughing when Cammon lifted his head and seemed to be listening. Senneth watched him, eyebrows raised. There were a lot of people crammed into the narrow streets of Lochau; it would be impressive if Cammon could pick out a handful of individuals over the general chaos.

"Group of riders just crossed into the city," Cammon said. "Soldiers, it feels like. Maybe seven or eight of them."

Kirra and Senneth exchanged glances. "Probably Halchon," Senneth said. "Let's go check our hair."

They slipped back into their own room to see if they needed to make any improvements. Kirra was wearing her usual red, trimmed today with heavy ivory lace. Senneth had opted for black and gold, the king's colors, in a very narrow, formal dress of drastically simple cut. Her hair was too short and too wayward to respond well to styling, but Kirra had manufactured a black band

and used it to hold stray locks back from Senneth's face. The look was severe but striking.

"I wonder if he'll recognize me," Senneth said, gazing at herself in the mirror.

"How well did he know you before? Weren't you only seventeen when you disappeared? What did you look like then?"

Senneth continued to eye her reflection and didn't answer any of the questions.

A soft knock fell on the door. "Serra Kirra? You and your—your companion have a visitor." It was the clerk's voice, and he sounded unnerved. "Marlord Halchon has asked—has asked for you. Both of you."

Kirra grinned at Senneth. "Could it be? Our visitor specified you by name, and our landlord is startled to find how illustrious his guest is."

"Halchon never did have any discretion," Senneth said and opened the door.

Indeed, the clerk was standing there, looking most uneasy as he waited for the women to appear. That might have been, Senneth thought, because the men of her traveling party were also waiting in the hall, two of them heavily armed and looking like threat personified. But it might have been because Halchon had asked for Senneth Brassenthwaite.

"Thank you," she said calmly to the clerk. "Tell him we'll be right down."

"He's in the private parlor," the clerk said, speaking to Kirra but giving Senneth quick, disbelieving looks.

"Thank you," Kirra said. "How many men does he have with him?"

"Four in the parlor, two outside the door. I didn't check to see if there were more in the courtyard. I could—"

"Never mind," Senneth said. "Tell him we'll be there momentarily."

She waited till he was out of sight, then she issued quick orders. "Donnal. Take bird shape and await us on the roof. If there's any problem here, go directly to the Danalustrous ship in the harbor and get word to Kirra's father. Cammon. I want you to wait in the hall right outside the parlor. If any trouble threatens, interrupt us immediately. Justin, Tayse. You come in the room with us."

"Will he allow that?" Tayse asked.

Senneth smiled grimly. "Oh yes. His own men are there. He will expect to see us defended as well."

"What do you want me to do?" Kirra asked.

"Just stand there and look noble. Unfortunately, I think this is my interview. He's come to hear what I have to offer."

She caught Kirra's sharp look and Tayse's puzzled one. She smiled. "Well, let's see what Halchon Gisseltess has to say."

TWO soldiers were guarding the parlor, both wearing the crest of Gisseltess: a falcon clutching a red flower in its talons. Four more soldiers with the same insignia stood just inside the room. Senneth and her companions stepped through the door, Senneth trying to make her own carriage as regal as Kirra's—which, perhaps, meant she was really imitating the supercilious Casserah Danalustrous. It was comforting to feel Tayse so close behind her, even though she did not turn to look at him. She could see the soldiers inside the room cast calculating looks his way and knew that his appearance, as always, was formidable. Just now, she needed a formidable presence at her back.

Halchon Gisseltess stood gazing out the window, his back to them, and did not turn around immediately. Senneth took the opportunity to study him. He was dressed in riding gear: leather pants tucked into black boots, a short wool coat on his back. His hair was slightly ruffled from wind, but still thick and heavy as it fell to his collar. Streaks of silver lightened its blackness, but he had not grayed as much as his sister had. Then again, he was ten years younger than Coralinda. Just over forty. A powerfully built, powerfully stubborn, and powerfully dangerous man.

"Halchon," Senneth said, when she was tired of the tense silence in the room. "I'm so glad you could find the time to see me."

Now he turned, but she was braced for the hard slap of his personality as all his attention came quickly to bear on her. His eyes were midnight black, his square face not nearly so handsome but just as fierce as she remembered it. This was what her raelynx might look like if it took human shape and aged for a couple of decades.

"Senneth," he said, and his voice was beautiful and hard, like an exotic wood or an edged blade. "It has been too long."

Not long enough, she thought. "You've been busy, these past years," she said. "I hear tales of Gisseltess prowess and Gisseltess products across the whole of Gillengaria."

"I oversee a very rich property," he said. "And I have considered it my duty to make it flourish. I think even Brassenthwaite and Danalustrous would acknowledge that Gisseltess is among the greatest of the Houses."

"As it always has been," Senneth said. "Yet these days there are—rumors—that perhaps Gisseltess is overreaching itself. Striving for roles and honors that, strictly speaking, the House does not deserve."

He smiled, a charming, feral smile such as a raelynx might produce. "That's the Senneth I remember," he said, and his tone was admiring. "Straight to the point, and no pleasantries beforehand. I knew you could not be in this room five minutes without going on the attack."

"I have not attacked you," she said, keeping her voice very calm. "But I *am* here to ask you questions. We have been on the road several weeks, my friends and I. And we were not traveling long before we came across Gisseltess soldiers interfering in matters that seemed more rightly to belong to Helven and Fortunalt troops. It led me to wonder how far your influence extends these days—and how far you want it to spread."

"I want to rule the country—surely that cannot come as a surprise to you?" he replied instantly. "I have always been ambitious. I have always wanted to acquire more land, more money—more influence, as you say. If the conditions were right, I would happily take over the management of all the southern Houses—and the middle Houses, and the northern Houses, and Ghosenhall itself. Is that what you wanted to hear me say?"

"Only if it's true," she answered.

He laughed. "And do you think it's true?"

"From what I have seen, it is certainly possible," she said. "I suppose what I really want to know is why. And why now."

He was holding a glass of some kind of amber liquid; he took a meditative sip and set it down. "The why and the why now are the same, I suppose," he said. "We have an aging king on the throne. Beside him sits a mysterious queen, and somewhere in the shadowy recesses of his palace flits a strange young princess whom very few have ever seen. The succession is in danger, Senneth, and I am not the only one to say so. A royal line in turmoil puts a country in chaos. A country in chaos puts a crown up for grabs." He shrugged. "I am just the man to grab it. So I ready myself for the opportunity."

"There is no proof yet that the king is ill or his daughter unfit," Senneth said. "You move too soon."

"Better too soon than too late."

"And if the king yet produces an heir capable of ruling? Princess Amalie or a half sibling born to Queen Valri? Don't you worry about being at the center of a bid for treason?"

"Well, the queen has produced no heir as of yet," he said, sounding amused, "and, the situation being what it is, she may never have the opportunity."

"So that is enough for you. That is reason enough to arm for war," Senneth said. It could hardly be a surprise after the revelations of the past few weeks, but still she found herself unable to credit a philosophy so simple and so brutal. "You doubt the strength of your king, but without proof, and without consultation, you plan to steal the throne from him—and claim it is to ensure the stability of the realm."

He shrugged. "Oh, I have already admitted I am ambitious. My motives are not entirely altruistic. But I tell you plainly that if this king dies without an acceptable heir, and no plans have been made to install a ruler in his place, we are headed for civil war before his bones are even cold in his grave. I have moved up the timetable by a few years, perhaps, but war has been plotted in the background ever since Amalie was born."

"Your sister speaks of a holy war and seems to care not at all about kings and princesses and shaky successions," said Senneth. "Yet she is poised to cause almost as much damage as you are."

Halchon gave her a wide smile. "My sister's passion has been convenient," he admitted. "We pursue the same ends for different reasons. I could not have asked for a better ally. But it is not she who will rally forces and command troops. If there is a war, it will be fought at my direction."

"'If there is a war,'" Senneth repeated. "What would it take to make you draw back from your plotting?"

"Concessions I doubt the king would be willing to make," Halchon said. "But you could pass along my concerns to him and see what he has to say. If he is eager to avoid bloodshed—if he is indeed tired and worried about the future of his country—he may be willing to make a treaty with me. I am ready to be reasonable."

"Then tell me your conditions," Senneth said. "I return to Ghosenhall as soon as I leave Lochau."

"Name me heir," Halchon said. "It is as simple as that."

Senneth felt her eyebrows lift. "And don't you wonder—just a little—how the marlords of the other Houses would feel about Gisseltess being suddenly raised to such a position of prominence?"

Halchon shrugged. "I am willing to make an alliance. I am willing to take a bride from some northern House and spawn children of mixed blood who will take the throne after me."

"You already have a wife," Senneth said.

"Wives are easily disposed of," he said.

Senneth felt her blood, always so warm, turn frosty in her veins. "You are willing to be quite ruthless to attain your ends," she said in a neutral voice. "Don't you worry that by invalidating your current marriage—by whatever means—you will anger your wife's family and dismantle an existing alliance?"

"I almost married a Nocklyn girl," he said conversationally. "But that very circumstance held me back. So I married from within the ranks of Gisseltess nobility. I was thinking very far ahead, you see. No one in Gisseltess will turn against me."

Her skin turned chillier and chillier. She thought she knew what was coming very soon, but she could not keep herself from asking more questions. "Your sons?" she asked against a dry throat. "They won't be furious if their mother is cast aside?"

"They will be given high rank in the new court when they are old enough. And the powerful Houses will seek them as husbands for their daughters, as a way to ensure some connection to the court and some hold over me. I do not think they will suffer much."

"I do not think the other eleven Houses will be satisfied by such a measure," Senneth said. "I do not think they will so happily give over control of Ghosenhall to you."

"They will if I choose the right bride," he said. "They will have no choice, for the alliance will be too strong."

Colder and colder—ice in her bones. "And what alliance would you pursue?" she made herself ask.

Halchon's night-black eyes glanced at Kirra and returned to Senneth. "Danalustrous would do," he said, "but that would be my second choice. Malcolm Danalustrous is a tricky ally in the best of times. I cannot be so certain what course of action he might take, even to avert a war."

Senneth couldn't bring herself to look at Kirra, who merci-
fully stayed mute. "And if not Danalustrous?" she said.

He fixed her with that midnight gaze, impossible to look away
from. She had hated a fair number of people in her life, but none of
them as much as she hated Halchon Gisseltess. "Brassenthwaite,"
he said. "You."

There was absolute silence in the room.

Halchon continued. "It was the marriage I wanted nearly
twenty years ago, and it's the one I want now. Your brother is a
more reasonable man than Malcolm Danalustrous. I think he
would grasp the advantages of the match right away, just as your
father did. And seeing Brassenthwaite fierce in support of the
throne, I think the other Houses would fall quickly in line to accept me. To accept you and me," he amended.

She could not look at Kirra, at Tayse, but she could feel their
astonished attention focused on her as they solved some of the final mysteries of her life. Her throat was so tight she was not sure
she could speak, but she was making a supreme effort to appear
normal, to appear detached. "It has been a long time," she said,
"since I acted at the direction of my brothers."

"Much has changed since then," he said.

She found a little strength and infused it into her voice. "And,
if you recall, I was not eager to marry you the last time the alliance was proposed."

"It's different this time," he said.

"How so? I am even more independent now than I was at seventeen."

"It's different now because if you don't marry me, the whole
country will be plunged into war," he said. "I think you have a soft
enough heart to want to see such a tragedy averted. Put aside your
personal feelings about me, and make a marriage that will save
the kingdom."

"I would rather see you dead," she said calmly.

For a brief, shocked moment, everyone in the room absorbed
her words. Halchon was the first to react—with a short, dry laugh.
"I wonder what it is about me," he said, "that you find so unpalat-
able. You can't be afraid of me, because Senneth Brassenthwaite
fears nothing on this earth."

"You terrify me," she said. "You always have. It is a struggle
for me to stand even this close to you."

He seemed more amused than offended by this reply. "And

perhaps that is what draws me to you so irresistibly," he said softly. "Your so very obvious desire to escape. I find myself wondering—I have always found myself wondering—what it would be like to hold you so tightly that you could not break away. Would you scream? Would you shatter? Would you succumb? If you were my bride, you know, I would be able to discover the answer. I might be able to discover it anyway."

And he took three quick steps closer and placed his hands around her throat.

For Senneth, the world became a place of stark shadows streaked with patches of light. The pressure on her throat was so great that she could scarcely breathe, but she could not even gather the strength to wrench away from him; she could not clench her hands and summon fire. It was as if his very touch was anathema—as if he was made of moonstone—as if he possessed a magic that was of a composition completely antithetical to her own. She could not struggle, and she could not strike. She could only stare at him, wreathed in night and errant brilliance, and listen to the roaring darkness.

A flash of silver cut across her vision, and a bulky shape loomed suddenly behind Halchon's body. "Release her," said a low, taut voice, "or you die."

A second longer the stranglehold lasted, then the fingers relaxed from around her throat. Senneth stumbled aside, coughing, shaking her head to clear her vision. Soft fingers were laid across her arm, and she felt Kirra's healing strength pour through her muscles. She stood a moment, bent half over, collecting her thoughts and her energy.

When she straightened, she saw a grim tableau: Tayse with his bared knife against Halchon's throat, the Gisseltess soldiers arrayed around Tayse, their own weapons drawn. The minute Tayse released Halchon, the four of them would cut him down. No alarm had been raised, so she did not think the two soldiers outside the parlor had run inside the room. At any rate, she knew without turning around that Justin had his sword out and was guarding the door.

"Back away from him," she said in a hard voice.

The Gisseltess soldiers looked at her as if she was mad.

"Drop your swords and back away from him," she repeated, raising her hands as if in invocation. When they did not respond, she splayed her fingers, feeling the fire running down her wrists and palms. One of the soldiers yelped; the other three loosed curses and exclamations. All four of them let their swords clatter to the floor.

"Against the walls," she said, and the soldiers tripped over themselves to do as she commanded. "Don't move," she said, and sent her hand in a small wave through the air. The temperature in the room flashed upward by ten degrees. It would take very little to set the furnishings on fire.

"Kirra. Get Cammon. Collect our things. Justin. Bring in the two soldiers from outside—and keep them here. Tayse—you'll have to watch him until we're ready to go."

"We can take him with us," Tayse said.

At that, unexpectedly, she smiled. "Oh no. I think he'd be much more trouble than he's worth."

"We could kill him now," Kirra said. Those were the first words she had spoken since they walked into the room. "Save ourselves a war."

Senneth allowed herself a quick look at Halchon. He stood unmoving within Tayse's close hold, his face unreadable, watching her. He appeared neither angry nor afraid, but his black eyes snapped with calculation.

"The only ways to avoid this war are so distasteful that I cannot bring myself to do them," Senneth said softly. "But I will not be the one to shed blood without provocation. I am not Halchon Gisseltess. I will not kill willfully just to get what I want." She glanced at Kirra. "Now, fetch Cammon. We have to leave."

Kirra's light footsteps pattered out the door, and then came the heavy tramp of soldiers' feet as the two outside guards came in. More commotion, more exclamations of outrage—it was almost with impatience that Senneth washed them with heat and demanded that they stand by their fellows.

"You could just ask my assurance that I will keep them from harming you, and end this ridiculous situation now," Halchon suggested.

Senneth didn't even look at him. "Tayse. Can you disable him without truly hurting him?"

"Yes."

"Then that's what you'll want to do if he gives you any trouble. Justin—can you get all their swords? We'll take them with us, at least part of the way."

"They'll have more than swords on them," Justin said.

"Then take whatever you can find."

A few of the Gisseltess guards muttered at this robbery until the metal hidden in their boots and up their sleeves began to heat like branding irons. Then there were oaths and the clink of daggers being tossed to the floor. Senneth listened to the sounds of Justin scooping up blades of all descriptions. He had ripped a curtain from one of the windows and began to wrap all the weapons into one rather untidy bundle. But mostly she kept her attention on Halchon.

Who watched her with an unwavering concentration. "Truly," he said. "I give you run of the city. Walk out of here now and expect no retribution from me."

"Your sister made me the same promise," Senneth said, "then sent riders after us within the day. Somehow the word of Gisseltess fails to carry much weight with me."

Halchon smiled, and Senneth felt the chill all the way across the room. "My sister lacks subtlety," he said. "But I have no reason to wish you dead. You are my chosen bride, after all. I can see beyond petty differences of personality to the greater good of the kingdom—and the succession."

Senneth couldn't keep her eyes from lifting to Tayse's face. His expression was so cold and so furious that she was surprised he could keep himself from slicing his knife across Halchon's throat. Almost, almost, she wished he would do it. "Lay aside that dream, if you abandon no other," she said, keeping her voice very soft. "You will never marry me, Halchon. You will never take me at all."

"We shall see," he said.

There was a knock at the door and then quick footsteps entering. "Ready to go," Kirra said crisply. "I've sent Donnal ahead to tell Captain Abernot we want to pull out now."

Senneth nodded. She was still watching Halchon, who was still watching her. "I'm going to put a spell across this door," she said. "You won't be able to leave, and no one else will be able to enter, for six hours. You'll be unharmed as long as you don't touch the windows or the door. I'll carry your offer to the king."

He laughed. "Most generous of you, Senneth. But then, you were always warmhearted."

"It was what you wanted from me," she said. "Fire to melt your ice."

She lifted her hands, clenched and flexed her fingers, and warded the window frames with fire. The Gisseltess soldiers moved uneasily away, muttering and rubbing their exposed hands. Then she nodded to Tayse, who released Halchon—roughly enough to fling him against the line of his own soldiers. The five of them hurried through the door, pulling it shut behind them, and Senneth again called up phantom flames to make the aperture impassable.

"Will it really hold six hours?" Kirra asked.

"I don't know," Senneth said. "My magic is not so strong around Halchon, it seems. But I think it will hold long enough for us to get free of Lochau."

"Horses are saddled outside," Cammon said. "Let's go."

CAPTAIN Abernot was not delighted with the news that he had to cast off immediately, against a not entirely propitious wind, with the possibility that Gisseltess warships might be launched against him before the fall of night. But he made sure the horses were quickly stowed below and that all of his passengers had been assigned quarters.

"The first few hours may be choppy," he warned. "If you find yourselves inclined to be sick, please avail yourselves of your chamber pots."

He was a short, stocky, heavily whiskered man with bright blue eyes and skin worn red with wind, and his mix of deference and authority instantly appealed to Senneth. "Thank you for taking us on board," she said gravely. "We will try not to be any trouble."

"It's trouble marlord Malcolm would want me to be put to for his daughter," the captain replied. "And he doesn't mind befriending Brassenthwaite, either."

Senneth tried not to sigh. "Thank you again," was all she could think to say, and she retired to the room she and Kirra had been given.

Within minutes, they were under way, though the pace at first seemed agonizingly slow. From her porthole window, Senneth watched the wharf of Lochau fall away, and the limited view she had showed no Gisseltess ships in pursuit. The ride picked up speed as they moved into open water, but the captain had been right: The waves were rough, and the motion of the ship over the water left Senneth feeling violently unwell.

Too much stress over too many days, she thought, and threw up in the chamber pot. More than once. She was never so glad to see night come and feel the water grow calm under the hull of the ship. She stretched herself out on the narrow bed, wondered briefly what had become of Kirra, and let herself be rocked to sleep.

CHAPTER
33

IT took a week to sail from Lochau to Dormas. The first day of that week was a great improvement over that first night. Senneth woke up in the morning feeling more or less normal, though she ate breakfast cautiously. Tayse and Justin made only brief appearances that day; they both looked pale and disdained all offers of food. Over a hearty lunch in the ship's tiny galley, Cammon confided to Senneth that he'd never been seasick for one minute during his long voyages with his parents.

"I'm usually sick the first day out of port," Senneth admitted. "At least, I was when I sailed in the past. But I was hoping maybe I'd gotten over that unpleasantness."

"Is Kirra downstairs vomiting?" he asked.

"No. I don't know where she is. Donnal either."

Cammon grinned. "Well, you know they're all right then, since they're no doubt together."

Senneth nodded. "That's what I'm hoping."

She made a slow circuit of the open deck, clinging to the rail and making sure she stayed out of the way of any sailors engaged in their own tasks. The ship moved north at a steady pace that was impossible for her to gauge, but the wind blowing incessantly against her face led her to believe that it was fairly brisk. She stood for a long time at the prow, watching the restless water split against the hull and foam up the sides of the wood. She could not tell if it was lingering winter or just the wind of passage that made the air so cold against her face. To her right, Gillengaria was a low, constant presence of shadowy blue and huddled brown. It comforted her that it was never completely out of sight, remaining always close enough for her to feel its magic tingle along her bones.

Kirra and Donnal reappeared in early evening. Senneth, who had napped away the late afternoon, had returned to the top deck to breathe fresh air again. One moment, there were two gulls perched precariously on the upper rail; the next, Donnal and Kirra stood on the deck, clutching the railing and swaying rather unsteadily to the motion of the ship. Both of them looked drenched with spray and soaked with mischief.

"Oh," Senneth said. "That's where you've been."

Kirra laughed and shook back her tangled hair. "Rough water always makes me ill," she said. "In human form. We slept on land last night, and followed the ship all morning. But the sea seems calmer now."

"The King's Riders have proved to be particularly vulnerable to seasickness," Senneth said. "But Cammon is completely unaffected. Of course. Nothing seems to bother Cammon. I felt horrible yesterday, but I seem to be doing well enough today."

"We're making good time," Donnal said. "Another five or six days, and we'll be in Dormas."

"Then on to Ghosenhall," Senneth said. "And what a story we'll have to tell there."

THAT night, Kirra slept on board, taking the narrow bunk across from Senneth's. The cabin was so small that from their bunks they could have reached out and clasped hands had they wanted to. Starlight filtered in through the porthole window, making a round, watery shape on the floor.

Kirra waited till they had both managed to get as comfortable as possible before speaking into the darkness of the room. "You never told me," she said. "That it was Halchon who wanted to marry you—Halchon you ran away from."

"It's an old story," Senneth murmured. "From another life. He wanted to marry Senneth Brassenthwaite, and I have renounced her." She thought a moment and sighed. "Or tried to renounce her.

She seems to be manifesting herself again, like some kind of unwelcome and persistent ghost."

There was a rustle as Kirra turned impatiently in her bed. "But Senneth—*Halchon Gisseltess!* He seems obsessed by you—if he's been pining after you all these years—"

"Pining after the Brassenthwaite connection."

"That doesn't seem to be all of it," Kirra said. "He was—he seemed to be—it's you he wants. It's a very personal thing."

Senneth was silent a moment. "I couldn't do it," she said very softly. "I had met him maybe a dozen times before I was sixteen. Our fathers had decided when we were very young that Halchon and I should marry. It was something I had known almost as long as I had known my name. But I—he frightened me. And you didn't know me when I was sixteen, but very little frightened me then."

A smile in Kirra's voice. "Nothing frightens you now."

"Oh, now I am old enough to realize how many terrors there are in the world and how few of them I can really keep at bay. But when I was sixteen—I was afraid of no one, of nothing. Except Halchon Gisseltess. And I decided I would not marry him. And I decided I would take another lover as a way to repulse him. And I was glad when I was shamed with an illegitimate pregnancy— glad because surely no proud nobleman would consent to marry a woman who had been so obviously unchaste. But Halchon— Halchon came to my father's House and reworked the dower settlements and made arrangements for the baby to be cared for by one of the lesser gentlewomen of Gisseltess. 'This baby will not be mine, but I will not want to lose track of it,' he told my father. 'I will see it raised and determine whether or not it may be useful in the future.'"

"That's a little chilling," Kirra said.

"Yes—everything he says and does leaves me trembling with cold. So I knew that, once my baby was born, I would have to leave my father's house. I thought to go seek shelter with some of my grandmother's family in Kianlever. She and I had talked about it, because she hated Halchon as much as I did. I would have the baby, I would leave my father's care, and I would lead the quiet, confined life a woman leads among the Thirteen Houses. Or so I planned . . ." Her voice trailed off.

Kirra knew the rest of that story; no need to go into it now. "What I don't understand," Kirra said, "was what happened yesterday. When Halchon grabbed you. Why didn't you turn him into a pillar of fire?"

Senneth drew her blanket closer to her chin. She, who was never cold, shivered even at the thought of Halchon's touch. "I can't. There is something about him—that smothers my magic. Do you know how there are some rooms you can walk into—or caves—or cathedrals—where the sound seems deadened? There are no echoes, and your voice scarcely seems to carry three inches from your lips? Halchon is like that, for me, at least. A dead place. A place where my magic won't light. I could tell that, even when I was sixteen."

"You can't marry him," Kirra said. "Even to avert war."

"I think war would come anyway," Senneth said soberly. "Or how could I forgive myself for telling him no?"

THE rest of the week on board ship passed in a similar fashion, though Justin and Tayse were up and walking around—somewhat unsteadily—the third day they were at sea. For Senneth and her party, as soon as health was restored, tedium quickly set in. They were used to hard riding and constant vigilance, and they chafed a bit at the enforced inaction. Tayse encouraged them all to take the rare chance to catch up on missed sleep, but the bunks were so uncomfortable that it was difficult to follow that excellent advice. Mostly the six of them gathered in one room or another, crowding together on the narrow bunks and the cramped floor, and played cards or talked idly or complained about the boredom.

If Senneth and her friends climbed up to the top deck for a little change of scenery, Captain Abernot and his sailors were polite but not enthusiastic. Senneth knew how unwelcome an unexpected guest could be when there was work to be done, so she made sure to keep out of the way when she encountered any of the crew. Cammon, though, volunteered early on to help out, and, after watching him tie a knot and hoist a sail, Captain Abernot allowed him to work with the other sailors when he wished. Justin followed Cammon's lead and offered his services when the wind was strong or it looked like other hands might be needed. Senneth wasn't sure if the captain appreciated or tolerated these volunteers, but as far as she could tell, they did no harm, and so she allowed them to continue on in their efforts.

Kirra and Donnal were as often gone from the ship as present, having one way to entertain themselves that none of the rest of them possessed. Senneth saw them take dozens of shapes before the journey was done, from gull to hawk to fish to eel. "Better be careful some hungry sailor doesn't snare you on a line and fry you up for dinner," she admonished Kirra one night after that young lady had come back to their cabin sleek and wet from a swim in the ocean.

Kirra grinned and ran her fingers through her matted hair. "Oh, I'd turn human as soon as the hook went through my lip and he started hauling me back toward the rail," she said. "He'd think he caught a mermaid or some other creature of the sea and be so startled he'd drop his line in the ocean."

"If he didn't shoot you with a crossbow instead and let you bleed to death in the salt water," Senneth said.

Kirra laughed. "I think Captain Abernot has put a moratorium on shooting gulls and catching fish, during this stage of his journey, anyway," she said. "He worries just as much as you do."

Of Tayse, during this long, dreary week, Senneth saw almost nothing. Unless the six of them were together, eating or gaming or talking. He kept to his cabin most of the time, clearly a man who was not happy to be water bound. It was obvious he considered them all safe for the first time since they'd set out on this journey, so his own ferocious vigilance was eased. He did not feel the need to set a guard on Senneth's door, or watch her every movement, or be aware of, night and day, exactly where she was.

Senneth missed the unfailing attention, bitter as it had sometimes been. She knew she would miss it even more once they arrived at Ghosenhall and Tayse left her life entirely.

The few times she saw him outside of his cabin and strolling the deck alone, he mostly kept to the stern of the ship, watching the water unroll behind them. She knew without asking that he was guarding their back trail, making sure no fast-moving Gisseltess ships raced out of the southern waters to menace them on their journey. He could not entirely ignore his own protective instincts.

They had been on board ship six days before Senneth took the chance to speak to Tayse alone. It was early evening, and her traveling companions would soon gather in the galley to eat their meal half an hour before the sailors began arriving in their own dinner shifts. The sun was very low over the western horizon, about to disappear into the farthest edge of the wrinkled sea. The breeze was fitful, but cold as always. Tayse stood braced against the back railing, his coat gathered around him, his gloved hands loose on the top bar.

Senneth came to stand beside him, taking a casual stance, pretending that it didn't matter to her if he greeted her with a smile or a scowl. He did neither; he glanced down at her with little expression on his face at all, and then moved over somewhat to make room for her.

They stood there a moment in what Senneth hoped was companionable silence before she spoke. "Any ships in pursuit?" she asked lightly.

He shook his head. "Not that I've seen, or Donnal or Kirra. I've asked them to look when they go out on their adventures."

"Ah. Then they aren't just playing like children when they turn themselves into sea creatures and water birds."

His face relaxed in a faint smile. "Well, I imagine it's more playing than reconnaissance, but I trust them to at least patrol the seas for enemy ships."

"Captain Abernot says we should make land tomorrow. I have to say, I'm looking forward to it."

"Yes," he said, the word so heartfelt that she laughed.

"And are you looking forward to returning to Ghosenhall as well?" she asked. "This has been a long journey for you, I know."

He looked down at her, his dark eyes hard to read. The smile was gone. "I will be happy to be back in a place I know with people that I understand," he said at last, the words very slow. "But this has been a journey it will be hard to walk away from. I think the roads and stops along the way will stay with me longer than they usually do."

"You have not traveled enough," she said. "Or you'd know that every journey makes its own map across your heart."

"You have traveled too much," he said. "Or you wouldn't think that life holds only such journeys."

"It is true," she said, "that I have chosen to make the road my home. But no other home seemed feasible."

"You could join the Riders, as Justin has suggested," he said. "It wouldn't take much training to make you good enough. And the king would welcome you into their ranks."

"But would the Riders?" she asked, amused. "I am an element that does not mix so well with certain others."

"It might take some time," he admitted. "But you would win them over. Most of them."

"Oh, Tayse," she said, leaning against the railing and watching the sea ruffle and calm behind them. "You don't want me as a Rider, troubling you with my presence. You're worried about my safety. You think that once you're not beside me, I'll tumble into danger as I round every curve in the road. I'll promise you to be careful, and then you can watch me go with a light heart."

"Hardly that," he said, his own face turned toward the south.

"I have to confess," she said in a low voice, "that I was glad you were in the room with me when I confronted Halchon Gisseltess."

He was silent a moment. "I would have killed him."

"I know." She, too, held the silence briefly, and then she sighed. "But it's better that you did not."

"You're afraid of him."

"Yes."

"What can he do to you? He doesn't have the power to compel you to marry him, does he?"

She laughed. "I don't think so, but if I hear that his wife has mysteriously disappeared, I think it will be time for me to go to ground."

He looked down at her again, his eyes very dark and serious. "It is time for you to talk to your brothers, I think," he said.

She had not expected such a comment from him, and she felt a strong wave of indignation. "And I think you don't know anything about it."

"When you and Kirra were dividing Houses for the war, all your calculations centered on Brassenthwaite's fealty to the throne. If your brothers think *you* will be on the throne, it might change their sense of loyalty."

"My brothers have no interest in me anymore."

"I doubt that," he said dryly. "Certainly once they find Halchon Gisseltess still wants the alliance, they will find you very interesting indeed."

"I have renounced my Brassenthwaite heritage and my Brassenthwaite relations."

"But they have not renounced you," he said. "If Senneth Brassenthwaite is going to be at the heart of this war, she had better know who her allies and enemies are."

She stared up at him, for that was putting it more plainly than she had ever managed to phrase it to herself. She *was* at the heart of this war, one way or another—because she was a mystic, because she was powerful, because she would fight for her king with a wholehearted passion. But Halchon's proposal had put her at the center of conflict in the political arena as well. If she could thwart him, if she could sway Kiernan, she had obligations she had not foreseen—or had chosen to ignore.

"I hate my brother," she said.

"You've changed since you were seventeen," Tayse said. "Perhaps he has, too."

"He will not take my side."

"You don't know whose side he is already on."

She leaned forward, scrunching down over the railing, resting her chin on her hands as they clasped the bar. "And my grandmother's dead," she said. "And my mother betrayed me. There is nothing for me in Brassenthwaite anymore."

"There is a kingdom at stake," he said. "You have to go."

Senneth did not reply. She kept her eyes before her on the curling lines of the wake, watching the water fold over on itself and then smooth into an eternal blue. He was right, of course. She had to go to Brassenthwaite. Though it was the very last journey she wanted to make.

THEY arrived at Dormas in the middle of the following afternoon. It took nearly two hours to get their belongings packed, the horses off-loaded, and the raelynx set in a rented gig—just till they got out of the city, Senneth promised Cammon. The rest of them all stood on the wharf for a few minutes while Kirra finished giving Captain Abernot messages for her father.

Cammon seemed uncharacteristically nervous. "What if we see Kardon?" he asked, pushing his shaggy hair from his eyes. "He'll recognize me. What if he wants me back?"

Tayse looked down at him with a lurking smile. "What makes you think we would give you back?"

"I wouldn't want you to have to fight for me," Cammon said shyly.

Justin laughed. "We fight for everybody, in this group," he said. "Haven't you noticed that by now?"

"Anyway, you're safe enough. We won't be in Dormas long enough for anyone to recognize us," Senneth said.

But of course her words were to be disproved less than a minute later. While she and her friends waited patiently on the pier, a knot of horsemen clattered by—then came to a sudden, tangled halt as voices cried out a surprised welcome.

"Tayse! Justin! Is that really you?"

"Hey, it's Justin! And Tayse! Why are you in Dormas?"

Seconds later, they were surrounded by a small group of men and women jumping from their saddles and greeting the soldiers with strong handshakes or playful punches on the shoulder. Senneth thought she counted eight of them, but they moved so quickly and talked so rapidly that it was hard to sort them out. Not hard to know instantly who they were, though: King's Riders, dressed in black and gold, and sporting the arrogant rampant lion on sashes across their chests.

And not hard to see that these were the people that Justin and Tayse were most completely comfortable with. Justin was wrestling with some attractive young man about his age, clubbing him about the head and ducking the good-natured blows aimed at him in return. Tayse was standing between two older men, talking with great animation—actually smiling. Actually laughing.

Cammon glanced over at Senneth. "True friends," he said with a smile. Senneth nodded and dropped her gaze to the planks below her feet. She was wondering what it would be like to have Tayse's affection so casually and willingly given.

"But are you done, then? With your mission? Weren't you supposed to be off touring the southern Houses or some such thing?"

The artless question caught Senneth's attention and made her lift her eyes. Not so good to be gossiping about such a topic in such a public place. Even through his thicket of friends, Tayse managed to give Senneth a reassuring glance. "Still on the mission, escorting friends of the king's," he said in a soft voice. "And it's not to be talked of just now."

"But who are—where—are *these* the king's friends?" said the good-looking one who had been roughhousing with Justin. Young and tactless, but Senneth couldn't blame him. His gaze rested first on her, then, with patent disbelief, on Cammon and Donnal.

"Mind your manners," came the sharp words from one of the older men standing beside Tayse. "You're pretty disreputable-looking yourself, and the king seems to hold *you* in high regard, though I don't know why."

A muffled laugh from the crowd, and the young man shuffled his feet. "Sorry," he muttered.

"These are some of my companions of the road," Tayse said in a calm voice. "But *she's* the one who's led us most of the way."

"Ahhhh—" came from more than one throat, and Senneth knew without looking that Kirra must be making her way down the gangplank. Kirra would have seen the knot of soldiers and guessed as quickly as Senneth who they were, and she had no doubt assumed her most regal air and most golden aura. "Danalustrous, that one."

"And you're still not done riding?" one irrepressible soul asked. "*I'll* come join you if you need another sword."

"Thank you," said Tayse, sounding amused. "So far we have managed to defend ourselves tolerably well without you."

"Where are you headed now?" inquired one of the older men. "Or shouldn't I ask?"

"Ghosenhall," Tayse said.

"So are we!" the Rider exclaimed. "Can we travel together? Or is there a reason you should be a smaller party on the road?"

Senneth felt her heart grow tinier and harder inside her chest. No reason at all their party shouldn't be augmented by Riders. In fact, Tayse was certain to see that as a good thing, an extra ring of protection around the companions he could never make safe enough.

"We'd be happy to have your escort," Tayse said. "In truth, we've drawn more—attention—than I had expected. I'd like to think that, this far north, we would be wholly unmolested, but I wouldn't mind sharing a few watches for the last leg of the journey."

"Excellent," said the other Rider. "How much time do you need? We're ready to leave now."

"So are we," said Tayse. "As soon as we mount."

Kirra had by this time joined the group and bestowed her radiant smile on all the newcomers. Even the women seemed dazzled by her obvious charm. "Tayse, have you found friends?" she asked lightly. "And all this time I thought you didn't have any."

More laughter for that. Tayse was grinning. "Plenty of friends, though they're astonished that I'd spend so much effort guarding *you*," he replied. "They've offered to escort us back to Ghosenhall, and I've accepted, assuming you have no objection."

Like Tayse, Kirra was quick to realize that Senneth did not want the Brassenthwaite name spoken in this crowd, and she had no hesitation in accepting her role. "How could I object? I'm happy to be surrounded by King's Riders. When can we leave?"

"Now," Tayse said, swinging himself to the back of his horse. Three of the new Riders hurried forward to offer Kirra help into the saddle. Kirra dimpled and allowed one of them to lift her up.

Senneth briefly exchanged glances with Cammon, who was grinning, and Donnal, who was seething. "Time to go," she said. She managed to mount her horse without anyone's aid, and then they were on their way.

CHAPTER
34

THEY were in Ghosenhall six days later. Cutting through Storian lands and traveling on the well-maintained highways of the middle regions, they made excellent time, better than Senneth would have expected from such a large group. She had reluctantly concluded that she must keep the raelynx confined to its cage for the whole trip, now that their numbers were so expanded and it would be harder to keep track of it during all the confusion of travel. Cammon begged her to release it but did not seem to think he would be able to change her mind. Their progress was slowed a bit by accommodating the cart that carried the wild creature, but even so, they accomplished their journey very efficiently.

Kirra quickly became the darling of the camp as all the male Riders jostled for a chance to flirt with her. Donnal scowled through most of the journey, dropping back toward the rear guard to avoid watching her smile and laugh with the strangers. "Don't change shapes—don't draw attention to yourself," Senneth warned him, so he stayed in human form, but he glowered so much she thought he might as well have been a bear.

Cammon enjoyed himself thoroughly and proved to be almost as popular with the Riders as Kirra. This was no doubt because of the way Justin treated him, like a younger brother of whom he was inordinately fond. The women among the Riders instantly adopted him and fussed over him like adoring aunts. Senneth could not help but smile to see him so happy, practicing new sword moves in the evening, listening raptly to the tales told around the fires. Yes, she should probably leave him in Ghosenhall, whether or not she sought out a mystic to train him. The Riders would take him in, one way or another; he would be safe among them.

As for herself, for this leg of the journey, Senneth made herself as inconspicuous as possible. She did not go quite so far as to conjure the spells that would make her disappear, but she never spoke unless someone else addressed her, never made overtures to any of the other Riders, never offered to start a fire, and didn't even bother to keep the campsite warm at night. She guessed that their new companions assumed she was Kirra's maid or impoverished companion, when they thought of her at all, and she was content to have it that way. Everyone was civil to her, though completely indifferent; she thought, if she wanted, she could slip away entirely.

Except that, on the day she was feeling most glum about her near-invisibility, Cammon sought her out to ride beside her for two solid hours. Except that, over every meal as she was being most outrageous, Kirra would send a look and a smile her way. Except that, when a Rider accidentally bumped Senneth on horseback, Justin was instantly beside her, calling the other young man by all sorts of furious names and making sure Senneth was entirely unhurt.

Except that, every night as he made his circuit around the campfire, Tayse looked first for her. And every morning as they all mounted up again, Tayse watched to make sure she was steady in the saddle before he took to the road. And half a dozen times during the day, every day, Senneth would look up to find Tayse turned on his horse, glancing back at her. She had the eerie sensation that if, at any point during the night or day, she cried out in sudden terror, Tayse and Justin and Cammon and Kirra would be at her side almost before her voice had sounded.

Donnal, of course, would be at Kirra's side, but Senneth had no quarrel with that.

The knowledge that, even lost within this larger party, her small group of friends were still tightly bound to her made her squelch the urge to vanish. But she could not say she truly enjoyed any part of that final trip.

• • •

THEY reached Ghosenhall on a sunny day that showed off all the charms of the royal city. It lay on a wide, flat plain and stretched out over the gentle land like a pretty mistress too lazy to rise from bed. Most of its buildings were low and rambling, built of warm granite or a honey-colored marble; in the public districts, the streets were wide and well-maintained. Parks and fountains and flower gardens were spread liberally throughout the streets, and though none of them were particularly beautiful at this time of year, they did contribute to the city's open, uncrowded air. There were people everywhere, hurrying down the ample boulevards, calling out to each other, shouting at careless drivers, announcing their wares, waving to the Riders. Yet everything was so ordered and civilized that it was a joy to travel through the streets.

The royal palace was situated at the center of town, on a slight rise of ground that allowed it to be seen from almost every corner of the city. It, too, was built of a rusty granite, heavily ornamented by spires and arches and turrets, and it consisted of so many wings and additions that there seemed to be no formal plan to its construction at all. It was situated at the center of a huge compound that was completely encircled by a high wall; the gates were guarded by royal soldiers. Inside the wall were so many fenced gardens and ornamental ponds and graceful follies that it was said even the head groundskeeper could not keep track of them all.

Senneth could not help it. She loved Ghosenhall, and she particularly loved the palace. If she would ever have any temptation to marry Halchon Gisseltess and pursue the throne, it would be for the pleasure of living here every day of her life.

As expected, their party was greeted cordially at the gate and instantly waved on through. "Here's where we part," Tayse said to the other Riders once they passed into the courtyard. "For I think Justin and I must be present when Kirra makes her report to the king."

Cammon pressed forward. "What about the raelynx? Should I stay out here with it?"

Tayse glanced first at Senneth, who shook her head. "No. All six of us must go in together," he said.

"But I'm worried. He's been caged so long. Is there someplace that we can set it free?"

Tayse's friend, one of the older Riders, looked skeptical. "We'll take it back to the stables with us, but I don't know about setting it free just yet."

"Maybe tonight, then," Cammon said. "After we're done with this audience." He sounded impatient, and everyone listening had to smother a grin. "You can tell me someplace safe that I can let him out for a while. I'll stay and guard him then."

"We'll figure something out," Tayse said. "But first we must go in to meet with our king."

The other Riders drifted away, waving and calling out farewells. The six of them continued on up the long path of crushed white stone that led to the door of the palace.

"Couldn't we get cleaned up first?" Kirra asked. "I don't feel quite fit for royalty just yet."

"We'll see what Milo says," Tayse replied.

"Who?" Cammon said.

"Milo. He's the king's secretary, and he decides who has an audience with King Baryn and who does not. And when."

Cammon crowded his horse closer to Tayse's. For the first time on this long journey, Senneth thought, he looked a little awed. "You aren't going to leave us, are you?" he asked anxiously. "You'll be with us when we go in to see the king?"

Tayse smiled down at him. "I won't leave you," he said. And then, as if he couldn't help himself, he glanced back at Senneth. "Not just yet."

As soon as they approached the door, a pack of servants came swarming out. Some lifted their bedrolls and saddlebags from the horses; others helped the women from the saddle; others gathered up the reins and led the horses away.

One man stood on the threshold, framed by the open door, and waited majestically for them to climb the two flights of quarried marble stairs. He was of medium height and heavyset, mostly bald, and he wore both his elegant clothes and his air of authority with perfect ease.

"The king has been expecting you," he said. "He wanted me to direct you to the visitors' chambers to freshen up, and then escort you immediately to his private rooms. Follow me."

And without waiting for a reply, he turned on one well-shod foot and proceeded down the hallway. Justin mouthed the word "Milo" and pointed at his back. The others grinned, nodded, and followed.

All of them except Cammon had been inside these halls before, so they did not waste much time gaping at the high, fluted ceilings, the expensive tapestries, the life-size statues in marble and gold. But Senneth could not help but smile a little at Cammon's obvious amazement at the richness of the furnishings and the gorgeous proportions of the architecture. In all of their travels, they had seen nothing like the king's home.

"And it's like this throughout the palace," she told him, "one hallway more gorgeous than the last. The part I like best is the sun room, which is entirely covered, ceiling and walls, with gold leaf over carved wood relief. Exquisitely beautiful."

"What must it be like to live someplace like this? All the time?" he asked, his eyes wide.

"Oh, you get used to it after a while," Justin said airily. "It becomes as familiar to you as a poor man's hut is to him. You don't even notice the gold and the paintings and the ornamentation after a while."

Senneth smiled. "This from a man who lives in the barracks."

Justin grinned. "Well, I got used to *those* quickly enough."

They spent twenty minutes in the small, elegant chambers reserved for visitors, doing what they could to improve their appearance. All Kirra had to do was run a comb through her hair and mysteriously change the fabric of her coarse riding dress to a heavy silk, and she looked beautiful. Senneth contented herself with washing off most of the grime of the road, taming her hair with a wet brush, and changing into a clean blouse and skirt. The men washed their faces; Justin and Tayse shaved, and Donnal trimmed his beard. Soon enough they looked as presentable as they were going to manage, and Milo was back in the doorway.

"The king will see you now."

KING Baryn was awaiting them in a small room warmly furnished with plush chairs and accessories of deep, rich colors—a room meant for intimate conversation with close and trusted friends. He turned to face them the instant the door opened, and the smile on his face was genuinely welcoming. Senneth had always thought he looked like he should be a toy maker or a cobbler or a gardener—anything but a king. He was tall and thin, with wispy gray hair that no royal valet had ever been able to style. His face was ruddy and perpetually cheerful; his wire-rimmed glasses always slid far enough down his nose that his brown eyes could peer over them at a world that he seemed to find continually fascinating.

"Senneth! My dear!" he exclaimed, throwing wide his arms and taking her into an avuncular embrace. "And Kirra! Look at you, the very jewel of Danalustrous. I always think your sister must hate you for your hair."

Kirra laughed. "She does."

The king turned to shake hands with each of his Riders. "Justin. Tayse. As always, my faith in you is justified."

"We had some incidents along the road, which you'll hear of," Tayse said.

The king nodded. "But you're back, and safe, and your companions are alive." He came to a halt and tilted his head to one side as he regarded the others. "Now, I don't believe I know these young men."

"Donnal," Senneth said. "From Danalustrous. Malcolm doesn't trust anyone, even Riders, to protect his own."

"Very wise," the king approved.

"And Cammon. We picked him up in Dormas. He's a mystic."

"Excellent! So happy to have you here. Come, come, sit down. As you see, there are drinks and various foodstuffs over on the sideboard. Help yourselves, and then let's talk."

The men hesitated, but Senneth and Kirra, less abashed by royalty, went straight to the buffet and filled their plates. Soon all seven of them were munching on sugared fruit and delicate pastries. They had just chosen their seats and drawn their chairs into an irregular circle when there was a knock on the door.

"This must be Valri," the king said happily. "Come in!"

The woman who entered brought an immediate, appraising silence to the group. She was young—no more than Kirra's age, Senneth thought, which would make her about forty years younger than her husband—and coldly beautiful. Her skin was a delicate white, her short hair a rich and sultry black; her eyes were the color of spring grass, astonishingly green. She was small and exquisitely formed, and everything about her gave Senneth the impression of a doll—porcelain, exaggerated, perfect, unreal.

"You wanted me to join you?" she asked in a neutral voice, glancing around the room.

"Yes, yes, sit with us," Baryn said, motioning her in. "You know Senneth and Kirra, I believe." All the women nodded at each other. "Tayse and Justin, of course. This is Donnal, from Danalustrous, and Cammon from—well, they found him in Dormas, but I feel certain his origin is more exotic than that."

"Hello," Valri said coolly to them all, and took her seat beside the king. She folded her hands in her lap and sat very straight and looked as if she would rather be almost anywhere else in the world.

"Now," the king said. "Tell me what you've learned."

They all looked to Senneth, who had been debating what to say. She had not expected Queen Valri's presence at this conference, but she supposed it didn't matter. The king would repeat to her anything they said, anyway, if it was true that he consulted her on all matters of state. A fact which displeased many, especially those who believed she was a mystic . . .

"I'll start with our general conclusions, and then go back and tell you the whole story, if you want to hear it," Senneth said. "It seems clear that some of the southern Houses are arming for war. Gisseltess appears to be the main force behind it, but Fortunalt and Nocklyn are ready to join forces with Halchon. Martin Helven talks like a loyal man, but the country he commands seems more ambivalent. Ariane Rappengrass stands firm as your ally but is surrounded on all sides by potential traitors, so she is not in a very good position to offer you much aid."

"I knew some of the Houses were restless—but war—" Baryn said.

"It might not come to that," Senneth said quietly. "But if it does, it appears likely a war would be fought on two fronts—the political and the religious. The southern territories are being overrun with Daughters of the Pale Mother, who are preaching a gospel of fidelity to the Silver Lady and an exorcism of all things magic. Mystics in the southern regions are being abused, ostracized, and sometimes killed, and there is a great rash of piety through the major and minor towns. Coralinda Gisseltess has reopened the Lumanen Convent and installed upwards of five hundred acolytes there—and surrounded herself with a formidable guard that appears to be made up of private soldiers from the southern Houses as well as some lesser noblemen. She and her brother Halchon seem to have different motivations but are working together toward a common cause."

"Deposing me and putting Halchon on the throne," Baryn said calmly.

"Exactly."

"And their reasons for such a drastic act?"

Senneth could not keep herself from sending a quick, troubled glance at the motionless Queen Valri. "The one that would seem likely to carry the most weight with the other nobles is the issue of the succession," she said. "There are—questions—about Princess Amalie. Halchon and others have spread the idea that, because she is so rarely seen in public, she is not fit to rule. And since you and Queen Valri have no children, if Amalie is indeed unfit—well, they say they worry about the stability of the kingdom."

Baryn nodded. "You know the story, I think—or perhaps you do not. Amalie was only a little girl when she and her mother were riding through the marketplace in Ghosenhall. A band of brigands attacked them—ignoring my wife and concentrating almost solely on my daughter. Trying to kill her, kill my little girl. Well, there were Riders accompanying them, so you know the outcome of that encounter—all the outlaws dead, Pella and Amalie safe. But I never did learn who sent the assassins, and I was terrified to risk the incident occurring again. Ever since then, I have kept Amalie confined very closely to the palace grounds— or heavily guarded any time she has gone out in society. It seemed the best way to keep her safe. But perhaps, in some way, I have made her more unsafe. I must think on this."

"Sending her out into society may go some way toward mollifying the malcontents," Senneth said. "But I don't know if that will be enough. She is very young, and you—forgive me, sire— are aging."

"I'm old," he said with a chuckle.

"There is some fear that if you were to die suddenly, Amalie would be too young and inexperienced to rule in your place."

He tilted his head to one side and regarded Senneth out of his warm eyes. "A regent should be appointed, then, you think? I have been considering just such a move, I confess."

Kirra spoke up. "He would have to be someone acceptable to all parties," she said. "Someone strong enough to keep the Houses in order, but not so arrogant he will not listen to counsel. And someone you trust absolutely."

Baryn glanced at his wife; she shrugged infinitesimally, then nodded. "The man I have in mind is Amalie's uncle Romar," the king said. "Do you think he meets your criteria?"

"Lord Romar of Merrenstow," Kirra said consideringly. "I've only met him a few times, but I know my father holds him in high esteem—and my father, you know, dislikes almost everyone."

The king smiled. "Yes, that's what I enjoy so much about Malcolm—his impartial distrust of the entire population. Well, Romar is here visiting, in fact—you shall see him again at dinner and tell me what you think."

"The fact that he is a blood relation to Amalie is definitely in his favor," Kirra said, still mulling it over. "And while he is Twelfth House, he is not serramar to Merrenstow, which also is to his advantage—he will be seen as less ambitious, I think. If his character is sound and his personal charm sufficient, I think he would be a good choice."

"So we have disposed of the problem of the succession," the king said lightly. "For what other reasons might Halchon and his friends turn against me?"

"Magic," Senneth said bluntly. "Coralinda and her acolytes are spreading the message that mystics are profane and dangerous. You are regarded as a king who is most tolerant of magic—and you will have to expect that people will discover you have employed my services, at least for this mission. It is known that you welcome mystics into Ghosenhall—it is known that Malcolm Danalustrous is one of your staunchest allies, and that his own daughter is a sorceress. I think if you do not publicly renounce magic, even if you secure the succession you may still have a war on your hands."

"But if I renounce magic, I have a war on my hands anyway," the king said, "because Malcolm will certainly turn against me, and Kianlever may as well."

"Exactly," Kirra said. "We were trying to guess where the alliances would fall if magic became the divisive issue. I can't promise that the numbers are even, but certainly it would not just be you and my father against the other eleven Houses."

"Is Halchon capable of rebelling over magic even if the succession is secure?" the king asked. "Fomenting discontent merely because it serves his purposes, and not because he truly worries about the stability of the realm?"

"You know Halchon," Senneth said. "I think you can answer that for yourself. He has offered you a chance to buy his loyalty, however."

"I can hardly wait to hear his terms."

"Name him heir. He says he will then work with you to ensure a smooth transition from your reign to his."

"Halchon Gisseltess my heir!" the king exclaimed, even his mild voice betraying indignation. "His arrogance astounds me. And why would he think all Twelve Houses would willingly accept him as monarch after me?"

Senneth became aware of the weight of many sets of eyes trained on her. She glanced quickly around the room to see Kirra, Tayse, Justin, Cammon, Donnal, all watching her. She scowled and looked down at her hands.

Kirra spoke. "As to that, sire, he has a plan. He thinks if he—frees himself—of the encumbrance of his current wife, he can make a strategic alliance with a new bride and unite the northern and southern Houses."

Baryn looked intrigued by the politics, as if momentarily forgetting how closely they involved him. "Really? And where would he plan to marry?"

"Brassenthwaite," Kirra said baldly.

A long moment of awkward silence as the king ran through the possibilities and came to the inevitable conclusion. "Senneth?" he asked. Senneth nodded reluctantly. The king broke into a broad smile. "Really, did he ask you for your hand again? I hope that this time you did not turn him down in such a dramatic fashion."

"No, my refusal was fairly spectacular," she said ruefully. "But he said he would not despair."

"No, indeed, he must pursue you most diligently! It is his best chance at a coup, I think."

"I would not—I hope you don't think—Halchon Gisseltess—"

The king laughed merrily. Senneth could not help noticing that Queen Valri did not look amused in the slightest. "Oh, Senneth, I would as soon expect Tayse to knife me in the back as I would expect you to act in any way that would endanger me," he said. "Even if you didn't hate Halchon Gisseltess with all your heart, you wouldn't marry him to advance his claim to the throne."

Queen Valri spoke in her low, controlled voice. "Yet if Senneth thought such a move might prevent a war, she might be excused for acting in a way that seemed noble." Her voice did not make it sound as if such actions would seem noble to her.

"I will never marry Halchon Gisseltess," Senneth said flatly. "If I were going to betray my king, I would find some other way to do it."

"In any case, Senneth's a mystic. If he marries her, he has to placate the whole faction of fanatics he's roused to war," the king said. "He just might find himself in a bind there."

Valri lifted her impossible green eyes to Senneth's face. "You haven't said so, but I feel certain the question of magic has been raised for yet another critical reason."

Senneth felt a certain admiration for the cool way that the queen invited censure. "Yes, majesty," she said in a quiet voice. "I heard from more than one source that those who despise mystics are beginning to whisper that you are one as well."

The king lifted his delicate gray eyebrows. "Really? They're saying Valri is a mystic? Do they have any proof? Any instances?"

Senneth shook her head. "Not that I heard. And you know the way of rumors. People are charged with the crime that seems most heinous for that time and place. Malcontents trying to turn sentiment against the throne would naturally play on people's growing distrust of magic."

Valri gave her husband an unreadable look from her unnerving eyes. "I am proving to be a liability to you," she said in a low voice. She did not seem to mind that others could hear what she said.

"Nonsense," the king said. "You're essential to me."

"If my presence is rousing the Houses to war, I think you might find me dispensable."

Baryn reached over and took her hand in his. It was less a lover's gesture, Senneth thought, than the reassuring clasp a father might give his child. "The kingdom will fall before I put you aside," he said.

There was a brief, uncomfortable silence as the rest of them tried to pretend they had not witnessed this scene. Senneth could not help noticing that neither the king nor the queen had refuted the basic charge. "At this point," she said, "I don't suppose it matters. Even if, in some grand gesture to impress the nobles, you cast the queen aside, the damage has been done. If she has the power to compromise you, she has done it already. You are better off, it seems, standing united as you face the world."

"Exactly what I said," the king replied. "Valri knows I would not let her leave me."

Valri smiled tightly and trained her eyes on her shoes.

"So! Where do we stand?" the king asked in a conversational voice. "What is my next obvious step?"

"Announce your regent, make Amalie more visible, and confer with the lords you know to be loyal," Kirra said.

"And make shows of strength to the Houses you suspect of considering treason," Senneth said. "It might have some effect to send a few well-armed envoys into Nocklyn and Fortunalt. Let the lords know that you are aware of their machinations."

Tayse lifted his voice for the first time. "Send a delegation to the convent at Lumanen," he suggested. "It would not hurt the sanctimonious Lestra to get a taste of temporal power."

The king regarded him with some interest. "You speak as if you actually had face-to-face dealings with Coralinda," he said. "Is that possible? Time to tell me some of your adventures on the road!"

Tayse smiled briefly. "That one, at least, isn't much to my credit. I was overtaken by men in service to the Pale Mother, and thought it better to surrender than die in battle. They brought me bound to the convent and were happy to keep me captive. The Lestra herself came to visit me, promising to convert me to the ways of the Silver Lady. There was something about her—very disturbing. I think she would go to almost any length to prove a point. It was clear she was debating whether or not it would serve her best to kill me outright—or to taunt you with the news that she had captured one of your Riders."

The king was mesmerized. "But tell me! How did you win free?"

Tayse glanced at Senneth, for only the second or third time since they'd stepped inside this room. "Senneth, of course. Arriving at the convent gates and threatening to set the place on fire."

Cammon clearly could not contain himself any longer; his awe seemed to have exhausted its power to keep him silent. "And threatening to set free the *raelynx*," he said.

"Set free a *raelynx*?" the king demanded. He appeared to be hugely entertained. "Where did you find one?"

But Queen Valri seemed greatly startled at the word. Her green eyes lifted; she stared at Cammon. "You have a raelynx with you?" she said in a voice barely above a whisper. "Who answers to your command?"

Cammon nodded, then pointed at Senneth. "Well, Senneth's

the one who caught him first, of course, and she's the only one who can truly control him, but I'm learning. I can hold him for more than a day now, and not let him break free of me."

Valri's gaze traveled swiftly between Senneth and Cammon. "A raelynx?" she repeated. "But they almost never stray outside the Lirrens. And when they do—did you find it by the trail of slaughtered bodies it had left behind?"

"Almost," Senneth said. "We came across a small town that the beast was terrorizing. It's not full-grown yet, so it had not done quite so much damage as it could have. I want to take it back to the Lirrens once I—once we are finished with discussions here."

The king still looked amused. "And where is this terrible beast? Have you left it to wander around Ghosenhall, eating my subjects at will?"

"He's in a cage now, because Senneth thought it wasn't safe to bring him into the city," Cammon said. "But I thought—couldn't he run free here in the palace grounds? I can't stand to think of him cooped up as he's been for so long."

"I don't think—" the king began, but his wife interrupted him.

"Yes. My private garden," she said. "It is completely walled in. No one goes there except by my invitation. He will be safe there."

Senneth transferred her thoughtful gaze from Cammon's face to the queen's. *This is very interesting,* she thought. The king said in a humorous voice, "My dear, it is not the safety of the raelynx we are so concerned about, but the safety of the humans it might want to eat."

"It won't trouble me," she said.

Senneth could sense that Kirra's eyes had also come to rest on the queen's face and that Kirra was thinking very much what she was. Cammon just seemed relieved that someone with power was taking an interest in his beloved creature. "Can you talk to the guards, then?" he asked. "Because they won't listen to me."

"Yes," she said. "As soon as we're done here, I'll go see to its disposition."

The king laughed out loud. "Well, Senneth, I expected you to bring me back many interesting tidbits, but I certainly never expected you to come back with a wild animal at your back. I suppose it is true what they say about any bargain you make with a mystic."

Senneth smiled. "It will fail you or reward you in ways you never anticipated."

The king rose to his feet, and all of them hastily stood. "Tayse, I assume you can make provision for these young men in the barracks?"

"Yes, sire."

"Kirra, Senneth, you are welcome to stay at the palace as long as you like. The two of you will join me for dinner, of course. We still have much to discuss."

The king and queen were two steps from the door when Cammon blurted out, "But are you going to see about the raelynx now?"

"Cammon," Senneth said sharply.

Queen Valri looked back at him with a ghost of a smile on her red mouth. "Come meet me in half an hour," she said. "Ask Milo where my private garden is to be found."

"I will, then," Cammon called after her, but the door had already shut between him and the royal couple.

CHAPTER
35

SENNETH spun on her heel to look at those remaining in the room. Cammon still seemed distracted by thoughts of the raelynx, but the rest of them were watching her, their own faces showing various degrees of curiosity and trouble. She thought, with a moment of affection so intense that it resembled pain, that she had never trusted any group of people so much as those gathered here in this room.

"Well," she said. "And what did we make of that?"

"He wasn't surprised by anything you had to say," Justin said.

"Not even the bits about Amalie," Kirra said. "And I thought those accusations might have made him angry."

"But he's heard them before, or thought of them himself," Senneth said slowly.

"And already has a man picked out as regent," Tayse added.

"Which means," Senneth said, "that she possibly is *not* fit to rule. And that he knows it. And has made no provisions for what will happen upon his death."

"Because even a good regent can't rule forever for an incompetent heir," Kirra said.

Donnal shook his dark head. "Makes no sense," he said. "He's a good king. If he had no faith in his daughter, he'd be making plans for turning over the kingdom now. He trusts her, but he knows there's something about her that others will dislike or discredit."

Senneth looked at Kirra. "I don't remember the story of an attack in Ghosenhall. Do you?"

Kirra shook her head, but both Riders said, "Yes." Justin added, "It happened before I became a Rider, but they were all still talking about it. The day the Riders saved the princess." He grinned. "I've been waiting for my own chance ever since."

"What I found even more interesting than the king's reaction," said Senneth, "was the things the queen said—or didn't say."

"*Is* she a mystic?" Kirra demanded.

"Exactly."

They all gazed at Cammon, who first looked surprised and then thoughtful. "Is she?" he repeated. "I don't know. Not the way we are—the four of us." He waved a hand. "But she has—there's something about her—some kind of power. I don't know if it's magic. I can't read it. I can't tell what she can do with it. But she's—" He shrugged. "I wouldn't call her dangerous, precisely, but—"

"She has some kind of hold on the king," Justin said darkly.

Cammon wrinkled his forehead. "Nooo," he said. "I wouldn't say that. He doesn't seem like a man enchanted."

Donnal gave a little snort. "A man besotted. Young woman who looks like that—" He rolled his shoulders expressively.

Cammon shook his head. "No," he said again, "he doesn't love her."

They all stared at him. "You can tell something like that for certain?" Kirra demanded.

Cammon nodded. "He's not in love with her. She's definitely not in love with him." He shrugged.

Senneth lifted her eyes and glanced briefly at the others in the room. "So why did he marry her then?" she asked softly. "And what makes her so 'essential' to him?"

Tayse smiled faintly. "You're the ones invited to the royal banquet table tonight," he said. "Maybe you can find out."

Cammon seemed to bounce on the balls of his feet. "How soon does the queen have to go to the banquet hall?" he asked. "Is she in the garden now, do you suppose?"

"And that's another thing," Kirra said. "Why was she so interested in the raelynx?"

"*Just* what I was wondering," Senneth said. "Could it be that she's from the Lirrens, where raelynxes run wild? Is that why no one knows anything about her or what House she's from?"

"The Lirrens," Kirra repeated, incredulous. "You think the king married a Lirren girl? But that would be so—" She shrugged. "How odd."

"I've always thought the Lirrenlands were rife with a strange kind of magic," Senneth said. "Which might make the queen a mystic—of a sort."

Donnal looked unconvinced. "Or she might just be a Merrenstow girl who has a love for wild animals," he said. "You have to admit, many people would be fascinated to have such a creature brought to their doors."

"Maybe," Senneth said. "But I must say, I almost want to go with Cammon when he meets the queen in the garden."

Tayse gave her another one of those infrequent glances. "Or bring her with you when you take your wild animal back to the mountains."

She smiled. "Maybe I'll invite her along."

Justin looked as disquieted as Senneth had ever seen him. "So what happens next?" he asked. "To us—to you, I mean? We go back to the barracks and you stay in the palace tonight and then—what? Do you just ride away in the morning? Is this the last we'll see of you?"

Cammon looked stricken, as if none of these thoughts had crossed his mind. Kirra appeared to be faintly amused. Senneth smiled and put her hand briefly to Justin's freshly shaved cheek.

"It will be a day or so before I ride out again—maybe more," she said. "And I would never leave without saying good-bye. And I would never leave without seeing Cammon settled. Don't worry yet."

"But the adventure's almost over," Cammon said in a small boy's voice.

Now Senneth smiled at him. "This one," she said. "There are always more adventures."

KIRRA insisted they dress for dinner and went so far as to manufacture from their traveling clothes gowns of astonishing finery. For herself, she fashioned an outfit of gold and lace, and twined lace in her golden hair to heighten the effect. For Senneth, she designed a gown of Brassenthwaite blue, relatively unadorned, but featuring a deeply plunging neckline.

"Show off your housemark!" Kirra commanded when Senneth protested. "Wear that lovely old gold necklace to cover it, but let everyone know you are who you say you are."

"I don't *want* to traipse around as Senneth Brassenthwaite."

"Too bad," Kirra said unsympathetically. "Because, especially in this place, that's who you are."

"Can't I wear something just a little less conspicuous?"

"No," Kirra said. "Besides, you look beautiful. It's the perfect color for your skin. It even makes your eyes look blue."

"Well, they're not."

Kirra grinned and leaned in to whisper in her ear. "After dinner, you should go down to the barracks. Show Tayse how you look in a fine gown."

Senneth drew back sharply, both irritated and depressed. "He'd be even more likely to stay clear of me then," she said.

Kirra was smiling. "I think you underestimate your charms."

"I think you overlook the time," Senneth said, turning from the mirror. "We'll be late for dinner."

There were maybe twenty other nobles gathered in the drawing room adjacent to the dining hall when Kirra and Senneth arrived. Senneth thought she recognized one or two—older men who might have visited Brassen Court when she was a girl—but there was no one she knew well enough to address. Kirra, of course, was familiar with everyone there and moved effortlessly between knots of people, saying hello, introducing Senneth, asking after friends and relatives. Despite her claim to hate all such social gatherings, Kirra was clearly enjoying herself and completely at ease. Senneth tried to keep her face impassive when each individual lord or lady exclaimed, "Senneth *Brassenthwaite!* But I thought—it's lovely to meet you at last." She let Kirra make most of the conversation and allowed the rest of them to think her mannerless. She didn't want to be friends with them, anyway.

But she found her interest sharpening when Kirra led her up to a handsome, broad-shouldered man who looked just a bit impatient with the pomp and ritual of a formal dinner. He was tall, though not as tall as Tayse. His thick golden hair, which he wore unbound to his shoulders, was only slightly duller than Kirra's. His eyes were a steady brown, and his face was serious and intelligent.

"Lord Romar," Kirra said, drawing him away from a conversation he was auditing, and which did not seem to interest him much. "I am so pleased to see you again. You may not remember me—I'm Malcolm Danalustrous's daughter Kirra."

"Serra Kirra. Yes, of course I remember you," Romar said. Senneth thought he did not sound at all certain.

"I was at your wedding last year," Kirra said helpfully. "How do you find you like married life?"

"It is most pleasant, thank you very much." He seemed amused. "My wife is not with me, as I am here on political business, or I'm sure she'd be happy to renew her acquaintance with you."

Kirra's hand on her shoulder drew Senneth forward. "I don't know if you're already acquainted with Senneth Brassenthwaite or if you need an introduction."

His eyes showed a flash of interest but no surprise; no doubt, he had been briefed by his king. "Serramarra Senneth," he said, taking her hand in a warm clasp and looking at her with a lively curiosity. "I have had some dealings with your brothers and always found them most honest and forthright."

It was the polite thing to say; she couldn't bring herself to make the expected response. "You have the advantage of me. I have not dealt with my brothers in more than fifteen years," she said in a light voice. "But I'm glad they didn't make an effort to cheat you."

"Sen," Kirra hissed.

Lord Romar dropped her hand, but he appeared even more intrigued and not at all discomposed. A man who appreciated plain dealing, it would seem. "I have to confess, I was less fond of your father, but your brothers seem like honorable men," he said. "Very loyal to my brother-in-law."

"I'm glad to hear it," she said.

Lord Romar glanced between Senneth and Kirra. "I hear the two of you have just come back from some adventuring on behalf of the king," he said. "Are there any stories you can tell, or is it all secrets and political maneuvering?"

Just then a servant rang a small silver bell, and the whole crowd began to drift into the dining room. Kirra was laughing. "Some of the stories we can tell, I think," she said. "If we are sitting near you, we will recount the best ones."

But while Kirra was seated immediately to Romar's left, Senneth was half a table away. She had been given the place of supreme honor at Baryn's right hand, a fact which she could tell was causing no end of consternation and speculation among the other nobles at the table. She could not forbear giving her king a murderous look, which caused him to laugh out loud right before he introduced her to the people sitting nearest to her. High-ranking nobles of Tilt and Kianlever and Storian. Her peers, at least in theory, and she just might be related to the ones from Kian-lever, if she had time to work the genealogy. Senneth murmured appropriate phrases, and answered any questions addressed to her directly, but made no other effort to be gracious. She did not feel gracious. She did not want to be made over into a Brassenthwaite heiress after spending literally half of her life escaping that iden-tity. She decided on the spot that she would never attend a formal dinner again, in Ghosenhall or any of the holdings of the Twelve Houses. The decision restored some of her equanimity, and she ate most of her meal in a more cheerful frame of mind.

She excused herself from the activities planned for after the meal—cards and music, it seemed, entertainments that everyone else appeared to be looking forward to—noting that she was tired from the long journey.

"Come see me tomorrow," the king said as she prepared to leave the dining room. "At two hours past noon. We have things to discuss, you and I."

She could not help but return his smile. "Yours to command, sire," she said, giving him the best curtsey she could manage.

His voice was full of satisfaction. "Every Brassenthwaite is."

IN the morning, Senneth was awake early and quickly dressed in a set of her travel clothes. They had been cleaned and pressed by the palace servants, so they did not look quite as disreputable as they had for the past few weeks. She asked the footman at the door—and then two or three different gardeners and groundskeep-ers as she passed—where Queen Valri's private gardens might be found. The compound comprised several hundred acres; it was easy for anyone to get lost.

Eventually she located the queen's own property, which looked to be maybe thirty square yards enclosed by a high brick wall. Tendrils of last year's ivy trailed over the brick from the other side; a few thin branches from ornamental trees poked their heads up over the wall. Senneth circled the enclosure till she found the scrollwork metal grate set in the north side, but she did not have the key to open the lock.

She pushed her face through the bars and peered in. A tangle of shrubs and vines and exotic bushes met her eyes. In summer, this place must be thickly overgrown with plant life. Now everything was brown and dusty-looking, patiently awaiting the advent of spring.

"Cammon?" she called. "Are you in here?"

A rustle of dry branches and Cammon appeared, bounding over to her like a happy puppy. "Senneth! You're awake early."

"Not as early as you," she replied, amused. "How's our wild friend?"

"Wild," he admitted. "Calmer today than he was yesterday when they first set him free. But he keeps pacing and then every once in a while he gives that howl—you know the one I mean—"

She nodded. "Good thing the garden is so far from the palace."

He laughed. "That's what I thought."

"How'd you get in?" she asked. "The gate's locked."

He pulled something from his pocket. "The queen gave me a key."

Senneth's eyebrows rose. "She did, did she? She must have taken quite a liking to you."

Cammon grinned and unlocked the gate. Senneth slipped inside quickly, and he locked it again behind her. "She took a liking to the raelynx, and she could tell I cared for it. That made me her ally."

Senneth glanced around, looking for the raelynx. For a moment, she couldn't spot it, which made the back of her neck prickle. There was no way it had managed to overlook her arrival, and she did not like the idea that it was lying in wait, close enough to spring on her. But then she spotted the wave of russet through the densely overgrown bushes, and she saw it sitting about ten feet away, watching her, its tail twitching ominously back and forth.

"Has he been fed since we arrived?" she asked.

Cammon nodded. "A few squirrels had made their homes in the garden. They're gone now." He shrugged, showing little sympathy for the short lives and violent deaths of those unfortunate creatures. "And the queen had raw meat sent in this morning. Venison, I think."

"So she really came here yesterday afternoon? To see it?"

Cammon nodded.

"What did she say?"

Cammon spread his hands. "She asked how we'd found it, and how old we thought it was, and how you managed to use it to scare off the Daughters of the Pale Mother. The whole time she was talking to me, though, she was watching the raelynx, and it was pacing around the garden, and pouncing on game and acting very edgy. I was a little worried that her presence would stir him up so much that he'd attack her, but I had a pretty close grip on his mind."

Senneth turned to look at him. Cammon was never particularly good at hiding his emotions, and she could tell that something had happened yesterday to trouble or excite him. "And then?" she asked.

"And then she—Senneth, it's hard to explain. It was a lot like when you would transfer control of him to me, or I'd give him back to you, except I didn't know she was going to do it. She just—she took him from me. All of a sudden, he wasn't in my head anymore, and I could see by the expression on her face that *she* was the one holding him. And the raelynx didn't like it at first. He let out one of those terrifying screams, and he started pacing even more tightly. You know how he gets, with his ears down and his tail going. But she just stood there, so quiet, not moving at all. It was like she wasn't even breathing. And then the raelynx started to calm down—stopped pacing, sat back on his hind legs and just watched us for a while.

"And then," said Cammon, his voice trembling a little, "it stood up again and came over to us. Like a dog or a housecat. But it was snarling a little—you could see its teeth. I backed up to the wall, but the queen just stood there—had her hand out, as if she would stop it. And it sat back down. And then it lay on the ground and stretched out, right at her feet. It was close enough to lick her shoes. I swear, for a moment I thought she was going to reach down and touch it on the head, but she didn't. She just stood there a long time looking down at it while it looked up at her. And then suddenly she spun around and left the garden. And the raelynx jumped up and acted like he wanted to attack *me*," Cammon concluded, with some grievance in his voice, "but I had hold of its mind again before it could come any closer."

Senneth's emotions were an unworthy mix of admiration, speculation, and jealousy. She turned her attention back to the raelynx,

who was on his feet and prowling through the undergrowth, sending occasional calculating glances back their way. "That's very
impressive," she said in a neutral voice. "And while she was proving her mastery over the raelynx, did you scent any magic on her?
Sense any kind of sorcery at all?"

He spread his hands. "The same as yesterday. I think there's
power there, but not any that I understand. Not the same kind of
magic as ours."

"Would you trust her?" she asked softly. "Because you have an
especially good instinct for knowing when someone is a friend
and when someone is an enemy."

He looked at her, though she kept her eyes on the raelynx.
"Senneth, I can't tell."

She nodded and didn't answer. She had brought all her energy
to bear on the raelynx, the wild creature she had forced to accompany her over hundreds of miles of dangerous terrain, giving it a
hasty mental promise to take it home and set it free whenever the
time would prove convenient. It was no happier here in this pretty
prison than it had been pacing alongside them as they rode to Gisseltess. She could feel its uncertain temper, its watchfulness, its
never-stilled hunger. She closed her mind upon its own.

It responded with a cry of protest and leapt forward by a dozen
paces, its tail lashing furiously back and forth. Its tufted ears lay
almost flat against the red fur of its head, and its eyes were hot
with fury. Senneth cleared her mind, made her thoughts limpid
and cool, and invited the raelynx closer. It hissed and snarled and
sat back on its haunches. Senneth extended one hand.

"What are you doing?" Cammon asked somewhat fearfully,
but she ignored him. She opened her mind even more, made it a
space of freedom and joyous motion, and bade the raelynx enter.
He resisted for a moment, then came with a sudden, menacing
fluidity to his feet. Putting one paw daintily, almost hesitantly, before the other, he came closer and closer to where Senneth and
Cammon stood at the gate.

When the raelynx was only a few feet away, Senneth sank to the
ground, her hand still outstretched. The raelynx stepped forward a
few inches at a time till he was close enough to devour Senneth's fingers with one quick bite. Delicately, he pushed his red face forward
and sniffed at her hand. She could feel the tickle of his whiskers
across her skin.

Then he opened his mouth and brushed his tongue across her

palm. She felt as if she had just been kissed by a mouthful of knives; her eyes watered with the momentary pain. She kept her arm extended, but he did not lick her again. Instead, he settled his full length on the ground before her and began to rumble with a deep purr of satisfaction.

Senneth turned her head slowly to glance up at Cammon. He was staring down at her with an expression that showed equal portions of delight and terror. She could not help herself. She laughed out loud.

CHAPTER
36

ONCE they had left the garden and locked it behind them, Senneth and Cammon headed off toward the gates that separated the palace grounds from the city.

"I want you to meet someone," she said. "I think you'll like him."

The day was cool but sunny, and Ghosenhall, as always, was a treat for all the senses. They stopped three times to buy food being sold by street vendors: dried fruit, warm bread, fried sausages. They admired the uniform arrangement of shops in the merchant streets, the well-tended parks, the handsome statues that guarded occasional corners.

"I like this city," Cammon decided.

"Yes," said Senneth, "it's the jewel of Gillengaria. There are parts of it that are not so savory—Justin could tell you about those—but most of it is a treat and a treasure."

They had walked more than an hour from the palace wall by the time they arrived at their destination, a stately three-story house in a residential district that featured similar well-constructed buildings on every street. They had only taken two steps up the flagged walk when the front door opened, and a tall, thin, totally bald man came dashing down to meet them.

"Senneth!" he exclaimed. "I had heard you were back in Ghosenhall, but I was not sure you would have time to come by and see us!" He took her in a hard embrace, pulled back to look at her, and then hugged her again. When he finally released her, his face was full of admiration. "You've grown even stronger," he said. "I can sense it. It's like you have fire in your veins, not blood."

She smiled at him. He was maybe ten years older than she was, though his face looked even younger than hers, and his eyes were a pale gray that gave him a strange, otherworldly air. "Jerril, I want you to meet Cammon," she said. "We picked him up in Dormas and found him to possess most extraordinary skills. He saved our lives more than once while we were on the road."

Jerril turned instantly to Cammon and laid his bony hands on the young man's shoulders. Cammon looked up at him with an expression both wary and hopeful. Senneth thought that nature had made Cammon a happy boy who embraced all new adventures, but experience had taught him how bitter those adventures could be. She could not tell exactly what Jerril was communicating by touch, but Cammon's face grew more radiant, bright with wonder, the longer Jerril stood there looking down at him.

"So!" Jerril said at last, dropping his hands back to his sides. "A sensitive—and a very strong one at that. I can see why this one would have been quite an asset to you as you traveled in hostile territory."

"Are there any hostile territories in Gillengaria?" Senneth asked innocently, and Jerril rewarded her with a laugh.

"Forgive me for expressing aloud what I have deduced from reading people's emotions," Jerril said. "What is the phrase the melodramatic persons use? These are parlous times."

"Or they will be soon," Senneth said. "I think we have a period of grace before true trouble begins."

"Then you have time to come in for tea?" Jerril asked, still laughing. "Perhaps a little luncheon? Lynnette and Areel will be most excited to see you."

"I have to start back to the palace very soon, for I have a conference scheduled with the king," Senneth said. "But I thought you might entertain Cammon for a while. Show him the treasures of your house. Explain to him—" She shrugged. "What you might be able to teach him."

"Then Cammon is come to us as a student?" Jerril asked, sounding most pleased.

"That's up to Cammon—and you, of course," Senneth said. "He needs training, and I would rather trust him to you and

Lynnette than to anyone else I know. But I'm not sure he's ready
to leave his friends up at the palace. Two Riders and a raelynx. A
most unusual set of companions."

"A raelynx?" Jerril repeated. "That must be an interesting
story."

"Justin said I could stay with them," Cammon said, but he
sounded uncertain. "They'd find a place for me. Tayse said so, too."

"Well, you must naturally stay where you feel most comfortable," Jerril said. "But we'd be happy to take you in here. We only
have two other students at the moment, and the house feels almost
empty. And we don't live so far from the palace grounds, as you
must have noticed if you walked here this morning. You could
study with us and see your friends quite often."

Cammon glanced up at Senneth. "What should I do?" he said,
rushing his words. "I want to do both."

She laughed and gave him a quick hug. "Why don't you spend
the afternoon with Jerril and his friends?" she suggested.
"And maybe spend a few more days here next week before you
make up your mind. You know I would not leave you anywhere
that was not safe—you know you can trust my friends, and be
happy here."

"Oh, I know," he said. "I can tell that already."

"Then spend the day here," she said, "and come talk to me
tonight. You don't have to decide anything yet."

"All right, I will," he said, sounding quite cheerful. "I hope
you have a most interesting conference with the king."

She laughed, a bit ruefully this time. "I'm sure I will."

QUEEN Valri was with Baryn when Milo ushered Senneth
into a small, comfortable room that clearly functioned as the
king's private study. The dark blue furnishings seemed well-
worn; the desk was cluttered. The window gave out over a lovely
view of garden and lawn, but it was clear the king rarely had time
to gaze out when he was in here working.

When Senneth stepped inside, the queen was standing beside
the king's desk. He sat in his plush chair, looking up at her over
his wire-rimmed glasses. Both of them appeared quite serious.

Senneth instinctively edged back toward the door. "I'm sorry,"
she said. "I'll return later."

But King Baryn smiled at her. "Nonsense! I've been expecting you. Besides, Valri is here to discuss a matter that might be of some concern to you."

Valri had also turned her head to look at Senneth but, unlike the king, she was not smiling. "I am petitioning my husband for permission to keep the raelynx."

That brought Senneth all the way into the room. "Keep him? But—here at the palace? In that garden? I don't—I know you think you can contain him there, but he—I'm not sure that would be such a good place for him."

Valri nodded, as if she did not find this speech either disjointed or disrespectful. "Deep in the palace grounds we have a small stand of woods. Full of enough game that sometimes my husband and his friends go hunting there. I would have this fenced in and guarded, and I would keep the raelynx there. It would not be true freedom for a creature such as he, but it would be better than the garden." She drew a deep breath. "And then, when I have the time, I will take the raelynx to the Lirrens and release him into the wild."

"You could go now, or later this year," the king murmured. "You do not have to wait."

The queen looked down at him with some unreadable message in her green eyes. "No. I would not leave you."

Something peculiar going on here. Senneth wished Cammon were beside her to decipher the undertones of the conversation— though Cammon had already said the queen was impervious to his magic. Well, she might be for now. But once Cammon had trained with Jerril and Lynnette for a few months, he might learn a thing or two about how to scan even the most protected mind. Then Senneth would be curious to see just what Cammon might learn about the queen.

The king raised his hand in a gesture that might have been affection and might have been resignation. "Very well. You may keep the raelynx." He glanced back at Senneth. "Unless Senneth has some objection."

"It is not for me to object, sire," Senneth said quickly. "I am happy to turn over his care to someone else."

The queen watched her a few moments with those fabulous eyes. Her expression had softened, but she did not look particularly happy or even grateful. "Thank you," she said quietly. "I will care for it most attentively." And with that, she nodded to her husband and left the room, closing the door behind her.

The king offered Senneth a whimsical smile. "I suppose you think me a most indulgent husband," he said.

"That's not what I was thinking," Senneth said.

He laughed and waved her to the chair across the desk. She sat. "You are thinking, 'What was that fool about, to marry a woman young enough to be his granddaughter?' There are many who think that, though very few of them dare to say it to my face."

Senneth was grinning now. "Actually, I never wonder why an old man marries a young woman. I do admit to curiosity about what would make a young woman marry an old man."

"But I am the king!" he said. "I commanded her! What could she do but obey?"

He seemed to be joking, but Senneth wondered if perhaps he was telling the truth. "She seems most devoted to you," was all she could think to say.

"I could not manage without her," he replied, and now there was no trace of laughter left in his voice.

"Then I am glad she is here," Senneth said.

He nodded and tapped a finger against his desk. His mood had quickly changed; now he appeared to be thinking over some serious proposition. "So! Since you are relieved of responsibility for returning the raelynx to the Lirrens, you are now free to carry out some other commission for me, are you not?"

Senneth laughed. "I stand ready to serve, sire."

He peered at her through his spectacles. "I am not so sure you will be interested in this next task I have to propose."

"But you are the king," she said, gently teasing. "You have only to command and I will obey."

"You are the least obedient of my subjects, and if you do not like my proposition, you will burn down my palace!" he exclaimed. "I am well aware that you do only what you want—and what your conscience bids you. I do not flatter myself that I can bend you to my will."

"What is it you want me to do?"

"Chaperone Amalie as I introduce her to society."

Senneth felt a thrill of horror along every nerve. "What? You want *me* to—oh, sire, I am the wrong person for such a job."

"But you are the one who told me I must make Amalie more visible! I thought if I sent her to a few of the more important functions at the Twelve Houses this spring and summer—"

"Yes, and I think it is an excellent idea! But I am not the right one to sponsor her. I haven't been at a society function for seventeen years! I don't know how to dress or what to say—or even who most of the people are! *And* I don't like them! You would be better off with—well, with Kirra. She would be an ideal escort for the princess."

"Kirra can't set a man on fire if he attempts to harm my daughter," the king said.

Senneth stared at him a moment. "Ah," she said slowly. "So you would not want me to pretend to be anything other than what I am. You want a respectable companion—who has the ferocity of a Rider. And you want everyone to know that your daughter is protected."

"By the most gifted mystic of our time," the king completed. "The more tales there are about you, the happier I am to see you standing at my daughter's side. No one who knows you would attempt to harm Amalie while she was under your protection."

"This is a heavy burden, sire," Senneth said in a low voice. "This is a commission more difficult than I had imagined."

"Well, you can think about it for a few weeks," he said cheerfully, "and let me know your decision when you get back."

Now she felt an even deeper sense of foreboding. "Back from where?"

"Where do you think I would want you to go next?"

She closed her eyes and wondered how her life had brought her, so inescapably, back to the very point she had abandoned so long ago. "Brassenthwaite," she said on a sigh.

"Yes. Will you go?"

She opened her eyes. "Are my brothers expecting me?"

He made a gesture of equivocation. "Let us say, rather, they know you are alive and well and engaged in delicate operations on my behalf. And they know it would please me for a rapprochement to be achieved between the quarreling members of their family."

"I can't stand them," she said flatly.

"Kiernan is not your father, Senneth," the king said in a quiet voice. "He is more thoughtful than you remember. He has told me more than once how deeply he regrets your father's cruel and hasty actions. He searched for you, you know."

"He did not."

"He did. Even while your father was alive, and with more urgency once he was dead. It was Ariane Rappengrass who first told Kiernan you were still alive. Malcolm knew," the king said, with a little smile, "but he wouldn't tell anyone. That's Malcolm for you."

Senneth leaned back in her chair because her bones felt like they needed some support. "And Nate's an idiot."

"Again, not as true as it might have been seventeen years ago. They are not easy, delightful men with witty conversation and elegant manners. But I trust them, Senneth. They are good men. They deserve that you give them another chance."

"I'm sorry I ever came back to the palace," she remarked. "I should have sent Tayse back with Kirra to make our report and headed straight on into the Lirrens with my raelynx."

The king grinned. "Will you go to Brassenthwaite?"

She sighed again. "Yes. I will go. When do you want me back at the palace? Because I will not need to linger with my brothers."

"Two months, maybe three," he said. "We will open the season with a ball. I want you beside Amalie as she makes her debut."

Senneth nodded. "Very well. I'll go to Brassenthwaite and return directly here."

"But Senneth," the king said, and his face was so serious that she was sure he was about to say something outrageous, "do not travel to Brassenthwaite alone. You need an escort to ensure your safety on the road—and to offer you a little consequence when you arrive at Kiernan's doorstep."

Her eyes narrowed now. Who had been gossiping with the king? It could only have been Kirra. "Take an escort?" she said in a mild voice. "Anyone you would suggest?"

He was unable to keep the sober look; he was laughing out loud. "Oh—I thought—perhaps one of my Riders? You have met one or two of them—perhaps you could select one for yourself. Or, if you like, I could make a recommendation—"

She jumped to her feet, not willing to endure such teasing even from her king. "I am well able to care for myself, you know," she reminded him. "You'd better hope so, if you think to entrust your daughter to me."

He was still smiling as he rose more sedately. "Yes, but all of us fare better if we have someone nearby watching over us," he said. "It is simply the way the world works, Senneth. But you have been solitary so long—you don't seem to remember what it's like to have a friend at your back."

"No, but I have a king who is ordering me to remember," she said in some exasperation.

He gave her that kindly toy maker's smile. "Then I command you," he said solemnly. "Go find one of my Riders and tell him I have decreed he must accompany you to Brassenthwaite. So the king proclaims."

CHAPTER
37

TAYSE leaned against the fence surrounding the training compound and watched the other Riders battle. He had spent the morning in a hard workout against Coeval and Hammond, who had not lost any of their sharpness while Tayse was on the road. He had acquitted himself well, both on foot and on horseback, and Coeval had murmured approval when Tayse parried a particularly ferocious assault.

"You must have seen some real fighting on the road, not just pretend battles," Coeval said, wiping sweat from his face.

"A little," Tayse said. "More often we just showed a willingness to fight, and that was enough to stave off an encounter."

"Yes, but the day one Rider isn't as good as the lion on his sash, that's the day every half-trained soldier in the kingdom thinks he'll try his hand at fighting one," Hammond grumbled.

Tayse laughed and scrubbed a towel over his own dripping face. "But that day will never come," he predicted.

It was good to be back among the Riders. The night before, he and Justin had been greeted by the whole pack of them, the rest of the fifty. The Riders had clustered around them in the great open room of the main barracks, asking questions, tossing out insults, clapping one or both of them on the back if they were close enough. They had all stayed up past midnight, drinking beer—but not too much, since Riders never overindulged—and swapping stories. Before the night was through, Tayse had spoken to each one individually, the many men, the few women, had renewed the deep and silent covenant that was the bond between elite fighters. *I am your friend. I will not fail you at your darkest hour.* For this, more than the prestige, he had always wanted to be a Rider—for this utter, bone-deep sense of commitment to a unit and an ideal. Back in the barracks, back among these people who were so like him, he was where he belonged; he was reminded of who he was.

But he knew he was no longer that man.

His father had joined the group of revelers very late in the evening, as a few of them had started to drift off to their beds. Tayse had looked for his father right away, of course, but Coeval had told him Tir was off delivering a message for the king. "He'll be back tonight, though," Coeval said, and he was.

Tayse hadn't seen him enter the room. Tir was a big man, but adept at stealth; he just materialized beside Tayse as Tayse sat on one of the stools and laughed over his mug of beer. "You're back," Tir observed, and toasted his son with his own glass of beer.

"This afternoon," Tayse replied.

"Good trip?"

"Successful. Everyone home safe. But the news we brought back wasn't good."

Tir nodded. "The news isn't your responsibility."

"Any trouble here?"

Tir shook his head. "Not yet. But there will be."

"So we've learned."

That was it—that was the extent of his conversation with his father that night as the Riders welcomed back two of their wandering members. That was the type of exchange that had always been enough for Tayse, covering the essential points, wasting neither time nor words. *Back from my job safe, my skills equal to the demands upon them.* What else was there to say?

Father, I've met a woman, and she's changed my life. She's changed me. This is not enough for me anymore. I do not know how to forget her—I do not know how to go back to being the man I was before. I feel the way I felt when I was a small boy and I picked up my first practice sword, and it was too heavy for me to wield. "I cannot do this," I thought. That is how I feel when I am away from Senneth. "I cannot do this."

But he could not say that to Tir. He could not say that to any of the Riders.

So instead he drank his beer, and slept in his small, spare room, and woke in the morning and worked out against the two best Riders on the force. And felt his muscles respond in familiar, conditioned ways, having lost none of their strength or agility, and thought optimistically, *Perhaps my heart, too, will remember its old routines*. But he knew it was not true.

Senneth would leave this place in a day or two, and though she had promised she would say good-bye, he thought it possible she would forget. He thought it possible he would never see her again.

Though that, at least, seemed impossible.

A weight beside him on the fence, and he turned to see that Justin had come to join him. Tayse smiled a little. That was one thing, at least, that had not altered. Justin had always sought him out, made no secret of the fact that he wanted to emulate Tayse in every particular. Even the long journey to Gisseltess and back had not made Justin lose his faith in Tayse. That was a balm, of sorts.

"Where's Cammon?" Tayse said. "I haven't seen him today."

"I checked with the gate guards. He left with Senneth this morning."

Ah. "Well, she said she wanted to see him settled," Tayse said. "She probably knows some mystics in Ghosenhall she wants to introduce him to."

"Better for him there than with us," Justin said. "I suppose."

"Cammon has some growing to do before he decides where he wants to be," Tayse said gently. "He'll be back."

Justin turned so his spine was against the fence, and he rested his elbows on the top railing. "We've only been back a day and already I feel restless," he said. "I don't know how I'll sit still for the next few weeks—or few months—just training in the yard and waiting for something to happen."

"Something will happen," Tayse said. "That's why you must keep training."

"When is Senneth leaving?" Justin said abruptly.

"I don't know."

"She promised to say good-bye."

"She did."

"I wish she wouldn't go, though."

Tayse knew the feeling. "She has her own appointed tasks. Different from ours, but just as important."

Justin made a quarter turn and stared straight at Tayse. "She shouldn't leave *you*," he said.

Tayse was left absolutely speechless.

"Or you shouldn't leave her," Justin added. "I haven't worked it out yet. But you shouldn't be apart."

And he had thought there was no one with whom he could discuss this. It astonished him that Justin had noticed so much during their journey to Gisseltess, because Justin hadn't seemed to be paying attention to anyone's emotions but his own. He gave Justin the answer he'd given himself already more than a hundred times. "I'm a Rider. She's from the House of Brassenthwaite. We don't belong together."

"You're the two strongest people I know," Justin said. "It feels right when you're side by side. It doesn't feel right otherwise. I don't know how to say it." He waved a hand. "Cammon could say it. But Cammon's not here, and Senneth is leaving, and none of it makes any sense to me."

"It always feels like this, a little, when you come back from a hard mission," Tayse said. "You're at loose ends. You can't get back to the order your life had before. Give it a week and you'll feel more normal."

Justin stared at him. "By then, she'll be gone."

"I know."

Justin shook his head. "Tayse, you never make mistakes. Never. Any Rider would follow you on any desperate mission. I would do what you told me even if I thought it would mean my death. But you're wrong about Senneth. Don't let her leave."

Tayse turned away from him to stare blindly out into the training yard. His heart was slamming against his rib cage, and his head thrummed with tension. If he had expected a lecture from anyone—which he had not—he never would have believed it would come from Justin. "I have nothing to offer to a serramarra of Brassenthwaite."

Even his cold voice and stony face did not deter Justin from making one last comment. "But you have everything to give Senneth."

AFTER dinner in the barracks, Tayse slipped outside and did a slow walk around the perimeter of the palace compound. It was a habit he had picked up years ago, shortly after coming back from one of his first missions for the king. On the road, of course, Tayse was accustomed to circling the campsite at least once during the night, checking to make sure all was well, that no unexpected danger threatened. Here in Ghosenhall, there were plenty of other guards appointed to watch the grounds, but it gave Tayse a sense of rightness to make that nighttime circuit even in this place. It was also an exercise that helped to calm his mind and weary his body whenever he was having trouble sleeping.

Walking at a good clip, he took more than an hour to follow the fence all the way around. He spoke idle words to the guards he encountered along the way, none of whom were surprised to see him. The moon rode high overhead, a small and stingy sliver. The slight breeze was cold enough to make him glad he'd worn his coat, but it carried a faint green scent of spring. Or so he imagined. It seemed he had been hoping for spring ever since the onset of winter.

Done with the outer circuit, he made the inner one, walking the uneven ground all around the palace. Lights flooded from the kitchens, the bedrooms, the dining hall. The formal dinner must still be under way, all the king's guests making merry downstairs while their servants yawned in the bedrooms upstairs. Tayse wondered who sat at the table tonight besides the king and the queen, and Kirra and Senneth, and the handful of nobles who were always attendant at the palace.

Not that he cared about any of them except Senneth.

For a moment he let himself imagine what would happen if he climbed up the wide stairs, nodded to the soldiers at the front door, and stepped inside the palace. He could follow the sound of laughter to the dining hall or the music salon or the ballroom where the guests were gathered. He was a Rider; he had entrée into every corridor and chamber of the palace. He would bow to his king, make a slightly less sincere bow to his queen, and then locate Senneth in whatever gorgeous and bejeweled crowd had gathered. He would make his way past the beautifully gowned women, the sumptuously clothed men; he would not pause to inhale the rich perfumes or marvel at the glitter of housemark gems. He would find Senneth, and he would bow so low before her that Valri would be jealous and the king would be outraged. He would take her hand in front of all of them, the marlords and the marladies and the royals, and he would tell her, "I love you."

But though he stood there for five minutes, ten minutes, watching the guarded doors, he could not make himself start forward and climb the steps. He could not bridge the distance; he could not make the leap. He could not change himself so far as to ask her to change for him.

When he turned to go back to the barracks, she was standing a few feet away on the lawn, watching him.

For a moment, he thought it was illusion—hallucination—a flickering manifestation of his own hopeless desire. But then she moved, took a few steps nearer, and he was swept with that wash of physical heat that always warmed the air around Senneth. By that alone he knew she was real.

She was dressed in a slim column of antique white, a lace-colored dress that matched the hue and texture of her hair. Even on this cool night, her arms were bare; the deep neckline of the gown showed the contours of her body more than her riding clothes ever had. She was as bright and unattainable as starlight.

"Senneth," he said, because she seemed to be waiting for him to speak. "What are you doing out here this night?"

"I grew bored with the king's party," she said. "So I came to look for you."

"For me?" he said, and strangled his sense of pleasure. "Did you need something?"

She shrugged a little. She seemed unhappy or unsure of herself, troubled by events. "I miss all my companions of the road. I've taken Cammon to the house of some mystics, and he's been gone all day, though he promised to come back and tell me what he's learned. Donnal has disappeared, disgruntled because Kirra has become—oh, you should see her! Even grander than she was in Helven and Nocklyn. It's fun to watch her, because she is enjoying herself so much, but it's not very easy to sit and confide in her. And you and Justin are off with your friends, and even the raelynx is walled up in a garden and it's—I'm lonely, I suppose. I didn't think such a thing would happen to me. I've been on my own so much that I'd forgotten what it was like to come to depend on others."

"Maybe that's not such a bad thing," he said.

"What? That I'm unhappy?"

"No," he said, laughing. "That you find yourself missing friends. Maybe you'll find yourself making more of them."

She sighed. "And what about you? Do you find yourself happy now that you're back at the palace, back among your fellow Riders?"

He chose his words carefully. "Justin seems to be feeling much the way you are," he said. "I told him that the end of every mission brings with it just such a sense of—disorientation. Of malaise."

"Even for you?" she said, as if she didn't believe it.

"Even for me. This time, at least. But I also told him the feeling would pass."

"Yes," she said. "You would tell him that, I suppose."

He did not mention that he was pretty sure it was a lie. "I cannot imagine you will give yourself much time to brood about it," he said. "You're a restless woman. You must already be planning your next journey."

A twist of the mouth for that. "In fact, I expect to be leaving in a day or two," she said.

"And where will you be going this time?"

She came a few steps nearer, and now she was close enough to touch if he had courage to reach for her. On her face was a mix of emotions it was hard to sort out: irritation, resignation, amusement, and something that might be hope. "Brassenthwaite."

"Ah."

"Under duress."

He smiled. "At the king's behest?"

"Yes. He wants to see me reconciled with my brothers."

"Well, he's a smart old man. He knows what's best for the kingdom. And it might be best for you, too. You'll see."

She hesitated a moment. She was toying with some of the lacy edges of her dress and seemed to be reviewing some past thought or experience. "I have fought in sea battles and land battles," she said at last, slowly. "I've faced down angry soldiers and predators with no thought but to kill me. I've been sick. I've been solitary. I've been hungry. I've been afraid more times than I can count. But I've never been as afraid of anything as I am to walk back into Brassenthwaite to face my brothers alone."

The words were out before he could stop them. "Take a friend," he suggested.

She stilled her hands by flattening them on the front of her gown. "Will you come?" she asked.

He stared at her a moment in the dark. There was so little moonlight that she was only visible because of the color of her dress and the candlewick of her hair. Yet he could see the tautness of her face, the apprehension in her gray eyes. He could tell that she was afraid of one more thing, and that was the answer he might give. And that knowledge undid him, cut through all his careful bindings of class and caste and calling; that anxious expression turned him soft.

"I will," he said in a quiet voice. "I will accompany you to Brassenthwaite, and from there to any other region in Gillengaria, and from there to any country across the sea, named or unnamed. I will protect you with my weapons and with my skill and with my life. Neither your brothers nor your enemies nor strangers upon the road will offer you harm while I am living."

"I want more from you than that," she whispered.

"I know," he replied.

Now she lifted her hands, hesitantly, and the gesture was full of such uncertainty and such supplication that he could not endure it. He closed the short distance between them. He wrapped her in his arms as if she was a child who needed succor and he was the only avenger for miles. Fire flashed between them; he thought for a moment the flimsy gown had gone up in flames, but it was just the heat of her body, or the excitement of his, or the reveling of the night around them, and nothing to be concerned about. He kissed her, and that was the end of it. No more pretending, no more holding back. Life changed by love, life sparkling now with its own peculiar magic. He tightened his hold and let the transformation take over. When he lifted his mouth from hers, he knew, he would be a different man.

He kissed her until the world was changed, and even that was not long enough.